Time to Move On

Time to Move On

Grace Thompson

ISIS
LARGE PRINT
Oxford

First published in Great Britain 2007
by
Robert Hale Ltd.

Published in Large Print 2008 by ISIS Publishing Ltd.,
7 Centremead, Osney Mead, Oxford OX2 0ES
by arrangement with
the author c/o Johnson & Alcock

British Library Cataloguing in Publication Data
Thompson, Grace
    Time to move on. – Large print ed.
    1. Badgers Brook (Wales: Imaginary place) – Fiction
    2. Large type books
    I. Title
    823.9'14 [F]

ISBN 978–0–7531–8140–9 (hb)
ISBN 978–0–7531–8141–6 (pb)

Printed and bound in Great Britain by
T. J. International Ltd., Padstow, Cornwall

CHAPTER ONE

Seranne Laurence closed the door of the van in which she had been given a lift, by pushing against it with her hip. A small, slim figure, she wobbled on high heels with which she tried to compensate for her lack of height, and took short, impatient steps. Her arms were holding a shallow cardboard box which meant she couldn't see where she was placing her feet. When she reached the kerb one trim leg hovered until her foot touched the road surface. An elderly man nearby paused holding his breath until she had regained equilibrium.

In the box were blocks of margarine, a packet of ice-cream mix and two dozen eggs. The tea rooms she ran with her mother had used dried egg powder for two days and today they could claim fresh eggs again. Like most food, eggs were still rationed in 1952, seven years after World War Two had ended.

She was in a hurry, running across the road after the van had moved off. They needed to make cakes before the tea rooms opened for business at ten o'clock and she increased her speed, stumbling with her awkward load. When the dog ran towards her, barking hysterically and startling her, she lost her grip on the box, tripped and staggered across the pavement trying to steady it. She fell against the garden wall of the house shouting at the animal in rage. The shouts turned to groans as the box hit the wall awkwardly before sliding slowly to land against her waist and allowing eggs to smash and shed their contents over her feet.

Never a tolerant person, Seranne glared around, looking for someone to blame.

"Hey! You!" she called to the owner of the dog who was trying in vain not to laugh. "That dog is dangerous! You should keep him on a lead!"

"I'm sorry but —" The rest of the apology was lost as the woman gave way to mirth. Several passers-by had stopped and were also highly amused. The dog enjoying the fun ran towards her again.

Seranne screamed. "Keep him away from me," while the dog unconcernedly began licking the egg from her feet.

"Can I help?" the old man asked.

"Did you see that? The dog ran at me and I dropped it all and what are we going to do about the eggs? They're rationed you know. This woman has to do something!"

Accepting there was nothing he could do, the elderly man walked away.

"You were trying to run carrying a large box. Hardly anyone else's fault," the dog owner shouted back. Relenting a little, she came over and picked up the sticky box and without thanking her, Seranne snatched it from her and walked the few yards to the door of Jessica's Victorian Tea Rooms.

2

Across the road a car had slowed down and stopped. With dread, Seranne looked away, hoping she had been mistaken and the man was not the one she knew. The driver, a dark-haired man in his thirties, had seen the incident and he too was smiling. Seranne risked a second glance and recognized him with dismay. He was the man who always chose the corner table in the tea rooms, a regular customer who was polite but rarely said more than convention demanded. Yet there was something fascinating about him and Seranne had begun to look forward to his visits. Why did he have to be passing at this exact moment? Her embarrassment was exacerbated when a woman called, "The red sale price label is sticking out of your blouse, mind. You can't act dignified with the label showing!"

Renewed laughter followed her through the door, accompanied by the roar of the MG sports car's powerful engine as the man drove away.

She threw the box and its sticky contents on the kitchen table and pulled at the label revealing the reduced price, ten shillings and six pence, on her blouse. What will that man think of her, and why did she care? He was only a customer and he didn't even leave generous tips.

She went into the kitchen but her mother wasn't there. She was probably sneaking out to see her latest boyfriend. There had been several over the years, since divorcing her stepfather, each one more unsuitable than the last. Just as well Jessie was out; she didn't really want an audience looking like this. It was bad enough that the dog owner and the man who tried to help and the man who sat at the corner table had seen her at her worst. She told herself it didn't really matter and tried to believe it. Calming herself, she took off her messy clothes and had a second bath before dressing in fresh clothes, by which time she had begun to see the funny side.

Her mother, Jessie Laurence, appeared as she was taking the first batch of scones out of the oven, and she put the utensils she had used into the newly fitted large sink and laughed as she explained the disaster. Turning away from the sink to share the joke she was quickly aware that her mother wasn't really listening. "Is everything all right, Mum? You look flushed and anxious." Probably boyfriend trouble, she mused. "Not bad news I hope?"

With a serious expression on her pretty face, Jessie tried to smile. "No, in fact I've some wonderful news."

"You've managed to get the pretty new china we need for the tea rooms?"

"No, dear, better than that. I'm going to marry Paul."

Seranne stared at her mother in disbelief for a long moment. "You can't marry Paul Curtis! You haven't known him for more than a few months! And —"

"And he's younger than me? Is that what you were going to say?"

"No, er — well, yes. He seems to enjoy the company of younger women. Younger than himself, I mean. I've often seen him at the local dances and he seems, I don't know, a bit of a flirt, not the kind of man to settle in to life here in the flat above our tea rooms."

4

"That's where you're wrong, dear. He's had all the travelling and excitement he wants and now he's searching for comfort and security."

"Sounds exciting," Seranne replied sarcastically.

They went up to the flat above the tea rooms, to the beautifully furnished sitting-room filled with antique items, many of which had belonged to Seranne's great-grandmother. A few modern pieces blended perfectly with the old. The clock that had belonged in the family for four generations, the carved oak side table on which were displayed silver treasures bought during their short marriage by her mother and her father. A tea set displayed on the dark oak Welsh dresser had been chosen by them too. How could her mother consider sharing these memories with a stranger?

Jessie stared at her daughter then said, "Just give him a chance, I think you'll be happy for me once you accept you are no longer the whole of my life." The pointed remark was given with a smile.

Seranne smiled and hugged her mother affectionately. "You're right, Mum. I can't expect us to go on like this for the rest of our lives, running our tea rooms and living up here like a couple of part-time hermits." She looked again around the beautifully furnished room. "But it will be a bit cramped."

"We'll manage, at least for a while," Jessie replied.

"Perhaps I could move into the smaller room, and use my bedroom as a second sitting-room?"

"Thank you, that's an idea worth thinking about. But not yet. Let's wait until we've lived in it for a while, plenty of time later to start shifting things about."

"How long? Have you thought about when you and Paul will arrange the wedding? Perhaps in the winter months when we aren't so busy?"

"Oh, it's all fixed. We've booked the ceremony. It's two weeks from Saturday, the eighth of November."

Seranne was too surprised to produce a verbal reply, she turned away, thankful for the knock at the door offering a reprieve. Leaving her mother to put away the last of the breakfast things she ran down the stairs to open the door for the baker. It wasn't who she expected. A baker, but the wrong one. Tony Hopkins was a baker in the small town of Cwm Derw and his sister Babs was one of Seranne's closest friends. He held out a wooden tray on which, resting on greaseproof paper, there were some filled bread rolls and a couple of fancy cakes.

"Morning Tony," she greeted him, as he pushed past her into the kitchen. "What's this? Still trying to convince me we'd be better served by Hopkins's bakery?"

"No, although if you want a trial run . . .?"

"No thanks, Tony," she replied as he put the cakes on to a plate.

"I'm here with a message from Babs. She sent these little treats for your elevenses," he said, already on his way back out. "She wondered if you fancy setting her hair for her tomorrow night? I think she's got a date but she won't tell me." He grinned as he stepped into the van. "I bet it's that useless lump of lard, Keith."

"That's muscle not fat!" she protested laughing. "I'll see her at seven," she called as the van moved off, and his arm came out and waved acknowledgement. They were always in a hurry, Tony and Babs. Tony worked long hours at his parents' bakery while Babs ran the shop.

For a moment his appearance had allowed her to forget her mother's news. She wished he'd had time for her to talk about it. Then the door reopened and he came back waving a piece of paper. "Forgot to give you this. It's an invitation to come a week Saturday and stay the night, there's a party for one of Mam and Dad's friends and we'd like you to come."

She offered him a cup of tea and he glanced at his watch, then at her worried expression and sat down. "Is something wrong, Seranne?"

"Sort of. Mum is getting married and I think the man is most unsuitable."

"Why?" he surprised her by asking. "Is he unsuitable, or are you afraid of the changes he'll cause?"

"Both," she replied honestly. "He's too young and I'm so afraid of Mum making yet another mistake."

"This is the wrong way round," he said staring at her. "It's usually the mother who doesn't want to let go. Don't be afraid of change, Seranne."

"I'm not afraid to let go, or of making changes, as long as they're the right ones."

"Babs is just as bad," he went on between hasty sips of hot tea. "Mum, Dad and I want to make changes in the business but Babs blocks us every time."

"Why does everything have to change? If things are going well why mess them up?"

"Because they could be better?"

When he left, running to the van as though to make up for the minutes he had wasted, Seranne adjusted the oven and began to gather the ingredients for sponge cakes. The movements were so automatic that the tasks allowed her to consider the changes to her life Paul Curtis's arrival would cause, while her small efficient hands dealt with the preparations for the day. Her movements were swift, the tasks carried out with the smoothness of familiarity.

She had worked in the tea rooms all her life, even as a small child she had undertaken certain responsibilities. Jessica's Victorian Tea Rooms had been opened by her grandmother and had continued in much the same way ever since. She and her mother had worked together in almost complete harmony, both wanting the best for their customers, offering a welcome, serving only the very best food, even in the difficulties of the war years.

Pretty, hand-embroidered cloths covered the tables. The originals had been made by her grandmother and great-grandmother, and as they had gradually worn out they'd been replaced by those made by her mother and herself. Shelves around the walls held china teapots of various styles and these were interspersed with beautiful plates. Subtle rose patterns adorned the walls and curtains, and Jessie often likened it to a garden, although the potted palms and trailing ivys had long since been banished.

They had been determined to hang on to traditions in a changing world and so far they had succeeded and found customers who appreciated the timelessness of the place. It was a bit shabby as replacements hadn't been easily found for breakages and wear and tear, but they had managed to retain the atmosphere of elegance that still appealed.

She looked around, straightening a tablecloth, adjusting a chair, a plate, and sadness overwhelmed her. Once Paul Curtis moved in, things would change. Her mother would allow him to make decisions. It had happened before with other men whom Jessie had briefly believed to be her one true love. She wondered if this time she would be able to contain her temper. It wasn't something she found easy. Pushing aside her melancholy thoughts she returned to the kitchen and began setting trays with china ready for their first customers.

An hour later, several sponge cakes were cooling, scones were displayed on pretty china plates and two platters of sandwiches were arranged under their glass covers. The place smelled of freshly ground coffee and she had discarded her working overalls for a neat white apron with a notebook and pencil attached to the pocket. She was ready for business. She glanced at the clock. In a few minutes Jessica's Victorian Tea Rooms would open its doors. She heard her mother's footsteps descending and braced herself with a smile.

Jessie looked uneasy, knowing her daughter was upset by her announcement. She didn't know what to say to ease the difficult moment.

Aware of her mother's unease and knowing humour was usually the best way over difficult moments, Seranne asked, "Can I ask a question, about Paul?"

"Of course, dear."

"Is he any good at washing up?"

"Living in a room with a landlady to spoil him that's very unlikely," Jessie said with a chuckle. "D'you know, that's one of the reasons I'm so happy to be remarrying. I like looking after a man, making sure he has his favourite meals, that his clothes are immaculate and always ready for him."

"As long as Paul is ready for slippers and pipe," Seranne warned.

As soon as the door was opened, several people walked in: two ladies who always met on Wednesday morning before they did their midweek shopping, a mother who came for a coffee after taking her children to school, an elderly man who lived alone and depended on them for tea and toast for his breakfast.

Seranne glanced at the table in the corner by the window. She wondered whether the dark, serious-looking man would come. After the embarrassing moment when she lost control of the eggs, she half hoped he wouldn't. He occasionally called in for tea and scones, and always chose that particular seat, where he could observe without anyone looking in his direction, and from where he could look out at the street. She knew nothing about him, not even his name, but was drawn to him by curiosity, attracted by his slow smile and the look in his brown eyes. Accepting the fact he had seen her at her worst, covered in egg, arguing with people in the street like a fishwife, she determined to greet him with a smile, look confident, pretend it hadn't happened. Crossing her fingers as each customer entered, she dreaded someone taking his favourite place, stupidly convinced it would prevent him coming in.

The first hour started slowly but by eleven the place was full. A dozen conversations filled the air and the buzz of voices and the occasional burst of laughter excited her. This was how she wanted to spend her life, creating a place where people felt at home, for a little while at least, where they could relax and enjoy the food she and her mother prepared. She hoped Paul Curtis didn't intend to spoil it.

She heard the sound of a powerful engine and glanced at the door. She was tuned in to the sound of his MG. Oh dear, at the very last moment his table was occupied! She hurried across to see to the newly arrived customers and was relieved when they stood to move to a table near the window. Two people were leaving and she hastily stacked their dishes and efficiently filled her tray, flicking the odd crumb from the table before hurrying into the kitchen, where used dishes stood in regimented order waiting to be washed.

She heard the till give its *ching ching* as customers paid, then her mother asking, "What would you like this morning, sir?" She brushed her hair back, refixed her silly hat which her mother insisted she wear, glanced at her reflection in the mirror placed for them to see into the tea rooms, and went out. He was looking at a newspaper but as she entered he smiled and nodded before his gaze returned to his paper. Was his smile wider than usual? Was he remembering her battle with the eggs and the recalcitrant dog? Deep breaths and she went on with her work trying to pretend he wasn't there.

Jessie took his order, a scone with the jam and cream served separately, as he liked it, and a cup of tea. He didn't stay long leaving a tip as usual and nodding his thanks as he left. Seranne waited and at the door he turned and smiled. She sighed. "And that's my excitement for the day," she whispered to Jessie.

"His name is Luke. I heard someone greet him as he came in," Jessie whispered back.

They closed at one o'clock on Wednesday and often went to the wholesalers hoping for bargains in china or glass to replenish their stock, depleted by years of shortages, but today Seranne wanted to talk to someone.

She didn't drive, so she would make the journey to Cwm Derw on two buses. She expected her mother to go to the wholesalers as usual, but as she left, Jessie was dressed in one of her smartest suits, hair and make-up immaculately done, waiting for Paul.

Babs closed the bakers' shop at one but Seranne didn't expect to be there until half past two. She wished she had phoned. Babs might have already gone out for the afternoon. Fortunately Tony was passing and he stopped to give her a lift. Babs was still at the shop when they arrived, having been held up by a flurry of late customers. Seranne helped her wash the shelves and put the cardboard cutout of a sad baker boy showing a "Sorry, we're closed" notice in the window.

"Mam's got a new boyfriend," she began when they were finally finished.

"That's hardly surprising. She's had several in the past and they don't stay long. She gets tired of them very quickly, doesn't she?"

"Usually, but this time they've booked their wedding."

"What!"

"She doesn't have a ring and she's only know him a few months but they are getting married at the register office on the eighth of November, would you believe."

"Well I suppose, if it works out, it will be nice for her. After all you'll probably marry one day and otherwise she'd be on her own."

"Of course she wouldn't. We run the tea rooms together and that wouldn't change."

"But she's still young . . . ish!"

"She's forty. I'm twenty-two. She was only eighteen when I was born."

"Twenty-two and I'm three years older. Time we were married, Seranne. Are you sure you won't marry my brother?"

Seranne put on a mock serious expression and said, "Even Tony would be better than being on the shelf, I suppose." Then they laughed. It was a long-standing joke between them.

"What about this party a week Saturday night? Or we could go to the local hop this week instead of my date with Keith? We aren't that passionate about each other any more and I'd be glad of the excuse to cancel."

"I don't feel like dancing."

"A good reason to go then, you misery!"

"All right. Better than watching Mum and Paul canoodling."

Babs sighed. "I could do with a nice canoodle, couldn't you?"

On Saturday it was again Tony who obliged with transport and the two girls set off with the intention of having a good time. They both enjoyed dancing although they didn't go as often as they would have liked because of the very early start to their days. There were several girls there they knew and with their mood set for fun they found laughter easy.

To their surprise, Paul Curtis walked in and almost immediately began to dance with a young woman, whispering in her ear, making her laugh. Angry, the mood ruined, Seranne waited until Babs had joined a group of their friends, then left the hall and spent the rest of the evening in the cloak-room, blaming Paul for her ruined evening.

The following morning, after staying the night with Babs, she refused a lift home and left early to get home by bus. Being Sunday there were fewer buses and after several long delays, she wished she hadn't been so insistent on refusing Tony's offer of a lift. But she knew this was the only morning when Tony could sleep later than usual. Besides, she needed to be on her own, to decide what — if anything — to say to her mother.

She kept thinking of Paul flirting with the young girl and feared for her mother, who seemed to be about to make another mistake. She got off the bus some distance from home, unable to sit any longer, filled with the need to walk. It wasn't far and the crisp cold morning made it almost pleasurable. Mist shrouded the trees, frost glistened on the pavement and she felt her feet slide, unstable on the three-inch heels of her dancing shoes. Stupid to walk in them. Why hadn't she carried some sensible ones?

Muttering to herself, walking cautiously, rather like a drunk, she stepped on to the road and made her way across to where a light glowed from above the dark windows of the tea rooms. She wondered if her mother knew where Paul had spent his evening and the temptation to tell her was strong. Surely she ought to be told? If she were to marry him, and find out too late that he was a womanizer surely that would be worse than making her face it now?

She felt a chill of guilt knowing that her resentment towards mother's plan to marry was not really because she thought Paul unsuitable. The truth was she was afraid. Her mother was the only person in her life apart from a few friends; no relations, not even a distant cousin. Her mind kept filling with imaginary scenes. None were pleasant. She was taken by various routes into the future, each one a trip to loneliness, while her mother and Paul went off together, their lives filled with laughter and happiness.

Her resentment towards her mother marrying was because she was afraid of being left alone. How selfish was that?

She stood on the pavement hesitating about going in. Ignoring her freezing cold feet in the flimsy shoes, she walked past the flat unwilling to go inside, then back again to stare through the windows of the tea rooms, wishing it would all return to normal. She crossed the road, wishing there was somewhere to go for an hour or two while she calmed her restive thoughts. How could she pretend everything was all right, knowing Paul had been out dancing while her mother — his fiancée — had sat at home unaware? Surely she had to tell her. Not for selfish reasons, but to save her mother from making a big mistake.

"You're wandering around as though you're lost, but as you live across the road that can't be true." The voice startled her and she turned to see the man from the corner table looking down at her, his smile barely visible in the early morning gloom.

"I was thinking!" she said, embarrassment making her voice sharp.

"Don't let me interrupt, then."

He slowly backed away, arms open in apology, and on impulse she added, "I'm thinking about my mother."

"Oh? Is it something I can help with? I'll listen if you want to talk."

"She's getting married."

"That's good, isn't it?"

"The man she's planning to marry was at a dance in Cwm Derw last night."

"Cwm Derw? That's a long way to go for a dance."

"My friends have a bakery there."

"Hopkins?"

"Yes, and he was there, dancing and flirting with a young woman."

"You're probably jumping to conclusions. Men and women dance together and have fun together without automatically misbehaving."

"We've seen him there before."

"You're wondering whether or not to tell your mother?"

"D'you think I should?"

"Most definitely not! You can't interfere in the lives of others, without knowing all the facts. I've had experience of how devastating that can be." With that he walked away, leaving her wondering what sadness he'd experienced and also, whether in her mother's case, her *not* talking could have a more devastating result. Still uncertain about what to do, she went up the stairs calling to her mother.

"I caught the early bus," she told Jessie when she went inside.

"Oh? Did you enjoy the dance? You must have seen Paul there."

"Paul? Well. I — I thought I saw him but presumed I was mistaken."

"No, he was with friends celebrating their daughter's twenty-first birthday. Something arranged a long time ago. I was invited, but thought it better not to go."

Seranne wondered whether she would dare tell the man at the corner table he had been right. He had saved her from storming in, in her usual quick-tempered way, telling her mother she was being fooled and upsetting her. She was grateful not to have made a terrible mistake.

Her mother was in the kitchen dealing with a fresh batch of cooking the following morning when the man she now knew as Luke came in and made his way to his usual place. Self-consciously she went to ask for his order and at once said, "You were right, about not telling my mother. She already knew."

"Good, I can understand how difficult it must be for someone like you to hold back."

"What d'you mean?"

He looked into her eyes, laughter in his, offended injury in hers which quickly changed to embarrassment when he said softly, "Are there omelettes on the menu? I saw you quarrelling with a small terrier a few days ago."

"Yes. Well. He startled me and eggs aren't easy to replace." She took out the small notebook with its dangling pencil and said, "One of our scones with jam and cream served separately? Thank you, sir." There was just a slight edge to the "sir".

Her mother went out that evening and Seranne sat in the living-room doing neat darns on some of the worn tablecloths before ironing them. She thought about Paul and wondered whether this time her mother might have got it right.

Jessie had been married three times, firstly to Seranne's father, who had died when she was a baby in 1930, then to Simon Laurence, who gave Seranne his name when he adopted her. They were divorced when she was ten and he had dropped completely out of their lives. The third was Peter Wood who had disappeared during the war, but Seranne suspected he hadn't died, but had resulted in another divorce. Since then there had been several friends but none lasted very long, to Seranne's relief. Although each one was different from the last, there was always the fear that they would stay and make changes to her life. She knew the fears were selfish, but running the tea rooms with her mother was all she had ever known.

From what she had gathered, Paul Curtis owned a small factory making leather goods, mostly shopping bags, travel bags and ladies handbags, but also wallets and shaving cases and manicure sets. He drove a smart Vauxhall car and dressed well. He obviously had money and certainly didn't lack charm. Perhaps he *would* be the one to make her mother happy. Perhaps too Luke was right, and it wasn't her place to offer an opinion. But however she fought it, the fear was still there. Tony was right, she was afraid of change. A third person would ruin the pleasant way she and her mother lived their lives.

Jessie was so happy as she planned her wedding that Seranne hid her doubts and pretended to share the excitement. She hated the way the flat was rearranged to make room for Paul. The furniture was shuffled around and several pieces were discarded. A small table that had been her grandmother's disappeared, taken by Paul together with her father's desk and chair while she was out, and she didn't get a sensible reply when she asked their whereabouts.

"Your mother didn't want them any longer," Paul explained. "Isn't that sufficient reason to find them a good home?"

She suspected him of selling them and outwitting him became a game. She arranged for Tony to collect anything her mother decided to discard for Babs to look after, ready for that distant "one day" when she might need them for a home of her own. A couple of armchairs and a painting that Paul declared he disliked were put in store before Paul could remove them, and if he was disappointed he didn't show it.

She had mixed feelings as her mother's bedroom was rearranged and prepared for sharing, drawers emptied and space made in the wardrobe for his clothes. New bedding had been acquired and Seranne found it embarrassing to think of her mother sharing a bed with this stranger who was coming into their lives.

She began searching the newspapers for evening activities to join, anything to avoid spending evenings in the flat. How could she sit there and make conversation while they stared into each other's eyes and wished her elsewhere? Yet there were things she and Jessie needed to discuss. They would still share responsibility for the tea rooms and that meant working together and discussing the day to day running of the place.

As the wedding day approached, Seranne discussed her worries with Babs on the telephone and Babs came up several times using the bakery van and encouraged Seranne to get all her worries out in the open. She tried to coax her not to be so afraid. "Why should anything change?" she insisted. "Paul won't interfere with the business. He owns a factory making leather bags. How can that give him the authority to advise on selling cakes in a café?"

"Tea rooms," Seranne corrected with a grin. "Mum hates it referred to as a café."

"I can't say I blame her when I think of the awful 'caff' we have in Cwm Derw. But come on, give them a chance. What are you buying them as a wedding present?"

"Heavens, I haven't decided yet!"

"Then let's go into Maes Hir on Wednesday. It's market day and there's sure to be something there that will suit."

"A pair of kippers?"

"That isn't the attitude. Come on, she's your mum and deserves something really nice."

They eventually found a charming White Friars glass vase and a pair of good quality towels, which a friend of Babs embroidered with "his" and "hers".

"I'll buy them something really special for their first anniversary," Seranne said as she wrapped them.

"You don't think they'll last that long, do you?"

"I hope they do, I really hope they will be blissfully happy, but there's something about Paul that makes me distrust him. I wouldn't be honest if I didn't admit to being worried for my mother."

The day of the wedding came around fast. The tea rooms closed for the day and many customers gathered to see the bride leave in a large Rolls Royce hired for the day by Paul.

Seranne wore a silk dress in pale honey, a charming contrast to her mother's gown in sky blue. Babs came as a second witness in a dress a few shades deeper than Seranne's. None of Paul's family came, although several gifts arrived with apologies for their inability to

21

attend. A three-year-old girl, the daughter of a customer, presented Jessie with a silver horseshoe and the local chimney sweep arrived to wish them good fortune.

It was a happy interlude, but coming back to the flat it became a rather sombre affair. Seranne and Babs had decorated the rooms and even the staircase with bunting and a few balloons, and they had prepared a buffet, but the guests were so few it lacked gaiety, the laughter seemed forced and the affair was low-key and almost sad. Seranne and Jessie had no known relatives and being so busy with the tea rooms meant they had little time for social events, so they had made few real friends. Neighbours and several regular customers made up the numbers and the result made them feel like strangers in their own home. Both Paul and Jessie were relieved when it was time for them to leave for their brief honeymoon in Tenby.

"Will you be all right in the flat on your own?" Tony asked Seranne, giving a stupidly large wink as he and Babs were leaving. "I'll stay if you like?"

"I'd rather borrow Mrs Baker's dog!" she replied, pointing them both towards the door.

She had never been in the flat on her own at night and as time for bed approached, she wished she had asked Babs to stay. She hesitated to undress and when she had pulled on her nightgown wearing so few clothes made her feel vulnerable and she was tempted to redress in her day clothes and sleep on the armchair. She went downstairs three times to check that the doors were locked and kept the wireless playing to give the illusion of not being alone in the almost alien building.

The hollowness of the empty rooms around her and the silent tea rooms below isolating her from the rest of the community made her heart race and she began listening for the sound of someone entering and threatening her. Like a child, she was in need of the reassurance of a small light. In her heightened state of anxiety, the sounds of the building, its creaks and sighs, seemed much louder than usual and it was a long time before she settled.

The following day was a Sunday and she had a leisurely breakfast sitting in front of the electric fire, still in her dressing gown. She smiled as she thought of her mother's disapproval. Jessie always insisted on a mannerly approach to mealtimes. A knock at the door surprised her. It was hardly eight o'clock.

Babs mocked her as she stepped inside. "Still in your nightie? Shame on you! Come on, we're going out."

"It's Sunday. Where is there to go on a Sunday morning in November?"

"Tony has the car as Dad doesn't need it, and we're going out for the day."

"I can't, Babs. There's the cleaning to do and —"

"And between us we can sort that in an hour. Tony is taking us to the seaside and we're having lunch with our Auntie Megan. Come on, it's all arranged."

Tony ran up the stairs a few moments later and the three of them started to deal with the usual Sunday routine. They settled for the absolute minimal and prepared for the unexpected day out. He drove them to a small cottage near the river in the Vale of Glamorgan and Seranne found herself hugged and greeted like a lost relative by Babs's Auntie Megan. When Uncle Richie came in from the frosty garden with leeks and some Brussels sprouts, the affectionate greeting was repeated.

While Auntie Megan prepared lunch, they walked along the river, Tony pointing out the various birds in the bare branches and describing the days out he and Babs had enjoyed as children. The chill wind made Seranne's face rosy and her eyes shone with the pleasure of the unexpected treat. The meal was huge and delicious and when she returned to the empty flat to await the return of her mother and her stepfather she was happier than she'd been for a long time.

She was filled with the smug feeling of having cheated by not following her mother's strict routine of Sunday cleaning. Tony hinted this wouldn't be the last. Perhaps Paul's arrival meant a freedom she hadn't known she lacked?

She set the table for supper for three and sat reading a book and it was a while before the sound of dripping water penetrated her thoughts. At first she thought the weather had warmed and turned to rain. Then she realized the sound was inside. Investigation soon led to the problem. In the kitchen, where the new sink had been installed, where old lead piping met new copper, there was a leak. She needed a plumber — and fast.

She grabbed a coat and set off for the house where the plumber who had dealt with the work lived. The house was ominously dark. He wasn't at home. Now what could she do? She stood irresolute, looking around as though a solution was hidden in the darkness. Nothing for it but to go back and continue catching the drips in a bucket. Surely her mother and Paul would be back soon, and Paul would know what to do? Time passed and in despair she phoned the bakery and asked Tony for his help.

He contacted a friend living near the tea rooms who came at once. When Jessie walked in, their kitchen was filled with tools and people: Tony and two friends — one the plumber — plus Seranne making tea and Babs trying to help. The floor was awash and while Babs and Tony mocked her, Seranne was scolding the plumber, warning him that she expected him to clear up the mess he was making.

Once the plumber and the rest had gone, Tony stayed just long enough to deal with the worst of the mess. As he reminded them, he had to start work at 4a.m. Seranne and Babs looked at the once immaculate kitchen, it looked a daunting task.

"Lucky we didn't spend all day cleaning, eh?" Babs whispered.

Ignoring their protests, Jessie helped, but Paul didn't do anything. He went into the room that was now his and Jessie's and prepared for bed.

Outwardly very little changed once Jessie and Paul were married, although a few more items disappeared without explanation. But for Seranne, his presence and the way her mother agreed with the small changes he suggested, without consulting her, was making her restless. It would never go back to how it had been, herself and her mother in complete harmony and the place running as neatly as a train on tracks, it would only get worse.

She lay awake many nights wishing she could leave, but where would she go? All she had ever done was help her mother run the tea rooms, the prospect of walking away and finding somewhere to live and a job to pay for it was overwhelmingly frightening. The awful thing was she and Jessie frequently argued and that was something that had never happened before. She knew she was at fault, her temper had always been easily roused and she knew she overreacted to practically everything Paul said. It wasn't his presence in their lives, she thought she could learn to cope with that, it was his interference in the business they had managed all their lives.

"There is too much waste," he had announced quite soon after moving in.

"How can you say that? We throw very little away at the end of each day. Making fresh cakes in small batches throughout the day means we only cook what we need." Seranne protested.

"Hush, dear," Jessie pleaded. "Paul is a businessman and he understands things we don't. He's trying to help."

Because of the difficulty of keeping quiet, Seranne took to walking each evening whatever the weather. The only evenings she stayed in the flat was when her mother and Paul went out. This they did often. He took

Jessie dancing and occasionally for a meal in some expensive restaurant.

He was always the first to rise and his first move was to go down and collect the post, tucking anything that came for him in his pocket to read in private. Seranne's dislike of him didn't wane and she began to be suspicious about his eagerness to avoid anyone seeing his letters.

Finding the sandwiches with less filling, and cakes made smaller and the jam dishes less full, made her anger towards him increase. Every day there seemed to be more so-called improvements about which she disagreed.

"Our profits are sufficient and we don't need to cheat our customers," she shouted one evening when she tried to make her mother see what was happening. "People are remarking on the reduced measures and some are already finding other places to eat."

"Quality is what they come here for and that hasn't altered," Jessie insisted.

"Quality and a fair price! You can't reduce the quantity and expect them to pay the same."

"Paul says we've been giving too much and we should adjust our prices to other cafés in the area."

"Paul has a factory making leather bags! What does he know about tea rooms?"

"I'm a businessman, Seranne, and I can see why you aren't making the profits relating to the outlay."

Seranne ran out even though it was past ten o'clock and slammed the door behind her. Too late she remembered she didn't have a key. Now she would have to knock and ask to be let in. Why couldn't she stay calm? Deal with Paul in a reasonable way, persuade her mother to agree, instead of charging about like a spoilt child?

She had nowhere to go. She couldn't call on Babs, it was too far to go at this time of night. Disconsolately she wandered along the pavement, wishing she had slammed into her bedroom instead of out of the door. When she reached the corner she sat on the garden wall where the woman with the small terrier lived. "Just start barking at me tonight and I'll be ready for your owner!" she muttered, looking at the house and almost wishing the little dog would give her an excuse for an argument.

"Talking to yourself?"

Startled, she looked around her and saw Luke, the man from the corner table, walking towards her. "I wasn't talking," she retorted. "I'm thinking aloud." Without giving him a chance to say any more she hurried back home to the side door and knocked loudly, her irritability apparent. He walked past and her mood was worsened by the sound of his subdued laughter.

There was no immediate response to her knocking and she walked away, childishly hoping to punish her mother by making her worry. It was cold and she walked down the side of the kitchen to shelter from a rising wind.

Inside, Jessie was held back from opening the door by Paul. "Let her get chilled, it might cool her temper making her wait a little while," he said, caressing

Jessie's back, holding her close to him. Jessie waited about five minutes then pleaded with Paul to let her in.

Luke was still smiling as he reached his car and jumped in. She really was a hot-tempered character, but there was something almost childlike about her that appealed. He wondered whether she had always been ready for an argument or whether something in her life was causing her irritability. Not that he would ever find out. He knew her as a waitress in her mother's tea rooms and it would never go further than that. His days of being attracted to young women were over. It seemed he would never be free.

He saw the side door of the tea rooms open but instead of seeing Seranne go inside he saw Paul come out. Curious, he waited. Paul stood for a moment outside, then walked to the corner and stopped again. He looked as though he was waiting for someone. Then he heard running footsteps and two men appeared, nothing more than crouched figures in the darkness, and to his horror, he saw them leap on the man and as one held him the other punched him.

"Hey! Stop that," he called and ran across to intervene. Paul received several more blows before falling to the ground.

Luke heard the attackers muttering in a menacing way as they leant over the man before one ran off. The other said quite clearly, "Pay him, or there's worse than that coming to you." After pushing Luke aside and aiming one more punch, the second man followed the first and was quickly swallowed up in the darkness.

Seranne got to Paul almost as soon as Luke and together they helped the distressed man back to the flat.

"Did you know them? Were they trying to rob you?" Luke asked.

"I'll phone for the police," Jessie said tearfully.

"No, don't do that. What good would it do? They're long gone and I couldn't even describe them."

"The police need to be told."

"Please leave it. I must have been mistaken for someone else, or perhaps they were just looking for a fight. They smelt of drink. They won't come back."

Luke said nothing of what he had heard, following his own advice of not jumping to conclusions, he would make enquiries though, using the wide network of relations he had spread around the area. Among his army of aunts and uncles and cousins there was sure to be someone who would know what was going on. He left soon after helping Paul into bed.

Jessie and Seranne sat silently staring at the walls.

"A flood and now an attack on Paul, whatever next," Seranne said as she stood to go to her room.

"Both your fault," Jessie said, pushing her aside and going to join Paul. "You insisted on the new sink and it was you going out in a huff that caused Paul to be there when those men were wandering around looking for trouble."

Seranne couldn't believe what she had heard. How could her mother say such a terrible thing? She sat on her bed, huddled in the eiderdown unable to sleep until the reluctant dawn showed through the curtains. She had known Paul's arrival would mean changes, but she had never dreamt of things going so wrong between her mother and herself that she would be blamed for the flood and the mysterious attack on Paul.

CHAPTER
TWO

Paul seemed unaffected by the attack. Although the following morning he was easily persuaded not to go to the factory. He sat near the fire and between serving customers Jessie ran up and down attending to his comfort. Seranne was uneasy, doubting his explanation of mistaken identity. Paul was in trouble and by marrying her mother he had involved them too.

Luke called to ask about Paul and was surprised to hear that he wasn't at work. "I'd have thought that with a busy factory to run he'd have made the effort. Self-employment doesn't allow much time off for illness, does it?"

Seranne agreed but managed not to add her own criticisms. Two days passed and he seemed fully recovered.

Luke began to make enquiries and what he learnt worried him. Paul had bought out his partner and carried a large mortgage on the business. Many of the staff had left and Paul was reduced to untrained people who surely didn't have the skills needed for the work. He also learnt that orders were falling, faults were bringing many items back for replacement and the once good business was in serious trouble.

Seranne found living in the flat with her mother and Paul a strain. Seeing them together, interrupting them with their arms around each other, kissing, hugging, it should have been a happy experience, knowing her mother was no longer lonely should have made her happy for her, but she couldn't warm to the man.

She was constantly apologizing when she came across them sitting close together, heads touching, hands clasped. They often put dance music on the gramophone in the evenings and danced together. As an outsider she had no alternative but to go either to her room or out to see a film she didn't want to see, when she would have preferred to be at home, listening to the wireless and talking to her mother about the following day's work.

She felt hemmed in with nowhere to go. Jessie was obviously ecstatically happy but seeing her so content didn't change how Seranne felt about her mother's choice of husband. She was more and more convinced Jessie had made a terrible mistake in marrying him.

Seeing him go into her mother's bedroom made her want to run away. It was so embarrassing despite forcing herself not to think of them both in the double bed.

"If it was anyone else but Paul Curtis I'd have happily accepted it, but I don't trust him. And Mum is so besotted she agrees with everything he says," she told Babs one day.

"The best thing to do is keep out of the flat as much as you can. Come to stay with us on Saturday night for a start," Babs suggested, but Seranne shook her head.

"There's such a lot to do on Sundays, and besides, I'd be afraid of what he was doing while I was away. He's already tried to make us discard the linen tablecloths and use paper ones to cut down on laundry, and he's taken away the beautiful china teapots and plates from the shelves to save washing them every week. Those things set the scene for a pleasant interlude, it's all a part of what we offer, but can he see that? No, he can't! I have the horrifying thought that he will ruin everything then leave her."

"You think your mother is so unlovable that you can't believe he married her for anything less than love?"

"No, I . . . I'm being overprotective I suppose, but she's made so many mistakes in the past I presume this is another to add to the list."

"Try not to show it, you could be wrong, mind. It has been known," she added with a smile.

Hiding her feelings was something Seranne didn't find easy. When she went into the tea rooms to begin preparations for opening one morning, she saw that the bread rolls to serve with soup, which they had always made on the premises, were already made and cooling and had been cut to about half the usual size. Her mother would have done the baking but it was to Paul she went with her complaint.

"What do you think you're doing persuading Mum to make the rolls so small? How can I serve that as a bread roll?" she asked, poking one near his face. "It's little more than a marble!"

"Seranne, dear, don't blame Paul, I made them," Jessie said. "It seems a good idea, they're often only half eaten and I thought . . ."

"*You* thought? Or was it Paul?"

Seranne knew she was upsetting her mother but holding her temper was simply not easy. Also, she wanted her mother to know how she felt so that when it all fell apart, Jessie would know she could talk to her about Paul. It had all happened before, with boyfriends who were wonderful for a few weeks and then began to lose their charm. The only difference was that this time Jessie had married the man.

Other changes were made, none of them discussed. "Why don't we serve scones on serviettes to save washing dishes?" An outraged Seranne shouted one morning. "Serve tea out of jam jars? Soup from pickle jar lids?"

"Don't be ridiculous, Seranne. You're acting like a child these days just because of a few improvements suggested by Paul and not you!"

They continued to work together but spoke only when necessary. Seranne stayed out of the flat as much as possible. One evening Seranne was coming back from a walk in the chill of the evening when she saw Paul putting a notice on the tea room window: "This establishment will be closed from midday on Saturday until Tuesday morning," it announced.

"Paul? What's happened, is my mother ill?"

"Not ill exactly, but if you and I don't manage to sort out our differences she might well be ill and very soon. Can't you see what you're doing to her?"

35

"What *I'm* doing to . . ." she began. "It's you, interfering with the way we run this place, lowering the standards for which we're famous." He said nothing and she asked. "How will closing the tea rooms change anything?"

"The three of us are going away for the weekend, staying at an hotel and perhaps we'll find a way of getting on together, for your mother's sake," he said. This is a treat for her and I want you to come, but not if we're going to continue this arguing."

"I have no intention of going anywhere with you and my mother. The fact is —"

"The fact is, Seranne, I'm worried about her. Did you know she was crying the other day, after you'd complained about the reduction in the size of a bread roll?"

How petty that sounds, Seranne thought, but that was just one incident among many. She looked up at Paul prepared to argue further, but she stopped. She heard echoes of her voice, high pitched and filled with resentment. What was happening to her that she could behave in such a way? All the years with her mother without a single disagreement, and since her mother's marriage she had allowed the situation to change her into a nagging woman. There had to be a better way of dealing with this.

"All right, I'll come," she said, doubtfully.

"You can pay for yourself if it will make you feel better," he said.

"Yes, I will!"

She packed a small suitcase with comfortable outdoor clothes, determined that apart from mealtimes when she would be calm and polite, she would leave them alone. Paul drove her mother's car to the hotel and the atmosphere in the car was tense, conversations limited. None of them wanted to be there, each was doing it for someone else and they were all longing for Monday evening when they would be on the way home.

Paul was attentive and at his most charming best and she smiled and ignored the anger bubbling inside as he treated her mother like a delicate china doll, the capable woman she really was completely hidden.

The weather had been awful, low temperature, rain and wind keeping most people indoors, and she had been forced to spend more time than planned with her mother and Paul, who were clearly making a great effort to please her. On Sunday morning, ignoring the warning of worse weather to come, she left the hotel and began to walk. She sensed rather than saw her mother and stepfather watching her as she hurried out putting her coat on as she ran, the wind trying to steal it from her, gusts almost succeeding.

This was more than a windy early winter's day, the weather was threatening. The clouds were a dark swirling mass so low it seemed they were being torn by the trees that swayed like dancers to the wind's wild, discordant music. She could feel rain on the wind, which was increasing in strength minute by minute and knew she ought to turn back, but an hour later she was still walking away, her speed increasing, far from the shelter of the hotel, along an unknown country lane.

There was something exciting about being out in the storm, the wind matching the turbulence in her head. She appreciated the freedom as she tried to sort out the difficulties between herself, her mother Jessie and her stepfather, Paul Curtis.

Coming away for a couple of days, leaving behind the routine of their work, had been a good idea and despite her constant resentment towards Paul she had enjoyed it. Away from the confined activities of the business, in the cold, quiet countryside, meeting the occasional lone walker and sharing no more than a few words had rested her. Now, as the time to leave drew near she felt tension rising with every remark Paul made, aware the fault was mostly hers as she misconstrued the most innocent of comments. How could she be expected to watch him interfere with the business she and her mother had nurtured? She would have to be a saint.

That the business was a success was in no doubt, so why change anything, she had argued and, pulled by both loyalties, her mother had become upset until it had reached the point where they could hardly bear being in the same room.

She had doubted her mother's wisdom in marrying Paul, considering him rather dull, but had expected things to settle down, with herself and her mother continuing as before, but Paul was spending less and less time at the factory and more time with them. That in itself was a mystery and a subject which he refused to discuss.

"Oh *why* did she have to marry him?" she shouted into the wind, as she fought against it, battling her way between trees that lined the long, dark lane.

The lane turned and began to rise as she passed an estate of new houses and bungalows on her right. At the top of the hill she staggered as she faced the wind that roared through the woodland on her right and whistled around the roofs and chimney pots of a few detached houses on her left.

She knew she wasn't far from Cwm Derw and wasn't surprised to see, with the aid of a torch, a signpost that announced she was approaching the town. She thought she might call on Babs and Tony. Even on a Sunday there was sure be a bus to take her back to the hotel, or Babs would take her in the firm's van.

The first flash of lightning and crack of thunder reached her as she was passing the houses set back from the lane and she instinctively ducked as though avoiding a missile. The rain increased suddenly as though being poured from directly above her and she scuttled towards the nearest gateway and ran up the path to huddle against the front door for the little shelter it offered.

Furious with herself for being so foolish, she stood there, isolated by the curtain of rain and the dull roar of its ferocity. She wished she had worn a mackintosh instead of the woollen coat. Changing position to ease the cold, wet garment away from her legs, she leant on the door and it gave way, catapulting her inside to land in an undignified heap in the hallway.

She leapt up and stared around in vain, the darkness complete. Her sight gradually made out a little of her surroundings and she knew she was in a hallway. Deciding it was best to announce her presence in case her uninvited arrival had alarmed the occupant, she called, "Hello? I'm terribly sorry but the door gave way and . . ."

There was no reply, only her own voice echoing back mockingly. The place had a hollow feel and she guessed it was unoccupied. She shone her torch through a doorway and saw a kitchen and her impression was confirmed. Shelves were bare and cupboard doors hung open revealing their emptiness. There was none of the usual clutter, just a long table and a few chairs. Although the afternoon was dark and cold, and no place would have looked bright and cheerful, it was not just missing its occupants, it was completely deserted.

After calling a few more times and shivering with the cold, she began to cautiously explore. Venturing into what was the living-room, which, like the kitchen, was sparsely furnished, she then tiptoed back and sat in the kitchen staring out at the wildness beyond the windows. Thunder and lighting were in unison, the storm was overhead. She took off her dripping coat and hung it over a chair, her shivering ceased and she relaxed.

She wondered if her mother was worried. Childishly she hoped she was. She thought gloomily about how her life had been disrupted by the appearance of Paul in her mother's life.

Although Seranne sometimes regretted giving up on a life of her own, failing to make friends as she concentrated on helping her mother at the tea rooms, she accepted the social limitations and was almost content. Now, several years on, apart from a few niggles of unease, she had begun to accept that at twenty-two her life was set and she would continue in the same way until she became too old to try something new.

As she sat in the kitchen of the old house, listening to the storm growling around the roof top, her thoughts cleared, like a headache of which she hadn't even been aware. She became less centred on herself, and realized with a pain of guilt, that by staying at home she was ruining her mother's chance of happiness. She was being selfish and unkind. Paul was her mother's choice and she hadn't the right to cause trouble for them. She had a mental picture of the three of them: Jessie, Paul and herself, as though she were an outsider peering in through a window, observing people she didn't really know, and felt the pain of her mother trying to make her understand. There, in that empty house, with the storm howling around its walls, she realized she had to leave the tea rooms and the tiny flat they all shared, and find a new life for herself. In doing so she would be allowing her mother and stepfather to enjoy their second chance. It would also give herself an opportunity to decide how she would like to spend her life. Surely she didn't have to depend on her mother as though she were a child? She was twenty-two, it was time she moved on.

She sat for a long time, fearful at the prospect of giving up the security of the only home she had known, but there were moments when she felt a glowing excitement at the world beyond the tea rooms opening out for her.

As the storm raged around the old house she allowed her thoughts to drift, daydreaming over the possibilities. At first, each idea floated away as she clung to the life she knew but gradually she accepted the truth. She had fallen into the trap of clinging to security, afraid to risk letting go.

Surprisingly, she was no longer cold, the chill of the night failed to penetrate the stout, stone walls. The atmosphere in the house was comforting and its age gave a sense of timelessness that soothed her. "Today's troubles will be history after the passing of a few days," it seemed to say.

Relaxed and at ease with herself, she became filled with happier thoughts about her mother and aware that life had given her mother a second chance, which meant a second chance for herself too. "It's time to move on," the soft murmuring of the house seemed to say, repeating it over and over again.

She became aware that the storm had passed over, the only evidence of it was the shushing murmur of the moving trees, which were shaking drips of rain down the windowpanes.

Putting on her coat that was unpleasantly cold and wet, she buttoned it and fished out a soggy headscarf from a pocket. Wet she certainly was but at least she looked sensibly dressed and less like an idiot who had ignored the early warning of the storm. With her coat clinging to her and chilling her again, she went down the path and turned left towards the village. Abandoning the idea of calling on Babs, she was relieved to see a group of people at the end of the lane, standing near a bus stop. Thank goodness she had brought her purse, she thought as she joined the small queue. The passengers were discussing the storm and she was encouraged to join their conversations, giving her a new sensation of being a part of the wider world outside Jessica's Victorian Tea Rooms. She didn't know where she was going, but knew she was on her way.

Although her wet clothes were far from comfortable, she felt light-hearted, as though a weight had been lifted from her mind. A decision had been made; she was leaving home, saying goodbye to the café where she had worked since childhood. The next problem was where she would go and what she would do, but that was a problem for tomorrow.

When she reached the hotel she saw her parents sitting at a table near the bar. Paul had his arm on Jessie's shoulder and she was laughing. Seranne was startled at how young and lovely her mother looked. It was as though she hadn't really looked at her before. It reinforced her decision.

"Mum? Paul? I've come to a momentous decision," she announced. She laughed at the anxious expressions and went on. "I'm leaving the tea rooms in your capable hands, and going to explore a little of the world."

Jessie looked hesitant, beginning to shake her head, but Paul smiled, stood up and hugged her and wished her "all the luck in the world".

There was no doubt he welcomed her decision, nor that her leaving would be a relief, but in her buoyant mood she hugged him back, appreciating his honesty.

The idea of coming away from the small flat and relaxing in the pampered comfort of a decent hotel had been Paul's but his plan was not altogether altruistic. He was in serious trouble. The factory had lost all of the managing staff and most of its employees and new ones were difficult to train. He had left too much to his managers and charge hands and now they were no longer there, he was unable to step into their place.

Using Jessie's money had saved him from the worst outcome and he desperately needed to find a way of paying it back. At least with bankruptcy avoided he could start again, open another business and once it was a success, he'd be able to look after her properly. She'd be able to give up the tea rooms and be cared for as she deserved.

The work had been less than perfect over the previous weeks, complaints were increasing and orders were becoming fewer each month. The results for August through to October had shown a serious fall in his once generous income and November was likely to be even worse. He had married Jessie believing he could increase her profits and hide the lack of the income he no longer earned. He loved her, she was so pretty and bright and she filled him with pride when they were together. But he had an ache in his heart when he thought about how he had cheated, pretending to be a successful businessman, when in fact everything had been about to collapse around him.

During their time away he had made a decision. He couldn't delay any longer, he had to act soon. The money that remained in his diminishing account and what he could get from the sale of the factory would be used to start a completely new venture. What that would be he'd not yet decided, but knowing he was looking for something fresh would open his eyes to possibilities and it wouldn't be long before he was earning again. Jessie might not even know how close he'd come to disaster. He would put the factory up for sale and there were several items in the café and flat that he could persuade Jessie they no longer needed. Every few pounds would help and he'd repay her once he was a success. There was no need to tell her until the new business, whatever it would be, was up and buzzing.

Seranne found the prospect of setting out on her own seriously daunting, it was one thing to make such a life-changing decision but entirely another to do something about it. A visit to the employment exchange encouraged her. There were plenty of jobs available, she just had to decide what she wanted to do.

"Coward that I am, I want to stay with what I know and look for work in a tea shop," she said to her mother.

"There's no hurry," Jessie assured her.

"Maybe not, but tomorrow I'm ready to start my search," Seranne said emphatically.

Meanwhile the work of running Jessica's Victorian Tea Rooms continued. Although November and December were generally quiet months, in the year of 1952 there was a determination among the public to make Christmas one of the best. Food rationing was still in force but one or two concessions from the government had given a few extras. Groups of friends and neighbours met at the tea rooms to discuss plans.

More than seven years had passed since the end of the war and families were used to sharing what they had. The exchange of goods in a barter system that had helped many to survive was still in existence. Queues still grew when something "off ration" appeared and the news of a bargain spread by mouth faster than any modern communication invented by man.

For Seranne and her mother things had always been a little easier. Although they didn't cheat on their allowances, leftover meals and cakes meant they were better fed and could afford to be generous with their friends. So as plans were prepared for Christmases at home, bookings were also made for parties to use the tea rooms for families and friends to celebrate. For once, this growing excitement didn't thrill Seranne. Having made up her mind to leave she was determined to do so before the year ended.

She couldn't explain why, but she couldn't put the small town of Cwm Derw out of her mind. She had seen it at its worst; dark clouds and heavy rain and even thunder and lightning, walking in soaking-wet clothes that had felt like an ill-fitting skin. That should have been enough to discourage a second visit, but the peace of that old abandoned house and the friendly chatter of the people on the bus journey back to the hotel had stayed in her memory.

On the following Sunday afternoon, leaving her mother and Paul to deal with the usual weekend tasks, she went again to Cwm Derw and stepped off the bus near the post office in the main road. She glanced over at Hopkins's bakery shop. Cwm Derw would be a good place to start out, with friends Babs and Tony there to ease her into the neighbourhood.

A bus trundled into sight and on impulse she jumped on and made her way to the house on the lane where she had sheltered from the worst of the storm. She stared up at its windows feeling a pull of welcome that warmed her and she went up to look inside, her heart racing with excitement. Nothing had changed, it was still unoccupied. She stood looking up at its gleaming windows and touched the old walls, feeling the warmth of them spreading through her and it was a long time before she turned and headed back to the main road.

Opposite Hopkins's bakery was a café, but being Sunday it was closed. There was a large notice stuck on the window advertising a vacancy for a general assistant. A bit different from running our own place, she thought, but curious, she crossed the road to look inside. It didn't look very attractive compared with Jessica's Victorian Tea Rooms, dull-brown paint and unadorned windows, but the food might be good enough to encourage customers, she mused. It would do no harm to talk to the manager and see what the prospects were of working there.

She turned away to recross the road and waited for an approaching car to pass, unaware of standing near a large puddle. As she waited for the solitary car to pass her, she was showered with dirty water that flew up like huge wings from the wheels. It drenched her from her head to her feet.

Gasping with the shock of it, she turned as though demanding to see someone who would commiserate. A woman stood near the post office and Seranne asked, "Did you see that?"

"No, and apparently you didn't see the puddle, or you'd have moved," the woman retorted.

"He should have slowed down!"

"Tell him that, if you can catch up with him!" She walked away.

An MG sports car was parked at the side of the road and as she watched, still glaring furiously to where the offending motorist had disappeared, a man approached the sports car and jumped in. She couldn't be certain but thought it was Luke. She had been splashed with muddy water and her coat was stained and dripping. Even her hair had been caught in the unexpected shower. She could feel rivulets of dirty water running down her face.

"What a mess I must look," she wailed as she tried to turn away to avoid recognition. Twice in a week she had visited Cwm Derw and twice she had been soaked. And if that onlooker was an example of the inhabitants, then she ought to accept her mistake and leave. The sooner the better!

The man stepped out of the sports car and hurried towards her. "Miss Laurence?" Luke said. "What on earth made you stand beside a huge puddle like that? You must have seen it?"

"How was I to know that an inconsiderate motorist was about to race through without a thought for others?"

"May I offer you a lift? I'm passing the tea rooms so it won't be out of my way."

He was the very last person she wanted to see her like this, and he was laughing! She pulled up her collar in an ineffectual attempt to hide her dirt-streaked face and began a blustering refusal. "I'm perfectly all right, thank you."

She was relieved when a voice called, and she turned to see a woman wearing an apron and slippers standing in the doorway of the post office. "Come on in, girl, and get dry. Terrible careless that was." In her rage, Seranne expected this woman blamed her too, but the woman added. "The man was driving like a maniac."

Seranne walked to where the woman was waiting and gladly accepted the invitation. Luke watched for a while then drove away, still smiling.

Seranne Laurence really was a quick-tempered young woman, but there was something appealing about her. Perhaps if things had been different, he might have enjoyed getting to know her, but he didn't want any more disasters in his life.

"I'm the post mistress, Stella Jones." Stella offered her hand, then began to peel the coat off her visitor. She ushered her into a warm, over-crowded room where a fire burned brightly sending its cheer flickering around the walls. Stella unceremoniously tipped a little dog off a chair and invited Seranne to sit. At once the dog jumped back up and settled on Seranne's lap. "Terrible spoilt he is," Stella said casually.

An hour later, Stella had learnt all she needed to know about her unexpected guest and had informed Seranne that the café across the road was looking for an assistant who could manage basic cooking.

"I'll have a word if you like, tell Mrs Rogers your experienced and not afraid of water — handy that'll be if you're expected to wash up," she teased. "Glad to have you she'll be, you having owned your own place an' all."

"I'll need to look for somewhere to stay," Seranne said hesitatingly. Although her plan was to move out before the end of the year, this was going too fast.

"Can you afford a reasonable rent?"

"I think so, as long as the wages aren't too mean. Although having been soaked twice on visits, perhaps I ought to choose somewhere else to start my new life!" She told Stella about being caught in the storm and sheltering in an old house on the lane.

"Such a friendly, welcoming house, even though I only saw it in the dark." She saw Stella was staring at her strangely and stood to leave. "If I do get a job in the café, is there a bed and breakfast place near?"

"Well, yes, but the house Badgers Brook is empty. I'll take you there if you like. Can you ride a bike?"

Being in business, Stella was one of the few people in the town to have a telephone; the owner of Badgers Brook, who ran an ironmonger's business, was another. Stella Jones made an excited phone call then announced that, "Geoff and Connie Tanner will meet us there in twenty minutes. Your coat will be warm by then if not dry." She shook it and changed its position on a clothes horse near the fire and took the cups and saucers they had used into the kitchen, singing cheerfully.

To Seranne's surprise, the house they were to see was the one in which she had sheltered on the day of the storm. Geoff and Connie were already there, a fire had been lit and cups and saucers and a few small cakes set out on the kitchen table.

"Connie never goes out without a picnic," Stella explained after introductions.

The place was warm even though the fire could not have been lit for long. Seranne wandered in and out of the rooms in a dream. There were a couple of beds and a wardrobe left by a previous tenant. Curtains were in place and the bedroom floors were covered with linoleum. Downstairs the floors were large slabs of Welsh slate and Seranne thought that only one or two rugs were needed to make it perfect. It was a heavenly place. From the kitchen window, she looked out on woodland on the opposite side of the lane just waiting to be explored, and at the front of the house facing away from the lane, there was a surprisingly neat and orderly garden.

"My Colin helps with the garden," Stella said proudly. "Him and Bob Jennings. Bob and Kitty will be your neighbours on the lane."

Seranne was amused at the way she had stumbled by chance on the place. But when she said so, Stella shook her head, "No, not by chance. This house invited you. Chooses its tenants it does."

Seranne smiled at the bit of whimsy and turned to Connie and Geoff aware of a bubble of excitement welling up inside her. "If you'll have me, I'd love to live here."

"We'll lend you a few pieces of furniture to get you started," Connie said with a warm, friendly smile.

"I certainly won't need more chairs, there seems to be plenty of those left by the previous tenant," Seranne said, pointing at the row against the living-room wall. "Enough to open a café of my own!"

"Oh, they'll come in handy," Connie replied. "Badgers Brook is a friendly house." Having agreed the rent, the only thing left was to apply for the vacancy at the café, which she still hadn't properly seen. She hoped it was more exciting than the view she'd had from across the road before being soaked by that careless driver.

They and their bicycles were given a lift back in Geoff and Connie's van, which smelled strongly of paraffin, and Stella and Connie went with her to look through the window of the café. The place was a long way from the beautiful tea rooms she and her mother ran. Tables covered with American cloth that was easily wiped clean, chairs scuffed and of several different styles. The walls were painted cream, but apart from a mirror to enable those in the kitchen to see the tables, bore no decoration. She wondered sadly whether she could work in such a place.

She went to the bakery opposite to tell Babs her news. Small, plump and, rosy cheeked, Babs gave a whoop of delight when she heard her friend would be moving to Cwm Derw. She called her brother Tony and they sat and discussed things until Seranne had missed her last bus. Tony offered to drive her home, but Babs insisted. "Tony gets up before four o'clock to start the baking. I'll drive you," she insisted. "Fantastic!" she said as they set off. "It'll be great to have you living near. And, I do think you're right to leave home and let your mum and Paul get on with their life."

"The café doesn't look inspiring but if I do get the job I might be able to change things, smarten it up."

Babs shook her head. "Mrs Rogers isn't one to accept change. Mind you, she hasn't met you yet, has she!"

When Seranne returned home she looked around their attractive tea rooms with some anxiety. Could she really leave all this and start again in that sad café and live among strangers? Then she called up a picture of the house on the lane and the smiling faces of all but one of the few inhabitants she had met and knew that whatever happened, she would not be among strangers for long. Stella Jones was right, by some mysterious way the house had invited her in.

Luke was best forgotten, he was just a foolish, half-formed daydream and not important. She seethed when she remembered the soaking, and the embarrassment of his undisguised amusement. Her coat needed dry-cleaning and she hoped the unsympathetic onlooker would soon suffer the same fate.

She went back the following day after a phone call and met the café manager, Mrs Rogers, who offered her the job. "From what you tell me your present position is a bit more glamorous than this place, so don't expect me to provide tablecloths and fancy cakes. It doesn't attract that kind of customer," Mrs Rogers said warningly.

Seranne was about to suggest that a little improvement would encourage a few more people through the door, but she stopped in time. This wasn't the moment. Taking things slowly she could do a lot more and besides, she didn't want to lose the job within minutes of being offered it!

"We buy bread and cakes from Hopkins's bakery and when there's time I sometimes make a few scones."

"I can do that. Scones are one of my specialities."

"Scones we sell but specialities are not on the menu. Right?"

She went to see Geoff and Connie at their ironmonger's store to pay her first week's rent and found them both serving customers at the worn wooden counter. To her annoyance, one of the women waiting to be served was the woman who had witnessed her soaking the previous day. She waited, staring at her until she saw her, then glared and turned quickly away.

"She's the woman who was so rude to me when I got soaked by that thoughtless driver," she hissed.

"That's Mrs Williamson-Murton. She's very unhappy. Don't let her worry you," Connie said.

"But she was blaming me! I got soaked! I was the one expecting sympathy and she blamed me," Seranne insisted.

"She lost two of her three sons," Connie explained. "How can she cope with such tragedies? Go in and make a cup of tea, we'll join you as soon as we've finished serving."

"But there was no need to be so rude!" Seranne pushed past two women customers, still irritated by Connie's apparent lack of sympathy, as a man standing at the counter picked up his order and faced her.

"Nice to see you again, Miss Laurence," said Luke, with a solemn expression. "Eggs, water, you do have fun."

She looked about to explode and he looked away, and it wasn't until he left the shop that he showed amusement. Seranne Laurence was attractive, but really pompous.

Inside, before she went through into Connie's kitchen, Seranne glared at his departing back.

Back in Jessica's Victorian Tea Rooms, Jessie and Paul were discussing Seranne's hastily made decision.

"Don't worry," Paul said, "it's probably a brief defiant gesture. She'll be back in a week or so. She'll miss you too much to stay away."

"If she doesn't, I'll need some help," Jessie said. "I can't run this place alone. And even if it is only for a few weeks, I'll need an assistant, and an experienced one too."

"I'll do what I can," Paul said.

Jessie ignored his offer, an amateur was not what she needed. "I'll ring the employment exchange and see if there's anyone available."

An hour later she had interviewed two girls and taken them both on promising to choose one of them at the end of a week. She still hoped that Seranne would be back and she wouldn't need either of them.

Paul's thoughts didn't echo Jessie's. He hoped Seranne would stay away. She would interfere with his plans for the future — a future that didn't include a dated, old-fashioned tea rooms.

Leaving Connie at the shop, Geoff took Seranne to Badgers Brook and with pencil and paper she made a list of what she would need. "Bedding, cutlery and china, cooking utensils. My mother will probably help me with enough to start with. After all, there'll only be me."

"Maybe, but don't be surprised if you need more. Badgers Brook loves visitors."

More whimsy, she thought with a smile.

A week later she moved in. Her mother and Paul brought a car loaded with necessities including some food to help fill her pantry. It was late when they arrived and too dark for her mother to see anything of the area. They did find Gwenny Flint's fish and chip shop open, and they sat in the kitchen of her new home and enjoyed their first meal.

Seranne wanted her mother to look around the house, get the feel of it, love it as much as she did, but Paul was impatient to leave and she was suddenly alone, in a house with only gaslight in a few rooms, and candles to light her way to bed. It was frightening and at first she wondered if she would manage even one night there. She made a hot drink and sat by the remnants of the fire and sleep began to overcome her. Locking the doors, pulling on the chain to put out the gaslights, she made her way up the stairs, undressed and slept soundly until morning.

She had arranged to start at the café the following week, planning to spend a few days settling in and exploring the neighbourhood. First on her list was to register with a grocer's shop for her food ration.

Mrs Harvey welcomed her and prepared her first week's food ration. When she saw the amount of food she would have to survive on she was shocked. The whole amount didn't fill a dinner plate. Having left all that to her mother she had no idea of how amazing the women were who had coped with shortages since 1940. She decided that most of her meals would be taken at the café!

Twice more Paul left Jessie in the tea rooms and drove to Cwm Derw with more of Seranne's belongings and every time she watched him leave, Jessie felt more dismayed. Any hope of an immediate return seemed less and less likely. Of the two girls she had employed, one seemed vaguely possible although she would need training, but she didn't want her there, she wanted Seranne back.

Paul comforted her and tried to help. He persuaded her that an older, more experienced woman would be a better choice and he introduced her to Pat Sewell, a widow with three children, who had worked in cafés all her working life. Jessie didn't take to her, she had the feeling the woman would expect a lot of her own ideas to be instigated, her own pushed aside, but Paul was very persuasive and Jessie did love to agree with him, make him feel he was in charge. She hoped one of the two girls she had on trial would do instead but had doubts.

Paul had begun to do the weekly accounts telling her that by taking those off her hands meant she had more time to spend teaching her individual ways to the new assistants. Jessie was forced to admit that neither suited and after Paul's repeated persuasions, she interviewed and employed Mrs Pat Sewell.

Jessie's first impressions were confirmed. Mrs Sewell was very confident, in fact, even during the original interview she was forceful with her opinions about how Jessica's Victorian Tea Rooms should be run. Jessie sighed and accepted that Pat Sewell was the best she could hope for at such short notice, and prayed that her daughter would some day return.

After one week in the Cwm Derw café, which she began to clean and freshen, Seranne offered to paint the chairs on her weekends. She bought paint and brushes from Geoff, explaining what she was doing.

58

"Good heavens, haven't you got enough to do? After moving in, people usually spend weeks changing things around and getting everything as they want it."

"Not Badgers Brook. It's perfect. Apart from adding two rugs and all my bits and pieces, there's nothing more to do."

"We'll come and give you a hand, if you like," Connie offered and the following weekend found them in the yard behind the café and, with Mrs Rogers looking on and pointing out where they had "missed a bit", the work was done.

That Mrs Rogers disapproved was in no doubt, but Connie and Geoff made the work fun.

"I'm hoping the atmosphere will improve if it looks more cheerful," Seranne explained to Connie in a whisper. "There's clearly no encouragement for customers to relax or stay longer than the time needed to drink their coffee and eat their food. Perhaps Christmas will give us the opportunity to liven things up."

"Will you be going home for Christmas?" Connie asked, as they were cleaning their brushes.

"Mum's café is usually very busy right up to Christmas Eve, and she always provides a free meal for people who live alone, on Christmas Day. We have our meal in the evening. So I expect I'll be needed."

"That's a very kind thought," Connie said, her face lighting up. "I bet there'll be plenty offering contributions if we tried it here in Cwm Derw."

"Make it a few days before and I'll be happy to help," Seranne said at once.

Later, she was glad she had made the offer. When she made a brief visit home, she found arrangements had been made for several people, including Pat Sewell, to help with the charity meal, and her help wasn't needed. To cover her disappointment, Seranne said, "Thank goodness, Mum. You see I've volunteered to help with something similar in Cwm Derw." She didn't explain that the date for the lunch in Cwm Derw would not be the same.

Connie commiserated when she heard. "It confirmed that you did the right thing in coming to Cwm Derw. It opened its doors wide and welcomed you in."

"And my home has closed its door behind me," Seranne replied.

"No, Seranne. Your home will always be there — if you ever want to go back."

During the following few weeks many of the local people introduced themselves to Seranne. Kitty and Bob Jennings, who lived next door along the lane called often and left little treats of vegetables, flowers and on occasions a small pie or a cake or two. Betty Connors who ran the Ship and Compass pub knocked on the door one Sunday afternoon bringing cakes and hinting about a cup of tea. They were followed by Stella Jones from the post office with her husband Colin and their little terrier, Scamp. Seranne soon realized what Connie had meant about the large number of chairs.

Betty explained that the place had always been a regular place for local people to "drop in". "But if you don't want that, you only have to tell us, mind."

"Heavens, I need you all," Seranne assured her. "I love being among friends." Risking being laughed at she added, "And in some funny way I know the house likes to be filled with people."

"It never takes a new tenant long to learn that," Connie said.

"When I worked with my mother there was never any time to meet friends. We were in the tea rooms from Monday to Saturday and Sundays were filled with preparations for the week ahead. Now I leave the café at six and forget about it until the following morning, I'd be lost if I sat here all alone every evening," Seranne said. She marvelled at how her life had changed. While she had shared responsibility for Jessica's Victorian Tea Rooms, she would never have imagined having such a social life, or living in a house where everyone immediately felt at home.

The plans for a Christmas Dinner for local people living alone went ahead and was arranged for Sunday, 21 December. It was to be held in the Ship and Compass and with Betty helping, Seranne listed the offers of food and decided on a menu. Several people offered chairs and china and at eight o'clock in the morning, help began to arrive. Alun Harris, who helped Betty run the Ship was already putting up the trestle tables and a small army of men and women walked in carrying quantities of food. One was the woman who had been so offensive when Seranne had been caught in the slipstream of that speeding car and momentarily anger flared again, but she turned away and went on basting the chickens given by the local poultry farmer and allowed her resentment to fade away. Betty was peeling vegetables and Stella and Kitty were setting out the long trestle tables running across both bar rooms in readiness.

"Hello Luke," Stella called.

Seranne looked up to see if it was the same Luke from the tea rooms. It was, and she felt her cheeks colour and she busied herself unnecessarily with the oven. In her agitation she was careless with the oven cloth and her bare hand touched the edge of the hot baking tin. She closed the door and jumped up, her eyes glaring as she looked around. The man stood beside her as she eventually straightened up and she looked into a face that was finding it impossible not to smile.

"I've burnt myself!" she said angrily, and at once he burst into laughter. He led her to the sink and thrust her hand under the tap. She pulled herself free, refusing to allow him to help and as Stella came in he walked away.

"Did you see that?" Seranne said loudly. "He laughed when I said I was hurt. What is the matter with the man?"

"Luke, come and say you're sorry," Stella said, but Luke was no longer there.

With second helpings of each course, and Betty having provided a glass of port for them all, it was almost five o'clock before everyone had gone. As Seranne was walking back to Badgers Brook with Kitty and Bob Jennings later that evening, a car pulled up beside them and a voice asked if they would like a lift.

"Yes, please," Kitty said at once, but Seranne had recognized the voice of Luke and hurried on. Kitty and Bob got in and Luke drove slowly until he caught up with the fast pace of Seranne. He asked again, promised not to laugh but she shook her head and hurried on. She'd rather have walked through a thunderstorm than accept a lift from that man.

Babs and Tony were at Badgers Brook one evening, having been invited for supper and to help Seranne decorate the room for the festivities.

"I'm not looking forward to Christmas," Seranne admitted. "I'd presumed I would go home, but perhaps because I didn't sound wildly enthusiastic or because Mum and Paul are hoping for a Christmas alone, neither of us persisted, and I ended up apologizing and explaining that so many invitations meant I couldn't leave Cwm Derw."

"You won't be wrong about that. Mam asked us to tell you we'd like you to spend Christmas Day with us, and there'll be plenty of other people wanting your company."

"Thanks, but can I wait for a while before accepting? You never know, Mum might come and ask me to go home."

She had tried not to be hurt when her mother easily agreed to her staying away, and she covered her disappointment with forced excitement at the prospect of her first Christmas on her own. Invitations did come but she refused the first few. Geoff and Connie invited her to lunch but she was convinced they didn't really want a stranger there. Stella and Colin, and Kitty and Bob, all offered invitations which were politely declined. She was sure that she wasn't really wanted on what was a family occasion. After more persuasion, she relented. To refuse would appear surly and unfriendly after everyone had been so welcoming and kind.

Christmas Day was spent partly at Stella and Colin's small room behind the post office and in the evening, she was invited to dinner at the Ship. Alun had cooked the meal and during the conversation, he explained that he had once owned his own restaurant. They talked about their differing experiences in catering. The café on the main road of Cwm Derw was hardly in the same league as his establishment but he offered suggestions and Seranne was interested, even though the place was not her own.

"I'll try the ideas on Mrs Rogers, but I don't expect she'll be keen. I quickly learnt that she doesn't like changes," she told him. She described the pretty tea rooms where she had worked all her life. "Glass-fronted shelves filled with dolls in Victorian dress, and china tea plates and beautiful vases of dried flowers above the picture rail. The gingham trimming and the linen tablecloths that are darned but still immaculately white, fine china Mum still manages to provide, even after the years of shortages."

"I don't think Mrs Rogers would cope with all the work that entails," Betty said. "But one day, when she retires you might be able to change things."

"I talk about starting a new life and I have to some extent, but my dream is one day to own a café just like Jessica's Victorian Tea Rooms. So my dream hasn't taken me far, has it?"

"Nothing's impossible, Seranne," Alun said. "Keep dreaming the dream, wait for the opportunity and if you really want it, you'll seize the moment and make it happen."

"And while you wait, be happy," Betty added.

Alun and Betty walked her home in the cold crisp air, and she went into Badgers Brook utterly content. She might have been forced to make the changes by the arrival of Paul Curtis, but the present was good and a future beckoned that was even better.

CHAPTER
THREE

Betty Connors had lived in the Ship and Compass all her life. The public house had been owned by her grandparents then her parents, and when they passed away it had been left to Betty and her brother Ed. He had not been interested in owning the place with all the accompanying problems and, after valuation, she had bought him out. Ed had continued to work for her until he had married Elsie Clements who owned the local guest house behind the post office.

Since Ed moved out Betty had found it difficult to find a reliable assistant. Some were useless and others were good but didn't want to stay. For a few weeks, Alun Harris, who had worked casually for Jake Llewelyn at the boat yard, had become at first an occasional help then had agreed to work for her full-time. She was delighted as he was experienced, having run his own restaurant, and was good with customers. She hardly had to explain a thing, he had fitted into the place as though born to it.

Even their sense of humour was the same and they only had to look at each other to share the fun of something said in the bar. She stood at the door of the cellar and listened as he moved things around making room for new stock, preparing for a delivery. He whistled as he worked and she hoped he'd stay for ever. She knew it was foolish to think that way. He was a qualified and experienced chef used to running something more complicated than a small pub in a small Welsh town, and would be off one day to revive his own career. But still, there was no harm in hoping, she thought as she gave the bar top an extra rub.

She went into the room behind the bar and turned up the heat under the kettle. It was time for their mid-morning cup of tea and a snack. Working through until two o'clock, they usually had something before they opened and then relaxed after everything was done, to sit and eat their main meal.

Today it was her turn to cook and she'd queued that morning and bought some fish with which she planned to make a potato-topped pie. She wasn't as imaginative as Alun, but he never criticized her plain and simple food. She'd been given a few extra eggs so perhaps she would make some real custard to liven up the remains of yesterday's sponge cake.

Her brother Ed called as she was pouring their tea and she added another cup to the tray. "How is Elsie?" she asked, always her first question. Ed's wife was suffering from a muscle-wasting disease that made her less and less able to help with the running of the guest house.

"Not so good. Yesterday was a good day and I think she did more than was sensible."

Betty handed him his tea as Alun came to join them. "Can I do anything?" she asked.

Ed shrugged his shoulders. "Not really. I'm coping all right, with the nurses coming in and making sure she's comfortable. We're quiet at the moment, only a couple of people staying and two cyclists expected this afternoon."

Betty shuddered. "Cycling? In this weather?"

"We don't get as many as we used to. More people are buying cars these days. I wish I had a car. It would be nice to take Elsie out sometimes — when she's well enough."

Alun threw his keys on the table. "Use mine whenever you need it," he said. "I don't use it much."

"There's mine too," Betty said reprovingly. "You know you only have to ask."

"How could I ask you? You've never approved of me marrying Elsie."

"What rubbish. It was nothing to do with me. I knew she was ill and I only wanted you to make sure you knew what you were letting yourself in for, that's all."

"She makes me happy. Right?"

"And I'm glad. Right?"

Alun stood up, aware that they were heading for one of their rows. "And I want to wash the front windows before we open. Right?" he said with a grin.

The Ship was busy that lunchtime and after they had closed and eaten their meal Betty said, "I think I'll go and see Elsie, perhaps take her a few flowers."

"I'll go for a walk. Even in this cold January weather Cwm Derw is a beautiful place."

"Think you'll stay around here?" she asked casually. "When you look for a place of your own?"

He stared at her and then smiled, his blue eyes seeming to stare into her mind to see what was there. "That's up to you, isn't it?"

"I don't want you to go," she said at once. "I've never had anyone so easy and pleasant to work with as you, Alun."

"Good," he replied. He was still smiling at her as she turned away and reached for her coat.

Elsie was sitting in her usual chair near the fire and Ed had just brought her a cup of tea and a biscuit. The affection between them warmed Betty as she sat near them both after Ed had brought another cup and saucer. Elsie was always smiling, her cheerfulness forbade sympathy and she brushed away any attempt at it in a light-hearted way. Elsie wouldn't live into old age, but Betty knew that Ed would never regret the time he spent with her and was building happy memories to comfort him after she had gone.

She sipped her tea and listened to them laughing about some of their more unusual guests, watching in delight at the way Ed jumped up the moment Elsie needed even the slightest help. She marvelled at the change in her brother. When he had helped at the Ship he had been unwilling to do more than the basic tasks, and managed to talk himself out of many that he should have done with easily found excuses.

She remembered once when the cleaner had failed to turn up and a delivery was expected and a phone call from one of his friends had him running through the door ignoring her demands that he stayed and did what she paid him for and be there to open up. She watched now as he helped Elsie with her food, doing more than was necessary and she delighted in his attentions, at the way they looked at each other. Their affection for each other was strong and she wondered at the power of love to change people so remarkably.

Alun had left Betty at the turning for the guest house and went on past a group of people waiting for a bus. He wore a heavy waterproof coat, wellingtons on his feet, a rather battered trilby on his head. A large man, he moved fast through the wet streets and headed for the lanes. He greeted those he knew with a lift of his hat and with long strides soon left them behind.

The drizzly rain didn't affect his contented mood. On the branches and leaves as he entered the wood he saw the glitter of raindrops and likened them to diamonds. Underfoot, the slippery mud in which the debris of long dead plants was revealed in the hint of many colours pleased his eye, and he even found the smells of winter exciting. Cwm Derw was a good place to live.

He stopped to look at the badgers' sett that had given the stream and the house their names. He paused again to pick a few branches of the chestnut that was showing the first hint of sticky buds, beauty waiting in the wings to perform its spring drama. Betty would enjoy watching the buds unfold.

There wasn't time to go far but he had half decided to walk through the lower part of the wood from where he could look down on the old farm buildings and the new bungalows that had replaced the animals in

Treweather's fields. Wandering idly he came close to the edge of the trees on the road opposite Badgers Brook. On impulse, he walked up the path to the door and the kitchen window intending to leave a few of the branches for Seranne.

He knew Seranne was working at the café so he was curious to see the silhouette of someone inside. Probably Kitty, who he knew looked after Seranne by getting fires lit, or opening windows on mild days to freshen the house. This wasn't Kitty, though, it was definitely a man. It was probably innocent but he knocked on the door anyway. No harm in checking.

A man opened the door, someone he hadn't seen before.

"Oh, hello," Alun said. "I just wondered whether the lady of the house was home. He stepped inside and put the branches on the kitchen table.

"No, I'm sorry, she's at work."

"I see. And you would be . . .?" he questioned.

"I'm her father."

"Oh, hello, I'm Alun Harris, I work at the Ship and Compass. I'll tell Seranne you're here if I see her, shall I?"

"Thank you." The man stood holding the door obviously wanting him to leave.

Still doubtful, but realizing he could hardly ask the man to leave his daughter's home, Alun stepped outside. "Nice to meet you," he said but the man didn't reply. The door closed swiftly behind him and Alun turned away from his intended walk and hurried back to the main road. He ought to tell Seranne, describe the man, reassure himself that the man was really her father. He headed for the café, after a glance at his watch with the aid of a torch. He needed to hurry, he had to be back and ready for the evening opening.

The café was busy, the windows steamed up from the cooking and the wet coats of the customers. He went in and explained to Seranne that she had a visitor. "He said he's your father."

"Stepfather," she corrected. "I wonder what he wants? Perhaps Mum is ill."

"I didn't ask." Alun didn't explain that the door had been closed before he'd had the chance. He was still uneasy and after explaining to Betty he got into the car and drove to Badgers Brook, parking on the lane a short distance from the gate.

Seranne left early after a word with Mrs Rogers and jumping off the bus, ran down the lane towards the house. A gaslight showed through the kitchen window and looking in before opening the door she saw Paul dozing in a chair. She went in and touched his shoulder to wake him.

"Sorry, I must have dozed off. How odd. That's something I never do. It's very quiet and peaceful here, isn't it?"

"Why are you here? Is Mum all right?"

He rubbed his eyes and stretched. "Funny that, me sleeping in the day."

"It's a very relaxing house, now please tell me, is she ill?"

"Not ill exactly, but I think she's a bit tired and I want to take her away again, just for a few days, a little holiday would be good for her and perhaps she'd get used to the idea of letting go a little, leaving more of the day to day management to others. And it's the quietest time in the tea rooms, isn't it?"

"Are you sure she's not ill?"

"To be honest, she was upset when you left and she hasn't felt really well since. Could you come and look after things for a week while I take her to the sea side?"

"How can I? I have a job here and I don't want to lose it."

"Don't worry, Pat — Mrs Pat Sewell — will run the place. She's fitted in very well. I just had to ask, you might have been hurt if I hadn't at least asked."

"You're sure she's capable, this — Mrs Sewell?"

"Pat. Yes, she and your mother get on very well. Different ideas about some things, but nothing they don't sort out between them."

"I'll come on Sunday and perhaps I can meet her and make sure all is well. Sorry I can't help, but it's difficult, having just started a new job."

"Relax, there isn't a problem, I just felt you should know." He stood up and stretched lazily. "This is a strange house. I never sleep in the day, but I slept and had some really vivid dreams. I was working in a shop selling beautiful china. Isn't that odd?"

"Beautiful china like my mother once had on the shelves in the tea rooms?" she couldn't help asking.

"Good heavens, no. Not old-fashioned gaudy Victoriana. This was smart, modern china, simple designs and smart lines. The windows were filled with quality pieces and, do you know, I can imagine that being a reality. I'm looking for something new and . . ."

There was a knock at the door and Seranne opened the door and invited Alun inside.

"I just wanted to see if everything was all right," he said apologetically.

Seranne thanked him and introduced him to Paul.

"It's good that you have friends, Seranne," Paul said. Turning to Alun he added, "But if you'll excuse us, I'd like to talk to my daughter-in-law in private."

Alun looked shocked at the curt response but he just nodded at Seranne and left. Seranne hadn't been in the village very long but she was a friend and deserved care. He realized there was nothing he could do, but there was something about the man that made him uneasy.

"This little holiday, it's a celebration," Paul told her and he looked away as he explained. "Your darling mother has insisted on becoming an equal partner in my business. She now owns fifty per cent of my leather goods factory. I didn't suggest it," he added hastily as Seranne drew a deep breath to complain. "It was your mother's idea and it's perfect. We're partners in every way and we're very happy."

He insisted on taking Seranne to the Ship for a sandwich before leaving and Alun waved across from where he was serving a customer, but Paul just nodded vaguely.

He was obviously in a hurry to get away and hardly giving her time to eat her food and drink the shandy he'd bought, he drove her back to Badgers Brook.

Seranne watched as he drove away, with a feeling of unease. She had never liked the man but couldn't explain why. There was always a question in the air, as though he hadn't told her all he was thinking, keeping the most important things to himself. The feeling was strong that day. Why had he come? She and her mother communicated by letter and telephone, so why was he telling her about their little holiday? Questions raced through her mind. Why drive over here to tell her? And why had he waited here at Badgers Brook when it would have been more sensible for him to go to the café where he knew he could find her? Why a holiday in January? Something about his visit was not right. She telephoned her mother from the phone box at the end of the lane and asked about the little holiday Paul had suggested.

"Holiday, dear? I don't know anything about it. Besides, how can I get away? Pat Sewell isn't experienced in my ways yet, I wouldn't like to leave her to manage the place. Unless you —"

"Sorry Mum, but as I explained to Paul, I really think it's better I stay away, give you and Paul a chance to settle into your new life." Jessie thanked her and then Seranne said, "Congratulations on becoming part owner of the factory. Mum, are you sure about this, I mean . . ."

"Seranne, dear, of course I'm sure. The accounts for the tea rooms should be half Paul's anyway and the money is really half his. It was just a gesture on my part to assure him of my trust and confidence. Your share in the business is protected," she added.

"That wasn't my worry," Seranne replied sharply. "I'm concerned about you."

"Then don't be. Paul will look after me, as I will him."

After the phone call she was more concerned than before. She would definitely pay her mother a visit on Sunday and hopefully meet Pat Sewell too.

Wednesday was her afternoon off and it was tempting to go home but Babs dissuaded her. "Best you act casual," she advised. "You'll learn more if Paul isn't on his guard. Besides, haven't we got work to do?"

During an afternoon off Seranne and Babs had gone with Kitty Jennings to the market at Maes Hir — Long Field — and bought some material to make seat covers for the chairs in the café. Rather grudgingly Mrs Rogers had agreed to pay for the material. "But making them is down to you, mind," she had warned. "And I'm still not sure they're hygienic. You can't wash them every day like wooden seats."

With Kitty helping, they used their afternoon to work on the new covers. The material was soon cut and tacked ready to sew on a sewing machine borrowed from Stella. Seranne had hinted that matching curtains might be nice but Mrs Rogers had firmly refused.

Trying to cope with her anxieties she filled every moment working at the café, even after the place was closed. The tatty table covers were trimmed and neatly fastened to the tables, fresh paper was bought to line the shelves. Two pictures she had found at the market were fixed to the wall. It wasn't much, but the place looked a little more inviting than before.

Mrs Rogers nodded approval, but still refused to consider curtains. "We don't want them to feel too much at home or they'd never leave," was her comment.

Sunday finally came and Seranne set off with some trepidation to see her mother. She was heading for the bus at the end of the lane when she saw one sail past and she ran after it but the driver didn't see her. Standing in the road she stamped her foot in frustration. Now she had a long wait for the next one.

In the way of impatient people in a hurry, she stayed in the road to look further for that first glimpse of the bus on its way and brakes squealed as a couple of cyclists swerved to avoid her. She glared at them, then as a car appeared from the opposite direction, she had to jump for the kerb. She didn't take any notice, not expecting to know the driver, so she was surprised when the car stopped and she heard her name.

"Seranne?" From the passenger seat Stella leaned out and beckoned. "You've got a lift if you want it," she invited. Seranne presumed the driver was Colin, Stella's husband, and let herself into the back seat.

"Did you see that? Those cyclists almost ran me over. They should have used their bell."

"You were in the middle of the road, mind," Stella said, adding quickly, "Going to your mother's, aren't you? Well, we're going there too, my friend lives just one street away from Jessica's Victorian Tea Rooms."

"Thank you. This is kind of you, are you sure it isn't out of your way?" They moved off and it wasn't until they stopped to let a car reverse out of a driveway that the driver turned and she recognized Luke.

"I thought I'd better stop and let you in, you being a danger to road users," he said with a wide, mocking smile.

Her instinct was to demand to be let out at once and she tightened her face into deep disapproval. "I thought it was your Colin driving," she told Stella haughtily.

"My Colin doesn't have a car," Stella said. "Shunts big-huge railway engines he does, but he can't drive a car. Luke is taking me to see my friend. Coincidence her living not far from your Mam's tea rooms. Goes there often she does." She chattered on and Seranne lowered herself back into her seat. Getting out here would mean a long delay and the temptation of a lift straight to her mother's door was too good to refuse. Catching Luke's eye in the rear-view mirror she was aware that he was still smiling.

"What is it about me that amuses you so much?" she demanded.

"I'm amused by your habit of looking around for someone to blame when you do something silly," he replied.

"Don't be ridiculous, I don't do that, do I Stella?"

"Leave me out of it. All for peace and a quiet life I am."

"Do you still go to my mother's tea rooms?" she asked.

"Sometimes," Luke replied, "but it isn't as interesting now the quick-tempered little waitress has left."

She wanted to ask him if it had changed since Mrs Sewell had taken charge but with him giving silly answers she decided to complete the journey in silence.

Luke had to call in to a bookshop, and while he was out of the car, Seranne learnt from Stella's chatter that besides owning a long-distance haulage firm and several shops, he was a director of other businesses, and lived not far from Cwm Derw. Although eaten up with curiosity, she managed not to ask a single question, feigning indifference.

When they reached their destination, Seranne surrendered to curiosity and asked Stella exactly where he lived. She waited until they were out of the car and Luke had driven off before putting her question, and insisted she wanted to know so she could avoid him.

"He's got a smart flat in Summerland Court," Stella explained. "Big family he's got, but his Mam is in a nursing home, poor dear. He's got two cars and a van. Busy beyond he is, looking after all his interests, but he always has time to help when it's needed."

Her mother had a tray set with biscuits and stood ready to make coffee. There was no sign of Paul, for which Seranne was grateful.

"What's this about a holiday, Mum?" she asked. "Paul says you're tired. Is that all it is? You aren't ill, are you?"

"I'm perfectly all right and it's Paul who keeps on about a holiday. I think he finds living here, with me 'on the job' and working long hours, a bit of a strain."

"Surely he knew what to expect? You've lived here all your life, and run the tea rooms for most of it. You must have explained what it entailed."

"Talking about it isn't the same as living it. He'll settle down, it's only an hour or two most evenings I need to get the preparations done for the next day, and keep the books up to date. In fact, he's offered to deal with the bookkeeping to save me that boring chore."

"Don't rush into anything. He'll get into the routine of your week soon, and it's best to keep everything in your hands so nothing is forgotten."

"That's what I told him. He's really very kind, Seranne. I'm so lucky to have a second chance." She turned to her daughter, looked at her for a moment and asked, "What about you, are you all right?"

"Fine. I'm slowly persuading Mrs Rogers to smarten up the café, although she'll never create anything as beautiful as our Victorian tea rooms. Chair seats this week, that's another step forward from scuffed chairs."

"Do you have any social life yet? Made any friends?"

"Lots of friends, although most are your age group rather than mine, apart from Babs and Tony."

"Such a pity you haven't brothers or sisters: even a cousin or two would help."

"Isn't it at least possible there are cousins? My father had a sister, didn't he? It's strange that she's never been in touch."

"Not really. They quarrelled and soon after they left school, she went into service and we didn't hear another word. She probably married and with the change of name and a few changes of address it's so easy to lose touch." She patted her daughter's hands, "I'm sure you'll start making friends as soon as summer comes. Winter is a time for enjoying the fire-side."

"You're right, Mum. And the neighbours frequently enjoy mine! Badgers Brook attracts visitors like no other place I've known."

Jessie passed on a few messages from friends wanting her to contact them, and gave her the post which had arrived for her, then took her to meet Pat Sewell. They met in the woman's home and she brought them tea and biscuits on a tray. The doubts Seranne had weren't fading and she swallowed the tea with difficulty. Pat Sewell was immediately on the defensive when Seranne asked if she was sure she could manage for a week after working there for such a short time.

"I've been a cook all my life. And I've run kitchens a lot bigger that your mother's tea rooms, so yes, of course I can manage."

"Won't you need help?"

"My oldest daughter will assist me and my youngest will come in to deal with the cleaning. All right?"

"Perfectly," Seranne said, hiding her concerns behind a smile.

Paul was there when they got back to the flat and they discussed the necessary details they needed to pass on to Pat Sewell. Lists were made and Seranne promised she would risk losing her job and come at once if she were needed.

"No, don't put yourself out, Seranne," Paul said. "But if she needs help Pat will telephone the café and ask you to come."

Seranne had the impression that Pat wouldn't phone even if the place blew up, but she agreed. "I won't come unless I'm asked," she promised.

At four o'clock as they were drinking yet another cup of tea, this time with cream cakes, there was a knock at the side door and Seranne opened it to see Luke standing there.

"Are you ready to leave?" he asked. "I promised to call for Stella at half past. And there's some cream on the end of your nose," he added casually.

Self-consciously rubbing her nose with a handkerchief, she invited him in, and he followed her up the stairs to where her mother and Paul stood waiting.

Jessie chattered to him about his visits to the tea room. "We see less of you these days," she said. "I hope you have no complaints?"

"None at all. I'm just passing at the wrong time of day."

As Seranne went into the bedroom to collect her coat, her mother whispered, "All your friends are my age, did you say?"

"He isn't a friend, in fact he's the most irritating man I've met," she retorted.

"Mmm, sounds promising!"

"How is Paul?" Luke asked as they walked to the car. "Has he been involved in any more fights?"

"No, but I still have the feeling that he's dishonest. And my mother buying a half share in his factory hasn't made me feel any better," she added.

Luke stopped and stared down at her. "You don't mean the leather goods factory?" She nodded and he asked, "How much do you know?"

82

"Know? Why, is something wrong? He's promised her a good return on the investment."

"I'm sure your mother knows what she's doing," he replied, but he frowned. How could she own half of a factory that had been sold weeks ago?

"What have you been doing?" Stella asked when they were on their way home.

"I've been to see a property and made an offer to buy it," Luke told them as they set off back to Cwm Derw. "It was a bicycle shop but I plan to reopen to sell saucepans and kitchenware."

"Why saucepans?" Stella asked.

"Food rationing is sure to end soon and people will be glad to go back to cooking in the traditional way. That will mean replacing all the things that are old and worn."

"When restrictions are finally lifted, won't money be spent on food rather than things to cook it in?" Stella said. "My Colin said he's going to buy the biggest joint of beef the butcher can supply, and I'm going to spread butter on toast so thick it'll look like an ice-cream wafer!"

Seranne said nothing. Saucepans? That's too mundane, she thought. Surely people will need luxuries after all the years of want. The man was wrong but why should she care? Stella talked about her friend, and Seranne opened up enough to admit that she wasn't too happy about leaving the tea rooms in the hands of Pat Sewell.

"Go on, your mother deserves a holiday and it's January, they can't be very busy."

"The place is crowded most mornings," Seranne disagreed. "There isn't the passing trade as in the summer, but locals meet there for a mid-morning chat and Mum and I used to be kept busy cooking fresh scones and making sandwiches most of the day."

"You ought to tell Mrs Rogers you can make scones," Stella said. "Hers are like sawdust and taste of bicarb!"

"I already have, but she isn't interested," Seranne replied.

Luke went through the main street and dropped Stella off at the post office, where Colin and the little dog Scamp came out to greet her.

"It's all right, I can walk from here," Seranne said, beginning to open the door.

Luke leaned over her and closed it. "It will take only a few minutes in the car."

He turned in the road and headed for the lane. At the front path, he stopped and turned to look at her. "If you're worried about the tea rooms, I'll take you there on your half day, just to reassure you, although I'm sure everything will run smoothly."

"Thanks but there's no need, the buses are very convenient."

"Hoity-toity."

"What?"

"That's what my mother will call you when you meet her."

"What are you talking about?"

"The dictionary says it means 'haughty and petulant'. Are you like that with everyone, or just me?"

"How dare you be so rude?"

"Oh, I don't think you're petulant, but my mother will." He was laughing again.

"Don't worry, if she's as ill-mannered as you, I'll never meet her."

"You'll win her round. See you outside the café on Wednesday," he said, as he drove off.

He tried to deny the pleasure he'd just had having her in the car. It wasn't any use hoping. Once bitten twice shy might be a well-worn cliché but like most clichés there was a grain of truth in it. He would never feel confident again, not after the last time. Best to forget her. If he could. Besides, he wasn't free. Neither consideration would affect his decision to make further enquiries about Paul Curtis, though.

Seranne went in and found the fire burning brightly. Kitty had been in to make sure the house was warm for her return. She put a couple of small potatoes in the ashes to bake and took out her sewing. Still angry with Luke she worked fast and with less than usual care. After she'd pricked her fingers several times she eventually dropped the cushion cover she was making back in the basket and glared around the room. It was then she admitted that Luke was probably right. She did often look around for someone to blame.

But now she was living alone, that habit will be easily lost, she thought with a sigh. Whenever she looked up there would be no one to share the moment with, neither good ones, nor bad. The thought made her feel lonely and she knew that even in the warm friendliness of this wonderful house, she needed someone to share her life. Such a basic need that most took for granted.

Betty slid the bolt across the pub door and switched off the outside light. The bar was its usual muddle of unwashed glasses and dirty plates. Cigarette ends littered the fireplace where the ashes had sunk low and mellowed into a pink glow. She could hear Alun singing in the kitchen and carried a tray of glasses through, to find him filling the huge sink with soapy water to start washing up.

"Go on, Alun, I'll see to these tonight, you go up. We're late tonight and I know you like to read a while before you sleep."

"Nonsense. These won't take long." He took the tray from her, his hands touching hers, his fingers stroking, holding them a moment longer than necessary. She looked up and he smiled at her. "Go and make our hot drink, what is it tonight, cocoa or Ovaltine?"

"Isn't this a dull existence for you, Alun?"

"I might have thought so once, but that was before I'd met you," he said, turning to start on the glasses. "I've never been happier."

She didn't know how to answer, and, afraid of making herself look foolish, she went back to the bar and collected more glasses. He didn't mean it, he was just being polite. How could someone like him feel anything more than friendship for someone like me? she thought, pushing aside foolish hope.

After she had cleaned up in the bar rooms and mopped the floor, she went through the kitchen and began to mix their drinks. He was singing, "The bells are ringing, for me and my gal . . ." and he said nothing more, just smiled at her as he thanked her for the hot drink. As they went their separate ways to their bedrooms, he patted her shoulder as usual and said goodnight.

She lay for a long time thinking about him, conscious of him being only yards away along the landing. Was she making too much out of what had only been a polite remark? Someone like Alun, who's a few years younger than my forty-seven years wouldn't be interested in someone like me, she told herself again.

Because she liked him, was attracted to him, that was the reason she had been flattered and encouraged by his words. That was it. If she hadn't liked him so much she wouldn't have given them a moment's thought. Time she stopped daydreaming like a schoolgirl or she'd lose him. And besides being a hardworking and utterly delightful companion, he was a very good barman.

The café in Cwm Derw remained open every afternoon, but Seranne was given an afternoon off. She had chosen Wednesday because that was the day of Maes Hir market and it was useful to be able to go shopping. On the Wednesday after her unsettling visit home, she stepped out of the café door to be met by Luke. He gestured towards the MG standing at the kerb. "Shall we stop on the way and have lunch?" he asked by way of greeting. "I'm starving and I doubt whether you enjoy eating in the place where you work."

"Thank you, but I was going back to Badgers Brook for a sandwich before setting off."

"No need." He opened the car door and gestured for her to get in. "I know just the place. You'll love it."

Prepared to argue, she changed her mind and slid into the passenger seat. She expected pretty tea rooms similar to Jessica's but was surprised when he stopped at a large shed-like building that was surrounded by lorries and cars.

"This place is for lorry drivers!" she said outraged. "What on earth made you think I would eat at such a place?"

"Because you'll like the owners." He took her arm as she protested and led her inside to the steamy, noisy place. A few people called to him and several waved a greeting. Finding her a seat at the table where there already sat a young boy and an overweight man dressed in cowboy shirt and denim trousers supported by a wide, ornate belt, he left her and went to the counter to order their food.

"Known Luke long, have you?" the man asked.

"Not really. He's just giving me a lift to visit my parents." She turned away to discourage further questions but the man persisted.

"He drove lorries for my father for years."

"Luke was a lorry driver?"

He nodded and waited until his mouth was empty then added, "Until he bought the firm."

Luke arrived with two plates on which there were some chips and a couple of sausages. "You've introduced yourselves, have you?"

88

Trying to look indifferent, Seranne shrugged vaguely.

"Seranne, meet my Uncle Pete and my cousin Billy."

"Your uncle?" She tentatively offered a hand which was lost in the huge grip of Uncle Pete, then gently taken by the shy Billy.

"Got to go, places to see, appointments to keep." The two stood up and with a wave were gone.

Seranne didn't know what to say, so she ate the food, and with more enjoyment than she had expected. "That was very good, thank you," she told him as she replaced her cutlery across the empty plate.

"She's a good cook," he said. "She's my auntie."

She wasn't sure whether or not to believe him. Wondering whether there were more surprises planned, she got back into the car. "Were you really a lorry driver?"

"I've done many different jobs and yes, driving lorries was one of them. I was also a conductor on the buses, and an apprentice carpenter, but I gave that up, I didn't have the necessary skill."

The day was full of surprises but the next surprise didn't come from Luke and it was more a shock. Jessica's Victorian Tea Rooms was closed.

She knocked on the door and rattled the handle but there was no sound from within. Using her key she went up to the flat and saw that everything was orderly as her mother would have left it. Downstairs it was not. In the tea rooms the tables were still littered with the remains of previous customers, the kitchen showed no evidence of having been recently used — or cleaned — and there was no sign of Pat Sewell.

"What on earth has happened?" she exclaimed.

"Are you sure your mother arranged for this Pat Sewell to run the place? It looks as though it's been closed for several days." He picked up a sandwich from one of the tables and ground it to dry crumbs.

"I know where she lives," she told Luke. "Shall I go round? She might be ill."

They walked to the modest little house and knocked on the door which was opened by Pat Sewell who was dressed in a thick jumper and a woollen skirt, neither very clean.

"Are you all right?" Seranne asked. "Seeing the tea rooms were closed we — I — wondered if you were ill."

"I'm perfectly well, but I could hardly go to the wholesalers for stock *and* work in the tea rooms, could I?"

"But I don't understand. Didn't my mother leave everything you need?"

"I needed a few things she doesn't keep. And the baker didn't deliver the scones this morning and —"

"Deliver the scones? We always make our own!"

"*You* might. I don't. Now if you'll let me get on — or I won't be able to reopen for the late afternoon teas."

"But what about your daughters, weren't they going to help?"

"Got jobs, they did. Typical that is, never here when they're wanted."

Ill at ease, but with nothing more to say, they walked away.

"Do you have the phone number of where your mother's staying?" Luke asked as they returned to the car.

90

"Yes, but should I telephone and spoil her holiday? Paul seemed to think she needed a break and it's only two more days before they come back. The damage is done now. It doesn't look as though she's opened up since Saturday."

"Perhaps you could leave a note then we'll come back and see them on Saturday evening, or Sunday morning."

"Yes, that's best." Then she stared at him. "But there's no need for you to come. This isn't your problem."

"Logically it isn't yours either. The tea rooms is your mother's business and you no longer work there."

"Of course it's my problem. I didn't stop being her daughter when I moved a few miles away, did I?"

"Put your eyes back in Miss Hoity-Toity, they're sticking out like lollipops!"

She turned to tell him off and was aware of how silly she had sounded so instead she said, "Sunday morning?"

"No."

"But I thought you said . . ."

"I'll ask Mrs Rogers if you can leave at midday on Saturday. It would be a good idea to see Pat Sewell in action, don't you think?"

"I can't have another half day."

"Instead of next Wednesday? I'll ask her. She's my auntie as well."

She laughed then. "I don't believe you!"

"Well, not an auntie, but she knows my mother and that's almost as good."

To Seranne's relief the tea rooms were open and very busy that Saturday. Pat was in the kitchen making sandwiches, some of which she was toasting. "Using up stale bread and charging more. Good idea, eh?" Leaving her to deal with the constant stream of orders, the customers' chatter interspersed with the cheerful ring of the till, they sat in a corner and waited until a young girl, whom they presumed was Pat's daughter, came and took their order.

Seranne sat in silence until the order came. A sandwich for her and, unbelievably, sausages and chips for Luke. "Sausages and chips?" she whispered. "These are tea rooms not a caff! What on earth does she think she's doing?"

Spearing a sausage, Luke took a bite, chewed and said, "Mmm, almost as good as my auntie's caff!"

"Not as good as my mother's cooking," Seranne retorted.

Leaving Pat and her daughter to clean up and close, they went for a walk around the village, where a couple of restaurants and a fine public house brought people long distances tempted by the quality of the food. Accepting that there was nothing she could do about the way Pat was managing the place, Seranne relaxed and talked about her childhood, pointing out the places she had known. The park where she played with friends, the tree from which she had fallen, causing a scar on her arm that had never faded, the muddy stream from where they had collected frog spawn and to which they returned the wriggling little tadpoles.

"I remember falling in a stream about as wide as this one after fighting with my cousin Harry," Luke told her. "And my cousin Frank pushed me off his swing once and I had a cut on my face that needed stitching."

"Have you really got all those aunties? And cousins?"

"Both my parents came from large families. Why, don't you have uncles and aunts?"

"None I know of. My father, that is my real father, had a sister I believe, so I might have a few cousins. But they quarrelled and lost touch years ago."

"Oh, is that where you get your temper from?"

Instead of a sharp retort, she smiled. "Maybe. I'll never know, will I?"

When they returned to the tea rooms on Sunday morning, the day was dull and lights shone in the flat above and voices called to them as they ran up the stairs. After the usual hasty declaration that the holiday had been perfect, Paul disappeared downstairs and came up with the cash box and the accounts book. Showing it to Jessie they declared themselves delighted with the way Pat had coped.

If Jessie noticed that the menu included chips, she said nothing. Seeing the note which she told her mother about finding the place closed, was still on the sideboard, Seranne picked it up and put it in her pocket.

Driving home, Luke stopped the car, looked at her curiously and said, "I'm impressed. I thought you'd be unable to resist telling your mother about Pat's failings. Perhaps you aren't so bad after all."

"Thank you, kind sir!"

"Now, now. Don't spoil it!" He leaned over and kissed her, then drove on. When he stopped at Badgers Brook, she wondered if he would do it again, but he didn't.

CHAPTER
FOUR

Betty listened as Alun came up the steps from the cellar where he had been whitewashing the walls. He was singing as usual. "Long ago and far away, I dreamed a dream one day . . ."

"Ready for tea?" she asked, as he appeared at the top of the steps with the bucket and paint brushes. "Go and sit down, I'll clean up." Ignoring his protests, she took the painting equipment from him and went to the outhouse where they kept the cleaning materials. Filling the sink she set to and cleaned everything, then went into the room behind the bar, where he sat waiting for her, a pot of tea ready to pour.

"I should have done that," he protested, gesturing towards the cleaned brushes.

"Nonsense, you've been down in that cellar since eight o'clock." She looked at him, noting the unusual faraway look in his clear blue eyes. "Anything wrong?" she asked.

"No, I was just thinking of how life takes you where it will. We can plan all we like but it sometimes seems that life is already decided for us and our puny efforts are blown away in a puff of wind. Eighteen months ago

I had a restaurant of my own and one greedy man — or fate — took it from me."

"One day you'll start again. You did it once so you can do it a second time."

Alun had owned a successful restaurant but had been robbed by his accountant, Ellis Owen, who had also stolen the profits from a clothing factory where he had been given control of the accounts. Ellis had died in an accident on the cliffs but the money he had stolen was still awaiting a court decision on its return. Fraud was difficult to prove when Alun's own signature had been trustingly written on all the relevant documents.

Betty poured a second cup of tea and offered the biscuit tin. Breaking into his solemn mood, she said, "Once the money comes through you can start making plans. I'll help if I can."

"You want me to leave?"

"Alun, you know I don't." She put a hand on his arm and he covered it with his own. "But I understand how much you want to return to what you enjoy."

"I enjoy working at the Ship. I didn't ever imagine I would, but I do." He smiled, then finished his tea and stood up. "But if I don't get the bar ready for opening, my landlady will send me on my way."

"Difficult boss, is she?"

"Terrible woman!"

They were washing the floor when Betty's brother called her and came into the bar.

"Hello, Ed, how's Elsie?" Betty asked automatically.

"Elsie's fine and we have seven people staying tonight and tomorrow, three of them walkers."

"That's good for this time of year, isn't it? So what's the long face for?"

Alun guessed they were in for one of their arguments and said, "Just look at the mud on the floor. I don't know how he does it but Colin Jones manages to bring mud all the way from his allotment and drops it off on our floor." He disappeared to get fresh water leaving them alone.

"Is Elsie really all right?" Betty asked softly.

Ed shook his head. "She seems to stay at one stage for a while and I begin to think she'll go on managing as well as she does, then the illness slips a notch further."

"I'm tied to opening hours, even with Alun helping, but I'll do what I can. You need more help, Ed."

"No. I can't take on anyone else. I don't want her to think we can't cope. Every time we arrange extra help she knows her condition is worsening. I'll cope for as long as I can."

Betty was touched by her brother's intuitive care. Elsie and he hadn't been married very long but they were obviously very happy. Such a pity they hadn't met earlier.

Neither of us found time for friendships, we were too content in the Ship, she mused later. Perhaps if Alun and I . . . but she stopped the thought there. She imagined them standing side by side looking in a mirror. She five feet four and overweight, Alun almost six feet tall and handsome with his beard and those remarkable blue eyes. He wouldn't have given me a second glance, she told herself sadly.

Pulling herself away from regrets and foolish dreams, she said, "Alun, I think I'd better go over there and see what I can do."

"I don't think Ed wants that, he just needs a shoulder to cry on sometimes. I think we should go for a walk instead."

"But there's work to do," she protested.

"Which you'd put aside for someone else but not for yourself? Come on, grab your coat. Wellies I think, don't you?"

Seranne had gone into work early and without putting on the lights in the café to encourage people to knock and demand to be served, she fastened the seat cushions on the newly painted chairs. It was only half past eight when she stood back and looked at the effect, which was disappointing. The dull walls and the old-fashioned counter detracted from the result and made the place look even shabbier by contrast. Paint was peeling around the door where it had been knocked by countless trays and kicked open by many feet. If only she could persuade Mrs Rogers to pay for some basic decorating, make it look more appealing, surely the business would improve and return the outlay?

She thought with regret of the neat, spotlessly clean tea rooms with its rose-bud curtains and tablecloths, and the valuable, ornate plates and teapots filling the shelves. She wished she were able to make the changes here, but knew from Mrs Rogers' reaction to the few she had suggested that it was not going to be easy, especially as every comment was treated as a criticism, which made Seranne feel guilty of rudeness.

"Daydreaming, Seranne? Shouldn't you have the kettles on and the door unlocked?" Mrs Rogers hung up her coat and rubbed her hands together. "Brr, it's cold out there. We could be in for some more snow. Thank goodness you turned on the heating." She stopped then and looked at the new chair covers. "Oh, finished them, have you? A bit bright, aren't they?"

"Not really, it's more that the walls are dull. D'you think we could —"

"No I don't, and get that door open. There's Mrs Greener on her way, coming for a cuppa before getting on the early bus for Barry. Goes to see her sister every week, you ought to know that by now. Opening a bit early for her isn't a problem for you, is it? Doesn't spoil your dream of turning this place into a rival to the Ritz?"

Swallowing a response to the sarcasm, Seranne invited Mrs Greener in and took her order for toast and tea. Mrs Rogers was in the kitchen, the toast already beginning to brown under the gas stove grill. She looked apologetic.

"Sorry I am if I'm not impressed with your ideas to smarten this place up a bit. But I'm only the manageress and all the owner looks at is the size of the profit." She placed the toast on a plate with a small helping of butter, which was mixed with margarine and some milk to make it go further, and handed it to Seranne to take to Mrs Greener.

The milk too was diluted, a pint of water to three pints of milk which was returned to the bottles and the cardboard lids replaced. Customers began to fill the tables and they were kept busy serving cakes and scones and sandwiches until the lunchtime crowd arrived, when they provided chips or boiled potatoes with sausages, spam, or whatever they had managed to buy at the wholesalers with their allocation of food. At two o'clock snow began to fall, silently enfolding the area in its beauty, hiding imperfections and giving dead flowers in the gardens an elegance.

Those who had to come out were enticed in for tea to warm them. Leaving Seranne to cope with the unexpected rush, Mrs Rogers took an hour off for a belated lunch, and when she returned she continued with the earlier conversation as though there hadn't been a break. "Truth is, Seranne, I'm reluctant to spend money unnecessarily. I'll be leaving here soon and I want to make sure I have a good reference in case I want to get another job. It's profit that counts with the owner and I want him to be satisfied I've managed that well."

"You're leaving? Oh, I'm sorry to hear that, Mrs Rogers." Despite her words, Seranne's heart sang. Perhaps if she applied for the vacancy for a manageress she could implement some of her improvements. "Where will you go?"

"Nowhere. My Gary isn't well, see. Wounded bad in the war he was and I'm staying home to look after him. The children are both working now and we can manage without my wage." She stared into space. "If we're a bit short I can always do a bit of cleaning."

"Will the owner keep me on, d'you think?"

"Sure to."

Seranne needed to talk to someone and she knew Babs would be pleased at the opportunity that had arisen for her. She and Babs had been friends since school, when Babs had lived near the tea rooms and had occasionally helped them. When Babs's parents had bought the bakery in Cwm Derw and they had all moved away, Seranne and Babs had kept in touch and remained friends. They told each other everything. Yet something made her change her mind as she closed the door of the café. If news of the vacancy became general knowledge there would be several more applications. Better to keep quiet until she had spoken to the boss.

It was six o'clock when Seranne walked across to the bakery with their order for the following morning. It would be Wednesday so they had extra teacakes and a few bread rolls. So predictable, so little to tempt customers to try something different. Babs and her brother Tony were in the kitchen behind the now closed shop. They were arguing.

"Sorry to interrupt, Babs, I just want to hand you tomorrow's list."

"Don't worry, we aren't going to resort to blows, even though I think Tony deserves a wallop!" Babs said.

"She wants to take a job she's been offered and I think her loyalty should be to the family." Tony said. He was holding the peel, the long-handled, spade-like wooden tool used for taking loaves from the ovens. He waved it wildly and added, "Selfish, she is. Someone ought to remind her about what she could lose."

"Her head if you don't put that thing down!" Seranne warned. "What sort of job, a rival bakery?"

"No," Tony sneered, "it's a pathetic job in —"

"Shut up, Tony!" Babs warned. "The job isn't even mine yet and might not be. So keep quiet, will you?"

Lowering his voice, Tony said, "You're too lazy to work for anyone else, you leave it all to me."

"You won't miss me then, will you?"

Leaving them arguing in a more subdued way, Seranne left them. Brother and sister, working close all their lives, they were in constant disagreement. Not like Mum and me, she thought sadly.

She made her way to the bus stop, along pavements covered with the fresh fall of snow, with mixed feelings. There was the possibility that she would lose her job when Mrs Rogers left, but there was also the chance of reviving the sad café and creating a more attractive place for customers to meet.

Excitement grew as her thoughts buzzed with ideas, of meals she could prepare that were just as cheap to provide but which looked more appetizing, of the cakes she would make instead of buying from Tony and Babs's bakery. Anxiety about being told she was no longer needed were pushed aside. Of course she would get the job, and she'd make the sad café into a success. She stood at the bus stop unaware of the cold. She was warmed by dreams of running the café the way it should be run and her eyes glowed with excitement.

As the bus loomed into view through the darkness and she jumped aboard, Betty's brother Ed walked around from behind the post office and headed for the Ship for the second time that day. He was walking fast, bending over in his haste and occasionally breaking into a run. He slithered on the pavement where someone had partially removed the snow allowing the early evening frost to harden it.

"Betty," he shouted as soon as he was in sight of the pub door. It was shut and he went to the side door, calling as he pushed his way in. Alun was in the passage behind the bar but Ed ran past him, calling for his sister. "Betty. You have to come. Elsie has to go to hospital. The ambulance is on its way and I'm going with her. Can you help with the late-night drinks and the bed changes tomorrow morning? The girl we've got is hopeless without someone keeping an eye on her."

"Can I help?" Alun asked.

Ignoring him in his anxiety, Ed ran towards Betty who came through the door carrying a mop and bucket. "Betty, I have to dash back, I've left Elsie with the girl. The bedding isn't sorted, the ambulance is coming and I have to go with her. Can you come?"

Taking off her coarse apron, Betty reached for her coat. "Go on, you, I'll follow as fast as I can." She gave a few instructions to Alun, who promised to open up, then calling after Ed, she hurried out.

When Alun arrived at the guest house soon after 10.30 that night, Betty was sitting in the private room, writing out the laundry list to put with the folded bedding.

"Are you all right?" he asked. When she nodded, he tied the sheets and towels in a bundle and fastened the completed list to it, ready for collection.

"The visitors are in and settled and no more are due until tomorrow evening," she said. "But I ought to stay."

"No point waiting for Ed and the visitors can manage until morning. Write a note and come home."

So, leaving a note promising to return in time to cook breakfast, they went to the door but they were stopped by the telephone. It was Ed, who assured them that Elsie was in no immediate danger and would probably be home in a day or so. "But she'll need extra care," he went on. "I hate doing this but I'll have to have an extra daily visit from the nurse. Besides upsetting Elsie with another reminder of her failing health it's going to be expensive."

"Let me know if I can help," Betty said. "I've got a few pound put aside for emergencies." Replacing the phone, she said to Alun, "I think Elsie has enough money to cope, but I had to offer. He's my brother. And families are important."

"Of course. But — I know it isn't my business, Betty — but don't make yourself short. Life can be very unpredictable. No one knows what their own needs will be in the future."

"Oh, I can't see me doing anything but run this place, can you?"

"I hope not. If ever anyone is in the right place, it's you."

More snow fell during the night and Betty trudged through it to reach the guest house in the morning. People were out even though it was very early. Deliveries had already made patterns of footsteps. Greetings were exchanged, passers-by waving and shouting encouragement even to complete strangers, children trying to build a snowman, stopping occasionally to pelt each other with snowballs. The sound of scraping came from all around as householders cleared the pavements, and they talked about the snow as though it were a rare event.

Luke was staying at the guest house, having got his car stuck in a drift near Treweather's old farm. When Betty arrived he had made morning tea for them all, and she thanked him and gratefully accepted his help with breakfast. Apart from one man who had taken the opportunity to leave without paying, everything went smoothly.

When she went back to the Ship and Compass, she found a letter for Alun among the morning mail. He received very few letters. Three or four had been brought to him from Jake's boatyard, where he had worked for a while before coming to the Ship. One or two had come from the employment exchange, but this one, in its long envelope, marked with the name of a firm of solicitors, looked official.

She went out and busied herself making toast and tea allowing him time to open it in private. When she went back he was staring at the pages and, determined not to intrude, she commented on the overnight snow that covered the garden and the rooftops, and he said he'd heard that a car was stranded in a hedge near Treweather's abandoned old farmhouse. "What could it have been doing in that lane? It doesn't lead any further than those old buildings," he said.

"That was Luke Beynon. He was looking at the old buildings to see if they were worth saving. Forgot how narrow it was I suppose. He walked back to the main road and stayed at the guest house."

"He has so many interests it's a wonder he doesn't forget where he's going," Alun remarked, playing with the letter.

"Something important?"

"Yes. I might be getting some of my money back," he told her, tapping the envelope agitatedly. "I can't believe it. Ellis Owen covered his tracks so well, he made it appear that I was the thief." He sat down heavily and went on. "He emptied my account and left me with debts it took me a long time to clear. The business was lost and no one trusted me enough for me to start again, even if I'd had the money. If I get some of the money back I'll be grateful, although having my name cleared is still the most valuable outcome."

"Congratulations, Alun. That's wonderful news. Will it be enough for you to buy a place?"

"Buy another restaurant, you mean? I don't know whether I want to. That man knocked the stuffing out of me. I don't think I have the heart to try again."

"Of course you have. You're still a young man."

He stared at her in the disconcerting way he had. "I'm only a few years younger than you, Betty. Can you imagine starting all over again if you lost this place?"

She wanted to say, yes, if he were beside her, but instead she turned away, and said, "I don't know, but I do know that you can. Strong you are, Alun, and hard working and very good at dealing with people. And with a vision of running a fine establishment of your own to urge you on, you can't fail."

"It wouldn't be easy on my own. I had a partner to help me last time. She left me when the extent of the trouble was revealed, convinced I was responsible."

She felt a fierce stab of jealousy that startled her. A wife? Perhaps even children? "That must have hurt," was all she said.

"What a pity you can't work with me," he said. "A fine team we'd make."

She couldn't reply. It was too close to her foolish dream.

From the bedroom window, Seranne looked out at the magical scene and gasped at the beauty of it. She went downstairs and turned on a gas fire and filled the kettle for tea. Then she reached for the shovel she had sensibly brought inside as a precaution and then looked at the long path leading to the lane. It would take a while to deal with that, but the prospect was not unpleasant.

The kettle boiled and she made tea and prepared some bread for toasting. Before she left she would ask Kitty if she could bring some shopping back for her, to save her venturing out. She would at least need bread.

After clearing a track through the centre of the path, she dressed in warm clothes and wellingtons, packed shoes and an extra pair of socks and went to see Kitty. The cold hit her as she pushed her way through the deep snow to Kitty's door. Only then did she think about the long walk in snow that faced her as she made her way to the café. The buses would need the snow ploughs and the gritting lorries out before they could move and with the snow still falling, it was unlikely they would be running in time for her to get to work on time. This end of the town was hardly a priority. But Mrs Rogers lived much further away and was unlikely to get there by 8.30. It was up to herself to open up.

"My Bob will get the path cleared and I'll go in and get the fire burning for when you get home," Kitty promised, after discussing the few things she would need.

Already chilled, Seranne stopped to add a second pair of socks and another cardigan and set off along the lane after taking a third pair of socks from the rail in case of disasters.

The wind had caused drifts and in places where the snow covered a previous fall, the icy cold snow was deep enough to reach above her wellingtons and fall inside. Thank goodness she had brought extra socks to change into. It was like a child's game, taking great strides and sinking with each step before hauling her foot free and taking another. She was exhausted when she eventually stepped inside the cold café.

Heating first, then the tea. She was late despite starting out early and there was no sign of Mrs Rogers. Several people were waiting outside and aware of the intense cold she invited them in. "You'll have to wait a while to be served, but it will be a little warmer," she said. One lady followed her into the kitchen and started to cut slices of yesterday's bread ready for toasting. Another went to the greengrocers with a list of her needs and returned followed by the delivery boy.

It wasn't long before the customers were sipping reviving tea and eating the warm toast, while Seranne quickly prepared soup to serve at lunchtime. She had a feeling this would be more acceptable than sandwiches on such a day. Where was Tony Hopkins with her bread and cakes order?

The lady who had helped, paid for her snack before going to see if the buses were running. Others admitted they weren't going to bother but would go straight back home. More customers arrived, several explained that their electricity had failed. A man walked in and at first she didn't look up. When she did she saw Luke, who asked for a buttered tea cake and she was immediately flustered.

"The car is stuck, I'm at the bed and breakfast which is in chaos this morning," he explained. "Elsie is in hospital, Ed with her, Betty is dashing from one place to the other and I'm in need of a cup of coffee and a bun."

"Sorry, but there aren't any, in fact not much choice at all until the baker comes," she said. Then she frowned. "Surely they aren't held up by snow? They're only across the road. I wonder what's happened, they're always here before this."

"I'll go and see," Luke offered. He stood on the step as he fastened his coat letting a blast of cold air into the café.

"Will you get a loaf for me and one for my neighbour?" she asked, then, as he hesitated, she shouted, "Shut the door! Please!" She looked around her as though in disbelief, sharing his thoughtlessness with the others.

He apologized and went out smiling. He returned almost immediately with Tony following, both carrying trays.

"Lucky to have this you are," Tony said. "You didn't give an order so we didn't think you needed anything."

"What d'you mean? Of course I need it! I left the order with your sister." Saying no more, she concentrated on putting the supplies in their places and serving the steady stream of customers. She gave Luke his teacake and he sat in the corner where he could watch her dashing between customers and the kitchen, taking money, handing out food and returning pleasantries.

He left at 10.30 and Mrs Rogers arrived, wet, cold and exhausted at half past twelve. When she had recovered and checked the till, she was impressed with what Seranne had achieved. The freshly made soup was popular and quickly sold out. Beans or spaghetti on toast, scrambled eggs, anything hot was gratefully accepted and they had the busiest day for weeks. At five o'clock, the snow had stopped but the roads were still treacherous.

"Best you go early, you've had a long day without even a break," Mrs Rogers said. "Be careful, mind, I haven't seen a bus so you'll have to walk. Watch out for cars that might skid."

110

Thankfully Seranne gathered up her shopping and prepared to leave. As she reached the pavement Luke stepped forward and took her arm. "I thought you might leave early so I came back," he said as he pulled her arm through his. He guided her past the bus stop where no passengers stood. The lane was very dark, there were few streetlights and none were lit. He began to talk about the frustration of having to leave his car and how difficult life was without one. "Do you drive?" he asked.

"No, I've never needed to, Mum always drove us. Why?"

"You seem so capable, it seems natural you'd have learnt. I don't think much would defeat you. Look at the way you coped today when the snow brought everything to a halt and you'd forgotten to order from the bakery."

"I hadn't forgotten!" she said, stopping and turning to glare at him. "I went there as usual and handed the list to Babs. But she and Tony were arguing as usual and she probably dropped it, or threw it at him!"

"Sorry," he said pretending to avoid a blow.

This time it was she who laughed. "He was waving the peel about like a furious warrior, threatening to knock her head off!"

Their shared laughter warmed her like nothing else had that day. It was natural to invite him in. After the long walk in the deep snow she could hardly abandon him on the doorstep. "I have to take this loaf to Kitty, my neighbour, but go inside, she's sure to have lit the fire for me."

"Nice neighbours," he commented as he slipped off his wellingtons, took her key and let himself in.

When Seranne returned he helped her off with her coat and wellingtons and offered her some socks which he had placed on the fender to warm. "Bliss," she murmured as she felt the welcome warmth.

She made tea and served a bowl of soup and they sat beside the fire wallowing in the comfort of a gradual thaw. He didn't say much but as he dressed to leave he turned to her and said, "When the weather improves, I can teach you to drive if you wish."

"Not in that sports car you won't!"

"No fear, I wouldn't trust you with my MG!"

"Why bother?" she asked. "I can't see me owning a car while I work for Cwm Derw's sad little café!"

"Is that how you see it, a sad little café?"

"I think it needs some attention, don't you?"

"Such as?"

"It's obvious, isn't it? New decoration, better menu, and home cooking instead of buying from Hopkins's bakery for a start."

"All right, don't get uppity."

"I'm not uppity Well, if I am, it's because you do ask some obvious questions sometimes."

"I'll try to remember not to," he said and she looked at him and saw he was smiling. "Driving lessons?" he asked.

"I don't know," she hesitated.

"We can't arrange anything until the snow clears, so I'll see you on Saturday evening, we can talk about it and make plans."

"I don't need to talk about driving. How will that help?"

"I'll tell you on Saturday."

She was smiling, excitement growing at the image of meeting him on what was very like a date. He was an intriguing man and despite her usual habit of pushing him away, the attraction was growing and she was disappointed when a day passed without seeing him. Saturday seemed a very long way off.

He was about to leave, his hand was on the handle when the door opened and Kitty slithered in, trying not to open the door too wide. She had a purse in her hand. "Come to pay for the shopping," she said with a glance at Luke. Then she looked at him again, and said, "Hello Luke, fancy seeing you here. How's the wife?"

"She's well so far as I know."

In the stunned silence her question had caused, Kitty sat down and bent forward to test the teapot in the hearth for warmth. "Shall I make a fresh cup, Seranne? You staying for another cup, Luke?"

"He's just leaving," Seranne said at once and ushered him through the door without a thank you for walking her home.

"How d'you know Luke?" Kitty asked. "I've known his mother since we were children at school."

"I don't know him. He walked me home because of the deep snow and no buses, that's all."

"He wasn't the young man who took you to see your mother?"

"Well, yes, but I still don't know him."

"Lovely boy."

"I'm sure he is. And I bet his wife thinks so too," she muttered.

"Or more fool her," Kitty nodded, startling Seranne, who hadn't realized she'd spoken her thoughts aloud.

The arrangement for Saturday that had been very like a date, had to be cancelled. It was no longer possible to see him, or even think about him. As always, anger was her first reaction. How dare he trick her into falling for him and keep the fact of his marriage from her? He was a cheat and a liar. The second, almost simultaneous reaction was disappointment, the automatic anger quickly becoming secondary to her disappointment. She had to make herself unavailable on Saturday. The meeting that had promised so much was no longer possible.

The snow stayed for the rest of the week but gradually the roads were cleared and buses rumbled along, their tyres hissing accompaniment. On Saturday Seranne arranged to go to the pictures with Babs, and left promptly to avoid having to meet Luke. She felt like a fugitive, imagining his gaze on her as she and her friend walked along the street.

"What's the rush?" Babs said trying to keep up with her. As they stood in the queue which slowly fed them through the doors and into the safe darkness of the cinema, Seranne told her about Luke's friendliness and the fact that he had a wife.

"Children too probably. What a cheek. Who does he think I am?"

At this Babs laughed. "A beautiful girl with two wealthy parents? Don't jump to conclusions, he could

114

be divorced. Lots of people are giving up on marriage since the war."

"Then why didn't he tell me?"

Thankfully the film began and the painful conversation stopped.

"What's this job you've applied for?" Seranne asked as they came out into the cold night.

"I can't tell you yet. I'm superstitious, see, and I'm afraid that if I talk about it I won't get it."

"Aren't you happy working for your family?"

"They want to make changes which involve most of our money. If it doesn't work out we could lose everything. Besides, like you, I'm afraid that if I don't start living my own life soon, I'll be stuck here for the rest of my life. I want to go out and try something different. You can understand that, can't you?"

"Of course I do. It's scary but I don't regret moving away. My decision was made easier by Mum marrying Paul."

"Mine is made easier by my irritating brother!"

"I might be job hunting myself soon," Seranne said. "Mrs Rogers is leaving and whoever takes over will want to chose her own staff. I have thought of applying for the job of manageress myself, I could certainly do it. I've done nothing else all my life. But I haven't been there very long so I wouldn't be considered."

"No, probably not."

Seranne was surprised by her friend's abrupt dismissal of her chances but presumed it was because her thoughts were on her own problems.

Walking back along the empty lanes on her own, ignoring the dry patches and instead squelching through the churned up slush that remained, Seranne couldn't help wishing that Luke was there to walk her home. The night was crisp, a chill wind moaned, and it was very dark. There was only the strange light from the patches of white snow on the verges to guide her, and the trees groaned and creaked in an alarming way, moved by an icy wind that cut through her clothing as it increased in strength. It was with relief that she stepped inside the old house with its own familiar creaks and groans and closed the door against the dark.

There was no sign of Luke on Sunday, for which she was grateful. Perhaps he would stay away now his secret was out. That should have pleased her but it only increased her sensation of loss. On Monday morning the order from Hopkins's Bakery again failed to arrive and Mrs Rogers went across to see why. Babs explained that Seranne hadn't given them her list.

"Nonsense, you must have lost it," she said.

"I didn't see her before we met for the pictures and she certainly didn't give it to me then. Ask Tony, he's responsible for deliveries."

Tony shook his head and gestured around the almost empty shelves. "There's plenty of bread left and I'll whip you up some scones. Babs might make some drop scones and pancakes, will that do?"

"It will have to, won't it? But take care and get it right for tomorrow or I'll go somewhere else. You aren't the only bakery in town remember."

Babs looked puzzled. "It isn't like Seranne to be careless," she said. "She was a bit upset, mind. That man Luke Curtis who's been trying to make a date with her is married. She was angry about that and was hurrying to get to the pictures without seeing him. Perhaps that was why she forgot?"

"Luke? Seranne and Luke? But surely —" Mrs Rogers queried.

"Hardly an excuse for neglecting her job," Tony interrupted. "The truth is, Seranne worked for her mother for too long and she can't manage on her own. Just like you," he said to Babs. "You'll never get a job, you're too used to leaning on Mam and Dad and me."

An argument was avoided by customers coming into the shop and pushing him aside, Babs turned and began to serve. Mrs Rogers returned to the café. They were very busy for the rest of the morning and she forgot her query about Seranne and Luke.

Elsie came home as the last of the snow melted away. Thankfully, Betty was no longer needed to help Ed during the busy periods of the day at the guest house. It had been hard to cope and without Alun, she knew it would have been impossible.

"Don't forget to thank him when you see him," she reminded Ed. "I don't know what I'd have done if he hadn't been there."

"All right, but he gets paid, doesn't he?"

"Not enough! He does a lot more than I pay him for."

"Fine, but remember he's only a barman."

"What's the matter with you? Aren't you glad I've got someone I can rely on?"

"Of course. I'm sorry, but you seem so wrapped up in how good he is, and there's me trying to cope with an ailing wife who won't ever get better. It makes you selfish, facing something like this — and don't say you warned me! I know you were against us marrying. Elsie is a lovely woman, a great companion and I'm not sorry I married her."

In the next room sitting on a couch from where she could see into the hall and also out at the street, Elsie hid her tears. Lies and carefully worded truths were handed out to her with smiles but she knew the situation, had read the books, talked to other sufferers and she knew that she wouldn't be able to stay home much longer. Ed would be all right; he would go back to the Ship with his sister. At least she didn't have to worry about him.

But there were other matters needing her attention. Everything was in place, she just needed to talk to her doctor and solicitor to make sure her instructions were clear and couldn't be overturned. She waited until Ed was out and asked the nurse to dial the numbers for her. Ed was always out during mid-morning and with the nurse's help she could get everything arranged.

Ed went into her room when he got home from his errands and found her sleeping. He sat in the kitchen unaware of the kettle boiling and rattling its lid. It was heartbreaking to see her going through this, aware of there being no escaping its end.

118

"Ed, dear, are you there? I can hear the kettle boiling."

"Coming my love. I'm making us a nice cup of tea." At least he didn't have to worry about the future. He'd have this place to keep him busy, with visitors to look after to disguise his loneliness when Elsie was gone. He hoped she'd be there for a long time yet, he didn't find it a chore looking after her, she was so sweet and rarely complained, but when she died, at least he wouldn't have to go cap in hand and beg Betty to take him back to the Ship.

CHAPTER
FIVE

Seranne was deeply upset by the revelation that Luke was a married man. If she were honest, he had never encouraged her to believe there was more than friendship between them, apart from that brief kiss, but surely if that's all they were he would have mentioned a wife and maybe even a child? Sharing their lives was something friends did, gradually being involved in their personality by what they learnt.

Over the first few days she jumped every time there was a knock at the door, or when someone walked into the café, but gradually she calmed herself, convinced that the truth being revealed had discouraged him. She tried to hold on to her anger but the fact was, she missed him. He was never a regular part of her life but the way he popped up now and then, and seemed to be there whenever he could be of help took the joy out of each day. He had been described as kind and someone who loved helping others, so that was probably all she had been to him, one of the "others" who occasionally accepted his help. But life was sadder because of those few words spoken in innocence by Kitty Jennings that day.

★   ★   ★

Luke was thinking abut Seranne. He had arrived for their Saturday date and had waited for an hour before accepting that she had taken Kitty's words at face value and no longer wanted to acknowledge him as a friend. Saddened but not surprised, he tried to put her a bit further from his mind but it was alarmingly difficult to do so.

Thoughts of Seranne led him to thoughts of Paul Curtis. Helping Seranne to accept her mother's new life had been the beginning of it, but from the little he had so far gathered, Jessie was now another reason for his growing concern. Talking to some of his widespread family he was disturbed by what he learnt.

The factory no longer belonged to Paul, it had been reclaimed by the mortgage providers. He was still acting the role of a wealthy successful man and Luke was beginning to suspect the money he was spending was Jessie's. Seeing Paul's car in Cardiff one day when he was visiting one of his own businesses, he waited for him, intending to strike up a conversation and maybe find out what he was doing there. He saw him approaching, carrying a large canvas bag, but then he disappeared into an antiques shop and Luke followed him in.

Standing back looking at some framed maps, he watched as Paul took from the bag several china plates and two elegant vases and a bowl decorated in a beautiful fruit design enhanced generously with gold, which looked, to his inexperienced eyes, like Royal Worcester. Paul was clearly selling them and Luke slipped out of the shop as new customers entered, before Paul saw him. The last time he had seen those items was when they were displayed on the shelves in Jessica's Victorian Tea Rooms. He waited nearby until he saw Paul leave then he went into the shop.

"Hello, Uncle Ray."

"Luke, nice to see you. Go in and make some tea, will you? I've been too busy to have a break today."

Luke fingered the newly purchased china and asked his uncle about them.

"A man called Paul Curtis sold them to me," Ray explained. "He's moving from a big house into a flat and has to sell off some of his treasures."

"And you're sure they're his to sell?"

"It's difficult to be sure, you know that, but yes, I think he was genuine."

"Will you hold on to them for a day or so, Uncle? I might be wrong, but they belong to his wife, so he's probably entitled to sell them, but she might not know about it."

Later that day, Uncle Ray rang the tea rooms and spoke to Paul, who assured him the items were his own. "If you're having second thoughts I'll cancel the agreement," Paul said huffily. "I think I can get a pound or two more elsewhere, it's up to you."

"No, no, Mr Curtis. Everything is fine. Thank you."

Paul smiled at Jessie as he put down the phone. "Honestly, some people! That was a customer trying to renege on a deal we made today."

"Someone local, dear?"

"No, I've been in Tenby all day and apart from him I had a very satisfactory day. So good that why don't we have a night out tomorrow? Perhaps a dance later?"

Luke called at the tea rooms late afternoon and saw immediately how differently it was being run. Pat Sewell had taken away all the trimmings that had given the place an air of elegance, including the beautiful china. The place was quiet, the few customers showed that it was no longer a popular place to meet. He ordered a scone and this was handed to him already filled and could not be described as fresh. Paying the woman's wage, and the reduction in custom must mean that any profit Jessie earned must be greatly reduced.

He saw Jessie as he left and she looked lovely. Dressed up and obviously just on her way out. "I'm meeting Paul," she explained. "We're going out to dinner then dancing. I have to dash, I've sold the car and the bus leaves in ten minutes."

"Can I offer you a lift?" he said at once.

She explained light-heartedly that Paul had pointed out the unnecessary expense of running two cars. "And here I am, in trouble straightaway. Thank you, Luke, I hate having to wait for buses, specially as rain is forecast."

"Perhaps you should have kept it. Paul can't be short of money, owning a factory making all those leather goods."

"Of course he isn't short, but it's silly to keep on extra expense, isn't it? Paul and I are always together except during the day, and then I don't need it."

"Business good, is it?"

"Yes. He's an excellent salesman. He was in Tenby yesterday and he was so pleased with the day he's taking me out as a sort of celebration. He's so

123

thoughtful, Luke. I'm very fortunate, having a second chance. Tenby is where we spent our honeymoon and Paul always says it's a lucky place."

"Tenby? I thought I saw him in Cardiff, but I must have been mistaken."

"Oh yes. He was definitely in Tenby, hence tonight's treat." Without a glance at the rather untidy place that used to be her pride, she waved to Pat Sewell and went out to the car.

Luke drove to Cardiff after dropping Jessie off at the restaurant where she and Paul were to meet and knocked on the side door of his uncle's antique shop. "I'm still doubtful, Uncle Ray, so will you let me buy them back? Then I can return them if there's a problem."

"More money than sense you got, boy," Ray muttered. Agreement was swift and the plates and the bowl were carefully packed and put in Luke's car. He was thoughtful as he drove home, wondering whether to tell Seranne of his suspicions but eventually decided to follow his own advice and not jump to conclusions. Best to wait and see what happens.

Seranne really wanted the job of managing the café and knowing that Mrs Rogers was leaving, she determined to make her mark. Over the following days she went to work early and by the time Mrs Rogers arrived, she had trays of freshly made scones ready. Once she made drop scones with a few currants and a squeeze of lemon juice. They were very popular and became a regular offering at teatime each day.

Mrs Rogers didn't accept all her ideas and the chair seat covers were taken away for washing and never returned. "Too much trouble," was Mrs Rogers' excuse and even when Seranne offered to launder them herself they never reappeared.

One morning, Seranne was told that the owner, a Mr Griffiths, was coming to interview applicants and Seranne made sure she was early and made her usual batch of scones. Tony came with the bread and cakes they had ordered and sniffed appreciatively as he stepped into the kitchen. "Making your famous scones are you?"

"The interviews are on this morning and I hope to impress Mr Griffiths," she said, showing crossed fingers. "I don't suppose it will make much difference, we've been very pleased with yours, but it's a lovely smell and customers like to think they're made on the premises."

"Have many applied for the job?"

"I don't know. Three or four? Mrs Rogers sent the names on to Mr Griffiths. I'm hopeful, mind, having worked here for a while."

"You know Babs has applied, don't you?"

Surprised, Seranne frowned. "No, why didn't she tell me?"

"Embarrassed I expect. If she gets it she'll be your boss."

"I'm sure we'd work together well, but I wish she'd told me."

"We want to make changes at the bakery, did she tell you? Dad, Mam and I want to build a new, larger premises and increase the business. Babs won't hear of it. We all own a share of the family business and she's afraid her investment will fall. Lacking in imagination, my sister."

"No one likes changes, but we sometimes have them forced on us, then you have to do everything you can to make them work."

Everything? A thought not spoken. Tony looked thoughtful as she went through into the café to unlock the door and let Mrs Rogers in. As he walked through the kitchen to collect the empty trays, on impulse he turned up the oven a notch or two before he went out.

A few moments later Babs came in, obviously aware that Seranne now knew of her application. "Sorry, Seranne, I should have told you we'd applied for the same job."

"Yes, you should. But I can't stop and talk now, we'll meet later. What time is your interview?"

Before Babs replied, Mrs Rogers called for some help and Seranne went into the café to collect used dishes and Babs went out through the kitchen and returned to the baker's shop.

The café attracted a large number of early morning people. Many came to meet friends and have a warming drink before visiting the shops. Some came instead of eating at home before going to work. The first of the scones were quickly sold and it wasn't until Mrs Rogers went to check on the progress of the next lot that she went into the kitchen and found them burning.

"Seranne! What were you thinking of? The gas is much too high and they're ruined."

Seranne rushed in and they were both staring at the smoking ruins, as Mr Griffiths walked in.

"It seems I've chosen the wrong moment," he said.

Things went from bad to worse as the interviews took place. Seranne was so nervous and upset by the burnt scones that she dropped a plate of beans on toast and gave a customer coffee when she had ordered tea. She was almost consumed with anger towards Babs. It was an effort to be pleasant to the customers. Whatever Luke might say, this time her anger was justified, there really was someone to blame. How could Babs do such a thing?

When Babs came in for her interview and waved at her, Seranne ignored her, convinced that it had been she who had turned up the heat in the oven. The opportunity had been there and who else would have done such a mean thing? How could a friend do that? As her friend left she overheard Mrs Rogers saying, "Don't worry, Babs, even though you're without real experience, I'll make sure Mr Griffiths knows how suitable you are."

Before the lunchtime rush, Mr Griffiths sat her down in the kitchen and asked her why she wanted the job. She had worked out the kind of questions likely to come up and had prepared answers, but the day had been so traumatic that her mind was filled with confusion.

Aware of her distress, he asked simple questions at first: how long she had lived in Cwm Derw and whether she liked living at Badgers Brook, and gradually she calmed down enough to explain about her mother's tea rooms and her own desire to improve the business by trying to emulate that success.

"So, burnt scones and food served on the floor instead of the usual plate isn't the plan?" he said, and she looked up to see he was smiling.

"I really don't know what happened. I'm sure I had set the oven correctly," was all she said. She would talk to Babs later and make her tell the truth.

"I have a few applicants to consider, and I'll let you know my decision by the end of the week," he said offering his hand. She thanked him and flopped back into her seat, exhausted.

"Don't worry," Mrs Rogers said. "I had a word and told him how excellent you are."

She might have found that comforting had she not heard her saying something similar to Babs Hopkins.

She phoned her mother and spoke at first to Paul, who seemed edgy and unresponsive to her complaints about her friend. "Don't give up your independence," he advised. "Better to work for Babs than lose your job." It was very clear that he didn't want her to return home.

When she spoke to her mother she was more sympathetic but echoed Paul's comments. Then she said, "Luke was here yesterday. He was more talkative than usual, asked a lot of questions. You didn't send him did you, dear? You'd tell me if you had any worries, wouldn't you?"

"Of course I didn't send Luke! I hardly know the man and wouldn't send anyone to spy. There's no need, is there? We tell each other everything, don't we?" She paused but Jessie said nothing. "Everything is all right, is it Mum? You aren't short of money, now the tea rooms aren't as busy?"

"Of course we aren't short of money. What a question. Paul is building up a list of new clients, planning to open a new business and the tea rooms is still a good business, less work for me, that was Paul's motive for the changes. We share everything, darling. And I'm blissfully happy."

Seranne was unhappy as she went home that evening. She hadn't tried to see Babs, better to let time pass or she would certainly quarrel with her and that would make difficulties if she had to work beside her. She reached the bus stop but walked on. She needed to empty her mind of what the day had held. She had set off with such confidence that morning but everything had gone wrong and she was returning with a feeling that everything had been lost. Her mother's brave words hadn't convinced her that things were satisfactory at home. After that dreadful interview she might not even have a job, let alone be offered the post of manageress.

Anger flared anew as she thought again of the scones being ruined by someone messing with the oven. It had to be Babs. That wasn't jumping to conclusions whatever Luke might say! Wanting the job herself and knowing that Mr Griffiths was due to arrive, the temptation must have been too much for her. It was probably the reason she had come, the hope of doing something to spoil my chances, she thought. The lane was dark and moisture dripped from the trees. A chill wind was blowing in her face. She began to wish she had waited for the bus. She would still have had to walk along the lane but she'd have been home sooner. Then a movement in the hedge made her stand and listen. A dark form crossed the road in front of her and she hugged herself with delight. A badger stopped, sniffed the air then went on its way. Two others followed and she stood there for a long time marvelling at the sight, her unhappy mood lifted by the unexpected encounter.

She was further cheered when she stepped into Badgers Brook. The house was warm and welcoming and she made a snack and sat beside the fire, lit as usual by her kindly neighbours, Kitty and Bob, and relaxed in the tranquillity of her lovely home. Anger completely faded and she was wrapped in the soothing atmosphere of the old building, comforted and at peace. It no longer mattered whether or not she was offered the job; whatever she had to do to earn her living, she would stay in this magical place.

She saw Kitty early the following morning when she went to ask if she needed any shopping brought. Still in her dressing gown, Kitty sat beside the newly lit fire and patted the chair beside her. "I saw your face when I asked Luke about his wife. You didn't know he was married, did you?"

"No, but it doesn't matter. We're only casual acquaintances, he walked me home because of the deep snow, that's all. Now I'd better be off," Seranne said briskly, "Or I'll get the sack instead of the job of manageress!" She stopped long enough to give her friend a humorous account of what had happened before the interview and left laughing, as though the disasters had all been nothing more than a joke.

She looked up at Badgers Brook as she passed. Such a wonderful place, it calmed her and made her concentrate only on the really important things. "And Luke isn't one of them!" she added aloud.

Friday came and went and there was no word from Mr Griffiths about the vacancy. On Saturday, she left work early and went to see her mother. It was after seven o'clock when she arrived and she was surprised to see the tables in the tea rooms hadn't been cleared and her mother was out. She let herself in and began to clear the debris of the day with some concern. This was something she had never know to happen. Her mother was never off duty until everything was clean and ready for the next day. Even on Saturdays, with a day off to follow, the routine had always been the same. She was further disconcerted to see that the leftover scones and cakes were from a bakery and not made by her mother.

The curtains were pulled across the large windows and it was a few minutes before she noticed that all the beautiful ornamental teapots and plates were gone. She didn't worry too much, they had probably been taken down for washing. She climbed up and washed the shelves ready for their return and was surprised at the dust that had gathered. They hadn't been cleaned for some weeks, she decided with a frown. What was going on?

She checked her room and found everything in order, even though she hadn't told her mother she was coming. That would never change. The room was hers wherever she chose to live. She sat surrounded by her familiar things and thought about Paul. He had married her mother so quickly. "Swept her off her feet" was a cliché, but that was what had happened, he had married her without giving her time to think, yet her mother seemed to be happy. So what is it that's worrying me? she asked herself. It was something more than the state of the tea rooms. Money was a concern. Paul didn't appear to be earning any unless the factory ran itself without needing his presence. He spent all his time driving around in that car of his or taking her mother out. He had persuaded her mother to employ Pat Sewell and was letting the café run itself down, so were they using her mother's savings? Would he leave her when they ran out?

It was almost midnight when the door opened and her mother and Paul came in, laughing as they came up the stairs.

"Mum, it's me," Seranne called.

"Darling! What a lovely surprise!"

"Sorry we were out, Seranne," Paul added. "I took your mother dancing again."

"I hope you didn't go into the tea rooms," Jessie said, rolling her eyes. "I'm afraid we left it all till tomorrow."

"And why not?" Seranne said, hugging her mother. "I'm sure it won't take long."

Jessie looked at her, head tilted and said, "You've dealt with it, haven't you? Oh I'm sorry, dear, you should have told us you were coming and we'd have made sure it was done."

"I'm glad I didn't because then you'd have missed a lovely night out."

"It's Pat Sewell's weekend off and I'm afraid we cheat a little and leave everything until Sunday."

"What about the books? They used to take us most of Sunday morning."

"Oh, Paul deals with all that," Jessie waved her hand as though brushing the irritation aside. "I don't have to look at them, thank goodness. He does the ordering too. He and Pat Sewell between them."

"After working every day? He must find it a bore."

"He's just told me he doesn't own the factory any longer. He sold it last week for a very good sum and my investment has done remarkably well. Isn't that marvellous? Until he decides on his next business venture we'll work here together, helped by Pat. She's a wonder, isn't she darling?"

Seranne glanced at Paul who looked suitably modest.

The following morning while her mother and Paul walked to the newsagent's to buy an extra newspaper — an excuse, she suspected, to go out and talk — Seranne looked through the books and explored the once beautiful tea rooms. Her worries increased and she was seriously alarmed at the changes in the way the place was being run. Economies, mainly instigated by Pat Sewell and supported by Paul had altered the character of the place. There was no longer a cleaner, and it showed. The tablecloths were no longer white linen, the windows no longer sparkled, the chair seats, like she had tried to persuade Mrs Rogers to use, were no longer there and the chairs were in need of a polish. Looking through the daily lists and the bakery accounts, the more expensive cakes no longer appeared on the menu. The cakes and scones, for which the place had always been famous, were being bought from the local bakery and were more expensive for a less attractive product, from the remnants she had seen. The only savings were in time, giving her mother more time to spend with Paul. She looked around sadly. Jessica's Victorian Tea Rooms had been reduced to nothing more than a cheap and shoddy café.

Later that Sunday morning, her mother took her for a walk before lunch while Paul stayed behind to deal with the weekly accounts. The day was cold and damp and the pleasure of seeing places she knew so well were lost beneath her worries. She didn't have the heart to call on friends as she had intended. She tried to persuade her mother to talk about the tea rooms, to explain why it had been allowed to run down.

Jessie laughed and said, "Paul says life is for living and after spending most of my life working, I deserve a bit of fun."

Everything her mother told her added to her concerns and when the rain began and they had to run back home, the weather seemed a reflection of her gloomy mood and she couldn't wait to get back to Badgers Brook.

Something was terribly wrong. Paul had taken over her mother's life and the constant reminders of how valuable Pat Sewell had become and the way Jessie deferred to her abilities, suggested it was she who was now in charge of the business. It was Paul and Pat who dealt with the books and the decision-making and she wondered how much longer the place could survive without her mother's guiding hands. That her mother was happy was in no doubt, but the once inviting tea rooms had lost its charm.

On her way back to Cwm Derw one of her mother's neighbours sat next to her on the bus. Seranne didn't need to ask questions for the gossip to be shared. Although cautiously spoken at first, it became clear that the tea rooms was no longer the most popular place for locals. It was also revealed that Paul had lost his business through neglect and indifference, it had not been sold, but handed over some weeks earlier to clear his debts.

What had really happened to the money her mother had invested? Paul must have used the money which Jessie had gullibly handed over, to bolster up his failing business. What could she do? There wasn't a soul she could talk to, except Luke, and he was no longer a friend.

On Monday morning a letter arrived for Seranne in which she was told, with many regrets, that her application for the position of manageress had been unsuccessful. It ended by hoping that she and Miss Barbara Hopkins would work well together. Now she had to decide whether she could work with a person who had ruined her chances. Babs was waiting for her when she reached the café and unable to avoid her, she glanced at her coldly and said, "Congratulations."

"Mr Griffiths said he thought your previous experience in a high-class place was a disadvantage when dealing with a small café like this one. I'm sorry."

"Are you? Is that why you ruined the scones?"

"Ruined the . . . what d'you mean?"

"Come on, you can't pretend you didn't turn up the oven and burn them."

"I didn't! How can you think that I'd do such a thing?"

"You were the only one in the kitchen, except Tony and he had no reason to bother."

Without a word Babs ran across the road back to the bakery and Seranne let herself inside, outrage tightening her lips. As she took off her coat, it caught a dish of duck eggs intended for making cakes and it teetered on the edge of the table. She leapt across the room and managed to save it, but at the same time knocked over a pile of tins she had taken out ready for greasing. The noise was alarming and seemed to go on and on as the pile slithered across the floor, paused, then slithered some more. A figure appeared at the door and Luke stood there laughing.

"What has upset you this time? Irate motorist? A dog? Wet roads? Burnt cakes?"

"Now they'll all have to be washed! D'you want something, or have you come to gloat?"

"Because you didn't get the job? Why would that please me?"

"I don't know. Everything that happens to me seems to be a cause for laughter."

"It's the look of outrage on your face. I don't know anyone else who can change her face from sunshine to thunder clouds in seconds. It's fascinating. You are fascinating." He stepped inside and began to rescue the fallen tins, and he pushed the eggs further away from the edge. Then he filled the sink with hot water and dropped the tins in.

"I can manage," she said haughtily.

"I came to tell you that my auntie, Mrs Rogers, won't be in today."

"What? But what am I to do?"

"Manage, I suppose." He was wearing that irritating smile again.

"Fine. I'll do what I can."

"Mrs Cassie Evans is coming to help. She's my auntie, too," he told her with a grin. "I'll see you later."

She dried the tins and glanced at the clock. Less than an hour before opening. She dashed around, putting the scones to bake, making a couple of large sponge cakes, preparing sandwiches and cutting slices of bread ready for toasting. She opened tins of beans and spaghetti and put them into pans, hard boiled some eggs and set the tables. As she opened the door to smile at and welcome the first customers, she looked across the road to the bakery. "How would Babs have managed what I just did?" she muttered rebelliously.

Mrs Evans arrived at eleven o'clock. A woman in her sixties, she wore her grey hair in a bun at the top of her head allowing feathery fringes to fall about her rosy cheeks and wearing a constant smile. Seranne disapproved of the waving hair but ignored it, this wasn't the time to criticize. Mrs Evans was soon helping to prepare the lunches and to Seranne's relief she was quick, needed telling only once, and Seranne was grateful for her speed and efficiency.

"Are you really Luke's auntie?" she asked as they were clearing up after closing.

"My mother had eight children. They all married, so Luke has seven aunties — including me — seven uncles and eighteen cousins. There's even more on his father's side."

"I'm an only child. It sounds wonderful to have such a large family."

"It is in our case, but not always. That Elsie Connors in the guest house had a sister but they haven't spoken for years. There's terrible, isn't it?"

"She's very ill, isn't she?"

"Yes, and it's only her poor husband and her sister-in-law, Betty Connors, who are there to help. Fancy being that stubborn when she's so ill. You'd think she'd forgive her sister for whatever she did all those years ago, wouldn't you? You haven't any family?"

"Only my mother and a stepfather. My father died when I was a baby. A stepfather adopted me but he left. Now there's Paul Curtis."

"And that's why you left home and came to Cwm Derw?" Mrs Evans asked shrewdly. "Probably the best thing to do."

"The trouble is, like Elsie Connors, it might be too easy for me to stay away." Especially now, when everything has changed, she thought sadly.

When she reached home she was aware that the busy day had given her very little time to dwell on the situation with her mother and the tea rooms, or Paul and his factory. The problem of working under Babs Hopkins returned but she forced herself to clear her mind of all concerns and enjoy the quiet evening. She put some potatoes under the fire to bake for supper later on. For now a piece of cake and a cup of tea would suffice.

A knock at the door pleased her. It would probably be Kitty. She opened the door smiling but the smile faded when she saw Babs, wrapped up against the cold in coat, boots, scarf and a pixie hood that was complete with a couple of bobbles bouncing around her head. With a show of reluctance, Seranne stepped back for her to enter.

"I'm not coming in. I just wanted to tell you that I didn't touch the oven and I can't believe you thought I could." Seranne began to apologize but Babs interrupted. "You really thought I could do that to you, didn't you? Well, I'm sorry, but I'll be in charge at the café from Monday and if you can't trust me I think it's best you leave."

"All right, if that's what you want. You'd better come in so I can explain the routine." Babs was about to turn away, but the wind suddenly blew around the house and hit her with a cold blast that almost lifted her off her feet. "What was that!" she gasped.

"Come on in, there's no point in freezing," Seranne said. Babs stepped inside and Seranne gestured to a seat beside the fire. Refusing to take off her coat, and

139

ignoring the offer of a chair, standing stiffly and unforgiving near the hearth, Babs glared at her one-time friend, waiting for her to speak. The wind howled around the roof-top for a few minutes then ceased.

"I've put a couple of potatoes to bake, they'll be ready in a while, if you're hungry," Seranne said.

As the minutes passed and Seranne discussed the daily routine, Babs still stood, fully dressed for outdoors. Their antagonism eased a little, although they were both uncomfortably aware that trust was no longer there.

"I don't know why I came in. There's something about this house, it's impossible to be angry for long. I intended to blast off at you then walk off in a huff," Babs admitted.

"Perhaps you ought to stay a while longer then."

"No, thank you. I won't stay and pretend you're forgiven!" Babs walked to the door abruptly.

"D'you think we could work together?" Seranne asked as Babs stepped onto the path.

"We can try." She didn't sound very sure and Seranne was left with the conviction that she would soon be without a job. The only thing she could do was continue the same as when Mrs Rogers was there; arrive early and start on the cooking, and hope things would smooth over.

In the Ship and Compass Betty watched as Alun prepared some bread dough. He had bought yeast at the bakery and was making them as an experiment to see if the customers preferred home baked bread rolls. Cheese and pickle or luncheon meat with mysterious origins were the only choices for filling but with a darts match being played that evening she was sure they would be appreciated. Specially with the last jar of her pickled onions.

They worked so well together that she tried not to think about him leaving and starting his own restaurant once his money had been released by the solicitor. Since her brother Ed had left, she'd had to manage with assistants who showed little interest and rarely stayed more than a month or two. With Alun it was different. The days flew past and she was happier than she had ever been before. Every morning she watched the post arrive, afraid it would include the letter which would delight Alun and fill her with dread.

She was taking sandwiches to the bar at lunchtime when Seranne came in. It was her first day working for Babs and she didn't look happy. She was carrying a packet of paper serviettes and a drum of table salt. "Sorry, I know you're busy, but I need to talk to you. Can I come in for a chat later?"

"I'll just take these out to the bar and we can have a cup of tea. Alun will manage for ten minutes. Will that do?"

"Thanks, Betty."

"You didn't get the job, then. How d'you feel about working with Babs Hopkins as your boss?"

"Not good. We started badly," she said, and explained about her accusations and the overheated oven. "This morning I was in early and started on the

141

cooking as usual, but when she came in she told me that was no longer my job. Instead of sharing the work as Mrs Rogers and I did, seeing what needed doing and getting on with it, I'm clearing tables, cleaning and taking money but nothing else. It's such a waste of my experience. I'm here now because I've been sent out to buy salt, as she insists that what we have is too coarse for the tables."

"Give it a week. She's probably very anxious, it's the first time she's worked away from the family business, even if it is just across the road. You can remember how scary that can be. She's afraid that you are so used to doing things your way she won't be able to act the big boss."

"It's hard, Betty. I've been in the business all my life."

"She might be getting revenge too. If she didn't tamper with the oven she must have been hurt by you thinking she could act so unkindly."

"If she didn't do it, who did? But you're right, I'll just have to give it time."

"A week together and you'll remember why you're friends. Why don't you invite her to come here tonight? There's a big darts match on and she'd enjoy watching her brother and father playing for the retailers taking on Colin and Bob and the allotment holders."

"I could make some scones if you like. I don't want to forget how it's done."

When she mentioned it, Babs said she might and although neither of them were keen to spend time together, Babs eventually agreed to go.

142

"Please yourself!" Seranne retorted. She had no intention of wearing sack cloth and ashes for ever. "I've promised to go early and help Betty, so I won't call for you."

"I'll be going with Mam and Dad and Tony anyway."

The first person Seranne saw on walking into the Ship with her tray of scones was Luke. She pretended not to see him and went straight through to the back room, where Betty was piling plates with bread rolls and pasties. Seranne ladled the pickled onions into dishes and put them on a tray to be taken through.

"I won't put the food out until they have a break, about nine o'clock," Betty told her.

"I'll come and help, shall I?"

"Don't avoid her, it won't get better without a bit of effort."

"Now what have you done?" Luke asked from the doorway. Seranne glared and was about to accuse him of eavesdropping when he added, "The scones in the café weren't as good today, did you forget the oven again?"

"Shhh," Betty warned, pointing towards the bar from where laughter and chatter filled the air. "Seranne didn't make them! They were from the bakery."

"She made these though," Alun said pointing to the tray. "And very good they are."

Braving the risk of another argument, Seranne went into the bar when the first rounds were being played. Babs was there but they hardly spoke. When Luke exaggerated the quality of the scones in her hearing Babs left. Her heart racing with the conviction that she would be unable to work at the café any longer, Seranne made her excuses and left soon after.

As she went to bed it wasn't the prospect of unemployment that held back sleep, but the state of Jessica's Victorian Tea Rooms. The very name was now a joke. Was that what the future was going to be, a café with basic appeal and economy being the priority? The thought saddened her as she remembered how her mother had worked to make the tea rooms a pleasant place to be. The ticking of the clock seemed extra loud and she soon found herself becoming emersed in the rhythm. The night outside stretched her imagination and made a picture in her mind of the animals that would be awake and searching for food. She remembered the badgers crossing her path, and wondered where they would be.

Useless to stay in bed, she got up and found her dressing gown. Better to accept her wakefulness for a while instead of fidgeting and trying to force sleep to come. The house was never quiet. The old fabric creaked and sighed and the wind whispered around its walls. She sat and was comforted by the sounds that were like a lulluby so late at night, and allowed her thoughts to wander.

She knew she could do nothing about her mother's business, it was just that: her mother's business. Jessie and Paul wanted a different life from the one she had known and she had to accept that. For herself, she knew that working with Babs Hopkins was no longer possible and she would have to find another way of earning her keep. But what could she do? If she told

Babs she was leaving, that would give her a week to find something new. It wouldn't be enough. All she had ever done was run a café and there was only one in Cwm Derw, which was no longer a possibility. Perhaps she should stay and forget she and Babs had once been friends, at least until she found another job. But that was cowardly. It would be dishonest too, to pretend all was well, then let Babs down, even if she had ruined her chance of getting the manager's position.

"Confidence", a voice seemed to whisper and she took a deep breath, knowing that her first move had to be to tell Babs she would no longer work for her. Then she would just hope something would turn up — something to allow her to stay in Cwm Derw and live in Badgers Brook.

She went back to bed, calmed by at least one decision having been made and slept wonderfully well. It was still dark when she awoke but she was rested and unable to stay in bed. Instead she rose and sorted out some of her household chores, the cold not affecting her, the house was never uncomfortably chilled, even in the darkest winter days.

She still had a key for the café and she left early without planning how she would spend the time. Leaving the café in darkness, she looked at the ingredients placed ready for the day's food. Should she start on the sandwiches? It was half an hour before Babs was likely to arrive. Will she be annoyed?" she asked herself. Do I care if she is? Why had she come so early?

She went to the small store cupboard outside and saw to her surprise that the bread had not been delivered. Tony always brought it before eight and it was now half past. She didn't want to go to the bakery so she satisfied herself by boiling eggs, grating cheese and slicing some sad-looking tomatoes. At nine she sat there wondering why Babs hadn't arrived. At ten past, a boy in white overalls knocked on the door with the loaves and he was followed by another carrying a wooden tray of assorted cakes.

"Where's Babs?" she demanded and was told that Babs wouldn't be in until at least eleven, as Tony had fallen and she was needed to do his work.

"Why wasn't I told? I do work here you know!"

The boys looked at each other saying nothing.

"Fine!" she said. "Tell her from me that I'm going for my lunch at twelve no matter what happens. And you can also tell her I'm leaving at the end of next week. Right?" She looked around expecting to see Luke watching. He was usually there when she did something stupid, and shouting at the young boys was as stupid as it gets. She opened the café door and called after them, "Sorry, boys. I know it isn't anything to do with you."

One of them waved in acknowledgement, the other waggled the empty tray. "Why didn't she tell me before?" she muttered as she opened the loaves and began making the sandwiches. She was glad she had at least begun the preparations. The scones and cakes were covered with muslin and the tall cake stands were ready to receive them and at 9.30, exactly on time she prepared her smile and opened the door.

It was difficult but she coped with the morning rush and was warming the plates ready for the early lunches when Babs arrived. She looked around at the neat tables and the clean orderly kitchen and said a cursory, "Thank you", to which Seranne didn't reply.

Forgetting what she had told the boys about an early lunch the two of them set to and served the lunches. Hardly a word passed between them and when they managed to eat a sandwich at about two o'clock, Babs said. "Look, Seranne —"

Hot-headed as usual, Seranne said, "No, *you* look. I can't work for you. I'm handing in my notice and will be leaving at the end of next week."

"Oh. That's a pity. I didn't touch the oven that day but if you don't believe me, then perhaps it's best you go."

"I'll take my break now, shall I?"

"Better than that, I'll pay you for this week and next and you can finish altogether."

"But how will you manage, if Tony is unable to work?"

"That isn't your problem, is it? I was made manageress and I'll do that, manage! That's something you can't accept."

Without a word, Seranne took the wages and left. She was barely holding back tears as she walked back to Badgers Brook, ignoring the bus again, needing to hide her stupid face from everyone. Luke was right about her temper being a joke. It was such a pity that she couldn't see it herself, until it was too late.

CHAPTER
SIX

It was strange to wake the following morning with no need to get up the moment the alarm shrilled in her ear. Seranne's first reaction was to reach for her dressing gown and get up but then realization came and she sank back onto the pillow. Instead of thinking ahead to the first routine tasks of the day in the café, she was faced with the unpleasant thought of looking for another job.

She walked up the lane and caught a bus to the main road and tried not to look across at the café, where a weak light struggled through steamed windows. It was not yet half past nine and a few prospective customers stood outside, leaning forward occasionally to peer through in the hope of the door being opened. She saw movement inside and curiously she stopped to look. A huge notice was displayed: STAFF WANTED. Regret filled her and she hurried on.

Perhaps she should go home? Her mother's tea rooms was certainly in need of her expertise. No, that wasn't the answer, she could no longer go home. It wasn't false pride that stopped her, or the embarrassment of knowing she had failed, but the realization that she had moved on. She no longer belonged.

As though she had picked up on her thoughts, when she telephoned her mother a few minutes later, Jessie said, "I love seeing you, you know that, but next time will you let us know when you're coming? Paul and I were so disappointed to be out last time. Let us know then we'll be sure to be in."

"That sounds very formal, Mum. Whose idea is that, yours or Paul's?"

"Well it was Paul who suggested I mention it. We go out quite often you see. We'd be so sorry if we missed you."

"It's still my home, Mum."

"And always will be, but now, with Paul in my life, the days are so full. It's really wonderful. I'm so happy, darling, I really am. So just tell us and we'll make sure you get a real welcome."

Seranne put down the phone with the uneasy feeling that all was not well. Nothing specific, just a slight strain in her mother's voice she hadn't been aware of before. She was trying so hard to convince me, she mused, but the effect was the opposite. She was so distracted with concern for her mother when she went to the employment exchange that she found nothing that appealed among the vacancies.

At two o'clock she went for a walk. She was too miserable to enjoy it as she usually did, her solitary state no longer enough. She felt cut off from her mother and very lonely. Signs of approaching spring went unnoticed. Birds pairing up after spending the winter in flocks, fresh green leaves like tiny spears appearing on the sunny banks. Bright sunshine that fell dappled by the still bare trees onto the woodland floor. Nothing succeeded in lightening her mood.

The following day, when she spoke to Stella in the post office, Stella offered Scamp, her little terrier, as a companion for her walks and she accepted with a few misgivings. She had never owned a dog and wasn't sure how he would behave.

On the first day he seemed to assert himself as leader and instead of walking through the lane toward the wood, he pulled her in the opposite direction. From the doorway of the shop Stella called, "He's off to our country cottage. Don't worry, he knows the way." Being towed along by the excited dog, Seranne had no choice but to follow. Country cottage? What on earth was Stella talking about?

Scamp led her to the allotments, where plots of land were neatly set out and dug ready for planting, each with its small shed. One shed door was open and it was to there she was taken.

"Hello," Colin said. "Scamp's brought you to see me, has he? Want a cup of tea?" He patted the little dog then turned to fiddle with a paraffin stove and a kettle. "Stella always makes sure there's the makings of tea. Her country cottage she calls it."

The shed wasn't like any other she had known. Inside there was a square of carpet, devoid of mud and grass as though regularly swept. The window was dressed with pretty curtains. Shelves held vases of artificial flowers.

"This is amazing," she said as she watched Colin open a tin from which he took cups and saucers and plates. A second container revealed biscuits and another a few small cakes. Chairs were unfolded and she sat and admired the gardens and sipped the tea Colin had made, enjoying the unexpected interlude.

She tried to coax Scamp to take a long route back to the post office but as before, he told her where he wanted to go and that was back home, where he jumped into his favourite armchair and slept.

During the next few days she called at the employment exchange several times and in between, she and Scamp explored the woods and surrounding fields. Several times she thought she had lost him as he disappeared chasing a rabbit or a bird, but he returned to her without trouble.

They were at the edge of the wood on their way home one day when she saw Luke. He was walking and seemed in no hurry. She didn't want to talk to him. Knowing he had a wife made it impossible to feel at ease with him. She would have been glancing around afraid of the wife appearing and attacking her in a jealous rage. She darted back through the trees and found her way blocked by an area of muddy water with a plank across it. As though she could already hear the angry shouts of Luke's wife she hopped onto the wood which immediately sank, her foot disappearing in glutinous mud. She shouted her dismay and heard footsteps approaching. Not the wife but Luke himself. Angry with herself, and with him for putting her in the situation, she presented a look of such fury that Luke laughed out loud.

"Oh, go away. Can't you see this isn't funny?" Which only made him laugh even louder. He offered a hand to help her out of the gooey mess but she refused and, struggling to free herself, put her second foot in the water. "See what you've done now!"

"What *I've* done?"

"Yes, you, creeping up on me like that!" She knew she was talking rubbish but couldn't help herself.

"Come on, take my hand and I'll help you out."

Reluctantly she did as he said and he helped her back to the road followed by an equally muddy dog.

"The car is around the corner," he said as they reached the lane. "But I think you'll both have to ride in the boot, don't you?"

"I can walk, thank you," she said rebelliously.

They reached the car and Luke bent down to take off her shoes and socks before helping her into the car.

"My feet are cold," she protested ungraciously.

Luke removed his scarf and wrapped it around her feet. Scamp jumped onto the driving seat from where he was hastily removed. Not before he had spread foul-smelling mud all over it. This was when Seranne began to laugh. Aware that her laughter was unkind when Luke was helping, she tried to stop but couldn't. Scamp barked, enjoying what he considered a game while Luke covered the seat with an old coat from the boot.

He drove her back to Badgers Brook, followed her in after tying a protesting Scamp to a tree at the doorway and put a match to the fire. "Go up and clean yourself," he said. "I'll make us a drink." Too cold and uncomfortable to argue, Seranne did as she was told, leaving Luke opening and closing cupboards as he searched for the things he needed.

"Why aren't you at work?" he asked when they sat drinking the cocoa he had made and Scamp was ensconced on his ruined coat in the kitchen. "You haven't left the café, have you?"

"Yes. I couldn't work with Babs."

"I see. You were upset because you didn't get the manager's job and went off in a sulk?"

"No, I didn't! Babs cheated to get the job and I can't consider her a friend any longer."

He persuaded her to explain, then said, "She says she didn't touch the oven?"

"She must have done. There was no one else. I didn't make a mistake."

"Heaven forbid!"

"What d'you mean?"

"Little Miss Perfect, so experienced, no one else can come near your expertise, can they?"

"I've been running a café alongside my mother all my life."

"A mischievous child might have gone in. Or you could have caught the control with your coat. You shouldn't jump to conclusions — about anything," he added looking at her strangely.

She wondered what he meant. He couldn't be referring to his wife. A man was either married or not and according to Kitty, he was.

"I'd better get Scamp back to Stella or she'll think we're lost." He offered to drive her but she refused.

153

"He'd be happy to walk," she said. Then seeing how dark it was, and how low the clouds were, she wished she had accepted. She added an extra jumper and some thick socks to what she was wearing, and two scarves, one around her neck the other, wide and thick, she wrapped around her head making her look like a colourful Egyptian mummy.

When she went out after stacking the cups and plates, the car was waiting. "I thought you might have changed your mind," Luke said amiably. She uncurled one of the scarves and got in. "You are inclined to speak before you think," he added, then he pressed the accelerator before she could jump back out, laughing at her angry expression.

She stayed and helped Stella to bath the dog then caught the bus to the top of the lane. She was aware how foolish she must appear to Luke. Always angry about something. She had never been as even tempered as she would have liked but he brought out the worst in her. She vaguely wondered why. It wasn't an attraction. As a married man he was strictly out of bounds. Any brief dreams about a romance had been swiftly put aside. So why was he so kind to her? Was he really the same to everyone he met? From the little she had learnt about him, he ran several businesses and was on the board of several others, so he was obviously not desperate for friendship. She wished she dare ask Kitty for more details about the man but didn't want to be misunderstood. He was married and that was definitely that!

She had several visitors that evening. First came Connie and Geoff, who called each week for their rent and stayed for tea and biscuits. Next came Kitty and Bob, who asked if they could borrow a couple of chairs as they had visitors the following day. The third knock puzzled her. It was quite late and she wasn't expecting anyone.

It was Tony and she glanced behind to see whether he had brought his sister. For a moment her heart leapt at the possibility she was going to be asked to return to the café, but he was alone.

Offered tea and a seat, he said, "Babs is struggling you know, and it's all my fault."

"How can you say that? She ruined the scones in a petty attempt to make me look inefficient and —"

"I turned the heat up."

"You? But why, Tony? Come on, aren't you covering up for your sister?"

"I wanted to spoil your chances because my parents and I want to buy a larger premises, bring in modern machinery and expand the business. Babs refuses to consider it. I thought that if I got her out of the way, Dad and I could get on with it. I wrote a wonderful letter recommending her for the job, my father gave her the finest reference. Then, seeing the scones that morning I couldn't resist the temptation to mess things up for you. I altered the regulo — I wanted her to get the job. But now, well, I don't think she'll last long. She doesn't know enough about running the business side of things. Making cakes in a modern bakery is different from selling them and making a profit."

155

She stared at him. "You haven't said sorry yet, Tony."

"I am. In fact I want to make a proper apology. Will you come out with me tomorrow night? Pictures maybe and supper somewhere?"

"There's no need for that, but you must put things right with Babs."

"I'd like to anyway. We've known each other a long time but we've spent very little time together. It would be good to talk to each other without my sister there. What d'you say?"

"All right, Tony. Only if I can choose the film, mind."

After he'd gone she felt a glow of contentment. She hadn't lost her temper or told him what she thought of him for ruining her chances with Mr Griffiths. Luke would be proud of me, she thought happily.

As for their trip to the pictures, they hadn't made a definite date and she could let it drag out until he lost interest. Tony and she had little in common, or they would have become friends long ago. She lit her candle and went up to bed.

She saw Luke the following morning as she stepped off the bus near the post office and told him about Tony's visit.

"What are you going to do?" he asked, gesturing towards the café.

She shrugged. "What can I do?"

"You could apply to the staff wanted notice."

"Don't be ridiculous! I couldn't do that!"

"Too proud, are we?"

"Of course not. But . . ." How could she explain that knowing she had been wrong about Babs just made

156

things worse? Apologizing then working with her, Luke was probably right, her pride wouldn't allow it. What was she doing worrying about what Luke thought of her? He was hovering on the periphery of her life, complaining about her temper, accusing her of jumping to conclusions without thinking things through, making her feel bad about things and causing her to mistrust her own feelings. He had no right to criticize. Calming down she wondered if perhaps Tony would help put things right. After all it was his fault the argument happened.

"Why don't we meet and talk about it, that often helps and you can hardly discuss how to apologize to someone with the person involved." He saw her hesitate and added, "Saturday evening? We could find a quiet place to eat, and talk for a little while then I'll drive you home."

That seemed a reasonable suggestion and she had to admit it appealed. She did need someone to talk to and, now she and her mother were no longer such close friends, apart from Kitty and Bob she had no one in her life to fill that category. Keep it casual and there was no harm, she convinced herself.

Her mind began to play with ideas about him as she went to the employment exchange for another attempt to find work. Perhaps Kitty hadn't realized that his marriage had ended in divorce? A divorced man? Was that an attractive idea? It was hardly a pleasing prospect. Trying to convince herself she didn't care, she decided that whatever had happened, he had been a failure.

Before Saturday came round she saw Luke again. This time he was talking to a young woman who was hand in hand with a little girl. The shock hit her anew. He was married, and for a moment she felt the usual surge of anger at his duplicity. Why was he hiding the fact? Then his words came back to her. Don't jump to conclusions. Was it a friend? Or someone asking directions? Seeing him with a woman didn't automatically make the woman his wife.

They met as planned and went to a small country public house, where they ate a simple meal of sandwiches. Luke said very little, he just asked an occasional question to encourage her to think things through.

She asked him if he had ever had to solve a similar situation. "Have you had a friendship that was in trouble and needed sorting?" It was the closest she dared to get to asking if he had a broken marriage behind him. Surely if he cared, even a little, he would tell her?

He smiled and shook his head. "Friends are too important to take chances. We need them all. I always try to make allowances, see the other side, although that's difficult at times."

Talking to him helped make up her mind. She would see Babs and apologize and hopefully return to work beside her. She thanked him as she stepped out of the car. He didn't come in and she wasn't sure whether she was disappointed or relieved.

Betty Connors was on the phone to the brewery giving her weekly order when she saw the ambulance drive around the corner behind the post office. She immediately guessed it was for her sister-in-law. "Can you hold the fort a while?" she called to Alun. "There's an ambulance and it's going towards Ed and Elsie's place."

Throwing off her apron and grabbing her coat, she hurried to her brother's guest house where she saw the ambulance parked with its doors open, and a stretcher being lifted inside. Ed was coming out from the house carrying a coat and a small suitcase. "Betty. Thank goodness you've come. I couldn't get through on the phone. Elsie's real bad. Can you see to the arrivals this afternoon?"

"Of course," Betty assured him. She watched as the ambulance drove slowly away then went in to see what needed doing. After ten minutes she rang the Ship.

"Sorry, Alun, but I'll be about an hour here. I'll be back for lunchtime opening, then I'll have to come back to see to the arrivals. Only four, thank goodness. Birdwatchers apparently. They won't be much trouble."

"Don't worry, love, I'll be all right until you get back."

The "Don't worry, love" pleased her and she felt like a young woman with her first crush.

Ed rang at lunchtime and the news wasn't good. Elsie was having difficulty breathing and would be in hospital for some time.

"I'll do what I can," Alun promised Betty. "Bob will help and Kitty has promised to wash glasses. This is an amazing place, I didn't have to ask!"

"I know. They all help whoever needs it, even the grumpy and ungrateful," she said with a laugh. "The customers are patient, too. A couple of them will come round the other side of the bar to help if it's busy."

"We can take turns going over to make the breakfast, the cleaner will cope with the routine and finding someone to help with the bed-changes shouldn't be hard," Alun said.

"I wonder if young Seranne would help us for a while?" Betty suggested. "She isn't working so far as I know."

"I'll ask."

Betty dealt with the urgent post and settled the accounts of the few guests without difficulty. Alun went over each morning and together they cooked breakfast, leaving the dishes for the cleaner, before dashing back to the Ship to start on their own morning's work. It was hectic at times but sharing the problems with Alun made it a joy rather than hard work. They dealt with everything together without having to make arrangements, slotting into the necessary chores with ease.

Ed stayed at the hospital, sitting in the uncomfortable waiting-room when he was not allowed in the ward — to the disapproval of the staff. Between visits he dashed home for bathing and changing his clothes and gave only a cursory glance at how Betty and Alun were coping. He did nothing to help, just left everything to Betty.

"A thank you for what you're doing for him would be nice," Alun said.

Betty shrugged. "Ed has always taken my help for granted."

"He treats you more like a devoted mother than a sister with a life of her own."

"I looked after him after our parents died. Too well, I suppose. I took on the role of mother instead of making him cope on his own. I thought perhaps he'd be different once he married but he's still rather selfish — except with Elsie. He's devoted to her. The way he is with me is my fault. The truth is, I was glad of him being here. I didn't want to be on my own. A different kind of selfishness maybe?"

Seranne was near the café, looking through the window and watching the shadowy figure of Babs dashing in and out of the kitchen, obviously without help. Swallowing her pride and apprehension she went in.

"Want any help?" she asked.

"You applying for the job?" Babs said stiffly. "You have to come for an interview like all the rest, mind."

"Tomorrow all right? Then I can spend today showing you how good I am."

"There's dishes want washing," Babs said gesturing towards the kitchen with a tilt of her head.

They worked together for the rest of the day and gradually relaxed into their old friendship. Whispering comments about some of the customers led to laughter and by the end of the day things were almost back to normal between them. As they cleared the last of the pots and pans Seranne asked, "Do I have the job?"

"If you say you're sorry I might consider it."

Seranne laughed. "That's what I said to your stupid brother!"

"You're right. He is stupid."

"I was too. I am sorry, Babs."

"I won't be staying you know. It's all too much for me. Accounts are a mystery for a start."

"I'll help with those. We can do everything together." The mention of accounts took her mind back to her mother and Paul. "It's my mother's birthday on Monday, and as we close at three, will you come with me to see her? I won't tell her we're coming, it'll be a nice surprise." Or a shock, she thought anxiously.

"I'll borrow the van," Babs said.

"Did you know your Tony has invited me to the pictures?"

"Wonderful, I always said he'll make a good husband."

"He will, but not for me, so if he does make a date, why don't you come with us?"

"Play gooseberry? No fear!"

"It will stop him getting the wrong idea," Seranne pleaded.

"I'll see. It depends what film you want to see."

On the way to see her mother, Seranne told Babs that she was worried about how rundown the place had become and when they parked outside, she glanced at the unwashed windows with increasing concern. Only two tables were occupied, each with two women who had obviously been shopping as their bags were beside them against the window.

Instead of going in through the side entrance they went straight into the tea rooms, Babs first. Paul and Pat Sewell were standing in a corner talking, heads close, Paul's arm around Pat's waist. Pretending not to see them, Seranne looked towards the kitchen.

"Mum? Paul? Anyone about?" The couple darted apart as though touched with an electric shock.

"Seranne, what a lovely surprise."

"Oh, hello Paul, I didn't see you there," she lied.

"Jessie's up in the flat, why don't you go straight up? I'll follow as soon as I've given Mrs Sewell her instructions."

"Remember my friend, Babs?" Seranne's heart was racing and her voice trembled high in her throat with the shock of what she had seen. She didn't speak to Pat Sewell, her voice wouldn't allow that. She was afraid she'd be sick if she even looked at the woman. Something was going on and it was more than the fading fortunes of the tea rooms. Don't jump to conclusions, a voice inside her warned and by the time they had reached the flat she had a bit more control.

"Hi Mum, happy birthday," she called. Her voice was still at the top of her throat and threatening to fail. But once she had handed her mother the parcel and flowers she had brought, her mother did the talking, then Babs joined in and she left them and busied herself making tea in the small kitchen of the flat.

She listened to the exclamations of delight as Jessie unpacked her parcels and the one brought by Babs. Paul came up with a few cakes and some dainty sandwiches on a tray. "I've just had to speak to Pat again about not washing the floor thoroughly," he said to Jessie. "I promise I was tactful though. I whispered so the customers didn't hear me telling her off."

Seranne cringed at the feeble explanation he had offered in case they had been seen.

"I'll have to do more," Jessie said. "It's been lovely having more time to enjoy, and I know you want to ease my load, but I miss it, darling. I really enjoyed baking and sandwich-making, serving friends and seeing customers enjoying what I do."

"You've worked hard for so long, it's time you took things easy and that's what I'm here for, to give you time to enjoy your life. Pat copes well enough — as long as I remind her of how you like things done, now and then."

"Any post for me, Mum?" Seranne asked and was handed a few letters from the box where her mother stored her mail. She glanced through. "Nothing of importance, but thanks for keeping it for me."

Paul seemed reluctant to go back down to the café and Seranne became aware that he was following her as she walked around the flat and showed Babs her room. Opening the door to the back bedroom, she said, "This is the office where Mum and I used to deal with the accounts and orders. Are you still using the same wholesaler, Mum?"

As she walked towards the huge desk that had been her father's, Paul quickly pulled her away and closed the door. "Don't bother your mother with such things on her birthday, Seranne."

164

"Paul, what happened to the teapots and plates from the shelves in the tea rooms? Some of them were mine, given to me by my grandmother."

"Mrs Sewell took them down. She doesn't have time for unnecessary ornaments."

"And the linen tablecloths?"

"Old. Almost threadbare, we threw them out. Look, Seranne, none of this is your business any more."

"My mother will always be my business. Marrying you hasn't changed that." She tried to ask her mother a few questions, but each time Paul answered for her, replying with the firm explanation that every change was to benefit Jessie.

Babs guessed what she was trying to do and she asked Paul to show her the tea rooms kitchen. "I run a small café myself you see and I'd be grateful for any tips you might have." Reluctantly he led her downstairs and into the kitchen.

"Brr, it's very cold in here, isn't it?" she remarked as they walked through the café which was now empty.

"We're having a bit of trouble with the electric fire," he explained. "Repairs are in hand, but the electrician is very busy."

Ignoring his attempts to stop her she went to look at where the pretend log fire was plugged into the wall and saw that the flex near the plug was old and frayed. Paul stood at the doorway into the kitchen and he pointedly looked at his watch. "I've arranged an evening to celebrate Seranne's mother's birthday, Babs. I'm sorry but we'll have to leave soon."

After a few innocent comments about the layout of the room and its well-scrubbed table, and pretending not to notice the dirty floor and neglected cooker, Babs said, "I'm impressed with how well you organize your time, Paul. You work every day as well as help run this place, don't you?"

"Not any more. I gave it up to give Seranne's mother a better life," he said. "This is a second chance for Jessie and I want her to enjoy every moment."

"She's a lucky lady," Babs smiled.

"And I'm a lucky man," he said earnestly.

In the flat while her mother cleared the dishes, Seranne darted into the office and quickly looked through some of the most recent letters. There were reminders for unpaid bills and the wholesaler was not the one they had used for years.

"Why aren't these bills paid, Mum?" she asked when her mother came to find her.

"Oh, it's nothing to worry about, dear. Paul says it isn't good business practice to pay a bill before the final demand, money in our account instead of theirs or something. I hated doing all that after your father died and I'm happy to leave it to him now, after all, he owned his factory so he knows about business. Seranne, I'm so lucky."

"So is he, Mum," Seranne said, unaware of the similarity of Jessie's and Paul's remarks.

On the drive home Seranne and Babs compared notes. "There's a cracked window in the kitchen and in the bathroom," Seranne reported. "The curtains in the café need a wash and the cheap, carelessly laundered tablecloths are a disgrace."

"The faulty heater in the café seriously needs attention," Babs warned. "And the kitchen wouldn't pass your inspection or mine. Crumbs and flour on the floor and piled up in the corner as though it hadn't been properly cleaned for days. A haven for mice and creepy-crawlies."

"What can I do?"

"Wait a while. I can't imagine your mother spending much longer sitting about being 'spoilt' by Paul, who's a bit of a creepy-crawly himself, don't you think?"

"Perhaps I should come home."

"A better idea would be to get your mother involved. She doesn't seem aware of the state of the place."

"He seems to have changed her completely. Love is said to be blind, but surely she can't look around and not see what happened to her once beautiful tea rooms?"

"I've never understood that saying, unless it means that a person needn't be beautiful to be loved."

"If Paul doesn't have a job, what are they living on? The café can't be taking enough to pay Pat Sewell and give them enough to live on. He must be using my mother's money. Money left to her by my father. Blind? She has to have gone crazy if she can't see what he's doing!"

Neither mentioned the closeness of Paul and Pat Sewell when they had made their unexpected entry. Seranne because she was desperately trying to persuade herself it was nothing important and Babs because she believed it was.

Seranne was thankful to return to Badgers Brook and allow its serenity to calm her mind and help her to put aside worries about which she could do nothing.

Tony and his father went to see an architect about building a new bake house. The money they had been putting aside, together with a small mortgage was enough for the large premises they envisaged and they were excited. As a family firm, the bakery was jointly owned by the four of them and with a majority of three out of four, they could at least start the process before trying once again to convince Babs that it was the right way forward.

Keeping her unaware of their plan was underhand and dishonest, but after many harsh battles in which Babs stoutly defended the principles laid down by her grandfather that small and reliable was better than risky adventures, she remained adamant that nothing should change. Tony and his parents eased their troubled consciences by assuring one another that, once there was something definite to show her, Babs would understand.

Her father and Tony were in the habit of going out in the evening for a drink before returning at eight, and she had been unaware of their lengthy discussions. Now, as she worked at the café and no longer drew a wage, they found it easy to talk and meet the accountant and the planning officers; the preparations were well in hand.

★ ★ ★

168

Betty and Alun kept Ed and Elsie's guest house running, as well as managing the Ship. It meant rising early and working late and using every spare moment between opening times and deliveries to go and attend to guests. Laundry, bed-making, shopping and cooking were all dealt with by staff but on days off and when someone was sick, they coped between them. It went on and on and there was no sign of Elsie being well enough to return home. That meant Ed being at the hospital during visiting hours and between times he seemed incapable of doing anything to help.

Alun didn't complain and Betty was grateful. "I know it sounds hard," she admitted, "but the business will be Ed's when Elsie passes away and I have to keep it running efficiently for him."

"I understand that," Alun said.

"But it's for my brother and you shouldn't be landed with all this extra work."

"You're doing it for Ed," he said with a smile. "I'm doing it for you."

"Thank you."

He shrugged away her thanks, then looked at her with concern. "You look worried and you haven't see Elsie for a couple of days, so why don't you go and see her this afternoon? Go straight after we close at two o'clock and I'll see to the clearing up."

Betty found Elsie in a bed with the sides pulled up and she looked so small and pale sleeping in what looked like a baby's cot, that Betty felt great pity. She had not approved of her brother marrying Elsie Clements, because she had not revealed how ill she was until it was too late for Ed to back out. He told Betty he hadn't wanted to cancel the wedding, but it was impossible for Betty to forget how Elsie had lied.

There were visitors at most of the beds, but the place was very quiet. The only sounds the subdued voices, the distant tapping of nurses feet as they went about their tasks and the rattling of paper as gifts of fruit and sweets were handed over. Heads nodded as she went in but there were no cheerful greetings from the few people she recognized, the ward was hushed by grief and despair.

Ed was dosing in an armchair nearby. He woke when Betty approached and whispered, "She seems better today, but she's sleeping a lot, so if you can stay a while, I'll go home and get changed and see if anything needs doing."

"Everything is all right but I'll certainly stay with her and give you a rest."

"I don't want a *rest* from my wife, as you put it!" he hissed irritably. "I just want to go home and change then I'll get back as fast as I can."

"Of course. I didn't mean that to sound like it did."

"You don't have to pretend. I know you've never been happy about my marriage. But I've been happy. Elsie has made every day a wonderful experience. You wouldn't understand about loving someone, would you?"

His harsh voice and the unkind words hurt, but she said, "I'm sorry. For goodness sake, Ed, I'm doing all I can and Alun too. Just go and see how well we've looked after things and stop picking a fight!" Elsie

170

stirred but settled again. "Go on, and for goodness sake take your time. There's no rush," she said, patting his arm to show her brief irritation was spent.

Alun had lent Ed his car and as he drove home, Ed was thinking about how he would manage if Elsie didn't come back home. It was easier when she was there even though she did practically nothing. She sat in her chair or in bed and managed the place, giving instructions and reminders, and praise. She was in charge and nothing was forgotten.

Spending so much time going to and from the hospital and not having her there when he got home was distorting everything and making the hours race by at times and at others seem to drag so he stared at the clock, willing it to hurry, waiting to leave for the hospital instead of catching up with some of the work. Betty would cope. She had never understood about Elsie, but she'd cope.

Elsie had been ill for all of their time together but he loved being with her. When her time came, he silently promised that the guest house would continue in exactly the same way as she had always run it. The business could afford an assistant and the cleaner could do extra hours. The rest he could manage. Betty was always there and she'd support him until he had learnt to cope without Elsie. Betty had time to spare and she loved being needed.

At the hospital Betty sat watching Elsie sleep. A nurse came and asked if everything was all right.

"How is she?" Betty asked. "Will she be coming home again soon?"

"You can never tell of course, but she is very ill."

After the nurse had checked the patient was comfortable and left them alone again, Betty moved and stretched. Elsie reached out through the rail of the bed and Betty held her hand. The grip tightened and then relaxed. It was several minutes before she realized that Elsie had died.

The nurses came and drew the curtains around the bed and after a few minutes they took her away. Betty walked up and down wishing Ed would come. She telephoned the guest house and the Ship but there was no reply. Then, when she tried the guest house again, desperate to see Ed and tell him the sad news, it was Alun who answered. "I'll go and find him," he promised. "Wait there and we'll come and join you."

Ed had taken Betty at her word and taken his time. Elsie would be pleased to see someone different when she woke. It would be a nice change for her to talk to Betty. He went through the house making sure everything was neat and orderly and checked that the kitchen was prepared for late-night drinks. Betty was so good at organizing. Perhaps she'll continue to come when Elsie came home? he wondered. She had Alun to help out and running the pub wasn't that hard. He was the one who'd need help. Elsie would need all his time, some spoiling, being reminded how much she was loved.

He went to have his hair cut and stayed for a chat with a few friends, before going back to the guest house to collect the few treats he had bought to take into the hospital. The phone rang as he was leaving, but a glance at the clock reminded him of how long he had been away and he ignored it. If it was important they would ring back. He didn't think it would be about Elsie. She was sleeping and would have Betty for company when she woke. And he would be back with her very soon.

He went to the shops and paid for his newspapers and put in the order at Mrs Harvey's grocery shop, then drove back to the hospital.

When he walked into the hospital he saw Betty and knew at once that the worst had happened.

"I'm so sorry, Ed," Betty said.

"Why wasn't I with her?" he wailed "Why did you tell me not to rush back?"

Betty sat him down and let him rage about the unfairness of it all. She had phoned Alun again and told him she would wait until the first stage of the procedures had been dealt with, then drive her brother home.

Ed was numb with grief and was unable to gather his thoughts. She drove him back to the guest house where the young cleaner had kindly waited to see how she could help.

"I have to go, Ed," Betty said. "We have to open the bar but I'll be back as soon as the first rush is over."

"Yes, you go. I'll have to manage, won't I? My Elsie's dead but you have to open the bar!"

She ignored the petulance in his voice and with relief, drove back to the Ship — and Alun. When she reached home, Alun said nothing. He just put his arms around her and held her. He rested his cheek on her

173

head and once or twice kissed her forehead. She was so grateful for his strength and comfort she didn't move for a very long time.

The following days went in a blurr of activity and phone calls as arrangements were made. Betty and Alun told the staff to refuse further bookings at the guest house for the following two weeks and Ed stayed there alone. He made it clear he didn't want people coming in offering condolences.

"They didn't bother with her while she was alive and you hardly bothered even when she was in hospital, so why should I have to listen to false sympathy now?"

He told everyone he wanted a quiet funeral and only a few ignored him and went anyway. Elsie had been unable to go out for several months and even before that her social activities had been seriously curtailed. Friends had lost touch, there was no family, and it was only a few neighbours and business people who followed the coffin that day. Even fewer went back to the guest house where Betty and Alun had provided a meal and at nine o'clock that night they left Ed alone as he had requested, and promised to call the following day.

"Is there a will, d'you know?" Alun asked, as they walked home.

"Hardly likely. With Ed as sole beneficiary, Elsie probably didn't bother."

"It makes things a bit easier, that's all."

"I hope having the business to run will make things easier for Ed. He'll have to get on with things. There'll be no time to sit and mope or dwell on his grief. That must be a good thing."

"We'll have to step back and not encourage him to depend on us too much. He's been running the place practically single-handedly for months and we mustn't make him feel unable to cope now Elsie's no longer there."

Betty shrugged. "I know I wasn't pleased when he married Elsie but now I'm selfish enough to be relieved that he has the business, and a life of his own."

Silently Alun agreed.

CHAPTER
SEVEN

A few days after the funeral of Elsie Connors, Ed received a letter from their solicitor, Mark Lacy. When he opened it, presuming it would be something confirming his ownership of the guest house, he stared at the few short sentences with casual interest. It simply asked him to go and see Mr Lacy, and Ed phoned to make an appointment. Although he didn't expect there to be any complications, he was still distressed by the death of Elsie and he asked Betty to go with him. "In case I miss something he tells me," he explained. "My head isn't clear at the moment."

Alun willingly agreed to deal with the morning preparations for opening and with Betty driving, she and Ed — still wearing mourning black — set off.

"This will be the final hurdle," Betty said. "After this you can make arrangements for the help you'll need and things will settle down. I'll be there to help with any problems, although I don't think you'll meet any. After all, you've run the business on your own for a long time now."

"I haven't. Not really. Elsie was ill but she was still in charge. I don't know anything about the accounts, she kept hold of all that."

"It can't be difficult. Poor Elsie didn't know she was going to leave you so soon or she'd have shown you everything," Betty said, although she was puzzled about Elsie's reticence to allow Ed to deal with the business side of things. He booked people in and managed the manual work, so why didn't he share the rest? "It can't be easy to face the fact of your imminent death," she said comfortingly. "I'm sure she'd have involved you if she'd known. Perhaps there's a note with the will."

"I don't think she left a will."

"Don't worry, the solicitor will sort it out. As her husband you'll inherit everything. It'll take a little more time, that's all."

The solicitor's office was above a shoe shop with an entrance at the side, but its importance showed in the well-painted door and the highly polished brass plate and door knocker. Ed rang the bell above the solicitor's name and walked up to where they found the door open and Mark Lacy waiting for them, hand out in greeting. He seemed nervous but when they were seated and he was behind his enormous desk he seemed more at ease.

"Firstly, let me tell you how sorry I am to hear about your loss," he began. Then the nervousness returned and he seemed unable to face them. He looked down at a document in front of him, smoothing it out, patting it, then said, "You are aware of course, that your wife left a will?"

"No, I didn't know," Ed replied, "but it must have been before we married and our marriage would cancel it, wouldn't it?"

177

"The will was made a few weeks after your wedding, Mr Connors and your wife assured me you were aware of its contents." Mark Lacy patted the document again. "I was told that you knew and understood."

"Understood what?" Ed stood up and tried to look at the piece of paper in front of the solicitor and Betty stood with him and held his arm. "Tell me for heaven's sake. She left a few gifts did she? That isn't a surprise, she was very kind. There was no need for her to tell me about them."

"The guest house will be easily transferred to my brother, won't it?" Betty asked. "No problems with that, is there?"

"The guest house is left to Mrs Connors' niece, er . . ." He was nervous and pretended to check on the paper. "A Mary Anne Crisp."

"But — but — I thought, as her husband — who is Mary Anne Crisp? I've never heard of her." He was shaking and Betty grasped his arm more tightly.

"Sit down, Ed, listen to the rest of what Mr Lacy has to say."

"The money left after everything has been dealt with is to be divided between you and Miss Mary Anne Crisp, apart from a few small bequests."

"You, Miss Connors, are to be given fifty pounds to thank you for the support and kindnesses you have shown. There are gifts too for the nurses and a member of staff". He looked up at Ed and added, "I have only done a preliminary assessment but I believe you will inherit in excess of two hundred pounds."

"But I thought there was more than that." Ed frowned. "Elsie didn't discuss the details but I understood she had several thousands, left to her by an aunt."

"That is shown in the purchase of the property and her more recent medical expenses, Mr Connor."

Ed turned and stared at Betty. He looked stunned. "But this can't be right. There has to be a mistake! The guest house must be mine. We were married, she wouldn't leave it to a stranger."

As though warning against an appeal, Mark Lacy went on quietly, "Besides the will, which makes her intentions perfectly plain, I have a note written by her doctor stating her to be mentally alert and quite clear about what she wanted, Mr Connors. There is also this." He picked up another envelope. "Your wife left a letter for you. Perhaps she explains it all in that." He offered the envelope to Ed, who brushed the man's hand aside angrily and it was Betty who took it and put in her handbag. "We have already set in motion the usual inquiries," Lacy said. "Appeals for Mary Anne Crisp to get in touch with us. When I have more information I will inform you immediately."

"You're wrong. There has to be a mistake. Elsie wouldn't treat me like this," Ed muttered.

Mark Lacy stood up and stepped towards him, hand outstretched. "When I have gone through everything thoroughly I will arrange another appointment and we can discuss it all fully. Until then, Mr Connors, I offer my sincere condolences and wish you well, and I hope this new stage of your life will be a good one. Good day to you both."

Dismissed, they went out with his good wishes echoing dully in their heads.

"I'm homeless, Betty," Ed said as they walked to the car. "Can you believe that? After looking after her, giving her every attention, loving her, this is how she treats me. I can't believe she'd be so cruel."

"Perhaps she wasn't thinking clearly, in spite of what the doctor wrote. She was very ill for most of your marriage."

"Her mind was as clear as yours." There was bitterness in his voice. "What am I going to do? I'll have to come back to the Ship and Compass, won't I?"

"We won't make any decisions until we know all the facts."

"Are you saying you'll let me down too? That you won't welcome me back home?" Betty declined to remind him that the Ship was hers alone. She had a painfully guilty feeling, because welcoming him home was not what she wanted. Not at all.

The bar was open when they went in but there were few customers. Alun was polishing glasses and talking to Colin Jones, who wore an old railways coat which he used for gardening, and she glanced at the floor to see that he'd left his usual trail of mud from the door to the bar and from there to the table near the fire. Today she didn't care. Ed's problem was her problem as well and she needed to talk to Alun in private. If Ed came back it would affect Alun too.

180

There was no opportunity as Ed went straight to tell him what had happened. She couldn't hear his words but from the whining tone she could guess what he was saying. Her heart was racing; she was afraid that Alun would suggest moving out, believing it was what she would want.

There were constant interruptions when she tried to talk to Alun, mostly when Ed came in for another session of stating his dismay and misery. When they did have an opportunity she hesitated, unsure how best to explain how she felt and that resulted in Alun believing she was hesitating out of embarrassment at having to tell him to leave.

As she served the desultory few, she was rehearsing what she would say to make him understand that she didn't want him to leave, not now, not ever. Putting all she felt into words was impossible, yet somehow she had to make him understand that when Ed had moved out, leaving her without help, she'd had to cope and, although she loved her brother, he now had to rebuild his own future and not expect to scuttle back to her, ruin her life, and expect everything to be made easy for him.

Another family in Cwm Derw was having problems. At the bakery, Babs had been summoned to a meeting, at which Tony and her parents told her they were building a new, larger, more modern bake house behind a larger shop they had bought, and they wanted her agreement.

"I *don't* agree," she said at once. "We've had this discussion time and again and I still believe we should stay with what we have. Extending and changing everything is a risk. We have a comfortable living here so why go for something new and unknown? It could be a disaster."

"All through the war and the years since, we've been restricted. Building was impossible and expanding the business was just a dream. Now it's 1953, Queen Elizabeth will be crowned on 2 June. A new Elizabethan age. Everyone is looking to the future and making plans. We want to move on."

"Why?" Babs asked again.

"I'm young and everyone wants to make his mark," Tony said.

"I don't."

Her mother looked away and her father coughed nervously. "Babs, love, if you don't want to be a part of this expansion, we understand and we're willing to give you your share of the money to do what you want."

"Buy me out?"

"I suppose so, but giving you the opportunity to leave what you no longer enjoy and start again is a kinder way of saying it. You chose to leave the business, to run that café so now you no longer take any interest in the bakery, it seems the best solution."

"But I am interested. In fact, I want to come, back and run the shop. I hate the café serving all those boring woman as they sit and gossip for ages over one small coffee and a bun. Seranne will make a far better manageress than I ever will."

"Too late," Tony said. "We'll soon be advertising the shop for sale and we'll move out as soon as the new premises are complete."

Brother and sister continued to argue, going over the same points time after time, neither willing to give in. They were different sides of a very high fence. Their parents sighed and left the room. This was a quarrel no one could win. By the time they parted, faces ugly with acrimonious fury, it was seven o'clock on a dark, cold March evening.

Babs refused to sit and eat the meal her mother had prepared, and ran from the house. There was a bus coming and she ran for it as though it was her last chance and got off at the top of the lane near Badgers Brook.

When she knocked on the door of Badgers Brook, pushed it open and called, Seranne greeted her with pleasure. "What a lovely surprise, Babs. Come in, Kitty's here, she brought me a helping of soup for my supper. Plenty for two if you're staying."

"Thanks, I'd love to." She went into the warm living-room where Kitty sat in an armchair near the blazing fire. "Hello Mrs Jennings, not interrupting, am I?"

"I'm just off to give my Bob his supper. But not because you've come, mind," Kitty said with a laugh.

Seranne set the table in the kitchen and served the bowls of lentil soup, flavoured with onions and a few bacon bones begged from the grocer. Babs said nothing until they had eaten and were sitting beside the fire nursing their cups of tea. "Seranne, I don't know what to do."

"Tell me about it," her friend coaxed.

Babs explained about her family's plan to sell the baker's shop and move into a new premises. "I disagree and tonight they told me they're going on with it without my consent. They offered to buy me out, give me my share of the money and let me start again with something I want to do."

"And?"

"I wanted to go back to the shop and sell bread and cakes, but it's too late. They're selling and I'm losing my home."

"Don't be so melodramatic. You can still live at home, unless you feel it's time to move on? And they will certainly find you a job. But it's a good time to stop and think how you want to spend the rest of your life. I left when I realized I was getting in the way of my mother's new marriage. It's a frightening feeling, like hanging over a river on a branch that might break off at any moment. But it doesn't. Young people do it all the time, leave the safety of home and move on."

"I don't want to stay in the café. Even with your help — which makes me realize what a cheat I am, applying for a job I couldn't do."

Seranne looked at her thoughtfully. "What if we could buy it, run it our own way, would that make you enjoy it?"

"Buy it? Buy the café?"

"I have some savings and with what your parents plan to give you we could afford it, although it would

184

be run on a shoestring at first. If you could make the bread, in fact do all the baking, we could advertise homemade cakes and bread and the smell alone would bring 'em in!" Warming to the idea she had been incubating for a while, she went on. "There's a lot we could do to increase trade, appearance for a start. It's never been made to look very appealing, has it?"

Their tea went cold as they sat there in the calm quiet of the old house and allowed their thoughts to tumble over the possibilities. The clock marked the hours unnoticed when they took out paper and pens and started working out what their idea would mean. By adding together their funds, the cost of buying the business plus the expenses of smartening it up seemed a possibility and their eyes glowed with the excitement.

"I'd need a larger room than the kitchen we have at present," Babs said. "Could we afford to extend? Even double it?"

"It's a question of permits for new building, but I can't see that it's impossible, can you? Things are far less tight than a couple of years ago."

"My family will know all about building permits!" Babs said, wryly. "They've been investigating for months."

"We wouldn't be able to do anything straightaway, we'd have to see how the finances work out, but . . ."

Babs laughed then. "There's me coming here for a moan because my family are making changes and just hours later I'm planning an expansion of my own!"

"There's a lot to find out, the first being whether Mr Griffiths will sell. I did hear rumours about him wanting to retire, which is why I had already been thinking about this idea."

"How can we run a business? I haven't the first idea."

"I believe that if you really want something, then all you need is determination and a small pinch of luck."

"My parents said this is a perfect time for making plans. It's coronation year, we're now in the new Elizabethan age."

"Maybe they're right and it's a time to be bold. There's excitement in the air although the coronation is a couple of months away. Already the streets are planning the decorations and the street parties. We could pretend they are for us too, Babs."

"I'm so glad I came here tonight, or I'd have flopped on the bed bemoaning my misfortunes, and waking up in the morning convinced I've been cruelly treated."

"It's this house," Seranne told her. "Badgers Brook takes away all negative thoughts and gives you a chance to think things out clearly."

They sat silently for a while, enjoying the peaceful atmosphere of the house. Its walls issued warmth and comfort and they both knew that it was this which had helped them make their important decision and was assuring them that everything would be all right.

Betty and Alun tried several times to talk about Ed's shock and disappointment at his wife's surprising decision. It wasn't an easy subject as each thought they could guess what the other was thinking. Alun believed that with her brother Ed back at the Ship, Betty would

186

no longer need him. She was certain to want him to leave, even if she found it hard to tell him so. He had to make it easier for her by telling her he was going away.

Betty was convinced that Alun had stayed as long as he had just for her benefit and would be relieved to be able to leave and find a place where he could return to what he did best, running a restaurant. They skirted around the subject in a casual way, neither able to explain how they really felt.

Ed was still bitter about Elsie's treatment of him and made it quite clear he wanted — and expected — to come back, but Betty insisted he had to stay at the guest house until Mary Anne Crisp was found and the place was claimed. He reacted like a child when she tried to remind him that the Ship was hers alone and no longer his home.

"You left me without a thought when you and Elsie decided to marry and I understood. After all, you had your own life to lead and only stayed because there was nowhere else you wanted to be. Until Elsie."

"But it's my home, Betty. I haven't known anywhere else."

"Until Elsie," she reminded him again. "You chose to take your share of the place and I became sole owner many years ago."

"You'll come and help with the breakfast?" he asked.

"Not permanently. Just until you find someone else to help."

It was very late when he went out muttering that the Ship was still his home, refusing to accept that he no longer owned a share of it.

Alun listened and was sad. He stepped outside leaving Betty to her thoughts. A heavy mist had fallen, blanketing the houses and reducing the street lights to hazy lollipops. It was late and his footsteps sounded extra loud as he walked along the street, past the post office and the houses where only a few lights showed. With no destination in mind he walked along the path leading to the allotments, the planting in precise rows hardly visible. A rabbit hopped across his view and he wondered if the gardeners would lose a few treats, but he didn't attempt to chase it away. An owl hooted and its melancholy sound persuaded him to return to where there were at least signs of people.

Walking past the guest house, still avoiding going back to the Ship, he was startled to hear someone call his name. "Ed?" he answered. "What are you doing out so late?"

"Same as you I expect, trying to decide what to do."

"You have to stay on, at least until the new owner is found, don't you?"

"Do I? When Betty wants me to go back home?"

"Is that what she wants?"

"Of course it is. We worked together for years until I gave it up to marry Elsie. If only I'd known."

"What would you have done differently?"

"I loved her you know."

"Then you would still have married her and looked after her, so what have you really lost?"

"I don't expect you to understand." Ed turned and went in, banging the door loudly.

Alun stared after him for a long time, the mist beginning to move in swirling patterns as the wind began to rise. He was chilled, having worn insufficient clothing for the late hour but the chill inside was the worst.

He knew he had to leave. Betty was showing anger towards Ed but her anger was misplaced, she was angry with herself for not agreeing to have him back at the Ship. She wants to help her brother but is hesitating because of me, he told himself. I have to help her by walking away. Even if it breaks my heart.

Ed reopened the door of the guest house and stood in the misty darkness looking out at the garden he had tended, making the guest house an attractive first impression for visitors. The lawn was neatly cut and the flower beds dug and raked ready for the annuals he had growing in the greenhouse at the back.

What hadn't he done? How had he failed her that she could cut him out like this? Her treachery was worse by not warning him. Perhaps if they had talked about it she would have reconsidered. She might at least have tried to make him understand, given him the chance to make plans. Then he shrugged. What could she have said that would make sense of what she had done?

Shivering, he went inside and up to his room, dejected and conscious of being completely alone. What price love? Cheated by his wife whom he had loved, and not wanted by his sister, who said she loved him!

189

Another man staring unseeing into the mist was Luke. He sat in his car, lights turned off and stared up at the puny lights showing in the flat above the the tea rooms. What was going on? This successful business had been destroyed and Paul Curtis had rented a shop in Barry which was promised to be opened in two months time to sell fine china. So far as he could ascertain, the man wasn't earning any money. He thought of the china that had belonged to Jessie's tea rooms that he had sold. What else had he taken from Seranne's mother to get his business idea started? And if money was his priority why had he ruined the business that had kept Seranne and Jessie in comfortable ease?

From his enquiries he had discovered that Paul had been borrowing wildly for months. When he had left the forces at the end of the war he had taken on a partner in the business left to him by his father. He had presumed the business ran itself as he had never done anything while his father had been alive and it soon suffered from his inability to do the necessary work. Money had been spent giving the impression of a wealthy man with no real need to worry about finance. Orders had fallen as he had neglected to take on the necessary work of running the place and all his best employees had gone.

Luke was almost certain Paul had used Jessie's money to narrowly avoid bankruptcy, which would have meant he'd be unable to start again. What was curious was the way he had persuaded Jessie to neglect her own business and instead spend time and money having fun.

An outside light came on and he watched as Paul came out and hurried around to where his car was parked. Cautiously, Luke followed. It was late and there were few cars on the road, which made it difficult not to be seen following. Illegally shutting off his lights for brief moments and slowing right down, then speeding up again, was all he could do. He hoped Paul was too intent on getting to wherever he was going. He stopped when he guessed where the man was heading. Then he waited until the rear lights were out of sight and slowly headed for the house where Pat Sewell lived. Paul didn't stay long and, reminding himself of his own rule about not jumping to conclusions, Luke drove away.

When Betty finished clearing the dishes from Ed's breakfast she picked up the letter she had taken from Mark Lacy and tried to persuade him to open it. As on several occasions before, he'd refused and in desperation, Betty tore it open and read it aloud. Then she read it again, more slowly.

Without an apology for not leaving the property for him, Elsie explained that having been left a large sum of money by an aunt she hardly knew which had changed her life, she had determined to do the same for someone else when her time came. She had been working as a cleaner in an hotel on the seafront in Tenby when she had been informed of the gift. Besides being unexpected, the money came with no stipulation about how it should be spent apart from the hope that the money was used to invest in a business and in turn would be passed on in the same unannounced way. The unexpected legacy had enabled her to buy the guest house and had made her financially secure for the rest of her life. Such a wonderfully generous gift was something for which she had never ceased being grateful and she determined to do the same for someone else. She explained, again without apology, that their marriage, when she knew she was seriously ill, hadn't altered her resolution.

"Right. I'm closing the guest house," Ed said firmly. "Why should I sit here like a lemon looking after it for someone I don't even know? I'll cancel the rest of the bookings, there aren't many for April anyway. And I'll move back next week."

Filled with guilt at what she had to say, she shouted the words, startling Ed with their ferocity. "No, Ed! Why should you expect to walk back into the Ship? Alun and I manage very well, he works harder than you ever did, and I don't want things to change."

"It's my home," he insisted.

"No! It isn't! I own it and I run it and you've never been more than a passenger!" Her voice rising even louder in anger, she stood and glared at him. "If you do come back — and I'll have to think about that — you'll rent a room and find a job to pay for it. I'm your sister, for heaven's sake. Not a stupidly tolerant mother!"

Betty told Alun what had happened and asked whether he had any objections to Ed coming back as a paying guest. "He'll have to find a job," she said. "I don't want him thinking he can come back and do a little work in the bar and be kept by me. Those days are gone and they went on too long anyway."

"He's your brother. You must want to help."

"Help, yes. But keep him? Like an overgrown child? No"

"What will he do?"

"Mark Lacy has asked if he'd stay at the guest house and keep it running for when the new owner is found. I've explained the simple accounts system. He'd have a home and a wage. But he's refusing to stay longer than a couple of weeks. He wants to come back here to wallow in self-pity."

Betty went to the guest house each morning to help with the breakfasts but she was aware that Ed was leaving more and more of the work to her. While Elsie was alive he had coped with the routine of bed and breakfasts efficiently, but once Betty was back in his life, he had relaxed, and allowed her to do more than she had originally offered. She returned to the Ship a few mornings later, leaving her brother sitting and staring at the pages of Elsie's letter as though they might read differently if he willed it so. She forgot his concerns as she walked back into her home, where Alun was whistling cheerfully as he set out the tables and chairs in the bar, where a fire burned brightly. It was time to make her own plans clear.

"Alun, come and have a coffee, I think there's something we need to discuss."

"Two minutes, Betty," he called.

To her disbelief, when he came in for their usual morning break, he was wearing outdoor clothes and carried a small shoulder bag.

"It's all right, you don't have to tell me or make it harder on yourself. I'll leave so Ed can come back."

"Alun! I don't want Ed back. I really don't. I hoped you'd stay and . . ."

"He's your brother and he needs a home and a job. You aren't capable of turning him away. Please don't be sad. It's time I moved on anyway."

Betty was speechless. She knew if she tried to talk she would burst into tears.

"I want you to know that I've never been happier than I've been working here with you." He leant over and kissed her cheek, she moved, tried to think of words to delay him, allow her to say her piece and their lips met. He hastily moved away and they stared at each other for a long moment before he turned and left the building.

"Where will you go," she called. "Where can I contact you?"

This time it was Alun who was unable to speak. Betty had been upset but he guessed that the tears were from guilt having to ask him to leave. With her brother back she must have been relieved at not having to ask him to go. He had helped her, made it easy but walking away was the worst thing he'd ever had to do. Worse than closing his restaurant and giving the keys to a stranger. He felt a furious dislike of Ed. The man was selfish and weak and depended on his sister's generosity instead of being strong and making his own way. At that moment if they'd met it would have been hard not to punch him.

Betty sat at the table and grieved for something she might have had. Alun must have wanted to leave. The affection they shared, which she thought was growing into love, must have been nothing more than kindness and friendship. He must have been waiting for an opportunity to walk away, and Ed's stupid insistence that the Ship and Compass was still his home had given it to him. If Ed had walked in at that moment, like Alun, she'd have wanted to hit him.

Ed's misery was increasing. He sat at the table in the kitchen of the guest house and glared at the pages of the accounts book. Picking up Elsie's pen, a gift he had bought for her, he scored the pages furiously, ruining the gold nib and tearing several pages. He threw pen and book across the room. Then he went to see Mark Lacy.

"I'm not willing to stay running that place any longer," he shouted.

"Will you stay for another week? It would be a great help, give me time to find a caretaker and maybe by then we'll have heard from the owner."

"All right, I'll see the guests in and be here to get their breakfast but I won't stay. I'm needed to help my sister in the bar," he said.

"That isn't possible, you have to be there at night."

Grudgingly Ed promised to stay, but explained that he would be in the Ship for the lunchtime and evening sessions. "It'll be hard mind," he said, "but I'll do it.

For Elsie," he added, hoping for sympathy and praise for his understanding.

Mark politely suggested that unless he had another job and somewhere to live, he might want to see if the new owner would offer both.

"My sister and I own the Ship and Compass," he lied. "So I have both. Right?" He glared at the solicitor and added, "I was never dependant on my wife for either."

Murmuring apologies, Mark showed him out.

Ed moved his things back into the room he had lived in before his marriage and settled to a bit of comfort and spoiling. He slept at the guest house but spent the rest of the time at the Ship. He made no effort to find work and gradually began to go into the bar and serve.

A week later, towards the end of April, Betty picked up Ed's washing, having cleaned and tidied his room, which he used for much of the day. Newspapers had been left unfolded, books spread around among plates containing half-eaten food and glasses and cups abandoned for her to clear away. The demand for sympathy about his wife's death had gone on too long. He couldn't continue like this, laze the days away and expect her to ignore his behaviour.

She missed Alun and grieved for his departure and as well as that, Ed was taking her for a fool. Anger towards her brother was growing. She'd had one chance of happiness in her hard working life and he had ruined it.

Depositing the clothes near the washing boiler, she went to stand at the door into the bar room. Ed was leaning on the bar chatting to a friend while several people were waiting to be served.

"Ed," she called sharply. "There are customers waiting."

Ed whispered something to the group of men around him and they glanced at Betty and laughed. Betty went forward and held her hand out for the money which they seemed reluctant to give. She suspected that as well as spending time talking to his group of so-called friends, Ed was supplying them with free drinks. Laughing at her at the same time was more than she could bear.

"Go down a fetch some bottles to fill the shelves, will you?" she said. "And while you're there check on the barrel, it needs to be up on the cradle today, ready for opening."

"I did all that earlier," he said, with a sigh for the benefit of his friends. "She's got no understanding of how bereft I feel," he told them. "It's only weeks since I lost my Elsie and my home."

Betty heard the words — as he had intended. "Go and get the bottles, Ed. We'll need them before the end of the evening." Her voice was harsh as she pushed him away from the bar and on his way. Then she turned to the men whom she suspected of being supplied with free drinks. "Now I'm asking you to leave. Immediately, please, and without any fuss and I don't want to see you here again." As one man prepared to argue, she gestured with her thumb into the back room where the telephone stood. "Go now or I'll call the police. Scrounging from my brother might not seem like a crime, but this is my pub and you're stealing from me. I won't have that and I'm warning you, nor will I put up with you causing a fuss when I tell you to leave." She looked across the room and called, "Bob, Colin, would you mind escorting these, er, gentlemen to the door?"

When Ed came back with some bottles he looked around for his friends and Betty said, "They've gone and they won't be coming back. I'll give you till the end of the month to collect your things and sort everything out, then you can go, too."

He laughed nervously but a look at Betty's face convinced him she was serious. "I don't want to stay here anyway and have you treat me like a servant, and my friends like criminals!" he muttered. "I'll stay at the guest house, I promised to do so anyway, until this Mary Anne Crisp turns up. I only came back to help you!"

"In that case you won't need a month, will you?" She stared at him coldly. "Shall we say now this minute? You can talk to Mark Lacy tomorrow and I'm sure he'll agree." She didn't sleep that night. Why hadn't she spoken to Alun sooner? Why had she allowed her brother to manipulate her and settle himself back under her roof? She wondered whether Ed had spoken to Alun and planted the idea that she had been glad of the excuse to ask him to leave.

Alun would certainly have cramped Ed's style, and he would have spotted him treating his so-called friends much sooner that I did, she thought sadly. Where had he gone? She wracked her brain trying to think of places he mentioned where she might find him. The only place she knew was Jake Llewellyn's boatyard in Barry, where Alun had worked for a while. Perhaps Jake knew where she'd find him. Then melancholy sank deeply into her heart as she thought he might not want to be found.

After long discussions starting with practicalities and ending with daydreams, Seranne and Babs wrote to Mr Griffiths asking if he would consider selling the café. A reply came at once stating that he had no intention of parting with it and if they were unhappy they could look elsewhere for employment.

"We could wait until your parents move out of the baker's shop, and into the new one," Seranne suggested. "If we could buy or rent it we'd be rivals and you'd certainly have your big kitchen too. Mr Griffiths won't like that but he wouldn't be able to stop us, would he?"

"Perhaps we could let him know that?" Babs suggested with a surge of hope. Later that day Babs called to see Mrs Rogers, who knew the Griffithses, even though she no longer worked for them. "Did you know Seranne and I offered to buy the café?" she said. "Mr Griffiths refused but it doesn't matter. We're thinking of taking over the baker's shop when my family move to the new premises. Exciting, isn't it? Rivals we'll be, but ours will be smarter, a tea rooms rather than a 'caff', more upmarket, so he'd better look out!"

Alarmed at the prospect of a rival café opening across the road, Mr Griffiths re-considered. At the end of April a solicitor's letter arrived offering them the business. The price was too high but they got Mark Lacy involved and eventually their offer was accepted. The negotiations were swiftly dealt with and they would soon be the proud owners of the premises and furniture and fittings of a café, to be called The Wayfaring Tree.

That weekend, Seranne went with Babs to see her parents, longing to tell them the news but not wanting to tell them on the phone. As before, Seranne didn't tell them she was coming, she wanted to see how things were, not have the problems disguised. Sundays had always been quiet days, with her mother and herself eating a simple lunch after spending the morning making sure the orders were written and the accounts up to date. Everything in the café below had always been left scrubbed clean and ready to open up on Monday morning, only requiring a light dusting before setting the tables and starting on the cooking.

She held her breath as she tried the door but it was locked and there was no reply to her knocking. She took out the key and let them inside. Surely Paul wouldn't object to her bringing a friend into what was still her home? It was 11.30 and she carried the details of hers and Babs's new venture for her mother to see and they talked as they walked up. Yet the place was silent, no door opened to greet them and when they reached the living room, abandoned plates of food lay around on the coffee table and other surfaces.

"Mum?" she called and at last, a sleepy Jessie appeared, wearing a dressing-gown, her hair lank and her eyes bleary.

"Seranne! What a lovely surprise. And Barbara, how lovely. But why didn't you tell us? We were out last night until heaven alone knows how late, and we overslept." She kissed Seranne and hugged Babs. "I'll see if I can rouse darling Paul."

Seranne and Babs didn't exchange a word but they both began clearing the litter of dishes, cups and glasses which they took into the kitchen.

Paul appeared and stopped them as they prepared to wash them. "Seranne, my dear, come and sit down, you don't have to do this. We don't fuss about such things, life is for living, not for worrying about what other people think, that's how we feel, isn't it Jessie? Relax and enjoy, that's our motto."

"And what about the tea rooms?" Seranne couldn't resist asking.

"Oh, we leave that to Mrs Sewell. She's a marvel."

Both went to get dressed and it was some time before they were able to discuss their new business venture and at once Paul took an interest. "If you want me to look over the books, see how healthy the business is, I'd be happy to help," he said, walking into the kitchen where Jessie was making tea and toast.

"Seeing the mess he's created since looking after our once thriving business," Seranne hissed to Babs, "I'd be more likely to trust a five-year-old."

Their breakfast dishes were piled with the rest and Paul followed Seranne as she walked around the flat and was clearly reluctant to allow her to go into the café, but she insisted, politely but firmly and, gesturing for Babs to follow, she went downstairs. The windows were even dirtier than before, the floor hadn't been swept let alone washed, the faulty heater cord had not been replaced and the windows that were broken hadn't been dealt with.

She mentioned these things to her mother, who took out a notebook. "I'll remind Pat tomorrow," she said, closing the book with a snap as though the petty problems were already dealt with. When she and Seranne were alone for a moment, she said, "Don't be angry, darling. I know I neglect the business but I'm so happy with Paul. Going out and having fun is something I gave up on for so many years and now, while I'm still young enough to dance and meet friends for meals and go to the theatre and cinema, well, I admit I find it irresistible. Paul is wonderful company and apart from a couple of evenings when he goes to the pub and has a few drinks with his friends and business colleagues we're together every moment."

"But the tea rooms, Mum. They used to be so beautiful, you did everything so well, but now . . ."

"Oh, Pat manages the tea rooms," Jessie said casually dismissing them as a triviality. "Not as well and you and I did of course, but what are a few overcooked scones and flat sponges in a lifetime? We gave them too much importance."

"Funny you should say that, Mum, because Babs and I are buying that café and my intention is to make it as near Jessica's Victorian Tea Rooms as I possibly can."

"Good luck, but don't make yourself a slave to it."

"Is that what you think it was? Slavery?"

"Compared to life with Paul? Oh yes!"

As Seranne and Babs drove back to Cwm Derw, Seranne mused about her mother's remarks. Since she had known Paul, Jessie's personality had changed beyond recognition. The work of running the tea rooms efficiently, making sure everything was perfect, that had been her life. Now she seemed to go from one entertainment to the next without giving the place a thought. Yet who was she to say her mother was wrong? Was it so terrible to include some fun in her life? Jessie had always worked hard: like Seranne, she had worked with her parents from the age of twelve. Surely she was entitled to enjoy the freedom? Neglecting what had once been an elegant and popular place for friends to meet was hardly a crime.

She tried to convince herself everything was fine, but there was an underlying fear that her mother's happiness would be short-lived, that Paul would become tired of her, enjoy this interlude and, when her money ran out, would leave her. She pushed the worrying thought aside and instead, remarked to Babs about how energetic her mother must be at the great age of almost forty-one, to practically dance till dawn with women twenty years younger!

"Being determined to keep up with Paul — who's at least six years younger — must be a good incentive,"

Babs said with a laugh. The flippant remark intensified Seranne's concern.

When they reached Badgers Brook, Luke was sitting in his car outside the gate. Kitty was leaning through the passenger window and she ducked out and waved when she saw them. "I've been trying to persuade Luke to come and have a cup of tea with us," she said.

"I have a delivery to make and I didn't want to leave it in the car unattended," he explained. He stepped out and from the boot handed her a cardboard box. Another was given to Babs and a third, the largest, he carried himself. Kitty hesitated about following and he said. "Go ahead of us and open the door, will you, Kitty? I don't want any of these dropped."

Seranne slowly opened the lid of the first box and moved the layers of tissue and newspapers that protected the contents. Impatiently Babs said, "Hurry up! What is it?"

The papers parted and revealed the china teapots that had once graced the shelves of Jessie's tea rooms. The rest were carefully examined and, seeing the china that had once decorated her mother's shelves made Seranne frown. "I don't understand?"

"Simple. Your mother and Paul sold them and I bought them back, in case you would like them for your new enterprise."

"But, how did you know about our 'new enterprise'? Oh, don't tell me, Mrs Rogers is an aunt. And I suppose the man who bought them from my mother is an uncle?"

204

"Uncle Ray, yes. You must meet him." He didn't explain that it was Paul who had sold them or that it was highly likely her mother had known nothing about it.

Like children at Christmas, Seranne and Babs carefully unpacked the lovely items and discussed where best to place them. "Thank you," Seranne's eyes were starry with delight. "We'll need some good shelves. You don't have an uncle who's a carpenter, do you?" she asked with a wide smile.

"Of course. Uncle Frank and my cousin George will fit some shelves for you."

"Thank you, Luke. I can't tell you how happy I am to have them. I presumed Mum had them stored somewhere and if you hadn't found them I'd never have known they were sold. Tell me how much they cost you and I'll get the money from the bank tomorrow."

"No rush. I'll have to pay my Uncle Ray first and he's notoriously slow sending out invoices."

The solicitor continued to advertise in the usual ways for the whereabouts of Elsie's niece, Mary Anne Crisp, but without success. He searched through the marriages in the area of her last known address but found nothing. There were no replies from newspaper advertisements, and sending someone to knock on doors failed to produce any leads.

He sent letters to the few people who might be connected with her but waited in vain for replies. He called several times on Ed, who grudgingly continued to run the business. Each time he called he checked that the accounts — in the new book — were up to date, and thanked him for his generosity in helping.

Having accepted the startling news that his sister didn't want him at the Ship, Ed knuckled down and did all that was necessary to keep Elsie's business running. He hoped that once Mary Anne Crisp was found, she'd agree to him staying on. As Mark Lacy had pointed out, at least that way he'd have a job and a home.

He no longer slept in the room he had shared with Elsie and even the living-room where they had spent much of their time no longer felt comfortable. The shock of her will made him feel an intruder there. A bedroom at the back overlooking the gardens of Franklin Terrace was large and he settled there with his wireless and the television which Elsie had bought not long before she had died. The television was such a novelty when so few local people had invested in one, he was never short of people to share his evenings.

It was only slowly that he realized he no longer had any real friends. Elsie had been the one who attracted people to call and Elsie had been all the friendship he had needed. Content with her he had allowed friendships to fade and those he knew from the Ship were gone once he no longer offered the occasional free drink.

He sat in his room until after 2a.m. one night, and began to realize how ashamed of him Elsie would be at the way he had treated Betty. They had worked together contentedly until he met and married Elsie and from that moment he'd been utterly selfish. Flattered by winning the hand and heart of Elsie Clements had in some way turned his head.

Expecting to go back to the Ship and laze his days away while Betty looked after him was unbelievable. Guilt began to weave its uncomfortable web around him. What had got into him that he could have treated her so badly? Telling Alun Harris that Betty wanted him to leave had been the worst. He must have been crazy. He wanted to go at once and apologize, but instead, perhaps he could somehow put things right.

Finding Alun wouldn't be easy. But he knew he had to try, for Betty's sake and for his own. Jake Llewellyn at the boat yard would be sure to know where to find him. But a phone call disabused him of that simple solution. He had no idea how to begin a search so enthusiasm faded and the noble thought was forgotten.

CHAPTER
EIGHT

Betty went through the routine of each day hardly aware of what she was doing. She was so tired that her body ached and her heart ached even more. Alun had left everything as perfect as possible, the orders had been placed, the cellar clean and organized ready to receive them. He had whitewashed the walls, the floors were spotless and she wondered vaguely when he had done these things. While she was at the guest house helping Ed probably — or more truthfully — doing Ed's work for him!

She had told Ed she no longer needed him and now Alun had gone and she was once more without help. She went out and put a vacancy notice in the window of the post office and wondered whether Bob Jennings and Kitty would help for a while. Neither were really experienced, but Bob had helped out once or twice and a lot of the work entailed tidiness and muscle rather than know-how.

"Why don't you ask your brother to help for part of the day?" Stella asked when the post office was clear of customers. "You can manage the bar as long as someone brings up the bottles and sees to the deliveries, can't you?"

"I can't. Telling him to go was one of my more sensible decisions. I need someone reliable." She looked at her friend afraid what she was about to say would sound harsh. "Because the Ship and Compass was our family home, Ed has always considered it his right to live there, and up to a point that's true. But I'm the owner. Ed was paid more than fifty per cent of the valuation, and I've worked hard to make the place a success. Ed had his money and spent it. I don't owe him free board whenever he needs it. Being my brother doesn't entitle him to take what he needs from me."

"Go and put the kettle on, Betty," Stella said, avoiding an answer. "We'll have a cup of tea while it's quiet."

Alun drifted for a while after leaving the Ship and Compass. He stopped when a town appealed and, after a couple of days, moved on. When he was near the seaside town of Barry, he went to the boatyard to see Jake but not to ask for his job back. He had only been a casual labourer, keeping the place relatively tidy, doing small repairs, answering the phone and sometimes dealing with irate customers. It had been all he'd needed at the time. A quiet place to lick his wounds when he'd lost his business.

Then he had found the Ship and Compass, and Betty Connors, and the friendly town of Cwm Derw and knew he'd hit upon a place where he could begin again. Betty's brother had spoilt that and now he was moving on with no destination in mind, to search for another place, a new group of people who might one day be his friends. Like the legend of Dick Whittington, there were voices in his head telling him to turn back. "Turn again Whittington, thou worthy citizen . . ." The words of the childish chant issued from his mouth in rhythm with his footsteps but he kept on walking away from it all.

Jake was pleased to see him but guessed he wasn't looking for a job and somewhere to sleep as before. "Good to see you," he called as Alun's tall figure entered the yard. "Oi!" he shouted to a young boy sanding an old clinker-built boat. "Put the kettle on and find some biscuits, will you?" He put down the curved needle and thread with which he was repairing a sail and stepped forward to meet Alun, smiling in pleasure.

"Betty given you the day off has she?"

"Not exactly. Her brother hasn't anywhere to live and she's taken him back. Pity mind, I was beginning to settle down in Cwm Derw."

"Ed? Why hasn't he anywhere to live? I thought he owned a guest house?"

"He thought so too, but his wife left the business to a niece no one has even heard of."

"That must have been a shock. Stella at the post office rang a couple of days ago and asked where you were, but I couldn't help her. What happened?"

Alun told Jake the course of events as they sat in the late April sun and drank their tea. When Jake invited him to stay for a few days, Alun shook his head. "I think I'll make for Swansea, find a job in one of the restaurants there. A couple of months then the summer season will start. Plenty of work then."

"Stay till then. I'll find you enough work to earn your keep. Go down and make enquiries then come back and stay a week or two." He showed Alun a boat he was building for a client. "It's a sailing dinghy and if it's successful I'll have an order for six more for a sailing school teaching eight to ten-year-olds the basics. Good eh?"

Alun was tempted, but he knew it would be an escape, he'd be hiding away from the real world and if he stayed too long he would never leave. Regretfully he declined. "But I'll come and see you from time to time, I don't want us to lose touch," he said.

It wasn't until long after he'd walked away, that Jake realized that, as before, he had no forwarding address. If Alun didn't come to see him, he had no way of contacting him.

Betty sighed as the middle-aged man entered the Ship a few days later. She sat in the bar waiting for him, her fingers crossed, praying that this one would offer her a reasonable hope of success. So far she had interviewed three men and a woman, Tilly Tucker, whom she had been tempted to employ, but all had eventually been rejected. The thought of the heavy work involved had persuaded her it would not be a good idea to take on a woman, even though she herself had managed much of the heavy work in the past. A pity, she thought, she and Tilly Tucker might have got on well.

This new applicant was the last of the people who had applied for the job, her final hope of getting someone to start the following week. She glanced at the clock standing in the corner, its slow bur-lip, bur-lip marching away with her life while she struggled to get it in some kind of order. He was going to be late. Not a good start. The pub opened exactly on time — or there'd be impatient banging on the door and shouts of complaint, she thought with a half smile.

She glanced at the piece of paper with the man's details written on it then looked up as the door swung open and he approached. As a prospect he certainly looked suitable. He wore a smart suit, his thinning hair was brushed neatly back and he walked in with an air of confidence, smiling, offering his hand.

"Les Gronow," he said. Betty gestured to the chair opposite her and began to prepare her questions, but before she could speak, he began his well-rehearsed introduction. "I haven't worked behind a bar for a long time, but I grew up in a pub and you never forget, do you? Keeping stock isn't a problem, I'm experienced at rotating to keep everything fresh. I'm able to read a balance sheet and I'm a whiz with figures, having worked as an accountant. I can't stand untidiness and not afraid of hard work and long hours, as long as the money's right. What wage are you offering, Betty?"

He'd hardly taken a breath and Betty was irritated and at the same time aware that she couldn't keep turning people away because they weren't Alun Harris. "Firstly, it's Miss Connors and secondly, would you allow me to ask a few questions of my own before we talk finances?"

Les was immediately subdued. "I'm sorry, Miss Connors. When I'm nervous I talk too much." He answered her questions more calmly and she was disarmed by his smile and obvious desire to please. She learned that he had spent most of his working life to date as a bookie, besides helping his parents with their small grocery store, where he now lived, since his divorce.

"A two week trial on both sides, will that suit?" she asked.

He gave her an address and a phone number where he could be reached and a few handwritten references which she placed in a file. Bob Jennings, as an ex-policeman, would advise her about checking them. Living alone she wasn't taking any chances.

There was also an illogical niggle of doubt over him being an accountant. Presumably unqualified as he'd said only that he'd worked as an accountant. It had been an accountant called Ellis Owen who had robbed Alun Harris, as well as two men who ran a clothing factory. In both cases he had been their accountant and had fraudulently robbed them and ruined their businesses. In one case, he'd convinced the police he was dead and had caused an innocent man to be sent to prison. As an unqualified accountant, she unreasonably thought, Les Gronow would need watching. Having turned away three men plus the woman Tilly Tucker, who had since found a temporary job in Hopkins's baker's shop, she knew she had to take a chance on this one. She couldn't continue putting in the hours needed to run the place alone. How she wished Alun would walk through the door. Life had been so wonderful with him to share it. The contrast between the noisy, busy bar and the silence when the door closed behind the last customer was enormous and she hated it. The building echoed her every move, a constant reminder that she was alone.

That wouldn't change. Les Gronow would continue to live with his parents and she would still be spending the nights alone in the large building. She shrugged, she'd done it often enough and she'd soon get used to it again. Nevertheless, the thought was not a pleasant one, and the temptation to ask her brother to come back was strong. She knew she wouldn't; not while there was the faintest hope of Alun coming back, and that hope would be a long time dying.

Before she opened for the lunchtime session she had a great many things to do, including arranging to check Les Gronow's references, but she ignored them and went to speak to Bob and Kitty. Then, decision made, she rushed back to open the bar.

Mark Lacy had failed to find Mary Anne Crisp. Endless enquiries and many false leads had left him with nothing at all. Many of the letters he had written had failed to produce even a negative response. Many were still outstanding and they came back in dribs and drabs in the morning post. Elsie's will hadn't given a time limit after which the instructions would change, but he doubted whether his enquiries would be successful however long he delayed. He had to slow down his search and hope that the post would eventually bring a solution. People married and changed their names, they moved on, and many had settled abroad in places like Australia and Canada. He hated failing to follow the instructions of a client but in this instance there seemed little more he could do.

At the beginning of May, the café in Cwm Derw changed hands. While the legalities had trundled on, Seranne and Babs had been busy preparing for its new look. Tony helped with the painting, and Babs's parents came over, offered advice and rearranged the kitchen to make their work easier. Although she had asked many times, Seranne's mother had not seen the place and this was a disappointment. Luke came, bringing some cups and saucers.

"A gift from my auntie," he said, brushing aside their thanks. "The one who runs the café for lorry drivers. She said they were too small and delicate for her clientele."

Seranne took out her bag. "Can we pay for them now, so we keep the books straight?"

"They cost me nothing, but I'd welcome an occasional cup of coffee."

"Why is he so kind to us?" Seranne asked Kitty and Bob who were giving the window a final polish.

"Luke has always been kind and he enjoys helping when he can," Bob said. "Getting seriously rich like he has can change people, make them mean, but not Luke. He's generous and I don't think he'll change."

Kitty gave her a wink. "Helping some more than others, eh?"

"But doesn't his wife mind?" Seranne dared to ask.

"Wife?" Bob said. "You mean Marion? Why should she mind? She's well out of the picture."

What did that mean? Seranne asked herself. Were they divorced? Separated? Or living together but apart? He ought not to make her heart race with excitement. And he shouldn't be spending so much time in her life. Now the wife had a name the thought of how she felt about him made her cringe with guilt.

They had arranged for Hope Bevan to make draped net curtains, and Hope had also painted the window with a delicate drawing of a wayfaring tree, the new name for the café. On the Sunday before they opened, they were busy from six o'clock in the morning, cleaning, rearranging and setting up the tables. The new chairs they had bought had been painted a week before, with Bob and Colin's help and were ready to put in place.

"You'd better make sure that paint is properly dry, mind," Stella warned with a laugh. "It wouldn't be a good start for your customers to stick to them!"

"Don't worry, we have new seat covers," Babs said. "They were made by Hope too and a perfect fit."

"Clever girl young Hope," Stella agreed.

During that last day, amid all the frantic activity, large numbers of people "just happened" to pass by, hoping to see what was going on at the café and the girls guessed that they would be busy on their first day even if only with sightseeing locals.

216

Seranne didn't think she would sleep that night and at nine o'clock she walked to the end of the lane and telephoned her mother. "Mum, I've just come from the café which we open tomorrow. Won't you come and see what we've done, wish us luck? We've worked so hard and I want you to see it and be proud of us."

"I'm sure it's all lovely, dear, and I love the new name. The Wayfaring Tree is perfect."

"But . . .?"

"But Paul is having to go away tomorrow, to see to some family drama and it's Pat Sewell's day off, so I have to get up and remind myself what it's like to run a tea rooms."

"You shouldn't have left it all to Pat Sewell, Mum. She doesn't have your ability."

"Oh, Pat's all right and Paul constantly points out that much of what we did, you and I, wasn't necessary. We made ourselves slaves for standards most people hardly noticed."

"I think they noticed all right, Mum. Can't you see that the place has been stripped of its charms?"

"Nonsense, dear. People only want somewhere to sit and gossip."

Seranne didn't say any more. She and Babs were starting their own place to sit and gossip the following day and until she was sure of it being a success, how could she tell her mother she was wrong? She would be tempting fate and could land flat on her face.

"We've decided to close for our half day on Wednesdays. It's the day a lot of the local people go into Maes Hir for the market. Shall I come and tell you how we're getting on?"

"That would be lovely. Bring Babs and we can have a girly gossip."

"We won't be able to stay long, there'll be plenty to do to keep it up to the standards you taught me, Mum."

"Just don't work too hard. You must find time for some fun, Paul has taught me that."

Seranne and Babs were at the café very early the next morning to start making the cakes and scones for which they hoped to build a reputation. When they opened the door at 9.30 a queue had formed and the tables were immediately filled. For the next three hours they didn't stop. Between serving the tables, one or the other went into the kitchen to make sandwiches and fresh batches of scones. They had seriously underestimated their success.

The atmosphere was subdued though and Seranne and Babs wondered how they could liven the place, encourage their customers to talk rather than whisper. The stilted atmosphere, the lack of laughter, was not what they had hoped for. Seranne knew some of the dampened mood was due to her. Even though many of the customers were known to her, she was unable to respond to their greetings and good wishes. Her face was set like concrete as the strain and anxiety of making this day a success pressed down on her spirits. This was clearly affecting the clientele, who remained stifled so the chink of cup against saucer was cautiously avoided. People came and went with only the soft murmur of voices. It was very worrying. She had persuaded Babs to invest her money in this place and if she had judged it wrongly, had set up a high-class tea rooms in a place where it wasn't wanted, she would ruin her friend as well as herself. The thought dragged on her all morning.

At 12.30, most of the "coffee brigade", as Babs called them, were gone. Toasted snacks were in demand and they realized they would soon run out of milk. This was made worse by discovering that one of their remaining bottles was sour.

"Really!" An outraged Seranne glared at the offending item as though it could speak for itself. "That dairy should be more careful. They must have muddled up today's milk with yesterday's! Can you manage while I go and fetch some, Babs? It's a disgrace and I'll tell them so!"

Laughter was heard and she looked up to see the smiling face of Luke.

"It isn't funny!" she said, which only made him laugh louder.

"Tell me what you need and I'll go and find it. Milk, I presume, and is there anything else you need?"

"Luke!" Babs said with relief. "Thank goodness. We need milk desperately and a few more loaves of sliced bread, too. And pasties if Tony has any left."

Luke nodded, grinned again at the still scowling Seranne and disappeared.

Betty called in and, seeing they were dangerously low in cups, saucers and plates due to having no time to wash them, sent two young boys across each carrying a box of her china for them to use until they could add to their own.

"Thank goodness for Luke's auntie, we'd have had to close and wash up if it weren't for the ones he brought," Babs sighed, piling more used plates precariously in the small kitchen.

Stella closed the post office for lunch and she came across with her little dog, Scamp, who was pleased to see Seranne and ran in before Stella could stop him. He greeted Seranne with enthusiasm then, as Luke walked in with the bottles of milk and some wrapped loaves and paper bags, Scamp jumped up and helped himself to a pasty from those left on the counter and, darting between Luke's legs, shot through the doorway at speed.

As usual, the look of outrage on Seranne's face made Luke laugh and the customers joined in. Seranne knew she ought to throw away the remaining pasties but the customers wouldn't hear of it and she ended up giving them away, which improved the atmosphere even more and the party-like mood continued through the rest of the day as the story was passed on to newcomers. She heard one lady tell her friend, "This place just makes you feel good. I can't imagine anyone leaving without a smile on their face." She turned to Seranne and raised her coffee cup in salute and added, "Well done, Seranne and Babs."

The last of the tension left Seranne, and she relaxed and began to enjoy herself. Luke and a no longer apologetic Stella stayed and had mushrooms on toast — declining the pasties with exclamations of horror, to add to the fun, even though they were newly delivered. It seemed the joke of Scamp's misbehaviour would go on and on into legend. The little dog had returned to sit under the table enjoying treats from various diners and was reluctant to leave when Stella went to reopen the post office.

Luke left at the same time as Stella but then surprised them by returning at five and staying to help clear up after closing. "Come to the Ship," he coaxed. "I know you're tired and want to discuss your first day, but you needn't stay long. I bet you've hardly eaten a thing and I've arranged with Betty for you to have a salad and some new potatoes and some of her home-made cheese."

It sounded perfect and they followed him like a couple of puppies, running and even skipping in their excitement as they congratulated each other on their wonderful start. Luke put an arm around Seranne as he guided them through Betty's side door and without a thought of the mysterious Marion, she put an arm around his waist and hugged him close.

Betty had prepared a celebratory spread which they ate with gusto, unaware until then just how hungry they were. When their excitement had cooled they began making lists of things they would need. Apart from the food order, Seranne remembered the tall tiered cake plates her mother had used for customers requesting tea and cakes. She doubted whether they were used by Pat Sewell, who would have considered them too much hard work, with the chrome frames to polish and the dismantling required to wash the plates.

She used Betty's phone and asked her mother if she could borrow them, and she also needed the recipe of Melting Moments — a coconut biscuit that used to be a favourite in Jessica's Victorian Tea Rooms. Luke watched her face, rosy with excitement as she told her mother about their first day at The Wayfaring Tree. Her eyes were glowing and when their eyes met she wrinkled her nose in a childish way that delighted him.

With Luke helping they did a rough assessment of their day's finances and were pleased. Even allowing for it being a day for the curious rather than prospective regulars, they had done remarkably well.

"Once you lightened up and stopped looking like a suspicious policeman in a room full of suspected criminals, the atmosphere was wonderful," Luke said, with a hand on her shoulder to show he was not critical, only aware of how tense she had been.

Seranne smiled and pushed him playfully. "I've never been so frightened in my life. My fears were for Babs more than myself. She trusted me and my idea with her money."

"I knew we were going to be all right," Babs assured her. "We'll make The Wayfaring Tree *the* place to meet friends and relax."

Luke agreed. "I'm really impressed with what you've achieved, and it will only get better."

She smiled at him, warmed by his praise.

Les Gronow the new barman arrived at the Ship fifteen minutes late full of apologies explaining that he'd forgotten to wind his watch and he'd lost track of time. Not what I was hoping for, Betty thought, dejectedly.

After a few queries he soon found his way around the bar and the customers liked his chatty and friendly manner. By the time they closed she began to feel hopeful that at least he wasn't completely useless. He was in a hurry to leave and as she finished up after he had gone, she wasn't fully convinced about his remaining. Perhaps she would leave that notice in Stella's post office a while longer. Putting away the last of the glasses she daydreamed of Alun walking past, seeing the notice and knocking on the door.

The Ship and Compass was more than the local pub, it was a place used for many local events and the coming celebration for the crowning of Queen Elizabeth II would be one of them. Meetings were held in the bar after hours where plans were made for the street party to which everyone was invited. Everyone was clutching at least one list. Hope had two, one for food and another for decorations including the essential bunting. Hope's mother-in-law Marjorie Williamson-Murton had a fistful, determined to be overall organizer, ignoring challenges from several others.

By doing a rough headcount they worked out what would be needed and people added their names and listed the food they would bring. Hope's husband Peter Bevan still had a cart which he had once used on a round selling grocery and Jason the horse was enjoying life in a field nearby. He offered them both for delivering tables and chairs and also for giving the children rides.

It would be a day the children would remember, everyone was determined on that and, because many people had invested in a television for the occasion and would want to watch the ceremony, the party would be four days later, on Saturday, 6 June.

Betty had her own lists and she began to wonder how she would cope with the extra work if Les Gronow didn't do his share. She glanced at his references and put them back in the drawer, she really should make enquiries, but they would have to wait. This afternoon the men were bringing her television and from what she'd heard, they would keep her busy until opening time. One on the roof turning the aerial and one inside shouting the result shown on the screen.

Jake called one day and asked if she'd heard from Alun. "He promised to keep in touch but I haven't heard from him," he said.

Betty shook her head. "Not a word. It seems he wanted to shake the dust of Cwm Derw from his shoes."

"I think he was sorry to go but felt you were forced by loyalty to have your brother back. That was a shock for Ed, wasn't it, him not inheriting the guest house?"

"Ed isn't back. Loyalty or not, I didn't want him here."

"But Alun told me you more or less asked him to go as your brother needed a home."

"No, that was what Alun decided. He obviously didn't want to stay, and the excuse of making way for Ed came as a relief to him. He was ready to leave, he'd had enough of me and the Ship and the quiet existence of living in Cwm Derw."

"I don't think so. I think you two have had your wires crossed."

"No, Jake. He wanted to leave, I'm sure of that."

"And you? Were you glad to see him go?"

Betty shook her head sadly. "I was beginning to hope he'd stay for ever."

"Barmy the pair of you," was Jake's response.

Luke's travels between his various businesses took him over a wide area and when he was passing close to Jessie's tea rooms he called there and ordered coffee and a cake. This arrived as a small cup of coffee and a sticky bun, having been offered the choice between a bun or a scone. Having seen both he decided on not the best, but the least worst.

Pat Sewell didn't recognize him and when he paid and left he walked around a while then went back for the coat he had intentionally left behind. It was now after closing time and he walked in and saw Paul and Pat Sewell in an embrace.

Luke lowered his head and pretended to pick something off the floor then looking away from where they stood, called, "Anyone there?" When he looked again Pat and Paul were standing far apart.

Pat asked, "Can I help you? We're closed you know."

"I believe I left my coat here." He gestured towards the table he had occupied and she strode forward and picked up the coat.

"Is Seranne's mother in?" he asked. "Seranne has asked for a recipe and I could take it for her. Some cake stands too, if you aren't using them."

Paul seemed to notice him for the first time and greeted Luke politely. He and Pat shared a glance and Luke suspected they were wondering if he had witnessed their close encounter. "I can call again if it isn't convenient," he said, smiling reassuringly.

Paul went to the stairs and called up, "Jessie, darling, Luke's here and he'd like a word if you aren't too busy."

Jessie appeared, dressed for something special, and greeted him affectionately. "Luke, how kind of you to call. There's a letter here for Seranne, will you take it for her?"

"Certainly. She mentioned she would like to borrow some of your tall cake stands and I thought I could take them for her."

"Of course you can. Where are they, Pat?" she asked.

"No idea. We stopped using them ages ago, didn't we Paul?"

Paul shrugged. "I think they might have been among the stuff we sold a while back, remember we discarded the teapots and the plates and the ornaments because they made so much work?"

Luke saw a flash of disappointment cross Jessie's face. She looked along the empty shelves, her eyes registering shock. "When were they sold, Paul? I don't remember that." Then, aware of Luke watching her, she smiled and said, "Of course, I remember now. Such a pity we didn't know Seranne was buying her own café, she could have used them."

The recipe was found and Luke drove back to Cwm Derw with a feeling of anger in his heart. What, if anything, should he tell Seranne? He asked about the letter Jessie had mentioned but Paul couldn't find it. Just as well, it would give him another excuse to call unannounced.

He drove to Badgers Brook and as usual found several visitors there. Betty was just leaving to open up, hoping that the new barman Les would be on time for once. Kitty and Bob were there with Colin, looking at seed catalogues and making plans for the garden and Bob's allotment. Scamp was asleep near the fire, having chosen a cushion which he had pulled to the floor to rest his head on.

He walked in and handed the recipe to Seranne while Kitty busied herself getting him a cup of tea. "I asked about the cake stands," he told Seranne, "but Paul sold them when he got rid of the teapots and plates."

"I wish they'd asked me. Even before Babs and I thought about opening the café I'd have wanted them. They were my grandmother's."

Remembering her mother's disappointed expression, Luke didn't think Paul had even asked Jessie, and had simply decided they were unnecessary work. "I'll look in a few second-hand shops on my travels," he promised. "I'm sure to find a few cake stands that will suit."

"Thank you. Were there any letters?" Seranne asked. "There wouldn't be anything important but I still get a few from people who don't know my new address."

"Jessie said something about a letter but Paul couldn't find it. He'll have it ready when you next call."

"But Mum always keeps the letters in the box near the telephone."

"Paul is different from your father, not as orderly and your mother has changed too. She finds life with Paul more relaxed, they aren't so particular about doing everything precisely on time, keeping everything in place." Reliving the shock of seeing Paul and Pat in each other's arms, he was anxious and was trying to convince Seranne there was nothing to worry about. "He'll find it in time for your next visit."

"It can't be anything important. Most people know where I am now."

"Why don't you phone and tell your mother you'll be there on Wednesday. I'll take you if you like."

"I don't like having to phone first."

"That's something else that's changed. Paul takes your mother out a great deal more than your father did." He still hadn't decided what to do about Paul's disloyalty and he didn't want Seranne to go in and find out as he had done. "So telephone and tell her we'll be there soon after three. All right?"

Betty drove to the Ship and saw with relief that Les had opened up. There were already several people in the bar and he was cheerfully exchanging comments with the darts players and a group of older men playing dominoes. She removed her coat, tidied herself and was soon working beside him.

The evening was fairly quiet and Les joined the darts players revealing a talent that had them trying to persuade him to join the Ship and Compass team. He declined and Betty wondered why. She assured him she'd have no objection to allowing time for him to play both home and away matches but he wouldn't change his mind.

He worked fast and didn't complain about the heavy lifting his job entailed, seeing the tasks that needed doing without being told. He integrated well with the regulars and apart from being frequently late arriving and always early to leave, she had no complaints. Perhaps she had chosen well. After all, no one could compare with Alun Harris and he was gone for good.

Alun had found a job in a small hotel with a restaurant that catered for outsiders as well as guests. Close to Swansea and Mumbles, it was a popular place for holiday makers despite offering very basic home-made meals, which in this instance was, in Alun's opinion, a synonym for boring.

He tried to persuade the owner to be more adventurous but his attempts were always frowned upon. "Driving away the regulars in the hope of attracting new is too risky," he was told, so he went on producing the bland food and accepting praise for something that made him ashamed.

He rented a room in a small guest house, and spent his spare time walking on the beautiful beaches and countryside of Gower and wishing Betty were there to enjoy it with him. Twice he started to write to Jake at the boatyard but each time he threw it away. Best to let it go and forget about Cwm Derw and Betty Connors.

He was standing outside a pretty tea rooms near the path leading down to the beach at Rhossili one day when he saw Luke park his car and set off towards the Worm's Head. He called before he thought about it, pleased to see a familiar face, and together they walked along the narrow strip of land with ancient strip farming fields to the left and the magnificent view down over the miles of sandy beach from Rhossili to Llangenith and beyond on their right. The late morning was warm and both men were in shirt sleeves and carrying a small rucksack.

Luke told him about the change of ownership on the sad café that was now The Wayfaring Tree, and Alun was interested to hear how well the two young women were doing and asked several questions. Then he told Luke about his dull occupation.

"I don't suppose anything would be the same after running your own restaurant," Luke said. "Taking orders and having to do things you know aren't correct, that must be hard." He looked at Alun, who nodded. "The Ship and Compass was frustrating and boring too, wasn't it?" he asked. "Isn't that why you left?"

"Strangely enough, I didn't find the Ship boring. I liked the atmosphere Betty created. Everyone knew everyone else, the events of people's lives were offered for discussion, people cared about each other, yet it was genuinely welcoming to strangers."

"Why *did* you leave?"

Alun shrugged. "Welcoming strangers only goes so far, I suppose. I realized that deep down I didn't belong."

"When you thought Ed was going to live at the Ship and help Betty?"

"Betty had to help Ed. He was her brother and I understand that."

"But she didn't take him back. Ed is staying at the guest house until the new owner can be found. After telling Ed to go, Betty managed on her own for quite a while. Damned difficult decision for someone as kind as Betty, Ed being her brother, but he was taking her for a fool, everyone could see that. Locals helped when they could but she had a hard time of it. She finally found a man called Les Gronow and he's all right, but he lives out and works strictly for the hours he's paid for and not a minute longer. She's on her own for most of the time and I don't think she likes it."

Alun looked at Luke in surprise. "But I thought — you mean, she didn't want Ed back?"

"Of course not, lazy so-and-so."

"If what you say is true, then I let her down as badly as Ed. But it's too late for me to go back now."

They were at the end of the mainland where they could look across at the tidal island called The Worm. The tide was high and seabirds screeched their objection to their appearance. Apart from the birds they were the only living creatures around. Alun stared across the sea, a frown on his face, regret in his heart. "It's too late," he repeated softly.

Luke looked at Alun and said, "Don't cut yourself off on an island of your own making, Alun. You have friends in Cwm Derw and they'd welcome you back."

"Betty's fixed up now, there's nothing for me to go back to. Come on, I'll treat you to a pint if the Worm's Head Hotel is open."

Back in Cwm Derw Betty was returning from a shopping trip having left Les to finish the lunchtime cleaning and arranging for him to open up if she was delayed. She had left the car and used the bus and when the return bus she intended to catch had been full, a customer offered her a lift so she was back earlier than expected. She'd be there before Les arrived. Just as well. He was never on time.

The side door was closed but not locked. Les must have come early for a change, she thought with surprise. She'd have to remind him about making sure it was locked. Unintentionally she went in without making a sound and gasped in disbelief when she found Les searching through her desk. The contents of a cupboard had been disturbed too, the papers and boxes were on the floor near him. He looked up and began a stuttering apology. "Betty, I had a call from the insurers and they wanted to know whether your valuation is up to date and —"

"Get out," her voice was calm. "And if you give me back whatever it is bulging in your pockets I won't go to the police. I should, but I can't stand the ordeal. But if I see you around here again, then I will." Her voice was raised as she repeated, "Get out of my sight!"

She stood barring the doorway while he took out a small silver inkwell and a cigarette box, also silver. When he began to push past she stopped him and pointed to his other pocket. He took out a silver and cut-glass cruet and two Georgian spoons. Still she wouldn't let him pass. His head held in shame, he handed her a small statuette, then patted his pockets to show there was nothing else. She stared at him and waited.

"That's all and I'm very sorry, Betty. It's for my wife you see."

"She'll be proud of you, will she? Stealing for her? This wife you told me you'd divorced?" She held out her hand and the second statuette was placed in it.

She locked the door after him and prepared to open the bar. It wasn't until much later, when everyone had gone and the house was still, that she broke down and cried. Once again she was on her own.

CHAPTER
NINE

Betty felt utter despair after Les Gronow had gone. She imagined him sneaking around the house marking treasures and making a mental list of what he would take, waiting for the right moment to grab everything of value. He probably had a buyer ready, waiting for him to deliver. She knew she should inform the police but embarrassment over her stupidity at not checking even one of his so-called references made her hesitate. Now several days had passed it was too late, they would think her even more stupid.

She told Kitty and Bob, who had enquired at the address he had given. She wasn't really surprised that no one there had heard of Les Gronow. Bob tried to persuade her to go to the police but she refused. "I just want to forget it," she insisted. She read through the list of applicants again and only one name gave her confidence. She decided to write to Tilly Tucker and persuade her to leave the bakery and come to the Ship. She at least knew where the woman lived and she was unlikely to rob her and disappear. Surely she'd had her run of bad luck?

She was distracted from her sad mood by preparations for the coronation celebrations on 2 June.

Whenever people gathered, the conversation quickly led to talk about the event. Every street had its own arrangement and most households were involved, either by cooking, helping with the enthusiastic decorations outside the houses, or lending tablecloths or chairs and tables. Anyone with transport was roped in to collect and deliver what was needed.

Seranne tried to persuade her mother to come and share the party, hoping for an opportunity to talk to her without Paul present, but Jessie refused, insisting that their new television, bought by "darling Paul", was too much of an attraction, even though the street party was not on the actual Coronation Day.

"She's avoiding me," Seranne said to Babs. "She won't talk to me in case she gives away something about Paul she's worried about. Why can't she tell me what's wrong? We used to tell each other everything."

"Marriage is bound to change that, she has Paul to discuss things with now."

"And a lot of good it's doing! He's stopped her thinking clearly and I'm worried that it will end in disaster for her."

"She knows you're there when she needs you," Babs comforted.

News of the Cwm Derw café's new management travelled fast and Seranne and Babs were kept very busy. The food they cooked was popular and they frequently ran out, and once Tony realized what was happening he came to help. Accepting the limitations of their small impractical kitchen was no problem and he cheerfully produced small fairy cakes each with its own individual decoration. These looked attractive and tasted delicious and the girls were grateful to him.

Luke sent his Uncle Frank and cousin George to put up the new shelves and Tony painted them to match the walls. The china that had once graced the shelves of Jessie's tea rooms was then proudly displayed, much to Seranne's delight.

Impulsively she hugged Tony and he held her close for longer than she expected. She was surprised when later that day he said, "What about that trip to the pictures I promised you. Anything you fancy seeing?"

She looked through the local paper and they argued light-heartedly between Abbot and Costello and a western until Tony said, "All right, love, comedy it is." Something in the way he said it startled Seranne and she went straight to Babs and insisted she went with them. "I might be imagining it," she admitted, "but I suspect your Tony is thinking of a kiss and cuddle in the back row."

In mock annoyance, Babs said, "You mean you don't want to be my sister-in-law?"

"Not if it means marrying your Tony. You don't have any other brothers you haven't told me about, do you?"

They met at the cinema on Seranne's insistence and it was only then that Tony saw his sister. "Spoilsport," he hissed.

Babs laughed. "The girl needed protection," she retorted.

To his further dismay she sat between them as they settled to enjoy the film.

★ ★ ★

Luke was on his way to see his mother when he saw Seranne waiting at the entrance to the cinema. Seeing Tony walking up made him groan in disappointment. He stared as Tony put a proprietorial arm around Seranne's waist but sighed with relief a moment later when he saw Babs join them.

Luke's mother was in a nursing home and he visited regularly. She always had lots of questions and this time she asked, "When are you going to find a girl? I want to see you married and settled again before I die."

"Don't talk about dying, Mum, you know how I hate it. As for a girl, how can I when I'm not free?"

"Marion, you mean? Forget her, she's done you enough harm. Not free? What rubbish you talk." He quickly changed the subject, as he always did and she sighed impatiently. "There is someone you're keen on?"

"Maybe, but it isn't possible."

"Since Marion, you've concentrated all your energies on making money, so when will you find someone to spend it on, instead of helping lame dogs over stiles?"

"When I'm free," he insisted.

He was returning from the nursing home when he saw Pat Sewell and he was curious when he saw she was talking to his Uncle Frank. He parked and waited until Pat had walked away then tooted the horn for his uncle to join him.

"How do you know Pat Sewell?"

"She used to live near us, until her husband died and she had to move to somewhere cheaper. I go into the café when I'm in the area."

"You've met Paul Curtis then?"

"Oh him? He and Pat have been friends all their lives, they care for each other but nothing more, if that's what you're thinking. Friends, that's all. He needs all the friends he can find, poor bloke."

"What d'you mean?"

"Well he's hopeless, isn't he? He inherited a good business from his father but ran it into the ground."

"Gambling? Having a good time? Wasting money on drink, or whatever?"

"No, he just isn't a businessman. A bit thick if you ask me. He should have worked alongside his father and learned from him but Paul was always convinced he knew best."

"What happened to the factory?"

"He spent too long making the items there was no longer a demand for and even when he was warned that plain, simple handbags were not what people wanted he carried on. He made wallets and comb cases, manicure sets, travelling cases for men and women, leather-covered mirrors and sewing sets, all sorts of gift ideas, but people are looking for something new and he refused to budge from the traditional lines that they'd made for years."

"I expect he's a bit dishonest too, spending money instead of putting it back into the business."

"No, Paul isn't dishonest, and he tried really hard to keep the place going. He just isn't any good at running the factory. All his best people left and he struggled on refusing to consider changes, even though he had the designers until practically the end. Probably didn't know how to change. He's a fool, but you can't help feeling sorry for him, poor bloke."

Luke was very thoughtful as he drove away. Could the man have teetered on the edge of bankruptcy by being a fool rather than dishonest? He had almost certainly used Jessie's money to save himself and that was hardly honest. Was it stupidity that had allowed the tea rooms to fail? He wasn't convinced.

The most inexplicable part was, why did Jessie allow that to happen? And what about the new shop he was planning to open? Nothing at all had happened there, the place was still closed and in need of decoration and the boxes he had seen were still in exactly the same places. It was more mysterious than ever after listening to Uncle Frank's surprising opinions.

Tony was thinking a lot about Seranne. The girl he had known all his life had changed, or his perception of her had. One of Babs's friends, hardly worth a thought, had become a desirable young woman. He went out of his way to please her, persuade her to notice him. She still treated him in exactly the same way as always.

Besides his early morning duties, Tony helped in the family baker's shop when their assistant Tilly Tucker wasn't there and in between, did what he could to help his sister and Seranne hoping that somehow things would change.

He was putting freshly baked loaves in the bakery window when Betty called in to place an order. He waved before disappearing into the bake house. Betty found Tilly behind the counter waiting to serve her.

239

"Oh, hello, I've written to you asking if you still wanted the job of barmaid. The man I chose didn't suit. Am I too late?"

"No you aren't. Here temp'ry I am, and if you'll give me a try I'd love to work at the Ship."

Betty called through to the bake house behind the shop. "Tony, can I have a word?"

"What can I do to help?" Tony asked wiping his hands on a white towel. "More bread rolls needed?"

"I'd like to know whether Tilly has a permanent job with you. I wrote offering her the job at the Ship but I don't want to poach her from you, Tony."

"No, she only came in while the regular is sick. She'll be finished at the end of the week."

"Thanks."

Tony moved closer and whispered, "Talk your head off she will, mind. Not gossip, she isn't one to talk unkindly about anyone, but I'm warning you, her tongue never stops."

Betty laughed. "I don't think that's a bad thing for a barmaid, do you?"

Arrangements were made for Tilly to see Betty after the shop closed to discuss details and Betty walked to the post office, once again wondering whether she had finally found someone on whom she could rely. She told Stella what had happened.

"Ever since that brother of mine started courting poor Elsie I've been trying to find someone to help and every time I've been let down. Except with Alun. If only he'd stayed."

"You should have made it clear straightaway that you didn't want your Ed back."

"Maybe. But he was so quick to go I just knew he was glad of the excuse."

On Wednesday, Luke arrived at The Wayfaring Tree in time to help the girls finish tidying up after closing at 1.30. It always surprised Seranne that he needed no telling, but joined in with the necessary tasks with ease, automatically knowing what needed doing and how they liked it done. At two o'clock they were on their way. Babs off home to her parents, and Seranne — with anxiety written on her face — to see what was happening at her mother's tea rooms.

Jessie was worried. She had been hiding her worries behind a smile for weeks and seeing the look on her daughter's face she knew she couldn't do that for very much longer. She had to face facts and the truth was beginning to dawn that leaving the running of her once beautiful tea rooms to Pat and Paul had been the biggest mistake of her life. But what could she do? She loved Paul and she would do anything to keep him, agree with anything just as long as he treated her like someone special, told her she was beautiful and adored.

A visit from a friend the previous day had brought things to a head. Matty Powell had been out of town for several months, visiting a daughter in America. When she called for a coffee and to see Jessie, the shock was enormous and Matty Powell wasn't the type to hide it.

"Jessie, what on earth has been happening? Been ill, have you? Taken to drink? Lost your sanity? This place

241

is the worse caff I've ever seen and I've seen quite a few!"

"Paul has made me stop working so hard and have some fun, that's all."

"Paul? Who is Paul?"

Taking her up to the flat, Matty asked questions which Jessie tried to answer while at the same time being loyal to Paul. Matty asked about Seranne and being told about her move to Cwm Derw, Matty looked thoughtful and, to Jessie's relief, stopped her barrage of questions.

Jessie walked down to see her visitor off and Matty pulled her into the drab place and made her look at the devastation of her once beautiful tea rooms.

"Paul might be the most wonderful thing that's happened to you, Jessie, but surely you don't have to let this happen to keep him?" She waved her arms to encompass the uncared-for mess of the room. It was closed and the tables had yet to be cleared. Listlessly, Jessie began to pick up some used plates.

"I do what I can. When Paul's out I come down and . . . do what I can," she ended aimlessly. "It's just that he enjoys spoiling me, telling me there's no need for me to work, that he'll take care of everything."

"And does he?" Jessie didn't reply and there was concern in Matty's eyes as she said, "I'll come again, soon, so we can see if anything can be done before you have to close down."

The stark warning behind the softly spoken words wasn't lost on Jessie. After Matty had gone she sat and stared unseeing at the walls, her head empty of thought.

When Paul returned, she clung to him and told herself everything would be all right. Paul had promised.

Matty phoned later and asked for Seranne's address but Jessie told her to stay away. The trouble was, Jessie didn't really want things to change. She liked being charmed by Paul. The flattery of walking into a restaurant on his arm and seeing the admiring looks that he engendered had never lost its initial excitement.

She was nervous when Seranne and Luke came on Wednesday, and hugged her daughter for longer than usual before offering a cheek for Luke to kiss.

"Is everything all right, Mam?" Seranne asked. Assured that everything was perfect, she looked around for Paul. "Isn't Paul here?"

"He won't be long. He's gone to talk to a new bakery supplier. We haven't been having good service from our present one."

"Pat gone with him?"

"She's the one running the place so it's she who needs to choose."

"Of course," Seranne said, with forced enthusiasm.

Luke kept the conversation going by telling Jessie how successful her daughter and Babs had been. "I'll come and fetch you one day, shall I? Then you can see for yourself."

"Don't worry, Luke, dear. Paul will bring me when he finds time. He's so busy. Did I tell you he's starting up a business of his own?"

"What sort of business?" Luke asked.

"Oh, you know how vague Paul can be. Something about selling catering equipment."

"Not china?"

"No." She frowned. "He hasn't said anything about china. Why do you ask?"

"No reason. Catering?" he coaxed.

"He definitely said catering equipment, utensils and pans and tins like we use here, and the larger things like chip cutters, fryers and fridges. What he can't stock he can order. He's arranging deals with the manufacturers."

She spoke brightly but Seranne could see she was on edge. When she or Luke asked questions her answers were vague and Seranne noticed that sometimes she was not really concentrating on what was being said. She sat there only half aware of them, as though listening for Paul's return.

In another attempt to start a conversation, Seranne asked, "Mum, has any post arrived for me? I'm not expecting any, most people know where I am by now, but Paul said a letter had come and he'd put it ready for when I next called."

Jessie shook her head. "There's nothing on the desk addressed to you. Perhaps he's forwarded it to Badgers Brook."

"Hardly, it was a long time ago and I'd have received it by now."

"I never see the post, Paul attends to all that, saves me bothering. He's so thoughtful. Don't worry, dear. It was probably unimportant."

"I'd still like to see it."

"I'll ask Paul when he gets home."

244

Luke went into the kitchen and set a tray for tea. There was a sad-looking sponge cake on the table and he carried it in with plates and server. "All right if I make us some tea?" he belatedly asked. Jessie replied vaguely and once again, Seranne was aware that she hadn't taken in what Luke had said.

Paul still hadn't arrived when it was time to go and Seranne was reluctant to leave. She stopped to wash the dishes, noticing her mother hadn't finished her tea or eaten any of the cake. She was only half alive when Paul wasn't there. As an excuse for another delay she wrote a note asking Paul to forward her mail, then they said their goodbyes amid hugs and promises to meet soon, and left.

"I hated leaving her, Luke," she said, as they turned the corner after which they lost sight of the tea rooms. "She seems so depressed, not like Mum at all."

"Where was Paul? She appeared to be anxious about him. Did you notice that she hardly turned her eyes away from the door and seemed to be listening for his return?"

"I did. My guess is that they've had a quarrel."

Luke thought of the scene he had witnessed between Paul and Pat Sewell and wondered if Jessie had found out about Paul's flirtation. If she had, then knowing they were out together must be breaking her heart. He agonized about whether or not he should tell Seranne but decided not. If it blew over, her knowing would make it harder for Jessie to forgive, and if it didn't, he believed that bad news shouldn't be delivered until there was no alternative.

He wondered what had happened to Paul's plan to open a shop selling china. He also wondered where Paul had really gone that afternoon. He had known they were coming, so was he avoiding Seranne? Things were looking desperate, could Jessie be about to lose her business and her home?

"I wonder why Mum changed from the regular bakery? We've dealt with Green and Sons for years."

Luke made a mental note of the name and spent the next few days trying to find out. Paul might be charming, but Luke didn't trust him at all. Reluctant as she might be to ask, Jessie was clearly in need of help.

During the following week, Betty watched as yet another trainee bar assistant went through her paces. At first Tilly faced a lot of teasing, but she clearly enjoyed it and gave back as much if not more than she was given. At the end of the first session she was quick and thorough with the cleaning and setting up for the next opening and Betty nodded approval and said, "No need for a trial period, Tilly, you're on the team." She was smiling but inside she wondered sadly just how long this one would last before finding a better job — or just losing interest.

In the bar that evening, Colin and Bob and a few other regulars were discussing the unexpected will that excluded Ed from inheriting his wife's guest house, and the mysterious Mary Anne Crisp.

"Elsie Clements as she was, lived here for years and it's strange we've never heard of this niece of hers,"

Colin remarked. "Crisp is an unusual name. If she was from round here we're sure to have heard it."

"Married for sure. She could be called anything now, although Mary Anne isn't so common either. Not local for sure, she could be anywhere, even one of them GI brides living in America."

"I knew a Mary Anne once," Tilly called over, having followed the conversation. "She quarrelled with her family and moved away. No one knows where she went. There's exciting! She might be wealthy and not know it."

"You ought to go and see the solicitor, Mark Lacy," Luke said, finishing his glass of beer. "Just think, you might be the one to solve the great Cwm Derw mystery."

"There's exciting!" someone mocked.

Betty was smiling as she went to answer the phone. She picked up the receiver with the constantly reviving hope that it might be Alun. It was Paul asking her to let Seranne know her mother was in hospital. She called to Luke and he went at once to find Seranne and take her to her mother, but it was Wednesday, the café was closed and from what he gleaned, Seranne and Babs had gone to Maes Hir market.

He drove to the busy little market town but despite walking around the market and the shops several times couldn't find them. He phoned and left messages with Betty, Stella and with Babs's parents at the bakery, then drove to the hospital to which Jessie had been taken. He asked several nurses but no record of her being admitted could be found. "Is there another hospital where she might have been taken?" he asked. "I might have misheard. A receptionist telephoned the nearest hospital but no one had a patient called Jessica Curtis. It was as he was leaving that he found her.

"I'm all right," Jessie assured him when he found her sitting in a corridor, waiting for Paul to take her home. "Paul overreacted, that's all. He gets so worried about me."

"What did the doctor say?" he asked, taking her cold hands in his.

"Nerves. Although I didn't think I was the type to suffer such a thing. I've always been a capable woman." She stared at him, held his gaze, anxious to convince him. "You believe that, don't you?"

"I do. Of course I do. From all that Seranne has told me about you, you can cope with anything life throws."

"Except the fear of Paul leaving me," she whispered. "Does that make me pathetic?"

"If Paul and you parted — and I can't see that ever happening," he added quickly, "you and he have something very special. But if you and he did decide to separate, you would cope bravely as you've always done, head up high, and you'd rebuild your life into something successful."

She was about to say something else; she leaned towards him, her hand came up to touch his lapel as she began, "Promise you won't say anything to Seranne, but —"

"Darling! I've been so anxious. I've searched all the wards and couldn't find you!" Paul ran the last few steps and hugged his wife and made soothing sounds a mother might make to her baby.

"They had no reason to keep me in, I'm fine, really, darling."

Luke stood and watched them for a moment then made his excuses. "I'm so pleased it wasn't anything serious and I'll go straight to reassure Seranne," he promised. "She must be home by now. He walked away, unsure of exactly what he would tell Seranne. He glanced back to see them wrapped in each other's arms, Jessie's small figure swamped by Paul's height making her look as helpless as a wounded child. He was frustrated, wondering what Jessie had been about to tell him. Now it was unlikely he'd ever find out. It had been a weak moment and Paul's arrival had ruined it.

It was as he reached the outskirts of Cwm Derw that he saw Seranne. She was sitting beside Tony in the bakery van approaching him and he tooted until they saw him. They parked and he told them all that had happened.

"I think I'd still like to go and see her," Seranne said and, to Tony's dismay, she went with Luke. Trying to retrieve something, Tony hugged her, kissed her lightly on the cheek, whispered reassurances on her mother's health, before driving away. Luke hid the possessive feelings engendered by the brief display of affection between them. If only things could have been different, he thought, helping Seranne into the car, if Marion hadn't — but that was something he had to live with.

When they reached the flat, Jessie was tucked up in bed, cosseted with hot water bottles. There was fruit and some magazines on the side table and Luke frowned. Paul seemed to want Jessie to become an invalid. He was further alarmed when Jessie began to cry the moment she saw them. Something here was very wrong, and accepting the risk to his growing closeness with Seranne, he had to do something before Jessie surrendered completely.

He tried to find a few moments alone with her, but Paul watched him and made sure it didn't happen. Frustration increased, making him angry and it showed. Paul and he glared at each other and although nothing was said, both had the other's measure, aware they were in conflict.

On the journey back to Cwm Derw Luke was quiet and Seranne was content to think about her mother and the way everything had fallen apart since Paul had come on the scene. So when he decided to take a chance and hint to her that things were not as they should be, she was receptive.

"I'm concerned about your mother," he began. "It seems to me that Paul encourages her to leave everything to him and she's given in, accepts what he advises even though she must know he's wrong." He held his breath expecting her to disagree.

"I've been thinking the same thing," she said to his surprise. "From the beginning he discouraged her from running the tea rooms properly, getting that awful Pat Sewell in and allowing her to ruin the business my mother and grandmother had built. Now she seems almost helpless, depending on him for every little decision."

250

"She isn't a weak person, I've known her long enough to know that. Love can change people, but why has she given up all she previously enjoyed?"

"I'm very worried, but what can I do? I thought I was doing the right thing when I left home but now I'm not so sure. She seems so afraid of losing him she won't disagree with a thing he says."

"Can't you persuade her to come to Badgers Brook and stay with you for a while?"

"I have invited her, but she refuses to leave Paul."

"She might be afraid of what he'll do while she isn't there. She must be aware of what's going on even if she's so afraid of losing him she pretends to ignore it." He thought again of the closeness of Paul and Pat Sewell but avoided mentioning it. Seranne had enough to worry her at present. And there was always the possibility he was wrong and what he'd seen had been innocent. Uncle Frank's explanation that they were long-time friends cast doubts on his previous suspicions.

They went back to Badgers Brook and Seranne made some Welsh rarebit with dried egg and the last of her cheese ration. Using trays, they sat in front of the fire and ate, a mood of despondency shrouding them as they were both aware of how little they could do unless Jessie actually asked them for help.

That night, while Paul was sleeping, Jessie went down and cleaned the neglected kitchen behind the tea rooms. She went back into bed without disturbing him and resolved to do the same every night until the place

251

was at least clean. Even if she could do nothing about all the missing displays and the pretty curtains that Pat had discarded if would be as clean as she could make it.

Beside his regular workload, Tony was busy overseeing the new premises. The bake house was being built in what had been the garden behind the shop they had bought. He visited the place at least once each day and pored over the plans and discussed the builders' progress with his father every evening. But he still found time to help at The Wayfaring Tree. Seranne began to look forward to his arrival, usually during the afternoon, when the place was filled with shoppers and friends meeting for afternoon tea and cakes.

He sometimes took some cakes he had made in the bakery and other times he baked in their small kitchen. One afternoon he made pancakes and drop scones which were always popular. He knew he did it for the pleasure of pleasing Seranne and talking to her, making her laugh. He disliked Wednesdays, when he had no excuse to call.

"We make a good team, don't we?" he said one Saturday, when the café was crowded and he was in the kitchen bringing out yet another batch of small fruit cakes. Babs had gone across the road to buy some napkins as their order had failed to arrive. They worked together with ease, and occasionally he touched her arm as he spoke to her. Seranne turned and smiled at him, her face rosy from the heat and he felt a rush of desire. The impulse to kiss her couldn't be denied and he put an arm around her waist and kissed her warm cheek. Then he turned quickly away before she recognized that the gesture was more than friendship and was embarrassed.

Babs arrived at that moment and she winked at her brother, who pushed her shoulder playfully. "Just a reward for doing well," he joked.

"Reward? A kiss from a bloke like you?" she teased.

The incident had unsettled him, but Seranne appeared not to have been affected. They had often hugged and an occasional kiss on the cheek was no great deal, and no reason for her to think anything had changed.

During the hours Alun wasn't needed at the hotel, he continued to explore. To fill what would have been lonely hours in his room, he walked around the villages and beaches of the Gower peninsular. Neither rain nor storms kept him in and with heavy waterproofs and a small rucksack, he explored all the roads and narrow tracks with the aid of a map until he felt he knew every corner, together with the legends and folk lore attached to them. At every new discovery he imagined walking it again with Betty, having her beside him to share the beautiful scenery would have made every step a joy.

He wanted to go back to Cwm Derw, but the longer he waited, the harder it became. He no longer imagined the way her face would light up as he stepped through the door, now he thought of walking in and finding someone else behind the bar, working beside her, laughing, his sojourn at the Ship and Compass forgotten.

Other faces passed through his mind and he wondered whether Luke and Seranne were together as he had once predicted. It was as he was thinking about Seranne and Luke that he saw Luke, and he was startled, as though he had willed him into existence out of his unconscious. "Luke," he called and as he waved, Luke saw him and ran across.

"Alun! So this is where you live? What good luck meeting you, now you can give me your address. Betty would like to know where you are, and Jake would too."

"I found a job in a hotel as I told you." He gestured behind him to where the sign read, "Sea View".

"Better than the Ship and Compass?"

"Not at all. The customers here are transient, few staying more than a week, many passing through on their way to somewhere else. At the Ship, Betty's customers are friends."

"You should have stayed. She's managing with a woman helping at the moment, Tilly Tucker. Hard on them sometimes with the heavy lifting and moving about they have to do." He stared at Alun and said, "Why don't you come and see us all?"

Alun nodded but didn't answer. They walked a little way along the road that skirted the six miles of Swansea Bay, then Alun asked why Luke was there. Taking a chance, Luke told him about his concern for Seranne's mother. "I'm going to see the wholesalers to find out why Paul no longer deals with them. Want to come?" He had an idea that getting Alun involved might be an obtuse way of getting him to return to Cwm Derw — at least for a visit and he had a suspicion that was what both Alun and Betty wanted. If he was wrong then there'd be no harm done.

The wholesalers selling equipment and ingredients to bakery businesses was not far from Swansea and the owner was willing to discuss his ex-customer. "Yes, Jessie Laurence. Married that Paul Curtis, didn't she? More fool her! She was a customer of ours, not big but she always liked the very best. As for why Jessie decided to deal with someone else, perhaps you'd better ask her that."

"Did you have a disagreement?" Luke asked.

Mr Green shrugged. "Not with Jessie, although I suppose you could call it that."

"You can't explain?"

Alun said, "Why don't you tell Mr Green exactly why we're here, Luke? If he knows the situation and how worried you are, he might be more helpful."

"The truth is, Mr Green, we think Jessica is no longer in charge. Her husband seems to have taken over and he's running the place into the ground."

"Why are you involved? What business is it of yours? I shouldn't discuss private business with a stranger. Not without good cause."

"I haven't any right to make these enquiries, but I care for Jessie's daughter and I'm trying to find out what's wrong so I can help."

The man hesitated for a moment, staring at Luke as though summing him up. Then he shrugged again and said, "The truth is, they haven't paid their account for months and Jessie always paid our monthly statement by return post. They ordered new equipment now it's becoming available, a new sink, a larger fridge, lighting, and they increased their regular order. Now they owe us a lot of money. There seems no prospect of us being paid, so we cancelled all further orders and have put the debt in the hands of our solicitor." He took out a few sheets of paper listing what had been supplied.

"He's probably sold the new equipment you supplied," Luke muttered angrily. "Apart from the sink, there's no sign of any of it in the kitchen. Thank you for being honest with us. I suspected something of the sort. Jessie's new husband has let the business slide and until now she hasn't seemed aware, or perhaps she doesn't care."

"I find that hard to believe. I'd have trusted Jessie with anything. Until these past months she was as reliable as anyone could wish. So what happened?"

"Paul Curtis 'happened'!" Luke said. "The real question is, what can we do about it?"

Luke and Alun went into a pub and ordered beers and sandwiches. They sat in silence, each mulling over the situation but neither coming up with an idea.

"The problem is whether Seranne would thank us for trying to help or accuse us of interfering," Luke said, and added, "Quick to lose her temper is Seranne."

"She must realize that things are seriously wrong."

"Yes, but facing problems is never easy. I think we're all inclined to hide our heads in the sand and hope the problem will go away."

"I'll come with you to confront Paul if you think it will help," Alun offered. "The first move seems to be to ask him what's happening."

Luke had an important meeting that afternoon but they arranged to meet the following day and drive to the tea rooms to talk to both Jessie and Paul. As they drove there, they planned their approach.

"I'll appear sympathetic and anxious to help," Luke said.

"And I'll stand watching, saying very little but obviously disapproving. They might think I'm a policeman," he added with a smile. "Paul has seen me before but no one really notices a barman."

It was mid-morning, Alun having managed a day off, and on their way they detoured and looked at Paul's empty shop — his "new enterprise". The windows had been partially whitewashed to discourage people from looking inside but through the carelessly applied screen they could see boxes of goods stacked at the back. There was no sign of Paul.

When they reached the tea rooms, to their surprise the place was closed. In fact, with the neglected appearance, it looked as though it had been abandoned. Luke knocked on the side door and when there was no reply, Alun banged harder. Eventually the door opened to reveal Jessie, still in her dressing-gown, her hair bedraggled, her face filled with fear.

"It's all right, Mrs Curtis — Jessie," Luke said. "I was passing and thought I'd call and say hello."

"Is Mr Curtis in?" Alun demanded, trying to sound authoritative.

"No, he's out on business." A nervous tic pulsed rhythmically in Jessie's cheek.

"May we come in?" Luke asked, moving towards her slightly, forcing her to step back. He waited for her to move upstairs and he and Alun followed.

"Why is the tea rooms closed?" Luke asked. "Aren't you well? Perhaps you should have stayed in hospital for a day or so." When there was no reply he asked, "Mrs Sewell, is she ill perhaps?"

Jessie cleared some dishes from the small table and took three clean cups and saucers from the dresser. "I'll make us a cup of tea, shall I?"

"Where's Mrs Sewell? Isn't she coming in today?" Luke persisted.

"She's gone with Paul. There's another business venture they're pursuing."

"I see. So you'll soon be running the tea rooms again? What a good idea, you managed the business so well."

"I don't know. I've lost interest in it to be truthful. I worked there for too long. It's time for a change."

An hour and two cups of tea later there was still no sign of Paul. Luke glanced at his watch and said, "Jessie, why don't you come back with us and see Seranne? She'd be so pleased to show you what she and Babs have achieved. I think she's amazingly clever but she insists it's all due to your teaching."

For a moment they thought she would agree but then she frowned and said, "Paul will be worried if I'm not here."

"Of course he won't. You can leave a note, and we won't be away very long. We'll bring you back once you and Seranne have had a chat. She misses you so much and would love to see you."

They were hopeful as Jessie went to get ready, and Luke took the opportunity to look around while she washed, dressed and combed her hair. On a sideboard there was a box labelled, "Seranne's Post", but apart from a library book reminder, it was empty.

Several drawers were stuffed with papers and in the time they had, they found a large number of outstanding accounts and reminders of unpaid bills, including those for electricity and gas and those from Green and Sons. A warning from Alun and they returned to their seats as the door opened and Jessie came in.

They were outside, getting into the car when another car drew up and an angry Paul stepped out. "What are you doing? Where are you taking her?" he demanded.

"Sorry, darling, but I'm going to see my daughter."

"Not now, Jessie. I need you here, there's something I need to discuss. I'll take you at the weekend, all right? You only had to ask me and I'd have arranged it, you must know that. Anything you want, you only have to ask me, darling."

"No, Paul," Luke said firmly. "It's all arranged. We'll have Jessie back before teatime." He put an arm around Jessie's shoulders and ushered her towards the car, where Alun held the door open. At the very last moment, with her hand on the open door she stopped, turned around and went back into the flat.

"Thank you for the offer, Luke," Jessie said. "You're so kind. But I'll come at the weekend with Paul. Give Seranne my love, will you?"

"Come on, Jessie, better you tell her yourself," Luke said in a final attempt, but Jessie smiled and put an arm through Paul's, leaned her head against his shoulder and they stood and waved as Luke and Alun drove away.

Determined to achieve at least one of his objectives, Luke drove straight to the Ship and opened the car door for Alun to get out.

"I don't think this is such a good idea, Luke. Betty might be embarrassed, thinking I'm hoping for my job back."

"If you're still worrying about her brother, look over there." Sitting in the spring sunshine, reading a newspaper, Alun recognized Ed Connors. Ed looked up and waved, then went back to studying the day's happenings.

Slowly, as though walking towards some dread punishment, Alun walked into the Ship and immediately looked at the bar. He was relieved when Betty was nowhere to be seen. He needed to take this in stages. Tilly Tucker was serving Bob Jennings and, in a corner near the open fire, a couple of the regulars were playing dominoes. Under the window on one of the old benches that had begun life in a church, a burst of laughter made him turn.

Jake was there, dressed in old corduroys and a cowboy-style shirt. "Here he is at last, and don't think we've forgotten it's your round," he called. Then he stood up and went to the door to Betty's living-room and shouted, "Come and see who's here, Betty."

Alun stared at the doorway smiling, his heart pounding, longing to see her but afraid the joy on his face wouldn't be reflected in hers. The doorway remained empty and he began to think she was refusing to see him. Then a voice behind him said. "Alun! What a lovely surprise." He swivelled around and standing at the entrance was Betty. Without thinking, he ran the few steps towards her and hugged her. The regulars cheered and he began to apologize for embarrassing her.

She held him close. "Never mind this lot, they never grew up," she said loudly. "Are you hungry? Will a sandwich do? Tilly, get these two a drink on the house, will you? Come and tell us your news. I've heard of you from time to time from Jake and Luke, but —" She laughed then, covering her face with her hands. "Gosh I'm gabbling aren't I!"

"Make him wait, we need sustenance over here," a domino player complained and Alun waved at them. "Always were the impatient one, Roy Johnson! And watch that Waldo, he's trying to look at your hand!"

Time passed in handshakes and the exchange of news. For Alun, it was an enormous pleasure reviving friendships and there was no doubt about his welcome. Between sharing parts of conversations and helping Tilly behind the bar, he and Betty exchanged glances their eyes glowing with undisguised happiness. They managed only half spoken sentences between interruptions as newcomers came in and saw him and welcomes began all over again.

261

It wasn't until the place closed that Betty and Alun were able to talk properly and even then their words were stilted by the presence of first Tilly, then Luke.

"Look, why don't we leave now and let Betty get on with her chores? We can come back on Sunday." It was eventually agreed that Alun would stay and help clear up while Luke drove Tilly home, then returned for him.

Betty and Alun dealt with most of the work in their efficient way while they talked. Then, as they passed each other in the confines of the bar, they stopped, threw down the things they were carrying and met in the kiss they both longed for.

When Alun left with Luke, promising to return on Sunday, they parted with the sensation that the miles were tearing them apart.

"Of course, if you really don't want to go on Sunday, I can make your excuses for you," Luke teased.

"Nothing will stop me now."

"Good. Now there's only Seranne's mother to sort out."

Talking to Seranne was always going to be difficult, Luke knew that. He also knew it was something he had to do. He would be at a business meeting in Newport the following day and wouldn't have a chance to see her, but Saturday was a possibility. He'd be back by the evening and she wouldn't refuse an invitation to go to the Ship and see Alun on Sunday.

Jessie knew Paul was upset. He didn't say anything, but he implied by his ultra-reasonable, tolerant manner that he was hurt. She tried to please him, preparing a good

262

meal, asking interested questions about his afternoon, and about the business plans. Flattering him about his foresight in changing from the tea rooms to something more forward looking.

"Seranne doesn't understand, she's never wanted anything other than the business she's always known," she said.

"So is that why she sends Luke snooping into my business and pretends it's out of concern for you?"

"Don't be angry, Paul."

"Darling, I'm not angry. Just disappointed that you'd go off knowing I'd be home longing to talk to you about all that happened. I've got my plans approved and you weren't going to be here waiting to hear about it."

"I'm here now, darling."

He turned then and hugged her and Jessie felt relief, but not quite as comfortably as usual. Why did she have to stay behind to wait, while Pat Sewell went with him to set up this new business? She loved Paul but the rosy glow didn't shine quite so brightly any more. She hoped Paul would take her to see Seranne on Sunday. Although it would be impossible to talk properly with Paul there. Perhaps she could persuade Paul that she needed to stay at Badgers Brook. With an aching heart she knew it was time to face up to a few things, and talking to Seranne would be the start.

CHAPTER
TEN

Alun gave notice at the hotel where he had been working since leaving the Ship and at the end of the week he moved back to Cwm Derw. He unpacked his few belongings in the room he had used before and went down to begin the evening shift, fitting into the routine as though he had never left. Friends greeted him with delight, at once beginning to argue about which darts team he would play for and insisted he owed them all a pint.

The situation with Betty was not as easy to solve. She was happy, he knew that but he was cautious not to rush things, he dared not presume that her obvious delight was something more. Their kiss was something he had regretted and the result was a lack of certainty.

Betty sensed his hesitation and, afraid of driving him away again, acted as though it hadn't happened, so although they worked together in harmony and shared meals, plus the occasional walk in their free moments, there was no sign of him wanting anything more.

The coronation street party was a welcome distraction. Everyone was involved and, as it would take place outside the Ship, Betty and Alun more so than most. The shed and garage were used to store the furniture as it arrived and Alun stacked everything so it would come out in the correct order. Food was on the kitchen table and the yard scrubbed in readiness.

"There'll soon be no room for you and me," Alun said. "We'll be sleeping on a park bench. Or Stella's country cottage!" He was smiling happily, glad to be involved once more in the community.

Fortunately the day dawned brightly and it looked set fair for a good day. People began arriving very early, lorries with chairs and trestle tables, women carrying tablecloths and decorations. They already wore dresses or aprons of red, white and blue. Piles of hats were placed on the bar-room tables and flags sprouted from every available point.

When the children began to arrive, shiny faced and dressed for the occasion, the union flag and hats were handed out to those who didn't have one and when Betty looked down from the bedroom window, she called Alun. "It's like a sea of colour," she said. The flags waved from corners and roof tops and lampposts. The red, white and blue hats bobbed in ever changing patterns as people moved the chairs into place and children chased each other round. The tables were dressed with plates of food and decorated with swirling wands of crinkly paper strips that were caught in the slight breeze.

"I wish everyone could stay this happy," Alun said, putting his arm on her shoulder.

"What is it? Is something worrying you?"

"Not a thing, I just feel so content I'm afraid something will happen to change it."

"Nothing will. There's no one here who wishes you harm, Alun. This is your home — at least, for as long as you want it." Afraid to say more she moved slightly away from his touch.

"Oh, I want it. I can't think of any place I'd rather be." His hand tightened on her shoulder and he was gone.

The children ate first, with Mrs Williamson-Murton armed with a handful of lists, marching up and down criticizing table manners, then it was time for the entertainment. There was cricket with Bob and Colin, and dancing with Hope and a teacher from the school, rides on Peter Bevan's horse, assisted by Hope and Peter's nine-year-old, Davie. Hope's ex-mother-in-law Marjorie marched around checking lists and appearing to be in charge. When some of the younger children began to leave she called them all to attention and handed out to each of them a china coronation mug, ticking their names off one of her lists. Then the adults took their places at the now untidy tables.

Ed sat on a bench within sight, but made no move to join in. Betty went over once to invite him but he shook his head. "I know when I'm not wanted," he grumbled.

Refusing to get involved in an argument, Betty said, "Please yourself," and walked away.

Seranne and Babs served teas and ate when they could, Seranne becoming exasperated by Tony appearing every time she turned around.

"My brother's smitten it seems," Babs teased.

"Will someone tell him I'm not? Please?" Seranne replied. "I'll trip over him in a minute!"

"Go on, give him a chance, I've always wanted a sister!"

Seranne looked up each time a car passed, hoping to see her mother. She had telephoned one final time and tried to persuade her to come but Jessie insisted she and Paul were too busy.

Dancing went on until late, the chairs outside becoming an extention of the bar, where Betty, Alun and Tilly were kept busy until closing time.

Tony appeared and touched Seranne's shoulder. "It's late. I'd better walk you home."

Desperate to think of an excuse, she was hardly aware of a car stopping at the kerb. Babs pointed to it and said, sotto voce, "Saved by the handsome stranger?"

"Hello Luke, you've missed the fun," she said, walking towards him.

"I've been to see your mother, as I was passing the area, in a vain attempt to persuade her to come," he said. He looked tired in the light from the street and the distorting coloured bulbs spread around the area added deep shadows. "I've just come back from Ireland," he explained as though reading her thoughts. "A business is starting up to make a new range of carpeting."

"There's some food left." She gestured towards the open door of the Ship, but he shook his head.

"I'll say hello to Betty and Alun then I'll drive you home, if you're ready to leave."

Mouthing a "sorry" to Tony and Babs, she collected her belongings and went with him to the car. She could see he was exhausted and he walked her to the door, telling her he wanted to hear about the party when he'd had some sleep. There were a few boxes she'd left in the car and he brought them in, sat down and was immediately asleep. She covered him with a blanket and sat looking at him for several minutes, unsure what to do.

The door opened and Kitty and Bob came in. They were hushed by Seranne, and tiptoed in to see Luke sprawled on the couch fast asleep.

"What can I do?" She gestured puzzlement with arms and hands spread wide.

Bob said, "I don't think he'll wake, and he's certainly not able to drive anywhere. Just leave him. Go to bed and I'll pop in later on to see that he's all right."

It was strange expecting to sleep with Luke in the house and she lay on her bed, fully dressed, determined to stay awake, but the long and busy day was too much and she slept.

The following morning she went down to see Luke sitting in the garden nursing a cup of tea, and Bob beside him, both talking in low whispers. She brushed aside his apologies and began preparing breakfast for the three of them. What a peculiar end to the coronation party, she mused, happiness lightening up her face.

Badgers Brook was rarely empty, but one evening the house was silent, and outside the only sound was birdsong and the soft rhythmic movement of spades turning soil. Colin and Bob were at the end of the garden digging an area where they planned to plant blackcurrant bushes in the autumn. There were already raspberry canes, a bed of strawberries and a few gooseberry bushes, and the addition was at the request of Seranne.

"I wonder whether she'll be here for the first fruit," Bob said, looking back to where Seranne sat studying a book on garden birds. "People rarely stay long."

"They bring their troubles and move on once they have sorted them," Colin agreed, "but Seranne's troubles aren't her own. It's her mother who has the problems according to Luke and Alun, and the house can't sort out people if they aren't here."

"D'you really believe the house helps?"

"I don't know how, but it seems to. It allows thoughts to settle, puzzles to untangle themselves. A bit like our country cottage, according to Stella. She believes that if a place makes people happy, then usually that's all they need to get their life in order."

"So how do we persuade Seranne's mother to visit your country cottage or Badgers Brook?"

"The usual way is to invite a few people around. Hey, Seranne," Colin called, waving an arm. "Isn't it time you had a few friends round? I'm inviting myself and our Stella, and Bob here will bring Kitty."

"Your mother hasn't seen your café," Bob added. "Why don't you invite her? She must want to see what you've done."

"She probably won't come, but I'd love to have friends here for lunch. Sunday lunch, so Betty and Alun can come, and Babs and Tony. But where will the food come from? A shilling's worth of meat won't make a roast."

"No need for anything formal," Bob said.

"We'll all bring what we can," Kitty said when Seranne mentioned it. "Just ask a few friends and the house will do the rest. You'll have a day to remember."

"Baked potatoes are easy," Colin suggested. "We could have a bonfire and bake them outside."

"Just make sure your mother comes," Stella said, when she was included in the plan. "She won't refuse an invitation to meet your friends."

Seranne shrugged sadly. "She probably will. She wouldn't come to our coronation party."

"She's got one of those television sets, hasn't she? It must be hard to leave home and miss something, but the novelty might have worn off by now. Ask her, tell her it's a celebration of yours and Babs's success. She won't refuse that."

Luke offered to drive up and explain about the planned Sunday lunch. "Better than phoning or writing a letter," he said. "Face to face she'd find it harder to refuse. I'll offer to go and fetch her, another reason not to say no. Whether Paul comes is up to him, but I think we must make sure your mother is here."

The thought of inviting her mother made Seranne uneasy. Partly because she was afraid of a refusal and she also feared that if Paul came, she wouldn't be able to talk to her. "I hope she comes on her own," she admitted to Luke, "but I can hardly tell her that."

Silently Luke suspected that Paul would use the free time to meet Pat Sewell; knowing each other for years didn't exclude the possibility of romance. He wondered if he could manage to follow them when they next went

270

out but realized it would be difficult, not knowing when or where. He could hardly sit and watch the place for hours each day in the hope of seeing them set off.

"Come on, Seranne, it's a wonderful garden and such a happy place. She'll come and she'll love this place," Kitty said, and the enthusiasm was so great, Seranne was laughing, swept up in the excitement of her mother's long-awaited visit.

Betty offered sandwiches and piles of Welsh cakes, the flat, spicy kind cooked on a griddle. Tony would supply bread rolls and Alun, a huge pot of soup.

Betty and Alun were both looking forward to the event. Each hoping that the day together would somehow cement their relationship. They were both so unsure, each afraid to admit their feelings for fear of embarrassing the other. The warmth that had begun when Alun first arrived at the Ship and Compass had never faded, only lack of confidence prevented it from flowering into love.

Luke was on his way to Machynllleth and he detoured by a few miles and called at Jessie's tea rooms. Fortunately Paul was out and he passed on Seranne's invitation, urging Jessie not to disappoint her daughter. "Paul as well, of course," he said. "But if he can't manage it, you must come without him. Seranne needs you there. She's longing to show you the café. She's worked so hard and is so proud of what she and Babs have achieved. All that's lacking is your admiration." He looked at Jessie, who was frowning. It was obvious from her expression that she was trying to make an excuse.

"I'm not sure, Paul is so busy, you see and . . ."

"She misses you," he said softly, "and she longs to show you her home and introduce you to her new friends." Without giving her a chance to say no, he went on, "So I'll call for you at ten o'clock. If Paul comes that's fine, but if he doesn't, bring a few things in case you decide to stay overnight. You'll love Badgers Brook."

"I'll try." She forced a smile.

"It's your daughter's day, a celebration of what she's achieved. You must be there."

Jessie promised, but Luke knew there was doubt in her mind. "Badgers Brook is such a special place," he coaxed.

"I have seen it, when Seranne moved in. It's only an old house, hardly special."

"Visit, stay a while and you'll realize it's magical."

He left convinced he had failed to persuade her. She would only come if Paul agreed. How had the brave, confident woman he'd learnt about from Seranne, changed to this nervous person lacking in self-esteem? He mused over the many aspects of love, which made his thoughts fly to Seranne. What he felt for her was love, but taking a chance on his feelings was difficult after his previous humiliation. Besides, he wasn't free from Marion, even after all that had happened.

Jessie told Paul about the lunch invitation when he returned, and waited for his response. To her delight he smiled, hugged her and said at once that they must go. "Your daughter wants you to see her and praise her success. Of course we'll go, darling."

"I know it's a Sunday," she said, "but I was afraid you'd be too busy. I can go on my own if you aren't free but I'd love for us both to go. Seranne would be so pleased."

"Of course I'll come. How would you get there if I didn't take you? You've given up on driving, haven't you?"

He spoke in a teasing voice but she felt a stab of dismay. Driving was just one of the things she no longer had confidence for. "Why do I need to drive, darling? I don't want to go anywhere without you."

"I feel the same, but I have to go out on business and you'd find it boring, so I go on my own and get back to you as fast as I can. Shall we eat out this evening, or will you cook?"

"I'll cook," she said at once. An evening at home was the most she saw of him since this new business venture began to take up so much of his time. She telephoned her daughter at the café and told her she would be there.

Seranne was disappointed to be told Paul would also be coming, but she only said, "Don't forget Luke will bring you if Paul can't make it. Or Tony or Babs will come, there are plenty of people who will help, they all want to see you."

"And Paul?"

"Of course. We want you both there. Oh, I'm so pleased that you'll be meeting my friends at last. I'm looking forward to it so much."

"So am I, darling. So am I."

Luke sat in his sports car at the end of the road wondering about Jessie's gradual lack of interest in the once successful café. The windows had been half-heartedly cleaned. The sills and the swinging sign were in serious need of paint and from what he had seen of the inside, nothing much had changed there, either. The place had lost its heart.

The business was completely gone and he wondered how much longer they would manage without any money coming in. Paul didn't appear to have a job and the business he referred to was a mystery. The shop he was renting was empty apart from a few unpacked boxes and there was no indication of the catering supplies Paul had envisaged.

He turned his head sharply when he saw Paul emerge from the side door and stride off around the corner where he usually parked his car. Fortunately Luke's car was facing the correct way and he switched on the engine and moved slowly towards the corner. As Paul's car nosed out of the side road he snatched up his trilby and clamped it on his head to hide his face, hoping Paul didn't recognize the car, although an MG didn't exactly fade into the background.

He followed Paul, cautiously allowing a lorry to come between them once and stopping for a motorcyclist at a junction. Each time he caught up easily and was within sight when Paul parked outside a small terraced house at the edge of the town. The door opened and Pat Sewell ran out and joined Paul, who then drove away, Luke following.

Fortunately Luke was able to stop near them when they parked and he sat watching them, waiting a few moments before shutting off the engine. For an hour he sat there and all they seemed to do was talk. Once or twice their heads came close together but if it was a sign of affection, it was short-lived. When he heard the engine start, he glanced across and saw them hug for a long moment, then the car turned and went past the layby in which Luke had parked. Shadowed by his trilby, he saw their faces clearly and they were laughing happily.

After dropping Pat back at the terraced house and waving as he drove away, Paul went back to the flat above the abandoned tea rooms. Watching them had made Luke late for his appointment and he stopped at a phone box to rearrange it. He was dissatisfied with his morning. He was no further ahead with his determination to find out what Paul was up to. That he and Pat were more than employer and employee was obvious, but how much more?

As Sunday drew near Jessie looked in her wardrobe wondering what to wear. She chose a summer suit in pale green with a cream blouse. Not exciting but if the weather was warm it would be suitable for an afternoon in the garden, and it was one of Paul's favourites. She was curious about the house her daughter now called home. Badgers Brook sounded countrified and she knew it was on a lane, but visualizing it was impossible even though she had paid a brief visit when Seranne had first moved in. "It can't be very grand," she said to

275

Paul. "When she rented it she was working in a café, she wouldn't have been able to afford much. It's probably a small and shabby cottage. We can take some flowers to brighten it up."

Paul agreed. "And a bottle or two, there won't be much to drink either."

"Perhaps I could make some scones. I was rather good at scones."

"She won't need your scones! She has a café, hasn't she? She'll make them herself."

"Of course she will, and they'll probably be better than mine."

Paul smiled, but she waited in vain for him to disagree.

It wasn't until Saturday afternoon that Paul told her he wouldn't be coming. She hid her disappointment well; she had been half expecting it. "Won't you be able to come if we planned to go later?" she suggested. "The invitation's for lunch, but we don't have to arrive early. According to Seranne, no one will be in a hurry to leave."

"I'll try, Jessie, I'll really try. I know how important it is for you. Look, why don't you go on your own? Didn't you say Seranne suggested you might like to stay overnight? It will be good for you to talk to her, meet her new friends."

"Luke did offer to come for me," she said.

"Perfect. I'll miss you, darling, I'll hate being here on my own, but she's your daughter and you need to see her, I understand that."

"You wouldn't mind?"

"Of course I wouldn't mind. Go and enjoy yourself." He looked serious as he added, "You won't discuss this new business of mine, will you? I don't want someone getting there first. Or our plans for reopening your tea rooms in a modern style. That's our secret."

"Of course not, dear. I'll leave food for you," she added, brightening as the idea grew. "And I won't stay. I'll be back before evening."

"No, dear, you must stay. Seranne will be at work on Monday so you can see how she manages her café. She'll be glad of some of your expert advice." He looked at her glowing eyes, the smile opening on her pretty face. "No later than mid-afternoon on Monday though, I couldn't bear to face a second evening without you," he added softly.

"How will I get back, the buses aren't plentiful?"

"Didn't you say Luke offered to take you and bring you back?"

She nodded, disappointed that he hadn't offered to bring her back himself. It wasn't that far. But he was very busy and she was being silly to expect him to spoil her like a child.

"Have we anything to take to Seranne?" she asked. "She said something about a letter which you couldn't find."

"I can't remember where it is. Probably unimportant and was thrown away. What about offering her some of your unwanted china? Now you're having a rest from the tea rooms it's filling the cupboards and making it difficult to sort out what we need to keep. When you reopen we'll have a fresh start with everything new. Mid-winter has some beautiful modern designs, and there are some lovely pieces coming in from places like

Czechoslovakia. We'll look into it as soon as I have my enterprise up and running. I have great plans, darling and one day I'll make you really proud of me."

"I always liked the rose-patterned china."

"Yes, and so do I, but we have to think modern and the smart new angular designs are what people will expect. Old-fashioned tea rooms are out of date."

"Being old-fashioned was its appeal."

"Not any more, dear. Trust me, I know what people want. This is the fifties, we're in the second Elizabethan age now, Queen Elizabeth is on the throne and we have to move on." He looked at the green suit spread on the bed. "You aren't wearing that, are you, dear? It's a country cottage, and you don't want to look overdressed, do you?"

In a rare act of defiance, Jessie smiled and said, "I'll take a chance. I doubt whether Seranne's friends will wear tweed and gumboots! I'll take a skirt and jumper in case you're right, but I always have a happy time when I wear this suit, so it's what I've chosen."

When he left, he walked back into the living-room and hugged her. "Jessie, darling, I love you. Always remember that."

She was puzzled by the seriousness of his expression as he left to hurry down the stairs and out to the car. He often told her he loved her, but there was underlying tension this time and it alarmed her. Perhaps she ought not to go to Cwm Derw. Then she reminded herself that he would probably be out for most of the day and the unease faded.

278

★ ★ ★

Ed had received an invitation to the Sunday lunch at Badgers Brook but he didn't think he'd go. Since the news about his wife leaving the property to an unknown niece became known, he felt as though everyone was laughing at him. The implications were that he had married Elsie in the hope of an inheritance, but the truth was that he had loved her. Even learning about her illness hadn't changed that. He had been shocked to learn of her growing helplessness but he had cared for her and had been happy doing so. So how could she have left the valuable business to someone he hadn't even heard of? Facing people and being aware of the expression of amusement on their faces while pretending to enjoy a friendly lunch was not possible. Besides, his sister would be there and she wasn't much better than Elsie, refusing to give him his job and home back.

Tilly came out of the Ship after the lunchtime session and saw him sitting on a bench reading a paper. She waved before walking across and sitting beside him. "You're Betty's brother, aren't you?"

"I am. And you're the barmaid who took my job."

"Oh dear, we are in a mood. I didn't take your job. It was offered long after Betty had told you to leave. She said you weren't doing your share. Right, was she?"

"I had just lost my wife."

"So you *weren't* doing your share. Grief is genuine, but it can only be used as an excuse for a while, then you have to get back on the treadmill and carry on."

"You've got plenty to say for yourself!"

"Want to hear some more?"

"No, I don't!"

"I know your wife left the guest house to a niece and the solicitor's looking for her."

"And I hope they never find her, right?" He was angry but Tilly appeared not to notice.

"Will the property revert to you then? If she can't be found?"

"Not according to the solicitor."

"Be glad to get it sorted though, so you can get on with your life. Best to know, eh?"

"Go away. What's this got to do with you?"

Tilly patted his shoulder and in a whining voice said, "Poor you, woe and self-pity personified. Not a pretty sight."

"What's it got to do with you?" he repeated angrily.

"Oh, I might be able to help. You never know, so it's best to be polite to strangers."

"What a misery he is, that brother of yours," she said to Betty later. "The fact is, I have an idea where this Mary Anne Crisp can be found, or at least where the solicitor might start enquiries."

"Then go and see Mark Lacy, get it cleared up for goodness sake," Betty said with a sigh. "Then perhaps Ed'll stop feeling sorry for himself. He's been looked after all his life. First by Mum, then by me and now he expects the same again!"

"The truth is, the girl might not be called Crisp at all. Elsie's sister, who was ten years older than her, never actually married Davie Crisp. She lived with the man, had his children but she remained Mary Anne Jones. The three children she had — a son and two

280

daughters — are all dead, but the son married and had a daughter, and named her after his mother, so she's the likely one to inherit. Better to make a few more enquiries before telling Ed, though. If I find her and she kicks him out, his chin will be down to his knees for the rest of his life."

On her day off Tilly went to see Mark Lacy and told him her thoughts about the girl they were trying to find.

"I have found a Crisp, but there's no record of a marriage and therefore, no issue. Searching for a family called Jones won't be easy, and we have no idea where Mary Anne comes into it, but at least we have a name and an area and an approximation of the date. Thank you, Mrs Tucker. I am most grateful."

Tilly went home feeling pleased with herself. Memory is a funny thing, she mused. So many things forgotten, drifting in and out of her head, but a conversation heard in whispers as she hid behind the couch, as her mother told a friend the guilty secret of a woman called Mrs Crisp who had a man and children but hadn't been "churched", had remained in her mind as clear as clear. Gossip might be wicked, but it was certainly more entertaining than some sermons, she admitted to herself cheerfully.

The weather was perfect for the Sunday lunch. Seranne woke before six and went outside still in her dressing-gown to drink her first cup of tea. The birdsong had woken her and from the trees and hedges around the garden they put on their finest performance.

The tranquil start to the day was spoilt when she began to wonder whether her mother would come. Luke had promised to bring her and she hoped they arrived early so there would be a chance to talk to her. There were many worries that she needed to discuss and once the rest of her guests arrived there'd be little chance of finding a private moment.

Bob and Colin came before nine o'clock and brought tables and chairs, borrowed from various people, and set them up on the lawn. Kitty came soon after with her contribution of food. Kitty was quickly followed by Betty and Stella, both arriving in the car with Alun, with boxes of food and sheets for tablecloths. Bunting was spread around the trees, with no real excuse apart from wanting Jessie to feel welcome. Everyone disappeared then, to return later as guests.

Sitting in the garden Seranne began planning what she would say to Jessie, how she would approach the subject of Paul and the abandonment of the tea rooms that had been in the family for three generations. It had fallen apart since the arrival of Paul. She had to make her mother see what he had done. Jessie's personality had undergone a change that was alarming, but how could she persuade her mother that it was due to Paul's influence without alienating her mother completely?

Then something happened to make her change her attitude towards both her mother and Paul. The worries in her mind, like snarled-up tangles of wool, seemed to unwind and everything became clear. He was her mother's choice and she was happy with him, happier than she had been running the business alone.

282

Looking around the garden, she was conscious of a lifting of her spirits. A robin searched the newly turned soil looking for worms, a blackbird sang from an apple tree, the day was calm and a peace settled around her. The magical place had set the mood for a perfect day. Why should she put herself up as judge, and try to persuade Jessie her life was in a mess? She no longer believed she should try. Paul was her mother's choice and if she no longer wanted to run the tea rooms, and instead devote herself to him, then the decision was hers. The house settled, making small sounds that calmed her even more and she felt the comfort and peace of the house settling around her as though it approved.

Luke arrived with Jessie soon afterwards and he didn't knock on the door but took her straight around to the garden. She ran to hug her daughter then stared around her in delight. "What a wonderful place you've found. A piece of heaven!" she said, staring at the beautiful old house, its windows glittering in the sun. She turned to look at the garden. "It's so peaceful!"

"Sometimes, if you're very quiet, you can hear the stream, it isn't far away, just across the lane and after rain it chuckles past quite delightfully," Luke said, giving Seranne a hug as she mouthed "thank you".

He went to talk to Bob and Colin who were first to arrive, and stood watching Seranne as she greeted the guests. She introduced her mother to them all and once Babs appeared, they left Jessie to mingle as they began to set out the food. Luke had disappeared but for an hour she was too busy to wonder where he had gone.

The low murmur of conversation interspersed with bursts of laughter was like music and she could see that her mother was enjoying the occasion, chatting with ease and making new friends.

It was as the first of the friends were leaving that Seranne asked if anyone had seen Luke.

"I think he said something about an appointment," Jessie said. "I was so excited about coming here I'm afraid I didn't listen properly."

"I expect he'll be back soon. He's taking you back home isn't he?"

"Not yet, dear. Can we go and see your café? The Wayfaring Tree, what a lovely name."

Leaving Betty and Alun sitting in the garden, they borrowed bicycles from Kitty and Bob and rode to the high street, enjoying the warmth of the late afternoon. For Jessie the first sight of The Wayfaring Tree was a shock as great as falling into icy water. She stared at the small premises and saw reflected a simpler version of the place she had allowed to fall into ruin. Seranne and Babs had chosen to copy the display of pretty plates on a shelf around the room — most of which she recognized as coming from her own tea rooms. The curtains were a charming floral design and the tables were covered with the same material. White china and white painted chairs were a delightful contrast. She thought of the once popular place she had owned and despair almost made her cry out in pain.

She had been obsessed with Paul, she had been blind to her own stupidity. And for what? A man who failed with his own business and would probably fail again.

284

His promises of helping her to start again were a nonsense. He had probably used most of her money in this latest project and she would have nothing left but an empty room.

Why had she allowed herself to be so manipulated that she ignored what he was doing? She had watched in silence as he had sold all her beautiful things with the promise of new, modern replacements. She had known she was making mistake after mistake, but had refused to accept what her mind was telling her. It was like coming out of a dark room into the painful agony of bright light. Aloud she said, "I've been so stupid."

"What did you say, Mum? Sorry I was putting some plates into the cupboard and I didn't hear."

"Nothing, dear. I'm just admiring what you and Babs have achieved. I'll have to persuade Paul to hurry up with our refurbishment. I can't have you leaving me so far behind, can I?"

After a tour of the small premises and a discussion on future plans, they rode back through the sleepy summer lanes and Jessie was silent. Seranne hoped the peace of the place was soothing her, unaware of the anger hidden behind her mother's serene expression.

Seranne's intention to talk about Paul and the neglect of the business had completely faded. It was such a perfect day and Jessie hadn't mentioned Paul at all. Until her mother wanted to discuss him, her stepfather was not a problem for her to wonder over. The thought was comforting.

When they returned to the garden there was still no sign of Luke. Bob and Jake were sitting next to Colin discussing the weather prospects for the following day, looking up at clouds, gauging the direction of the wind, arguing about the various old folks' tales good humouredly. Jessie went to sit among the others and began a conversation with Betty and Alun, holding back her anger, determined to go home and face Paul and demand a reinstatement of the tea rooms.

Luke had driven back to Jessie's tea rooms and watched as Paul moved backwards and forwards across the windows of the flat, wondering what he was doing and determined to wait until he found out. He sat in his car for an hour, wishing he was at Badgers Brook enjoying the lunch with Seranne. Another hour passed and then the side door opened and Paul came out carrying two large suitcases.

Luke stayed where he was and watched as Paul made two more appearances, each time with boxes which, from the way he handled them, appeared to be heavy. Another trip up to the flat, then he came down and stood for a few moments staring at the now full boot of the car before closing the lid and getting into the driving seat. He was obviously leaving.

Luke started his engine, his mind torn with indecision. What should he do, try to stop him? Follow him and report to Seranne? Paul moved off and, faced with no choice apart from ramming him, Luke followed.

This time he made no effort to disguise the fact he was following him and Paul increased speed when he recognized him. Luke stayed on his tail. Paul slowed down and beckoned him on, arm through the driver's window. Luke went ahead, jammed on the brake, forcing Paul to stop, and got out. Paul recovered and weaving his way around him, drove on. A car was approaching from a side road and only inches separated them. Luke put his foot down and overlook him again even though Paul moved from side to side to try and stop him. He stopped and ran back, grabbing the driver's door open and dragging Paul from the car. Paul fought him off and began to drive off again. As he edged around Luke's MG, Luke jumped in the passenger seat and leaning over, turned off the engine and pocketed the key. "Running away, are you? Having taken everything Jessie has that's worth taking?"

"What on earth do you want?" Paul demanded. "Get out and stop following me." He leant over Luke and opened the door. Luke calmly closed it again.

"Where d'you think you're going?" he asked.

"It's nothing to do with you!"

"Jessie's at Badgers Brook singing your praises. Whatever you're running to, it can't be as good as what you're planning to leave behind."

"You don't understand."

"Try me. Are you leaving Jessie for Pat Sewell?"

"Pat? Of course not. What on earth gave you that idea?"

"I followed you when you went to pick her up the other day. You were together in your car for a long time. It seems she's the one involved in this mysterious business venture when you ought to be talking to Jessie. So what else am I to think?"

Paul bent forward and buried his face in his hands, giving a low groan. "I've messed everything up, ruined it all and Jessie'll never forgive me."

"Tell me, then I'll tell *you* about Jessie."

"I've used a lot of Jessie's money, I was broke after losing my business. I sold everything I could find a buyer for, including some of the valuable china, which belonged to Jessie and Seranne. I had an idea that once I got on my feet, I could reopen the tea rooms, pay everything back. But it's all gone. The shop I planned to open to sell catering equipment has been condemned as unsafe and anyway, the agreements to stock some quality products have fallen through. The larger premises I'd been promised and the contracts to sell have both gone to someone else. I couldn't find the deposit you see. I've lost everything. What else can I do except leave? I've let her down so badly I can't face her. I love Jessie and I really believed I could make everything all right."

"And Pat?"

"Pat is a friend of many years and she's been trying to help. She lent me money too. It's all gone. All I own is an empty shop premises that needs huge amounts of work before it's habitable. How could everything go so wrong?"

"Too many irons in the fire by the sound of it. You start small and build, you don't take on so much that you can't finance it." He handed Paul's key to him. "Come back with me. Talk to Jessie. I said I'd tell you about her. Well, she's loyal, and loving and she'd rather you were there than face life without you, whatever the circumstances. Trust her — as you should have all along. She has managed a successful business all her life and she'd have helped, encouraged and supported you. Stopped you making stupid mistakes."

"It's too late."

"Trust her. Go back. I know it's what she would choose."

They turned around and drove back to the flat, Paul first, closely followed by Luke. In silence Luke helped unpack the boot and waited while Paul put everything back where it belonged. Then he said, "Come to Badgers Brook and bring Jessie home, Paul. You can tell her all that's happened and tonight you'll sleep, confident she's beside you, your partner in every way."

With the cars in convoy, they reached Badgers Brook and walked around the side of the house to the garden. By the time Jessie and Seranne had returned their borrowed cycles he had enjoyed a tour of the garden and house and was sitting drinking a beer and listening to the weather lore of Bob and Colin, while Kitty and Stella packed away the last of the food.

It was clear Jessie was not as pleased to see him as usual. She barely acknowledged his presence when he stood and walked towards her, turning to talk to the three men once introductions were completed.

"I've come to take you home, Jessie. I'm sorry I couldn't come earlier."

"There's no need, I plan to stay overnight."

"Please Jessie. Come home, there's been a bit of trouble and there's a lot I have to tell you." He was tense, having to talk with the two men sitting near pretending not to listen. Despite his pleading in a most uncharacteristic manner, Jessie was adamant. She was staying. She needed to calm down, knowing that if she talked to him now the result could be a serious breakdown in their previously loving relationship.

"Why don't you stay too, Paul?" Seranne suggested. "There's another single bed if you don't mind sleeping separately for one night." Jessie gestured her disagreement too late. Paul accepted with alacrity. This beautiful old house would be the perfect place to confess his failure and stupidity.

At eleven o'clock when the garden was dark and only an owl and a vixen, and the distant murmur of the stream disturbed the night, he stood outside with Luke, Seranne and Jessie. But without giving him a chance to say more than goodnight, Jessie was given a lighted candle and shown to her allotted room.

His own with its single bed was pointed out to him but when Jessie had gone up the stairs carrying her candle, having provided him with a torch, Paul settled on the couch near the still warm embers of the fire. He couldn't bear to sleep near Jessie without feeling her lying next to him. Yet within moments his worries eased away from him, the soft murmurings of the house as it settled were like a lullaby and he was soon deeply asleep.

Jessie couldn't rest. The calm quiet of the house had the opposite effect on her. Her thoughts clarified and she was impatient to get back to the tea rooms and start rescuing it from the neglect she had allowed to happen. She was angry with herself more than with Paul. It was her responsibility, and she had no one to blame for its demise but herself. It was up to her to return it to its former charms. She wondered how much — if anything — was left in their bank account.

At one a.m. she rose and dressed. She presumed Paul was in the small back bedroom so she was cautious as she stepped across the landing and went downstairs. She could see very little, but the fire found some unburned wood and a sudden flame revealed the figure on the couch. Holding her breath she tiptoed past, carrying her shoes.

Her jaw was tight with tension as she closed the door behind her and walked down the path to where Paul's car was parked. Thank goodness she still had a key. Would the sound of the engine wake him? With teeth gripped in a rictus of anxiety she started the engine and put the car into first. Along the lane a short distance she turned on the lights and moved up to second, then third and she was away. Finding her way created a few difficulties and several wrong turnings and it was four a.m. before she walked into the flat. All the way home she had been running lists and ideas through her mind. The sequence of dealing with the dirty place would have to be dealt with methodically. She had started once but that enthusiasm had quickly died.

She wanted to spend the rest of the night examining the stores and decide on the minimum she would need before reopening. Running through her mind was a list of ideas to put before the bank manager. As soon as she took off her coat, fatigue hit her and she fell onto the couch and was asleep before she could bring to mind the first item on her list.

Seranne woke suddenly and went in to see if her mother was comfortable. It was strange having extra people in the house and she presumed that was the reason for her unusual waking. She was not alarmed at first to find her mother's bed empty, presuming she had gone to join Paul in the small bedroom next door. Unable to resist she opened the second door and again found it empty. Curious now, she lit her candle and went downstairs. She didn't know why, but she went straight to the couch and saw the sleeping form.

"Paul?" she whispered, shaking him awake. "Where's Mum? She isn't in bed, I thought she might be with you. Why aren't you in bed?"

Bleary-eyed Paul stared at her for a few seconds then, "Not in bed? Then where is she?"

"Out in the garden maybe?"

Paul had only taken off his jacket and quickly retrieved it. Together they looked around the large garden, shining a torch around and calling, softly at first, then more loudly as alarm grew.

"Where could she have gone?" Paul was anxious now. "She couldn't have gone home, there aren't any buses at this time of night."

He touched his pockets and jingled keys. "I'd better go and look for her. But where do I start?"

It was when he went to the car and found it gone that realization hit. "She's driven back home! Why would she do that?"

Seranne didn't answer. She needed Luke. He'd know what to do. Walking up the lane in almost complete darkness was not alarming, she was too concerned about Jessie to think of imagined dangers. At the phone box, Luke's phone rang just three times before he answered. When she explained what had happened, he said, "I'm quite close to the flat and it's better if I go straight there rather than come and pick you up."

"You will find her Luke?"

"When I do I'll bring her back to Badgers Brook," he promised.

She hurried back to the house to find all the lights on. Paul was walking up and down, Bob was in the garden and Kitty, in dressing-gown and curlers was making tea in the kitchen.

When he reached the tea rooms, Luke let himself in through the unlocked side door and as soon as the door opened, he was aware of the smell of smoke. In the light of his torch he could see it thick and ominous. He started to run up the stairs but smoke immediately filled his nostrils and he dropped to the ground. Stay low, a voice in his head reminded him. Training to move around burning buildings was a well-remembered drill taught to children and adults during the early days of the war. He began to crawl up the stairs, calling for Jessie, praying she wasn't there. Why hadn't he looked for Paul's car? The instructions learnt so long ago reminded him that, if he were to rescue anyone, the most important rule was to keep himself safe. Any injured person was depending on him. He slithered back down the stairs but stopped at the kitchen door. If he opened it, the fire might engulf the place.

He went upstairs and grabbed towels which he soaked in the bathroom before going back and putting them against the bottom of the kitchen door, which seemed to be the source of the fire. He began to cough and his head felt dizzy. The smoke was beginning to affect him and he knew that time was already running out.

He went back to the stairs, calling, hoping the place was empty but knowing he had to make sure. The smoke was getting thicker and he lay as close to the floor as he could and almost flat on his stomach he crawled into the bedroom. To his relief the bed was empty, but, remembering those long ago lessons, he felt in the corners and under the bed before crawling back out. He had been warned that people hid in the most unlikely places where they think they'll be safe. Check everything first time, you might not have a second chance. The words ran through his mind like a mantra. He took precious moments to close the door.

He was coughing as the smoke penetrated the towel he had wrapped around his mouth and nose and the temptation to get out was strong but thinking of Jessie possibly trapped he went on. He crawled first to the bathroom then went into the living-room. Feeling in the darkness, longing to get up and run back down the stairs to gasp some fresh air, he forced himself to check the room thoroughly, feeling in every chair and every corner until he was quite sure the room was empty.

It's your one and only chance, the long ago voices in his head had warned, so search properly. You will probably die if you later have doubts and have to come back in.

He made his way across the floor convinced Jessie was not there but he persisted, hoping the staircase was still a safe exit. The source of the fire made that doubtful although the wet towels might have held it back for long enough. He heard the explosion of breaking glass as the pressures changed and he had to control his instinct to forget the living-room and get out. He heard the bell of the fire engine approaching and this with the black smoke that was threatening to choke him made everything unreal. He was afraid he was going to lose consciousness if he didn't get out soon. There was only the living-room to search. It was the most unlikely place at this time of night but he wouldn't be able to get back in; it had to be done now.

She was on the couch, head back struggling to breathe the foul air, and he felt the shock of disbelief. He hadn't expected to find her. Still remembering the rules about search and rescue from a burning building from all those years ago, he tied her wrists together with one of the towels and put her arms around his neck like a yoke. Crawling backwards, dragging her on her back behind him, he made his way back to the stairs.

He didn't hear the arrival of the fire brigade or the anxious voices outside. Dreading to hear the roar of flames as the fire broke through the now smouldering kitchen door, which they had to pass, he forced himself on.

His lungs were painful and he was gasping for air. Each sound that told of the fire's progress was a warning that their exit could be blocked at any second. He forced himself on, coughing, sweating with both the heat and fear. He tried to whisper reassurances to Jessie but couldn't manage it. He patted her shoulder each time he paused to find a breath of air, moving more slowly as fatigue weakened him. She seemed much heavier now. His neck hurt with the effort of dragging her — the roar of the fire was deafening and beginning to confuse him. He fought against the desire to stop and let everything go.

Pausing constantly to bend down and breathe the slightly clearer air near the floor, his progress slower with each second that passed, he made his way down. Welcoming hands met him and a fireman lifted the damp towel he had placed across Jessie's face and eased her arms from his neck which made him cry out in agony. There were murmurs of congratulations of which he was unaware, as she was carried to a waiting ambulance.

CHAPTER
ELEVEN

The first flames were visible by the time Jessie was carried into an ambulance. The fire had broken through the kitchen door and leapt across to the café area. The firemen quickly unreeled hoses and set to work. A front window cracked, the sound like a gun shot. All around the area, people had crept out of their beds to come and see what was going on. Police herded them back and Luke stood in the centre of the circle of curious onlookers imagining it was a film scene into which he had wandered by mistake.

He wanted to get back to Badgers Brook as soon as possible, to tell Seranne what had happened. That scene, where he held her in his arms and reassured her while she clung to him for comfort and love, that was like a film too, but unlike the fire, it was a fantasy.

As he was helped into an ambulance Luke told the fire chief that he thought the frayed cord on the heater might have been the cause. He was coughing, his neck was painful and stiff, his eyes were stinging and he knew that, even though his first thought was to get back to Seranne and reassure her about her mother, the sensible thing was to get some help first.

He looked at Jessie, so small, her face pale under the dirt and smoke stains. She smiled at him and in a small voice said, "Thank you," followed by a bout of coughing.

He asked questions of the ambulance men who assured him Jessie did not appear to be seriously harmed. "Thanks to you and your brave actions. She's conscious and able to talk a little — both good signs."

"Can you wait a while before contacting Mrs Curtis's husband and daughter?" he asked the policeman writing down the address where they were to be found. "I want to tell them myself. Aware that Mrs Curtis is missing, a policeman arriving will frighten them."

"Sorry, but we have to contact Mr Curtis immediately. Just go in the ambulance and get yourself checked over and leave us to worry about the family."

Still coughing and rubbing his swollen eyes, Luke went towards his car. "I have to see them," he insisted.

"At least wait until we can bathe your eyes."

"I'll get something at the chemist," he called back as he jumped into his car. "I'll be all right."

He couldn't drive very fast, his eyes were sore and he constantly blinked to clear them. At a newsagent's that was just opening its doors, he begged a drink of water and the man allowed him to wash the black streaks from his face and bathe his eyes, then he hurried on.

Unaware of the drama at the tea rooms, Paul was driving around the area with Alun. They both knew it was futile but futile activity was preferable to standing

298

and waiting for others to find her. Babs was at the café in case Jessie rang and Betty waited at the Ship. Seranne stood at the kitchen window waiting for someone to return with news. Kitty made tea.

It was almost nine o'clock when Luke reached Badgers Brook. He saw Seranne and called to her. "It's all right," he said at once. "She drove back to the flat in Paul's car."

"Why would she do that?" She stared at him. "Luke! What's happened? Your clothes smell of smoke — and your eyes . . . you're hurt!"

"Don't be alarmed, but your mother's in hospital."

"There's been an accident?"

"Try to stay calm, she's going to be all right. There was a fire and she's suffering from smoke inhalation, but she's safe and not seriously hurt."

"What fire? Was it the car? Oh Luke! Is she terribly burnt?"

"No, not burnt at all. She's going to be fine."

"And you? From the state of you, you were there too."

"There was a fire at the flat," he told her. "Your mother was sleeping and I managed to find her and get her out before the fire really took hold." She was staring at him as though the words didn't make sense. He wished his brain could arrange the words more calmly. Why couldn't he tell her without it sounding like news headlines? Then she ran to him and at least part of his wishful dreaming came true as she clung to him for reassurance.

"She was fully conscious and able to talk and the firemen told me they were positive signs. She's going to be all right."

"Thank you," she whispered. She was trembling and he held her more tightly.

Paul appeared only moments after Luke. The story had emerged and spread around the searchers.

Colin was intrigued with the way Luke had remembered the advice given more than ten years before. "Who'd have believed it? I remember being given a similar demonstration, but I don't know that I'd have remembered any of it in circumstances like this. Panic is more common than common sense! Well done, Luke."

Luke was tired and could barely keep his painful eyes open and it was Paul who drove Seranne to see her mother, borrowing Alun's car. Before they left, Luke warned Seranne not to blame Paul until she knew the full story.

Fear for her mother and the need to blame someone made her forget her promise before they left Cwm Derw. She listed Paul's failings and accused him of causing the fire by his neglect of the basic safety precautions but her voice faded after a while.

Paul didn't protest, white faced and anxious about Jessie, he agreed with everything she said.

On Bob and Kitty's insistence, Luke bathed and dressed in clothes borrowed from Bob. While he was doing so, Kitty cycled to the corner of the lane and phoned for a doctor. Still protesting, but relieved to have the assurance from the doctor that all he needed was sleep, Luke went to the small back room which

Paul had refused to use and, propped up on pillows, and with Kitty promising to look in regularly, he slept.

After visiting Jessie, and waiting until she slept, Seranne left Paul there and went to the police station.

"Investigations are underway," she was told. "But it's possible the fire was caused by a heater left on in the café, which had a dangerously worn cord. Exposed wires are a common cause of house fires, miss. In a place where the public are allowed, there should have been a regular check."

"There used to be," she muttered grimly, "until my mother began to leave everything to Paul Curtis!"

She didn't go back to the hospital, knowing that if she did, she would accuse Paul of deliberately causing the fire that almost cost her mother and Luke their lives. Contenting herself with a final phone call, she went to the bus stop and set off on the journey back to Badgers Brook, and Luke.

Luke woke once or twice and Kitty gave him sips of blackcurrant cordial and spoonfuls of honey to soothe his throat, which was now rather painful. She bathed his eyes and he drifted back to sleep. When he finally awoke and sat up, Seranne was sitting beside the bed. Wordlessly she hugged him.

"It's all right, it's all right," he soothed, as though she were the one recovering from the fire. "Have you seen your mother?"

"She's going to be all right, but if you hadn't been there, she wouldn't have woken up. The nurses told me that. How can I ever thank you?"

"We should thank that instructor who was preparing us to cope with bombing raids," he said.

Jessie was free to leave the hospital a couple of days later but she obviously couldn't go back to the flat. Investigations were not complete and the kitchen that had been the root of the fire had been seriously ravaged by the flames. The rest of the place suffered smoke damage and the building was uninhabitable. Paul brought her to Badgers Brook but he didn't stay. "I want to be on hand while the place is open, we don't want burglars on top of everything else, do we?"

"Will you be in trouble for not fixing the heater?" Seranne asked sharply.

"Why should I be? I had no idea it was in need of attention."

"I told you and so did Luke!" Her temper flared and Luke held her back.

"Not now," he whispered. "I don't think your mother wants to hear this, do you?"

"I'll be off, then," Paul said, smiling nervously. "I have so many things to see to."

"I'll come tomorrow and see what I can do to help," Luke said. "Where will you stay?"

"I'm not sure. I'll find a bed and breakfast somewhere, don't worry about me."

"I won't!" Seranne couldn't help saying.

"No accusations until we know the facts," Luke warned her when Paul had gone. "Think of your mother in all this."

"He's a criminal!"

"Or perhaps a weak and foolish man," Luke remarked thoughtfully.

Leaving Babs to run the café with Tony helping when he could, Seranne went to her mother's ruined flat with Luke the following day. It looked hopeless, the sight brought her to tears.

"I know it's a mess but you'll be surprised how quickly it can be restored."

"But it's ruined," she wailed.

"The damage isn't as bad as it looks. I'll find some men to clear it out as soon as the police and firemen give permission. New windows and shelves won't take long to fix. The insurance will cover the cost, so there won't be much delay."

"The smell will linger for ages."

"I can still smell the smoke on my clothes, even though they've been cleaned," he agreed. "But remember, no one was hurt. Your mother and Paul are safe. The rest is just down to work and imagination."

It was a few days later when Jessie began listing all they had lost that she remembered the letter which had arrived for her daughter several weeks before. "Paul found it but it was mislaid again and it wasn't until the day of the fire that I put it in the box with a couple of holiday postcards from friends I thought you'd like to see. It was one of those large, long envelopes so I thought it might be important."

"Do you remember who sent it? If it was official, the name is usually on the outside."

Jessie frowned. "I think it was more than one name, you know, like Evans Evans and Watkins."

"A solicitor, maybe? Although I can't imagine why a solicitor would write to me."

"Yes, it was something like Morgan and — Lace? Base? Chase?"

"Not Lacy, Mark Lacy? He's the solicitor with an office nearby."

"Lacy? D'you know, I think that was it. Morgan and Lacy. But what's the point of remembering? The letter would have been lost in the fire."

"There's no harm in talking to him. Perhaps I'm the lost cousin of a wealthy duke and my life will be changed by one telephone call," Seranne joked.

There was no phone in Badgers Brook, but the next day she rang from the phone box and explained about the lost letter. Mark Lacy arranged an appointment but he seemed vague about the reason. She wondered whether she would bother. Her mother was more important. Eventually curiosity got the better of her and she went.

"It's about the will of Mrs Elsie Connors," Mark Lacy told her when she had been offered a chair and a cup of tea. "I've been looking for a Mary Anne Crisp but without success. Then a couple of days ago, Tilly Tucker, who works in the Ship and Compass, called to tell me that she believed the name was incorrect and the young woman had never married and was in fact Miss Mary Anne Jones."

"Jones. That isn't an easy name to investigate in Wales," she remarked.

"Wasn't it your mother's name for a while?"

"Yes. My father was called Jones and when my mother remarried, my stepfather adopted me and I became Seranne Laurence."

"Seranne, a pretty name, was it your real name or were you christened Sarah Anne?"

"I'm Sarah Anne on my birth certificate but I've always used the name Seranne."

"Such confusion with these divorces and changing of names. It's been a difficult puzzle to untangle but at last, I believe I've done it."

"Good," she replied with a frown. "But why did you want to see me? I can't help. I've never heard of this Mary Anne Crisp — or Jones."

"On the contrary, I'm almost certain I'll have some interesting news for you very soon. There are just two details on which to check then I'll be in touch. If you will give me your name and address and where I can reach you by telephone, I'll say thank you and goodbye."

"It can't be about the guest house, though, can it?" she coaxed. "I've no connection with Mrs Connors."

He made an evasive reply but refused to say anything more. "I don't want to build up your hopes, Miss Laurence."

"Hopes of what exactly?" But he wouldn't be drawn.

She went outside and stood for a long time wondering about the mysterious Mary Anne Crisp. It couldn't have been anything to do with that. It had to be something completely different, a gift from someone. She frowned as she tried to think of someone who would leave her a small gift or memento, and failed.

A customer at her mother's tea rooms was a possibility, but in that case a solicitor would have been able to contact her without any difficulty. A connection with a father she didn't even remember was impossible. She knew nothing about him. Her adoptive father must surely have remarried and would now have children of his own and she would have been forgotten. Anyway, he wasn't a Jones. His surname and her own, was Laurence.

When her mother asked about the visit she shrugged and said vaguely, "I don't really know. Mr Lacy thought I might be able to help him trace a woman called Mary Anne Crisp but he didn't really explain how."

Jessie frowned. "I haven't heard the name, have you?"

"No, and neither has anyone else it seems." Bored with the subject she asked, "Have you seen Paul? Or Luke?"

"Luke phoned the post office, Stella Jones passed his message to Betty, who told Bob, and Kitty came to tell me Luke is coming here this evening." She was laughing at the convolutions of the delivery. "Who needs a telephone? They've both been trying to sort out the insurance and arrange for workmen to make a start on the repairs. I imagine Luke is coming with an update. The last time I spoke to Paul he assured me that everything will be underway by the end of this week."

Seranne busied herself preparing a meal. Vegetable soup with some bread rolls brought from the café. A few pancakes made with duck eggs and served with sugar and lemon juice, that would suffice. She dashed upstairs to change out of her rather formal suit she had worn for the appointment with the solicitor into something fresh.

When Luke arrived, he looked seriously in need of a change of clothing himself. His clothes once again smelt of smoke and his face was streaked with black smears. He looked tired and worried. He went straight upstairs to wash and when he came down he forced a smile. "It's been quite a day," was all he said. He didn't explain until the meal was over. Then, while Jessie dealt with the dishes he said, "More bad news for your mother, I'm afraid."

"Tell me."

"It's Paul again," he admitted. "Apparently the café was not insured. The payments have stopped and the arrears are weeks past the time when the policy could be reinstated. The company will not be paying out."

"But what happened? Paul isn't stupid enough to think it unimportant. He's had businesses of his own."

Luke declined to remark that they had all failed. Instead, he suggested, "Perhaps he simply forgot? When everything was in your mother's hands she was in control, and as they've gradually become Paul's responsibility, this one could have slipped through without either of them noticing."

"Rubbish! This is one of Paul's famous economies!"

"Don't lose your temper," he warned. "We don't know all the facts. It might be something your mother forgot."

"How likely is that?" She stood up and pushed his hand away as he tried to restrain her, and stormed into the kitchen. "Mum, Paul's forgotten to pay the insurance premiums. There is no money to repair your tea rooms. He's ruined you." She stopped suddenly as Luke came in behind her and shook her shoulder. "What are you doing?" she demanded.

"Stopping you playing the drama queen! Now sit down and listen, while I explain to your mother what little I know."

Seranne was so shocked at his action she did as he asked. More calmly, Luke explained to a white faced Jessie.

"We've been on to the insurance company and explained that the books and policies were destroyed in the fire. It took this long for them to get back to us because there *are* no policies. I'm so sorry. The insurance on the property ran out months ago and although several letters were sent, no attempt to rearrange it has been received."

Jessie started at him, waiting for the rest, a promise that a solution had been found, the error explained, that everything would be all right. Sadly Luke shook his head as though she had spoken aloud. Jessie opened her arms and Seranne ran to hug her.

"What will we do?" Jessie wailed.

For once Seranne held her tongue from accusing Paul of creating all their problems. "I don't know,

Mum, but somehow we'll get Jessica's Victorian Tea Rooms back again. Better than ever."

Later, when Jessie had gone to bed, Seranne said, "The only thing I can do to help is to sell my half of The Wayfaring Tree, it's probably worth a little more than we paid now we've increased the trade and smartened it up. Then I can use the money to get the tea rooms started again."

"Typical!" was Luke's response. "Let Babs down, after she's given up on the family business to share your idea. Don't worry about her, just do what you want to do."

"I don't want to give up the café. I'm proud of what Babs and I have achieved."

"Seranne, you have to accept that your mother has to live her own life. That means she is responsible for her own decisions and has to repair any damage her errors have created. She and Paul have to deal with this. We support them but we don't interfere."

"We?"

"Yes. Of course I'll help, but only that. No one has the right to march in and take over."

She giggled then.

"What's funny?"

"The thought of me wearing army boots marching into that mess of a building and taking charge."

Smiling with her, he urged, "Stay out of it, Seranne. Live your life, and try not to live theirs. Let them decide how best to sort this out."

"Is it possible, to sort this out?"

"Of course. But it will mean a lot of work and you and I can help with that, once they've decided what they are going to do." He left soon after and at the doorway he stared at her and said, "Keep that temper of yours in control when you see Paul. You won't help your mother by reminding her she married a man who failed her. She already knows that."

"But he's ruined her life and . . ."

"Hush, no two marriages are the same. Paul is her choice and I doubt very much if she'd want to change that."

"She's not stupid!"

"Love can make fools of us all." He held her, their cheeks touching and she felt the movement as he smiled before saying, "Even a hard-headed woman like you."

She felt the chill of loneliness as he walked down the path leaving behind just the faint musty smell of smoke on the night air.

When Paul came to visit Jessie, Seranne was at the café. When she went home for a brief visit between the lunch hour and the teatime rush, she found her mother in tears.

"What is it? Has something else happened?"

"Paul is so upset. He thought I'd dealt with the insurance and I thought it was on his list of things to do. I don't know where we'll get the money to start over again."

The confusion of responsibilities didn't explain it. The reminders would have come by post and must have been seen by Paul, who chose to ignore them. She held back the anger that threatened to burst from her, anger against Paul and his reluctance to spend money on the essentials. "Luke and I will help, you know that. And perhaps Paul too, as he's —"

"I know, he's partly to blame."

"Partly?" Seranne couldn't help saying.

"I've been too willing to leave it all to him. He knows what he's doing, it was only in this instant he was careless."

"Where is he now?"

"Trying to get some estimates for the cleaning and repairs. He and Luke are meeting later to compare notes and make a few decisions, I believe." She frowned. "Why is Luke so good to us, you and he don't appear to be more than friends?"

"That's all we are, friends. He's simply a kind man."

"Rich too."

"Not rich enough to sort out Paul's mess!" Her mother looked tearful and she regretted her outburst. "Sorry, Mum, but it's hard not to be angry with him."

"You don't understand how easily things can go wrong, you've never had a moment's worry, I've seen to that."

It was ten o'clock that evening when Seranne and Jessie were ready for bed that Luke arrived. "There's no easy way to say this," he said, holding Jessie's hands. "Paul didn't come as we arranged and when I went to the place where he's staying, he wasn't there."

"Then where is he?"

"He'd paid his account and left. Jessie, I went with him to the bank and arranged for replacement cheques and a statement. It seems that he's gone, taking the money that was left in your account."

To their surprise, Jessie didn't seem shocked. "Poor darling. You know, he's been doing all this for us, trying to make a better future for us, and now all his efforts have been in vain."

A glare from Luke prevented Seranne from saying what was in her mind. Leaving Luke and Jessie talking, she went to stand in the garden to cool her temper.

Seranne knew she could save money by leaving Badgers Brook, but the house was her safe, comforting haven. She and Babs were clearing up after closing the café and she told her friend, "I know I'll cope with whatever life has in store for me as long as I can go there each evening and draw strength from its old walls and peaceful atmosphere."

"Then stay, the rent isn't excessive and it wouldn't make much difference to an empty pot. Besides, you and your mother have to live somewhere."

"It soothes my pain and the way I feel about my mother is a wound of sorts. Sitting in that place, soaking up the history, with the memories of previous owners seeming to offer sympathy, is the only time I feel at peace."

"I can manage for a few days while you talk to your mother. I can go to the employment exchange for a temporary assistant. She needs you there."

"Thank you, Babs, you're a real friend, but no, I value the time we spend here and business is looking better every day. I don't want to risk that. Luke reminds me that their disaster isn't my responsibility. This is a mess for my mother to deal with, I can't do her thinking for her. He's right. For one thing, I'd be too tempted to suggest she tell Paul to go!"

"Do you know where he is?"

"Hiding somewhere, licking his wounds and telling himself it was all someone else's fault!" She smiled. "That's always my first reaction to a disaster, according to Luke!"

Everywhere around the town were the remnants of the street decorations put up to celebrate the coronation. People were loath to take them down and they hung limply and bedraggled from many lampposts as well as draped across windows and on walls. Even Stella's country cottage had flags flying from its roof, and Colin's runner bean had been tied with bunting instead of ordinary string. While Jessie searched for Paul, borrowing a car and driving around and asking everyone they knew for news of him, the sight of the abandoned, discoloured decorations saddened her.

It seemed the town was mourning the end of her marriage. Every corner of Cwm Derw that had once been filled with colour seemed to demonstrate with its drabness the futility of her efforts. She tried every guest house and small hotel and she grew more and more despairing. The echoes of happy celebration surrounding her seemed a cruel joke as she wondered with every day that passed, whether she would ever see Paul again. He was her third husband and a third failure. What was wrong with her? Why couldn't he have talked to her?

While Jessie tried to think of ways to finance the rebuilding of the tea rooms and her home, and grieved over the disappearance of Paul, Seranne received a letter from Mark Lacy, asking her to go and see him. What could he want? Only to ask more questions about a woman of whom she had never heard. She couldn't help and was far too busy to waste time.

"Go on," Babs urged, when she showed her the letter. "It says you could call any time this afternoon. What's the matter with you? I'd be unable to resist. You might have been left a legacy."

"A legacy? More likely to be a request to look after someone's cat!"

"Go on, for heaven's sake! If you don't care, do it for me! I'm so excited I just filled the pepper pot with salt!"

So she reluctantly agreed. She phoned and arranged to see the solicitor at three.

"I'll save the washing up for you," Babs grinned. "I don't want your inheritance going to your head!"

"Can you tell me what you know about your father, Miss Laurence? Your real father that is."

"Not much. I know he died when I was a few months old. Mum married again, to the man who gave me my name but that marriage ended in divorce."

"You knew he had a sister? Your real father that is?"

"Mum told me something about her, although I don't remember ever meeting her. I don't think my father and she were in touch, a quarrel that was never mended I believe."

314

"Do you remember her name?"

"I think it was Mary, Auntie Mary, but I've no idea what her surname would be. She must have married and, as I say, she didn't keep in touch."

"She was Mary Anne, and somehow, she began to be called Sarah Anne, the same as you. Mary Anne Jones, not Crisp. The man called Crisp never married her. She was your aunt, your father's sister."

Seranne stood to leave. "I'm sorry Mr Lacy, but I know nothing about all this, wouldn't it be better for you to talk to my mother?"

"This Mary Anne was also the sister of Elsie Clements who married Ed Connors, she was your aunt."

Seranne dropped back into her chair and stared at him. "Mrs Connors was my aunt? You mean I had an auntie living just behind the post office and I didn't know?"

"Sadly, Mrs Connors didn't know either."

"Now she's dead and it's too late. To think we might have been friends." Her shoulders drooped and she looked up at him sadly. "If only I'd known." Then she frowned and asked, "She really didn't know I was her niece?"

"No, I'm sure she didn't. Although she had been searching for you. It's the confusion of names you see. Your father's mother married twice more, and her sister called herself Crisp but remained a Jones."

"If only I'd known. Where is she buried? I can at least visit her grave and leave some flowers."

"That would be a nice gesture."

"Why are you telling me this? Is there something else I can do?"

"Just think of her kindly. You see, Miss Laurence, she left you the guest house in her will."

Seranne walked away from Mark Lacy's office in a daze. It was as though her mind had become numb, her thoughts refused to gel. How could this be? It was as though a voice from the dead had spoken. Her father and her Auntie Mary, two people she hadn't known had presented her with this unbelievable gift. But why? Surely there must be others who were more entitled to it than she?

She sat on a seat near the post office, unaware of what was going on around her. From time to time she peered guiltily around the corner to where the guest house stood. It was several minutes longer before she thought of Elsie's husband. Surely the place should be his? She couldn't accept it. What should she do? Her first thought was to go to the phone box outside the post office and talk to Luke.

When she told him what she had learnt, he congratulated her, but her response was far from thrilled. "Don't congratulate me! I'm horrified to think that this Elsie Connors who was my aunt, could leave a business to me, when it's her husband who has the right to it. I can't accept it, Luke. It wouldn't be right."

"Don't do anything until we've talked about it. Perhaps Mark Lacy will be able to explain."

"I must go back to him at once, explain that I must refuse it."

316

"No, please wait. I'll come to Badgers Brook this evening and we can talk it through."

"Will you ring Mr Lacy, tell him how I feel, ask for an explanation? Arrange a transfer or whatever it's called? You're right, I shouldn't go now. I'm so upset I wouldn't make sense of a single word."

"I doubt whether he'll talk to me. But I'll come with you tomorrow if you wish, although I think you should take your mother."

The following day Luke drove them and waited outside for them and it was Jessie who answered most of Mark Lacy's queries. Seranne's only question was, "Why did she leave her property to me?"

"The only explanation given is that Mrs Connors had been left a large sum of money when she was in her thirties. She had been widowed, and was earning a living by cleaning other people's houses, and living in one room. The money changed her life for the better. She determined to do the same for someone else. A surprise inheritance, was how she put it."

"But surely, once she married she made a new will?"

"Yes, but she insisted that her original plan remained. She hoped that the same thing would happen again after your time, that you would use the money to have a good life but treat it as a loan to be passed on to someone deserving and unaware." He smiled then and added, "Oh there's no commitment for you to do what she asks, just a hope that you will look after the money and do what she envisaged, giving the same request to a chosen recipient in your turn."

"But where did the money come from?"

"Her aunt Flora, from what I can discover. Mrs Connors, or Mrs Clements as she was then, used the money to buy the guest house and it has given her a good living. She hoped it will change another life and another after that, although, as I say, you don't have that as a stipulation to accepting the bequest. The guest house is yours."

It didn't take long for the news to get out. Seranne went to see Ed and he refused to listen to her explanation that the whole affair had been a complete surprise. His reaction was extreme anger. He told everyone who would listen that Seranne had deliberately tricked his wife into leaving the property to her. As she hadn't known the woman it was impossible to work out when, although truth wasn't allowed to get in the way of a good story.

Seranne was shocked by the amount of bad feeling towards her. Some people said loudly that they wouldn't use her café again, others sat in a corner, ate her cakes while whispering about her, eyeing her like a woman suspected of theft, which was what some insisted it was. Twice she went to see Mark Lacy and insisted he handed the business back to Ed Connors, the rightful owner, but he refused, insisting in his turn that it was his client's instruction and she must allow some time to pass while she thought it through.

Ed had said nothing to Seranne herself, but he put a note through the door of Badgers Brook stating that in the circumstances he wouldn't be running the guest house any longer. "The key will be with Stella Jones at the post office," the note added.

Luke and Seranne went that evening to look at the place. "And I'm going to search every cranny until I find a new will," she said firmly. "There has to be one. I don't believe she meant to deprive her husband of everything. No one could be so cruel."

The kitchen was neat and clean and on the scrubbed table was a note. She handed it to Luke with a groan. It was a list of everything that needed doing on the property, problems that seemed to start at the roof and reach the cellars, touching on everything in between.

Luke read the list and went with her to compare the listed items with the building. Luke pointed out that they were mostly exaggerations. "The biggest problem seems to be, who is going to run it if Ed won't help?"

"I can't. I have to work at the café. Babs can't run it alone. I don't want to close it down though. I still hope I'll find a second will and be able to hand it back to him."

"He isn't going to make this easy for you," Luke said grimly.

"I don't blame him," she said sadly. "If I take this place, which rightly belongs to him, I'll be nothing more than a thief."

They looked around each of the rooms, carrying the inventory given by Mark Lacy but not bothering to check against it. Every piece of furniture was examined for anything that looked like a will. In what was obviously the office, there were two spikes on wooden bases, one containing overdue bills the other the receipts for those that had been paid. Everything was up to date. They took out every drawer and even moved the furniture so they could look behind and underneath, but found nothing.

"I think you should talk to Ed Connors and offer him a home and the job of running this place."

"I don't want to take it! I haven't the right to it."

"You must, at least until the legalities are over. Then you can think again. Ask him to help for a while at least."

"He won't speak to me. He thinks I came here deliberately and, without him knowing, wormed my way into his wife's affections — although when I managed to do that I can't imagine. But it's what people are believing."

"Not everyone. Not even Ed, really. He's angry and saying things to feed his disappointment, and his humiliation," he added.

"Poor man."

Ed was sitting in Betty's living-room behind the bar, sipping tea and complaining. Betty listened patiently then asked, "Why have you left the guest house? Don't you have people coming in?"

"Let *her* deal with it."

"I can understand you being angry, but why don't you help her? She's as shocked as you."

"Pity for her!"

"What will you do?"

"I was hoping you'll have me here."

Betty shook her head. "No, Ed, I'm sorry, but I can't have you living here indefinitely. Go back to the guest house until everything becomes clear. This is a business and I have all the help I need at present."

"Can't I at least stay until I find somewhere to live and a job to pay for it?"

Betty was about to shake her head once more then realized that she was asking him to help Seranne, who unwittingly had taken his home and his job, and at the same time she was practically doing the same thing. She looked at him, drooping with misery. "Just for a while, then. Until you get things sorted. And," she added firmly, "you'll have to work for your keep. Agreed?"

He nodded and went into the bar. "I'll start by cleaning the top shelves, shall I? Then I'll bring up what you need for tonight."

Seranne went in later after further discussions with Luke and her mother, and found him wiping the tops of the shelves. "Mr Connors," she said hesitantly.

"Come to gloat, have you? Isn't it enough that you've taken my home and my living?"

Anger flared as murmurs of agreement rose from the customers. She had been searching for a solution to the situation, trying to find a way of returning the property to him and all he could do was alienate people from her without listening to a word she said. Any thought of an apology vanished. "This situation isn't of my making. I've come to ask you to stay on at the guest house until the ownership is clear," she replied. He wasn't going to make her feel guilty over circumstances she hadn't caused! Sharpening her voice, she said, "I would like you to continue to run the place and I will see that you are paid a good wage but only as long as everything continues satisfactorily. In a manner that your wife would expect."

Gruffly he said, "I won't go there again whatever wages you're offering. It's my home by rights, and you can't tell me different."

Disapproval was in every face in the bar. He had told his story and many people believed her guilty of deliberately setting out to deprive him of his rightful inheritance.

"So, you refuse to help? All right, I'm sure it won't be difficult to find someone suitable." She turned and walked out. Her intention had been to make him understand how unhappy she felt about inheriting the place, but her kind and sympathetic words curled up inside her. If he was that unreasonable he could sweat for a while!

Alun was walking around the corner when he saw her leave. Betty was outside the Ship opening the doors to the cellar. The delivery dray had just arrived, harnesses jingling, the powerful horses snorting and shuffling their huge feathery feet, already impatient to be off. Two men wearing thick leather aprons jumped down and began to unload her order.

Betty saw him and waved as he ran forward to help get the boxes inside. He took the first and carried it into the bar, while the men lowered the barrels down the slope into the cellar. He took the second load inside and was putting it onto the bar when Ed appeared. "No need for you to help, I'm here now and I'm staying. I've given up my home and my job to make sure she's got all the help she needs. So you aren't wanted. Right?"

Alun looked for Betty but she was nowhere to be seen. He waited a while but she didn't reappear. Surely she wasn't avoiding him again because of her idle brother's demands? Silently, he carried the rest of the order inside, then he waited in the living-room for Ed to come in. It was obvious he had something to say. He wasn't going to walk away again on Ed's say-so. But where was Betty? Why didn't she come in as she always did when he returned from an errand? Perhaps she was busy getting the barrels in the right place. Ed's announcement had been his own and not what Betty had told him. This time it wouldn't work.

"I know what you're up to," Ed said, pushing the door open angrily. "You've got nothing and my sister has this place. Makes a good living she does, and with you having nothing to offer, she's the best you can do."

Alun didn't say a word. Ed went back to the bar. The doors were closed as it was not yet opening time, but Alun did nothing to prepare, he just waited, watching the door. Behind him Ed continued to clean the shelves.

Alun turned as the outside door opened, a smile on his face.

"Alun," Betty called and beckoned him outside, pointing to where in a corner against the fence, the hard surface was covered with plant pots filled with annuals. "What do you think of building a real garden in this corner? I've seen some fuschias that would look good and maybe next year we could grow some roses too. What d'you think?"

He led her inside and with an arm around her shoulders and looking up to where Ed was rubbing enthusiastically on a mirror, he said, "Betty, I think it's a wonderful idea, I think you are wonderful and I want to stay with you for ever. Working alongside you is all I ever want." She moved closer and he took her in his arms. "I want to marry you. I know we'll be happy together for the rest of our lives, here in Cwm Derw."

She was still in his arms when there was a rattle of glasses being roughly handled and he turned to see Ed scowling at him. "I said you weren't wanted. He's got nothing to offer, Betty. He's another one like that Seranne Laurence, out for what he can get."

"No, you've got it wrong, Ed," Alun said quietly. "It's you who needn't stay. I'll be here for her for always."

A glance at his sister's glowing face convinced him. "Don't say I didn't warn you! That Seranne woman has been here, begging me to go and help, would you believe! After robbing me of all I have. The damned cheek of the woman! But I'll go, only because it suits me, mind!" He walked out, calling back, "Between Alun and that Seranne I'm left with nothing, he came with nothing and he's got it all."

"You're so right," Alun replied. "Everything I could ever want."

CHAPTER
TWELVE

Paul had no idea where he was going. He only knew he had failed Jessie and had to get out of her life before he destroyed her completely. He had wanted to do so much for her and if only the fates had been kinder he would have freed her of the need to work, given her a life of enjoyment. He knew he could make her happy, he loved her and knew that love was returned. All he had needed was a small slice of luck and that had been denied him.

He drove through Tonypandy, Ferndale, Aberdare, hardly aware of the roads he travelled, his actions automatic, changing gear, slowing for other road users, his driving immaculate although his thoughts were far away. Outside Merthyr Tydfil the engine began to stutter and looking down at the gauge he realized he was out of petrol. He parked the car, picked up the rucksack, which was all he had brought and, leaving the keys on the driver's seat, he walked away.

That night he slept in a barn and the following morning he was up before dawn and walking along the road, unaware that he was heading back the way he had come. A lorry stopped and offered him a lift and took him back to Pontypridd. Another lorry driver offered him a share of his packed lunch, then took him to Bridgend. He didn't care where he went, he had no plans.

He walked around the centre and looked in shop windows but would have been unable to explain where he had been or what he had seen. Late that day, another lorry driver stopped for him and offered him a lift to Llanelli.

"Llanelli would be fine," he said, thanking him.

He slept under a hedge that night, his head resting on his rucksack, his coat wrapped tightly around him. At five o'clock a farmer kicked him awake and sent him on his way. He washed in a stream and combed his hair. His beard was growing and giving him a wild expression. It was unlikely anyone would stop for him today, but it didn't matter, he'd stop somewhere, anywhere, and clean up and find a job. His thoughts were vague and he was unaware of being hungry.

He held out a hand as several lorries approached and he was indifferent as they drove past. Then a delivery van stopped, the driver leant out and called, "Where are you heading for?"

Paul shrugged. "It doesn't matter where, just as long as I get away."

"I'm heading for Tenby, that suit you?"

"Yes, thanks for stopping." He felt a slight lifting of his spirits. Tenby would be perfect. It was where he and Jessie had spent their honeymoon.

"Family problems, is it?" the driver asked as Paul climbed in.

"Family, yes," Paul agreed. "My fault really," he added softly.

"There's a decent café on the road not far from here, fancy a bite?"

Again Paul nodded. He hadn't eaten since driving away from Jessie, apart from sharing the driver's packed lunch the previous day.

Walking inside the large unprepossessing block-built building surrounded by a busy parking area, was like coming upon a protest meeting. The place was full and with each person having to raise his voice to be heard it sounded as though a dozen quarrels were taking place. Most of the tables were full. Paul handed the driver a ten-shilling note and found a table in the corner as three drivers were leaving.

The young man chatted easily and didn't ask questions, aware of Paul's distress. Paul ate with more urgency than enjoyment and when he had finished, his companion went back to the counter and brought back more toast, which Paul ate as the young man watched with obvious pleasure.

"My dad was on the road for a while, back a few years ago," he said as they were leaving. "He thought we'd be better off without him, silly old fool."

"Is that why you stopped for me?"

"Probably. Here, take your money, I'll treat you to that food. It was worth the money to see you enjoying it." He stuffed the note in Paul's pocket and, whistling cheerfully, set off for his destination.

★ ★ ★

After three days waiting for news and enquiring at the police station and the local hospitals, Jessie faced the fact that Paul had left deliberately and without any intention of coming back. When the car was found abandoned the fear of suicide filled Luke's mind. He drove around the area where the car had been found and gathering a group of friends together, walked the fields and hills searching for him. They found no trace of him. Using buses, walking or hitchhiking, he could be anywhere.

Jessie was staying at Badgers Brook and filling her time making plans for when she could rebuild and reopen the tea-rooms.

"It's all I know," she told Luke. "If I can borrow the money to get it running again, I know I can make it a success. Once my customers and friends know I'm reopening they'll return. I know they will."

Luke agreed and after discussing it with Seranne, he took both of them to meet a bank manager and offered surety for the loan.

"I think he still has the empty shop, he was planning to open it as a surprise for me," a tearful Jessie said, handing him the address. "It was due to open soon. He didn't own it but the rent is paid for six months. There might be something there which I can sell?"

Luke knew exactly where the shop was and the last time he had seen it there had been little sign of imminent opening, or of it containing anything of value. To save Jessie further disappointment he went there one evening, with Seranne.

"I feel guilty walking in and searching for something to help Mum, even though this must be at least half hers. I feel like a burglar, or worse. It's like searching for ghosts."

"It's like stepping into someone else's life, but remember it's your mother's life too. Come on, let's see what treasures he has in these boxes."

They opened three of them and groaned with disappointment. They were full of coronation mugs and plates, and now, with everyone having had their fill, they were practically worthless.

"We have to get your mother's permission, of course," Luke said, "but if we put a few sweets into each one, wrapped them in cellophane, we might sell them at the market."

"They won't make enough to buy a tin of paint." Seranne was distressed at the puny offerings. "These are the only things left by Paul? All that remains of their marriage? I knew he couldn't be trusted. He walked away and left Mum without a penny, leaving her to sort out the mess he made. I don't see how she can think of beginning again."

"I can. Your mother is strong."

"Strong? Falling for someone like Paul Curtis?"

"We can't choose whom we fall in love with, can we?"

Seranne was afraid to answer. That was something she wasn't ready to face. "You're right. My mother's no weakling, dependent on a man to make her life complete."

"That's a weakness? Depending on a man?"

She looked at him, in this shabby building, spending his time helping her to sort out the extreme difficulties her mother had encountered and in a sudden burst of honesty, she admitted, "We depend on you, don't we, Mum and me? I don't know how to thank you." She smiled at him and added, "I don't know why you're so kind to us, Luke."

"Don't you?" He stared at her and she looked away. How could she admit to the love that was in his eyes, and in her own? Loving a man who had a wife was strictly taboo and she would have to get out of his life soon or spend her days accused of breaking up a marriage.

He took her to a warehouse selling sweets and bought an assortment of lollipops and boiled sweets. For the rest of the day they filled the mugs with a few sweets or a couple of lollipops and she managed to stay some distance away, avoiding even the touch of his hand. They planned to visit Maes Hir market on Wednesday. "And I'll arrange for one of my cousins or aunties to take a stall at other markets during the week," he promised.

"Thank you. Mum will be grateful. She still hopes Paul will come back, you know."

"Yes, and so do I. We'll make a note of every transaction to show Paul exactly what we've done," he told her.

On Wednesday he took Seranne and Babs to Maes Hir and they set up their stall.

"This is where I started," he told them. "I bought the contents of a shop that was closing. Pens, notebooks,

330

calendars, postcards and birthday cards, and a huge supply of pipes and cigarette lighters. I did the same thing several times, bought something cheaply and sold it with a small enough profit to dispose of it quickly."

He showed them how to sell, talking to passers-by. "Interesting them enough to stop to look is the hardest part. Once they stop they'll be tempted to buy."

Their stock was disposed of by mid-afternoon and they went to one of the stalls selling snacks to celebrate their success. "Hello Auntie Vi," he said to the woman in charge.

"Not another auntie!" Seranne said with disbelief, smiling at the rosy-faced woman wearing a clean, white overall.

"Which one of you is Seranne, then?" she asked, handing them cups of tea and Welsh cakes. She was introduced, then she held her hand out for the money. "Auntie or not, he pays like the rest," she said, but she was smiling affectionately as she pushed away his offered money.

Betty and Alun were planning a wedding. "It will have to be a small affair," Betty said.

"That's hardly likely, is it? All your friends will expect an invitation and we have the perfect venue here, at the Ship and Compass."

"I'd be working hard for days getting everything arranged. Then there are sure to be people we offend by forgetting to invite them personally. And there's Ed. He'd hate us having a celebration so soon after losing Elsie and the guest house."

"We could just put up a notice, inviting everyone to come and drink our health? But, no, I think you're right and we shouldn't tell anyone until it's over."

"We can get away for a couple of days though, tell everyone we are heading for different destinations, put them off the scent. I'll arrange for a relief manager."

"What about the end of August?"

"Perfect."

As they began to discuss their plans, Tilly tiptoed away from the door and disappeared into the cellar. A small affair? Not if her name was Tilly Tucker.

With the money available, builders were organized and the work on Jessica's Victorian Tea Rooms began. Jessie stayed with a friend and oversaw the initial clearing and the necessary knocking down of the damaged areas. She discussed with an architect the rebuilding. She was busy every day and drove back to Badgers Brook a couple of times each week in the hope that someone had news of Paul.

She still had moments when she feared he was dead. But for most of the time she imagined him sitting in some dingy room, trying to rebuild his life as she was trying to rebuild the tea rooms. By comparison with his, her task was simple. If only he would trust her enough to come back, they could work it all out together.

Her friend Matty Powell turned up one morning as she was washing down one of the kitchen walls. "Good heavens, Jessie! The place looked bad enough last time I came. What happened?"

"Matty, lovely to see you. I'll put the kettle on, I'm dying for a cuppa. We'd better go up to the flat, there isn't anywhere clean enough to sit down here."

When she told her friend about the fire and her brush with death she went on to tell her about Paul's disappearance. "I wish I knew where he'd gone. If I could talk to him I know I could persuade him to come back to me. Ashamed he was, after all he tried to do he didn't have the necessary luck. Poor darling."

If Matty felt differently she said nothing. She let Jessie talk about her plans for reopening and kept away from the tender subject of the absent Paul. She knew from experience that agreeing with someone about the faults of a dear one could bring trouble later, when the faults were forgotten.

"Come on," she said briskly. "Lend me an overall or something voluminous and I'll give you a hand." Covered up with one of Paul's shirts that had escaped the fire, she went back down to the café and spent the rest of the day beside Jessie, cleaning away the smoke stains from the walls.

Seranne was still trying to deal with the shock of inheriting Elsie Connors's guest house. She had tried to speak to Ed, but apart from his brief comments about what was needed and handing her the weekly accounts, he walked away and ignored her. She went to two other solicitors and asked whether they had been given any papers belonging to Elsie, in case she had chosen a different firm to hold her final instructions. There was no sign of anything new. The will was firm and the place was hers.

The café she ran with Babs continued to increase in popularity and Tony still spent a few hours each day helping them. Occasionally the three of them went to the pictures and he always sat next to Seranne, leaning towards her to share the fun during a comedy and taking her hand when danger threatened the flickering characters on the screen. Once he leant over and kissed her cheek and Babs winked and whispered, "I knew it! You'll be my sister-in-law before the end of the year."

"Not a chance!" Seranne hissed back. If Tony heard he made no comment.

Paul found work in the kitchen of a restaurant not far from the seafront in Tenby. Around the corner was the hotel where he and Jessie had stayed after their wedding. He often sat near the hotel and thought of all his mistakes, the list passing through his mind like a series of indictments being read out in court.

If he had been asked what was his most disliked job, he would have answered without hesitation, washing dishes and pans. So there was some strange satisfaction in accepting the vacancy; he considered it a suitable punishment to scour dirty pans and scrape away stale food and deal with the resulting mess at the end of each shift.

Part of him hoped someone would see him and tell Jessie where he was to be found and another part knew he didn't deserve an end to his misery. He was fed at the restaurant and he put aside every penny of his wages once the rent of his room was paid. He tried not to think of the factory he had lost and the dream of opening a smart, modern shop selling beautiful china, or his most recent idea of supplying catering equipment.

Why had it all gone wrong? He had worked beside his father all those years, and taking on a partner should have made things easier. Was he simply incapable of running a successful business? Was this his true level? Washing up in a seaside hotel?

Luke described Paul and asked his aunt who ran the roadside café if she had seen him.

"Luke, I love you, but you must be *twp* if you think I'd remember one customer above the rest," she said with a laugh. "I'm so busy I don't look higher than the hand offering money. If people say hello, I say hello back but apart from a few of the long-time regulars I wouldn't know them if I met them anywhere but here."

Her young assistant disagreed. "There was a man travelling with Johnny Trevor. He comes in Tuesdays regular. I don't know whether the hitchhiker was the man you're looking for, but he could be. I'll ask Johnny. He loves to have a passenger and chats to them like lost friends."

Luke thanked them and left. He was dressed incongruously for the lorry drivers' café. Smart navy pinstriped suit, crisp white shirt, his shoes shining like glass. He was on his way to a board meeting of a company in which he had shares. Import and export was becoming increasingly important and this particular company was booming. He wondered vaguely whether he would have been equally successful if his marriage hadn't ended before it had begun. Probably not. He had been a lorry driver, and once he'd found himself on his own, he'd put every moment of his time into work, earning money, making plans.

Unlike Paul Curtis, he'd been lucky. As he'd told Seranne and Babs, he had started by purchasing the contents of a shop to sell at the local market, then he'd progressed to getting a loan to buy a house which he resold with a profit that enabled him to pay back the loan within months. He had borrowed more and used it to buy and sell houses, until he had enough to buy the firm for which he had worked. The haulage company still held its original name, he wasn't one to spread his name all over the towns. It was enough to know he was the owner.

Now, beside the haulage firm, he owned several small shops and a factory making wooden furniture which he designed himself. His success had led to him being invited to join the board of other, larger companies and now, at the age of thirty-five he was rich in money, but unable to find a private life to match his wealth.

After the meeting, he changed from the suit into casual clothes and drove around looking for a suitable premises for his latest plan. It needed to be close to a busy part of a town, a place where people passed, perhaps near a bus station or where there were popular shops like Woolworths. He found it in Barry.

Barry was a seaside town popular with visitors and he thought the population might be large enough to justify what he had in mind. An hour spent looking at the property on the busy main road with the agent, and a phone call to his architect to arrange a second visit, and negotiations were underway before he drove back to Badgers Brook to tell Seranne about his ideas.

"A china shop? Will selling china be enough for a business to survive?" she asked.

"I think the country is beginning to want better things. There are some beautiful porcelain tea and dinner services coming into the country now and British manufacturers are being allowed to compete. It will be a bouyant business once people start replacing all their boring old white cups and saucers."

On her afternoon off, he took her to see the shop, which he had already visited twice with his architect, and plans for some changes were set out on paper. Sitting on tea chests in the empty premises they looked through catalogues and discussed the stock he would buy.

"I value these conversations with you," he said. "In fact, I value every moment I spend with you."

Uneasy, wishing they could stay as casual friends, even though her heart was telling her something different, she moved ever so slightly away from him and said, "You know exactly what you want, so saying it aloud is all you need."

"I'm just speaking my thoughts aloud?"

"With someone to guess what you're thinking and encourage you to speak your thoughts aloud, anyone would do."

"No, Seranne, that isn't true, not any more."

Pretending not to understand him, she pointed to a page of Bunnykins children's china made by Royal Doulton and said, "That's something you ought to consider. Perfect for Christening presents from adoring aunts."

He turned a few pages of the suppliers' lists and said, "Glass too? Tell me. What am I thinking now?" He was smiling and she felt relief.

"I think you're thinking that anything beautiful would find a place in this new shop of yours."

"That's a part of what I'm thinking."

"Murano glass from Italy," she read. "Swedish Orrefors, Dutch Leerdam, British White Friars . . . But now we have to go. I've promised to cook a meal for Mum and Babs."

"And Tony?" he asked.

"Of course. You too, if you can. Even hotshot businessmen must have to eat."

They ate in the garden. Newly dug potatoes boiled and served with salad plus a tin of span cut very thinly and spread, fan-like on each plate. The conversation about china and glass went on long into the evening, but both knew it was a veil covering what they really wanted to say.

Betty and Alun waited until most of the regulars were in the Ship and made their announcement. "I'm going away for a few days," Betty said. "I've arranged for a temporary manager and I'm sure he'll look after you all as well as I do. Tilly will be here to keep you all in order."

338

"The problem is," Alun added, "I have to be absent for a couple of those days too. It's to do with the money coming to me from the restaurant," he explained, as grins began to spread from face to face.

"Oh, yes, for sure it is. Come on, Alun, pull the other one," Jack Gretorex said, and other murmurings began.

"I don't know what you're implying," Alun said, feigning annoyance, "but I can assure you that nothing untoward is planned between us. D'you think Betty would — d'you think I would — well, everything is respectable. It's just a coincidence."

Slowly the murmurings changed to apologies, except for an unrepentant Jack, who said, "More fool you then, Alun."

"D'you think we fooled them?" Alun asked, as they were cleaning the bar later.

"It's impossible to get one over this lot, but I don't think they really believe we're off on a naughty weekend."

"Amazing how wrong they can be," he said, holding her in his arms.

Looking for Paul was an automatic part of every journey Luke took. He stopped occasionally and asked strangers as well as some of his widely spread relations if they had seen him, carrying a wedding photograph of Paul and Jessie, borrowed from Seranne. When he called again at the roadside café run by his aunt there was news for him. The young assistant handed him a note written by the man who had given Paul a lift to Llanelli.

In revived hope he went there and asked around the various places where he thought Paul might have found work. After two days he gave up, thankful he hadn't mentioned the small lead to Jessie. Then a second lorry driver told him the man had gone on to Tenby. Johnny Trevor remembered the man well. "He told me he was Paul and he was running away from family troubles — of his own making he told me. I dropped him off at Tenby and told him I'd be going back to Llanelli in a couple of days' time if he decided to go back, but I heard no more from him."

Luke went into several cafés and public houses and even a few shops but no one remembered seeing Paul. Then he stopped a man who was sitting on a bench near a hotel who looked at the photograph then nodded. It was then Luke decided to tell Jessie what he had learnt.

Jessie came back to Badgers Brook dirty and tired after spending most of the day clearing what had been the living-room of the flat. As always her first question to Seranne was, "Any news of Paul?" Seranne shook her head.

They were sitting down to eat when Luke came. "Any news?" Jessie asked again.

"There's a possibility that he's in Tenby. Not a lot of help really, he could have moved on from there, so don't build up your hopes. It's probably a false lead like so many others."

With Jessie and Seranne asking questions, he told them the little he knew. "I showed the photograph of Paul to several people and one man thought — just

340

thought," he warned, "that he'd seen Paul sitting on a seat near a hotel several times during the past few weeks."

"I have to go there," Jessie said at once.

"I can take you on Saturday? I'm not free until then," Luke offered.

"No. Thank you, Luke, for all you've done, but I'll go on my own, tomorrow."

Luke didn't disagree. He had hoped all along that Jessie would be the one to find her husband. Jessie listened intently as he described the hotel, her eyes widening. "It's where we spent our honeymoon," she gasped. "How stupid of me not to go there. That's where he'll be, I'm sure of it."

"Shall I ask Babs if she can manage without me tomorrow and come with you?" Seranne asked, but she saw Luke shaking his head. "On second thoughts, it's our busiest day and I need to be there."

"Thank you, dear, but this is something I need to do on my own."

She set off on the bus the following morning and was in Tenby by ten o'clock. She didn't go straight to the hotel but to a café where she sat nursing a cup of tea, trying to think of the words with which to greet him. Half an hour later she walked up to the hotel and asked to see Paul Curtis whom she believed was working there. That was her first disappointment. They hadn't heard of him and didn't recognize him from the photograph or her description.

Throughout the day she wandered through the town, stopping occasionally and searching the faces passing in the hope of seeing him. Several cafés enticed her in, as her legs ached and her disappointment made her weary, but no one remembered seeing him. After phoning The Wayfaring Tree to tell Seranne what she planned, she stayed that night at the hotel and the following morning began wandering through the streets again.

Luke passed through Tenby on his way back from Pembroke and saw Paul sitting on the bench. He looked less than happy but was dressed neatly, his hair recently cut and his shoes shining with polish. At least he hadn't let himself go and was probably in employment, he thought with relief. He didn't want to be the one to find him. He knew that for them to have any chance, it had to be Jessie who made contact.

Unfortunately, Paul saw him and stood to greet him. "Don't tell Jessie where to find me," were his first words.

Luke didn't reply, having already done so.

"What makes you think she won't want to see you?" he asked.

"I've let her down."

"She puts it down to an impatient urge to please her. Plus bad luck and a bit of bad judgement. She'd help you out of the mess if only you'd let her. For goodness sake, Paul, stop treating her like a fragile doll."

"I was so excited at finding her I neglected the factory, left the running of it to incompetent people who were doing their best but had no experience. Then I took money from our bank account, cut down on everything of importance in the tea rooms and ruined the business, which I thought we no longer needed. I

342

lost most of it paying debts to avoid bankruptcy and in an attempt to start something new that would give us a wonderful new start."

"The china shop?"

"That was too expensive. I gave that up straightaway and tried the catering equipment because I didn't have to lay out so much money. I'd be taking orders from the stuff I displayed. But I dithered for too long and the franchise went to someone else. I still think the beautiful china was a good idea, but I just didn't have the money to stock it, at least with the kind of quality goods envisaged." He sighed deeply. "I wanted to do everything for Jessie, give her a life in which she didn't have to work, but I was too impatient, and overconfident."

As Luke listened to the man stating his failures in that matter of fact tone, without whining, accepting the blame he knew he deserved, knowing he had been very stupid, he had a strong conviction that although Paul might never be a businessman, his love for Jessie was in no doubt. "Look, I have to go now, but think about coming back. Jessie would rather life with you than without. She's already looking ahead. Builders have started on the repairs to the tea rooms and with luck, she'll reopen at Christmas."

"Then I'll stay away. She'll succeed if she hasn't got me to drag her down."

Luke didn't reply, there was no point in repeating what he'd already said. Now it was up to Paul. And Jessie. He handed him a note with his name and phone number and left him. He wasn't a superstitious man, but he crossed his fingers and hoped that now he had confronted him, Paul wouldn't move on.

Alun booked the register office marriage and they quietly made their plans. It was difficult not to share the excitement with others but they both felt this was the best way. Betty took a day off and went into Cardiff to buy a new outfit, choosing a slim-fitting dress in blue crepe with a peplum and a small bow. The coat was light navy with shoes and matching handbag. "Goodness knows when I'll wear all this again," she said, as she took it to her room.

"We'll give ourselves a few treats, theatre and dining out, an occasional weekend away. We aren't going to live like hermits, are we?" Alun said. "I'll want to show the world my lovely wife."

Luke said nothing to Seranne about talking to Paul. Jessie phoned her every day at the café. "She still hasn't found him and if she doesn't have any success she will come back here at the weekend," Seranne told him.

"Tell her to stay there over the weekend in case he worked during the week and might be out and about on Sunday," he advised. He was concerned. Could Paul have moved on, unwilling to risk being seen again?

Jessie finished breakfast and stood outside the hotel, wondering in which direction to walk. It all seemed so futile. If Paul were here they could be walking around the same area separated by a row of houses, a wall, a few steps, and still not meet. She looked around her

344

where families of holidaymakers wandered past with their children, carrying picnic baskets, fishing nets, buckets and spades. The smell of wet sand and seaweed mingled with other familiar scents teasing her nose with memories of long ago, when she had been one of those children, excited by the prospect of a happy, sun-filled day.

She was about to walk out into the morning sun when a man walked around the corner and sat on the bench from where he could watch the crowds. "Paul," she said aloud, instinctively stepping towards him. Then she stopped. What should she say? How should she act? Casually, as though he'd been gone just hours? Critically? Or simply tell him what was in her heart, that she missed him?

Although she had hardly moved he seemed to sense her presence and he turned his head. "Jessie," he murmured.

She ran then and he stood to greet her, their arms enfolding each other and no words were necessary after all. They walked along the pavement unaware of anyone else and gradually Jessie made him see that he was needed, and loved.

They ate lunch overlooking the beach and began to talk. Jessie didn't refer to his absence in a critical way as she explained about the loan and the work that was underway.

"You might be able to arrange a refund on the shop I rented," he offered.

"You wouldn't mind?"

"And there's the car, if you can find it. I left it somewhere near Merthyr Tydfil. So I can't drive you home. It will have to be bus — unless you fancy hitchhiking," he said.

"The car isn't lost," she said, embarrassed. "I sold it to help pay the architect."

"That was the right thing to do. You can manage without a car until the business is up and running."

She noticed he hadn't said, we can manage, and that worried her. Wasn't he coming home? "We can get all we need delivered, can't we?" she said firmly. "Come home, darling. I don't want to do this on my own. I need you."

He wanted nothing more than to go back but it wasn't going to be easy to walk into Badgers Brook and face Seranne and Luke. "I'll have to work a week's notice. I can't let the restaurant down, even though I'm only a lowly dishwasher."

"Of course. I wouldn't expect anything else of you."

"Will you stay here for the week?"

"It will be a second honeymoon," she replied. "I'll even help with the dirty dishes."

Betty and Alun left at different times on Friday, 28 August, Betty going by bus and Alun an hour later by car. She was waiting for him at a bus stop a few miles out of Cwm Derw and got into the car with her small suitcase, her eyes shining as she held up her face for his kiss. They had arranged to stay at a hotel and it was there that they changed into their new clothes for the ceremony.

Hidden by a group of people waiting for a later wedding, Tilly took some snaps with her brownie box camera and prayed they would be good enough to please the happy couple, who expected none.

Back to the hotel for the night, then the following morning Alun led her to the railway station where they set off for three wonderful days in Paris.

Tilly had hurried away from the register office afraid of being seen, and went back to the Ship, from where she had telephoned Tony to ask how he was getting on with the wedding cake. "Hurry up, I want it here before they get back but every flower has to be perfect, mind," she warned.

"It's roses all the way," Tony promised.

Paul had been told he needn't work the week and on Monday, filled with apprehension, he stepped off the bus at the end of the lane and walked down to Badgers Brook, carrying his rucksack, arm in arm with Jessie.

Having decided the only way to deal with his return was by acting as though nothing unusual had happened, Seranne said, "Hello Mum. Hello Paul. It's a bit of luck you being here, there's a bit of a party at the Ship tomorrow. It's supposed to be a secret, but Betty and Alun were married on Friday and Tilly found out, so we all have to be there to welcome them home."

"I don't think I can" — Paul began but Jessie squeezed his hand and he amended — "find a tidy suit."

"Dress casual, no one will notice anyway," Seranne said. "All the attention will be on the happy couple."

So his homecoming was eased and when he went up to his and Jessie's room that night, he knew that despite every stupid thing he had done, he was back where he belonged.

Ed refused to get excited by his sister's wedding. He had no intention of going to the party.

"Come on, Ed," Colin urged. "Betty did everything to please you when you married, even though she wasn't happy about your choice. She's your sister and you can surely make a bit of an effort for her."

Bob added his persuasions and grudgingly he agreed to "pop my head in and say best of luck, but I won't stay. Right?"

Their remarks had made him angry and he knew they had no idea of how hurt he had been over Elsie's will and his sister's refusal to help. Betty had pushed him aside for a penniless scrounger called Alun Curtis and he was expected to be pleased? How could they understand?

He went back to the guest house and looked at the bookings for the following three months. Why should he bother? The place should have been his. He wrote to the few people who had booked and told them the place was closed for repair, then he tore out the relevant pages and threw the ledger into the rubbish. In the kitchen practically every dish had been used and was piled ready for washing. The girl employed to help had left, complaining he was leaving more and more for her to do, and he hadn't bothered to replace her. "Why should I?" he kept muttering. He went into the room where he spent most of his time, and sat in front of the television not taking in a word.

He was unaware that his situation was the subject of discussion between Seranne and Mark Lacy, the solicitor.

"I have to do something for Ed but I don't want to give it up completely. I have a strong desire to do the same as Elsie and eventually leave it to someone without warning in the hope it will change their life."

"Perhaps you could become partners?"

"No, that would create complications worse than Elsie's will. I want to be free to leave it to whom I choose, yet give something to Ed."

"What if you keep the business in your name and, after Ed's wages and running costs are taken out, share the profits. How would that be?"

"That sounds a perfect solution. I can help Ed and still keep faith with what Elsie wanted."

"I think, knowing how er, unhappy Ed Connors is, that we should put in a few precautionary details. What if we made this a temporary arrangement to be reinstated after, say, a year? If he doesn't do what is expected of him, then you can rethink the idea." He was trying to be diplomatic, aware of how much this situation was worrying her. "I understand his disappointment over the situation is making him rather, er, unreasonable?"

"Not a year. I will be prepared to step in if this falls apart. Three years seems about right."

Mark shrugged but agreed.

They made an appointment with an accountant, explained their needs and he drew up the relevant arrangement. Mark checked it, and when Seranne received it she took it to show Luke. "Ed is sure to be at Betty and Alun's party. I'll tell him then," she said.

"He might not be pleased," Luke warned. "He still thinks the place should be his."

"I don't blame him for that, but Elsie must have had her reasons and I must respect them.

Mark Lacy also helped Luke as he arranged for the shop that had once been rented by Paul to be refurbished. It was his intention to open it as Paul had originally planned and to put Paul in as the manager. Like Ed, Paul was capable of managing a business but they both needed someone to be in overall charge so they didn't neglect the important things.

Under Luke's guidance, plans were presented for improvements to the guest house. Nothing major, just the garden behind the guest house to be cleared and made into a car park as more and more people were travelling this way. There were also discussions about adding a small bar for residents only. Ed was not included in these discussions and he continued to be difficult, bemoaning his fate to anyone who would listen. Seranne ignored him, certain that once everything was made clear he would understand.

"Ed isn't a businessman. It was Elsie who ran the place and he can't manage alone. He needs a partner to keep things running smoothly yet think he's in charge," Seranne explained to her mother.

350

"And it's the same for Paul," Luke assured Jessie. "With me overseeing the china shop and allowing him to make the day to day decisions, he will be content. You will have the tea rooms and Paul will have his success too."

"A perfect solution," Seranne agreed.

"Now, what about a walk?" Luke suggested, offering his hand to Seranne. She began to put on walking shoes but he shook his head. "Not that kind of walk," he said mysteriously.

He drove her to a beautiful house which, by the name, Eventide Home, she guessed was a home for the elderly. He walked in and led her to the lounge, where several ladies were sitting chatting. One elegantly dressed and upright lady, wearing a beautiful suit in lavender silk, he introduced, "Seranne, meet my mother."

After a few minutes he left them to go and find some tea and Mrs Beynon looked at her with obvious delight. "I'm so pleased you and Luke are friends, dear. He gets very lonely sometimes."

"Oh, we don't spent much time together," she said hastily.

"Thinking about Marion, are you?"

"Tell me about Luke," Seranne said quickly. "What was he like as a small boy?"

"Like all his friends, a bit of a handful at times, but he's always been considerate and I don't think anything will change that. After the Marion incident, he's concentrated on making money. He had to do something to fill his time, you see. Having a job wasn't enough. Since then everything he touches makes him more wealthy, but it was a substitute for what he really wanted, someone like you to love and look after."

Still uneasy, unsure of what Luke had told her, she tried again to change the subject. "Did he tell you he helped us to sell some things at Maes Hir market?" she asked. "He was so persuasive we sold everything."

"He was always good at that, dear. I remember once he filled a stall with baby and children's clothes. He was teased over that, I can tell you, but it was to help a man who was ill."

When Luke returned with a tray of tea the two of them were laughing as they exchanged reminiscences about Luke's childhood and Seranne's own.

They talked easily on the way back to Badgers Brook but Seranne was still confused by the casual way his wife was being dismissed. She didn't encourage him to stay, making the excuse that she needed to talk to her mother and Paul.

"All right, but I'll see you tomorrow. It's time you met Marion," he said as he closed the door.

The first thing Betty and Alun saw when they stepped out of the car was mud on the steps outside. "It looks as though Colin's been in!" Betty said.

"Who cares about a bit of mud," Alun replied. "But there shouldn't be anyone in at this time of day."

The second thing they saw was when they opened the door. They were met by a huge banner with letters sewn across a white background, which read

CONGRATULATIONS, BETTY AND ALUN. FROM ALL YOUR FRIENDS.

"How on earth did they find out?" Betty gasped.

With a laugh Alun said, "My guess is Tilly Tucker!"

The place was full but everyone moved back for a moment or two so they could see the bar, covered generously with food, its centrepiece a single tier wedding cake decorated with pink roses made by Tony from sugar given by neighbours.

Laughing and waving, they had to struggle through well-wishers kissing Betty, shaking Alun's hand and shouting the occasional ribald remark. They were so happy they were completely unaware of the resentments and anxieties rippling through the noisy gathering.

It was a long time before Betty saw Ed. He was sitting near the fire, stretched out so people had to give him a wide berth or risk falling over his feet. He was sipping a beer surrounded by the cheerful crowd, a scowl on his face to make sure everyone knew he did not share the celebration. "Where did he take you then?" he asked Betty. "Barry Island was it? He didn't have money to take you far, some honeymoon!"

"We went to Paris," she replied. "And he paid if it bothers you!"

"Lucky you!"

Kitty and Bob had brought a gramophone and records and despite the cramped conditions people began to dance. Seranne slipped into Luke's arms and they moved backwards and forwards in the limited space, just happy to be together. Tomorrow Luke had arranged for her to meet Marion and hear his explanation. She tried not to think about what would be said. Could she meet an ex-wife and not show her embarrassment? Divorced or not, she would feel like an immoral woman. Seeing Ed glaring whenever their eyes met, looking so accusing, didn't help. Trying to show happiness at Betty and Alun's wedding was not as easy as she had hoped. At least there was comfort in the way Paul and Jessie had sorted out their brief estrangement. They were dancing together and there was no doubt about their happiness at being reunited.

When the crowd began to eat, and relax into chattering groups, Ed still sat glaring and sipping his beer. Betty and Alun tried to talk to him but he turned his head aside like a petulant child. Seranne knew she had to tell him what she had arranged. She had the document in her handbag and, taking it out, she handed it to him.

"What's this, giving me the sack, are you? Well, I don't care. I'm fed up with looking after your interests." He threw the papers aside.

Betty hurried over to try and calm her brother. Seranne briefly explained herself then Alun picked up the form and handed it to Ed.

"I want you to have half of everything the guest house makes," Seranne said calmly. "An accountant has drawn up an agreement. After your wages and the outgoings are paid, you get half of the profits. After my time I'll do what Elsie asked, and pass the place on to someone who will benefit from an unexpected windfall."

354

Ed said nothing, he frowned as though unable to take in what was being said.

"That's very generous. It was what your Elsie wanted, Ed," Betty added. "Elsie was kind and thoughtful, and aware of how much a life could benefit from such a wonderful gift."

"Please yourself," Ed muttered. He handed his empty glass to Betty. "Give me a refill, why don't you, so I can sleep and forget about Seranne's thieving."

"Time you went home," Betty said beckoning to Colin and Bob.

"No need, I've closed the premises. I deserve a holiday."

Tony looked surprised. "Since when? I've been delivering as usual and so have the other people. There's bread in the outhouse and the butcher and green grocer want paying and so do I."

Alun stood with Bob trying to lift the man out of his seat.

"No," Luke said. "I think we should take him."

"Yes, you take me, you and Seranne, so I can tell you exactly what I think of your offer."

Without protest he stood up, accepted the support of Luke's arm and shuffled from the bar. At the door he stopped and waved at Betty and Alun. "I hope you have better luck than I did," he muttered.

"I think you can take that as Ed's version of wishing you good luck," Colin muttered.

Ed sobered up when they stepped outside. The air was warm for the beginning of September and he pushed away their arms and walked steadily around the corner from the post office and up to his door. "You needn't come in," he said.

Ignoring him they followed him in. "I don't think he's really drunk, just angry," Luke said, "but a coffee wouldn't hurt." He opened the kitchen door and stopped as the light revealed chaos. Behind him Seranne gasped as she saw the unwashed dishes and pans, the dirty cooker and greasy sink.

"What's been happening here?"

"He's done nothing for days," Seranne said in disbelief.

"Why should I?" Ed shouted.

"Because it's half yours, you fool," Luke said.

While the party continued at the Ship and Compass, Luke and Seranne set to and cleared the filthy kitchen. Besides the unwashed china, the fridge and the outhouse were full of stale food, hidden in boxes and beginning to decay. It was as they put it into the rubbish bin that they found the torn booking ledger. When they went to find Ed for an explanation, he had gone.

"We'd better get back to the Ship and tell Betty what's happened," Seranne said. "Trust Ed to ruin her special day."

"We'll go back, but she doesn't need to know about this today, does she?"

The party was still going strong having been reduced to Betty and Alun's closest friends. The bar was closed and the group had moved into the living-room. Slumped in an armchair, was Ed.

Betty insisted on knowing what happened and they told her about the negligence and the booking ledger they had found in the rubbish.

"Leave him to me," Betty said. "Tomorrow I'll make him see sense — if he has any!"

Luke had arranged to stay at the guest house although his booking had been thrown away with the rest. It was he who walked Ed home for the second time that evening. One of the bedrooms was unused and Luke lay in the bed, wide awake, no longer thinking about Ed, but wondering what would happen when Seranne met Marion.

Luke had arranged to meet Marion at a restaurant in Cowbridge the following evening. He called for Seranne at seven, and they set off in silence, each wondering what the situation would be at the end of the evening.

Seranne had no idea what to expect; Luke had told her nothing about the woman and she prepared to face anger similar to that handed out to her by Ed. She must be the most unpopular inhabitant of Cwm Derw, she decided, as the car took them closer to the woman she had replaced.

They were the first to arrive and they sat there unable to talk to each other both aware of how much their future depended on the next hour. As people walked in, Seranne's heart leapt. Was she the one? Or this one?

When a young woman came in leading a child aged about five, she looked away, and continued to stare at the doorway and hardly noticed the couple were approaching them.

"Luke?" the woman said.

Luke stood and introduced them. "Seranne, this is Marion Harper. Marion, meet Seranne. And this little lady," he said, bending to kiss the child's cheek, "is Helen."

Seranne stared at the woman and tried to imagine her as Luke's wife. She was plainly dressed and her hair was clean and neatly cut but hanging limply about her shoulders. Her clothes were also clean but simple and well washed.

"I think Luke would like me to explain why he has been helping me and my daughter," Marion said, offering her hand.

"I don't think there's any need," Seranne said, embarrassed. How could Luke put her in this difficult position?

"I presume you know we were to marry, and well, I met someone else just weeks before the wedding and I went away with this other man and left Luke standing at the altar."

"You weren't married? But I thought —"

"So did everyone else. The families said nothing, certain it would blow over as Luke told them it would. He was determined to find me and was convinced I would regret my mistake and we could marry secretly. I refused him a second time. Luke went away and I went too, with Helen's father and apart from the families, everyone presumed we had married and were living together in a distant town."

358

"But surely the truth came out?"

"Strangely enough it didn't. The wedding was a small affair, only six people present, even though it was in a church. Both families waited for Luke and me to come home, the house we had rented stood waiting for us and, well, time passes and the affair slipped from people's minds. Then Luke found me again and I was expecting Helen and the man who had promised to marry me was long gone."

"So then you married?"

"No, I could hardly expect a third chance, could I? Luke, being the generous man he is, helped us to get on our feet. He found a caravan at first, then, as money grew easier we moved into a couple of rooms."

"You and Luke?"

"No." Marion smiled. "It was over between us from the moment I ran out of that church wearing the white dress and veil. We both knew that. Just Helen and me."

"You see," Luke explained, "Marion and I had known each other for a long time and I couldn't feel free of Marion even though there was no chance of a reconciliation."

"He promised to help, until Helen and I were settled."

"And are you?" Seranne asked, helping Helen into her chair.

"I've met someone special, a man who loves Helen as much as he loves me. We're getting married."

They began to eat, even though Seranne was so confused she didn't think she could swallow a thing. But the presence of the bright little five-year-old helped and by the time the meal was over they were all relaxed, though Seranne had a thousand questions demanding to be heard.

It wasn't until they were driving home that Seranne asked, "Why didn't *you* tell me?"

"I tried, several times, but you were too quick to make up your mind."

"You warned me about jumping to conclusions, I remember that."

"Seranne, I'm so proud of you. The way you have accepted Paul and your mother being together, and how you've handled Ed, and your inheritance, and now, facing Marion not having all the facts. Where is that quick-tempered girl I first knew?"

"She's grown up I suppose."

They got out of the car near Jessica's Victorian Tea Rooms, to see how the work was progressing. A small dog leapt out of a gateway and barked at her. She squealed and tripped over the kerb, and Luke grabbed her as she began to shout. "Did you see that? The animal is dangerous and shouldn't be out without a lead. I'm going to complain." She was heading towards the gate where the dog was cowering, when she became aware of Luke's laughter.

"Not completely grown up, I'm happy to say," he said, gathering her once again into his arms.

Also available in ISIS Large Print:

Sarah's Cottage

D. E. Stevenson

Recently married to Charles, Sarah is furnishing a cottage in Scotland and starting on a life in sharp contrast to their wartime experiences. Their full entrance into village life is helped by Sarah's delightful grandparents, who have given them the land on which they have built their cottage.

They work together, collaborating in translations for a publisher. Charles embarks on more ambitious writing, his autobiography, yet increasingly it is not books but life itself that engrosses him and Sarah. In particular Frederica, the daughter of Sarah's frivolous and pleasure-seeking sister, commands their sympathy and love. One by one the characters of a large attractive family make their appearance but it is through Frederica that the nexus of family problems is finally resolved.

ISBN 978-0-7531-8080-8 (hb)
ISBN 978-0-7531-8081-5 (pb)

Love Out of Season

Ray Connolly

Perched between bleak moors and the cold sea, the North Devon Riviera Hotel is an unlikely destination for February. But, for the guests and staff there, it's about to become the setting for a weekend they will always remember.

Amy Miller has fallen in love with a famous married man and has gone into hiding at the hotel, pursued by the press. While waiting for her lover to call, however, she begins to question their affair. Then, into her life comes Tim, a musician. As the hotel prepares for its Valentine's ball and the tabloids circle ever closer, Amy, Tim and everyone else at the North Devon Riviera are about to discover that love — whether it's young love, old love, shared love or unrequited love — does indeed make the world go round, and sometimes in the most unexpected ways.

ISBN 978-0-7531-8022-8 (hb)
ISBN 978-0-7531-8023-5 (pb)

Lands Beyond the Sea

Tamara McKinley

By the 1700s, the Aborigine had lived in harmony with the land in Australia for 60,000 years. But now ghost-ships are arriving, and their very existence is threatened by a terrifying white invasion.

When Jonathan Cadwallader leaves Cornwall to sail on the Endeavour, he is forced to abandon his sweetheart, Susan Penhalligan. But an act of brutality will reunite them in the raw and unforgiving penal colony of New South Wales.

Billy Penhalligan has survived transportation and clings to the promise of a new beginning. But there will be more suffering before he or his fellow convicts can regard Australia as home . . .

ISBN 978-0-7531-8038-9 (hb)
ISBN 978-0-7531-8039-6 (pb)

Two Men and a Maiden

Winifred Foley

Forced to find another job to help support her family, Laura leaves the Forest of Dean to take up the position as maid to a Jewish family in London. She quickly settles in to life with the Cohens, befriending the daughter Rachel and catching the eye of both unmarried sons, David and Adam.

After a tragic incident, Laura returns home to the Forest of Dean, where she marries a promising young footballer. But after his untimely death, a surprise comes knocking. A surprise that signals a wonderful new life for her.

ISBN 978-0-7531-7970-3 (hb)
ISBN 978-0-7531-7971-0 (pb)